Deirdre Hart was born and grew up in the North of Ireland where she studied at the University of Ulster and Queens University, Belfast. She holds advanced degrees in social work and psychoanalytic studies and has worked in both the social work and the counselling industry for many years.

In her spare time Deirdre is a freelance writer who has won awards for poetry. She has three beautiful daughters who enrich her life and she now lives in Edinburgh with her husband, who is also a writer. She is currently working on her second novel.

THE
TRUST OF THE INNOCENT

Deirdre Hart

THE
TRUST OF THE INNOCENT

Vanguard Press

VANGUARD PAPERBACK

© Copyright 2009
Deirdre Hart

The right of Deirdre Hart
to be identified as author of
this work has been asserted by her in accordance with the
Copyright, Designs and Patents Act 1988

This novel is a work of fiction and does not reflect the actual practice of child
protection in the state of New South Wales or any state in Australia. Any
resemblance to actual events or persons living or dead is purely coincidental.

A CIP catalogue record for this title is
available from the British Library

978 1 84386 451 6

Vanguard Press is an imprint of
Pegasus Elliot MacKenzie Publishers Ltd.
www.pegasuspublishers.com

First Published in 2009

Vanguard Press
Sheraton House Castle Park
Cambridge England

Printed & Bound in Great Britain

Dedication

To Shane with all my love.
The story will always begin and end with you.

Acknowledgements

This book would not have been possible without the support of a number of people, especially Julie, who held on to her integrity despite the difficulties she encountered. Thanks to Mary Holmes for proof reading 'The Trust of the Innocent' and to Pegasus Elliot MacKenzie for giving me this wonderful opportunity. My parents, William and Susan have provided encouragement to me at all times and I am forever grateful. My family has continued to provide love and support despite the geographical distance between us. I would sincerely like to thank Dearhaile, Caoimhe and Aoibhin who encouraged me to follow my dreams.

For their enthusiasm, warmth and generosity towards me I would like to thank Dorothy; Steve; Diane, Kieron and Brandon. My thanks are also offered to Siobhan; Caroline Carmel; Joan; Geraldine; Rozel; Cath; Wendy and Karen. Finally I would like to thank David Lander who continues to fight against injustice wherever it may be found.

CHAPTER 1

Today was the first day of the rest of the mess. I groped towards the bedside table in an effort to reach the ringing alarm clock, knocking over a glass of water in the process and drenching myself. What a great way to start the day, looking like a drowned rat. Bugger! Just when I was getting used to yesterday, along came today. My inner child buried herself in the quilt, but the adult world intruded. Why couldn't people hibernate like bears? I wanted to stay cocooned in my quilt but the thought of what I had to face today dispensed any warmth which tog factor twenty might bring. Come on, brain, I urged, wake up. The brain is a wonderful organ you know. It starts working the moment you get up in the morning and doesn't stop until you get to work. Work! Who was it that said work was the curse of the drinking classes?

I stumbled into the en suite and took a shower, the hot water soothing my body and cleansing the last ravages of sleep. I dried myself and shivered as I walked to the wardrobe; it was cold today, a bit like my life really. I took ages to select an outfit, what sort of a colour. Hmm what did I feel like today? Would it be the blue or the red pill? I eventually chose a black skirt and a crisp white blouse. It had no imagination and I would look like a cocktail waitress, but they would have to do. I pulled them on quickly, noticing that the zip on the skirt was getting a bit tight. Amazing! You just hung something in your wardrobe for a while and it shrank two sizes. But, I comforted myself, at least I was in shape, that is if round was a shape. I didn't believe in working out, my philosophy was no pain, ever. I sat on the bed and slipped on a pair of strappy leather shoes which I took the trouble to admire. Shoes! The fat girl's friend. No matter how much your weight fluctuated your feet would always stay the same size. I've always believed that if the shoe fits you should buy it, and in every colour.

I caught a glimpse of myself in the hall mirror as I was about to leave the house. Ahhh! What was my mother doing there? Dear God, I'd forgotten to apply any make up. I couldn't face the world looking like this, I would be hunted down. I wondered how I ever got over the hill without getting to the top. I scrambled around in my handbag for my make up bag and attempted to try and make myself look a bit more human. As I squinted into the mirror to apply mascara I realised that wrinkled was not one of the things I wanted to be when I was grown up. I took a final look in the mirror before I left the house. I didn't look too bad I supposed, for someone who was thirty-seven, and at least I still had all my own teeth and my hair.

I drove myself to work, playing the usual game of chance in my head. If I could just get through two green lights in succession then it would be bearable. Today, like every other day, I prayed, please, Lord, let me prove that winning the lottery won't spoil me. My work paid my mortgage and kept me in shoes but I had one of the lowest jobs in the world. Are you ready for this? I am a professional child snatcher. Don't panic, it isn't as bad as it sounds. I work in the field of child protection, and yes, I have heard all the jokes before, how it is easier to get your children off a Rottweiler than a social worker. What were the other ones? Did you hear about the terrorist that hijacked a 747 full of social workers? He threatened to release one every hour if his demands weren't met. What do you call two thousand social workers at the bottom of the ocean? A start!!! How come they bury social workers three hundred feet in the ground? Because deep down they are really good people. Finished now? I know it isn't glamorous but this is how I earn my daily bread. I enjoy the work with children and families. But when people find out what I do for a living they always seem a bit taken aback, as if I'd admitted to serial killing on the weekends, or passing wind on public transport. They always tell me that it must be a very stressful thing to do. Yes, I reply, it's a thankless job, but I've got a lot of karma to burn off.

The negative side of this work believe it or not, was not the horrendous tales of abuse I heard, or the shocking things I saw, but the staff I was forced to work with. Most of them were more dysfunctional than their clients. I parked outside the building and summoned whatever energy Nescafe had provided to get me out of the car and moving towards the door. It wasn't an office. It was hell with fluorescent lighting. My boss, Kevin, was Lucifer in a suit, a cheap one. Millions of acrylics had died for it. You couldn't warm to him if you were cremated together. The Family Service Agency where we worked had already received two complaints of bullying by him and lucky me, I was his latest target. You know bullies and sperm have a lot in common. They both have a one-in-a-million chance of becoming a human being. Kevin was a legend in his own mind. He prided himself on his nickname, Mr. Teflon, because (he always laughed hysterically when he said this, yes, every single time) 'Teflon doesn't stick.' I read somewhere that bullies are often powerless in their home domain and he proved it. His wife used to phone him constantly and scream at him. He always stood there, tight-lipped, then he took his rage out on whoever was next in line, usually me.

After five long years of trying to cope with him I realised that while I had thought I wanted a career, it turned out I just wanted a paycheck. You will be asking yourself why I put up with this tyrannical behaviour, why I didn't just leave? I'll tell you. Kevin had promised that if I ever tried to get another job anywhere else he would give me a bad reference and would make sure it didn't happen. He meant it. Over time his repeated criticisms and fault finding had worn me down. It had got to the point where I was afraid to try.

Kevin had the social skills of a slug and the IQ of a table mat. How this man had been promoted to manager was beyond me; he couldn't manage a sandwich. He must have got there through assmosis. You know, the process by which some people seem to absorb success and advancement by kissing up to the boss rather than working hard.

Kevin wasn't a total failure, his boss Richard helped too. I had tried to explain to Richard what Kevin was doing but he refused to listen. Kevin was Richard's bitch. Have you ever noticed that at work the authority of a person is inversely proportional to the number of pens they are carrying? Well, Richard came fully supplied, but he had an intellect rivalled only by garden tools. When he opened his mouth, it was only to change whichever foot was previously there. If at first you don't succeed, try management, I thought, when I asked him a simple question and he couldn't answer. When he didn't know what to do, he would walk quickly up the corridor and look worried. I felt sorry for him. He had spent so much time trying to get rid of the halitosis only to find out that he wasn't popular anyway.

My work colleagues weren't much better. There were too many freaks and not enough circuses. Take Beryl. Please! She had a voice like a foghorn. Every time she opened her mouth I nearly jumped out of my skin. I spent many a happy moment visualizing the duct tape over her mouth. Her telephone manner comprised of answering a call with the word 'Wha?' She had delusions of adequacy and believed her level of success was measured by the number of sovereign rings and gold jewellery she wore. She was a Ratner's advertisement on legs. When she moved her head the numerous hooped earrings rattled against each other like a tin fence moving in the wind. She hadn't heard of dressing for success either. We were lucky if she changed her white Tesco two stripe trainers on a regular basis. If I was in charge I wouldn't allow her to breed.

The other manager, Gladys, was an information junkie. She slithered along the walls of the corridor and hung around listening outside doors. She would go up your rear end for a bit of news. Whenever anything happened to anyone in the office, she would always be found, sitting centre stage, listening intently and extracting all sorts of gory details. If she couldn't get news directly she tried to get it covertly. She kept a pair of slippers in her office and wore them during the day, only changing into her shoes if she had a meeting. I used to think she had painful feet, maybe she was crippled with bunions or something, but there was

15

nothing wrong with her, she wore them so she could creep up behind people without them noticing. That way she got to hear all sorts of stuff she wouldn't normally get a chance to. And a closed door was no obstacle to her either; she saw it as a challenge. She would burst in, hoping that she would find someone in a compromising position. It hadn't happened yet, but you never knew the minute.

Gladys had no life of her own and she lived it vicariously through other people. You know the type? Always giving out about the horrors of drink and yet she listened in complete fascination when someone described a drunken night out. She was one of those Sunday go to meeting type women, who are completely disgusted at the moral decline of the world, but she relished every juicy detail she heard of relationship break-ups and infidelity.

She didn't have far to look. One of her team was determined to shag his way round the office. John had been having an affair with Georgia, one of the women in my team, for months. Georgia still lived at home with her parents. We had become friendly when I first came to work in the office and she had stayed over at my house whenever we went out socially. Despite the fact that she was thirty her parents didn't allow her to smoke or drink but she did both. It was beyond my comprehension that they couldn't smell the smoke on her when she returned home as she spent most of her day in the smoke room reading magazines, or flirting with John. She didn't seem to have much life outside work, and she would even come into work on her day off so she could have a smoke.

Georgia had commenced her relationship with John one night when the staff had all gone out together for a few drinks. As she couldn't return to her own home with drink taken she had stayed at my house. I heard every bloody movement they made. I realised that she was only using me to be with John so I detached myself from her. I didn't want to condone home wrecking, but they continued their affair during office hours. Every day the pair of them sneaked off to John's friend's house. They would return, flushed faced and giggling. I knew that some of the other staff suspected what was happening but Georgia and John always denied it. They had to; they would have been sacked if it came to light. They were always playing practical jokes on each other, cutting the ribbon from each other's diaries, putting the contents of the shredder in each other's cars and hiding each other's lunch. It was so juvenile, and after a while it got to be a bit irritating.

Georgia should have known better. She wasn't the first and she wouldn't be the last. He'd fed her the age old line, you know the one, 'my wife doesn't understand me and we don't have an intimate relationship.' It all backfired on him when he had to shamefacedly announce that his wife was pregnant, again.

Georgia was devastated. Although she had been pleasant to me while the affair was ongoing, as soon as it ended she became hostile to me. As if it was somehow all my fault. She became friendly with another woman, Beth, who was twenty years older than her, and was married with a grown up family. I don't know what Georgia told Beth, but the pair of them started to gang up on me. Kevin loved it; he knew that when he wasn't there to torture me they would do it for him. I was getting it in stereo.

Over time Georgia and Beth's relationship grew. In fact their relationship grew to the point that when Beth went to Paris with her husband for their twenty-fifth wedding anniversary, Georgia went too.

Georgia didn't get much work done during the day as she was always in the smoke room, so she visited Beth in the evenings and at the weekends in order to complete reports that should have been done during working hours. Naturally she claimed overtime for this. Kevin did nothing. Even though he knew that it was causing resentment with the rest of the team, he was obviously too incompetent to address the issue. There was no work in her. Even though she had been qualified longer than me she was given the easy cases and she was always away on training while I did all the grunt work in the background. I had started out with nothing and I still had most of it left. I knew I had plenty of talent and vision, but after years of getting nowhere I just didn't give a damn anymore. I was beginning to realise that ambition was a poor excuse for not having enough sense to be lazy, like her.

Kevin would be back from annual leave today. He had given me a huge list of jobs to do before he left but he didn't tell me which one was a priority, he just let me guess. I had spent a lot of time at home making sure that all the work was completed and that he had no cause for complaint. Not that it would do me any good; if I completed a piece of work that pleased him, Kevin kept it a secret. Obviously leaks like that might earn me a promotion. Kevin always left the office without telling anyone where he was going. Still, it gave me a chance to be creative when someone asked where he was. Believe me, I usually came up with some highly plausible excuses.

He had a team meeting arranged for this morning. This was where I got the chance to reinforce my inherent dislike of stupid people. The meetings dragged on for hours and nothing was ever accomplished. I always tried to escape before Kevin got around to asking me anything. If I couldn't escape I would sit there wondering if I could get away with setting fire to my skirt.

We lined up and sat down in silence, every one of us suddenly finding the carpet of great interest. The secretary told Kevin that the office had now acquired its first scanner. 'That's great,' he said, 'how many channels does it have?' If he was any more stupid, he'd have to be watered twice a week. I asked a question about increasing caseloads and he replied with some incoherent mumble. It sounded like English, but I couldn't understand a word he was saying. He spoke in code as if he was working under cover for MI5. When he tried to communicate it involved a series of mumbles, and references to things that were happening which he couldn't reveal. Thanks, Kevin, we are all refreshed and challenged by your unique point of view.

He came into my office after the meeting. Georgia and Beth were having a cup of coffee and gossiping about what they had been up to at the weekend while I was toiling away. Kevin stomped over to me ignoring the rest of the team. 'I want that Smith report on my desk in ten minutes,' he snapped. I knew that he was supposed to have completed this before he went off on holiday but he needed me to do it for him; he believed that plagiarism saved time. He looked dumbfounded when I delivered the report to him ten minutes later. I smirked as I left his office; my overtime at home had achieved something.

He came back into my office while I was boiling the kettle for coffee. It was twelve o'clock and I still hadn't had breakfast. 'I want a report on this by this afternoon,' he commanded throwing a stack of files on my desk. No problem. Do you want fries with that? It was obviously something else he should have finished before he went on leave. Kevin only worked well when under constant supervision and when he was cornered like a rat in a trap. Right, there goes lunch time. I sighed. Some days it was just not worth chewing through the restraints.

I got stuck into the work. I spent the rest of the morning trying to prepare a report using words which had more than three syllables. I knew that Kevin would be out of his depth, sure he would be out of his depth in a puddle. But Kevin wouldn't leave me alone; he interrupted me constantly to inquire how it was going. He certainly knew how to aid my efficiency.

At least he had given me this extra work to do in the morning. Usually he waited until 5.00pm when I was leaving the office and then he brought more work to me telling me that it was a priority. He must have thought the challenge of a deadline would be refreshing for me.

'Aren't you having any lunch, Louise?' Susan asked me casually as she walked into the room. I wish!

'She's on a diet,' interjected Kevin as he licked the vinegar from his fingers. The room now smelt like a chip shop. 'She's on the Bobby Sands diet,' he tittered to himself. Jesus Christ! His teeth were brighter than he was. There was an embarrassed silence. Beth turned away; she didn't want to get caught up in

18

Kevin's tirade against me. She was in her late fifties and was just counting off the days until her retirement.

At least I had another job, where I worked part-time as a counsellor. I loved it. The clients were voluntary for a start so they were always pleased to see me, and the staff were wonderful. Working there made me believe that I wasn't as useless as Kevin had suggested. After suffering from Kevin and his cronies, I always looked forward to going there; it was worth giving up my free time each weekend. As if reading my mind Yvette interrupted my train of thought.

'So were you busy at work at the weekend?' she asked trying to lighten the atmosphere. She always took an active interest in my part-time job.

'Yes,' I replied, 'it was really busy and we....'

'Here, you,' interjected Kevin sharply, the gravy from his chips dripping from his fingers and down the front of his shirt. 'I don't want you talking about your part-time work with my staff.'

'But Yvette just asked me all about it,' I protested incredulously.

'You shouldn't encourage this type of thing. It's up to you not to talk about it, isn't it?' he scoffed. I bent down and took a book out of my handbag and started to read it quietly. There was no point even trying to converse with the rest of the staff when he was there. I was getting sick of his constant nit-picking.

As lunchtime ended I rose from my desk to go down to the main office. 'You, there,' he snapped his fingers at me. I looked behind me to see if he had left a dog somewhere when I realised he was indicating that he wanted to communicate with me.

'I saw what you were reading,' he hissed, 'I don't want you talking to the others about your academic achievements either,' he ordered. Why, because it makes you feel inadequate, you moron? I thought as I walked away in disgust.

Kevin complained when I left the office at five o'clock before he had returned from playing golf or whatever he did to fill his time. He always did his best to keep me late. Yeah, great Kevin, I thought as I hung around. I like the office and really have nowhere to go or anything to do. The man was depriving a village somewhere of an idiot. At the end of another miserable day I left the office to go home. I was looking forward to eating breakfast. I stopped at a local garage and bought the evening paper hoping that the employment section would offer some kind of distraction or promise for a new future. Well, you can always dream can't you?

I finally reached home and stretched the paper out on the dining room table while I waited for the kettle to boil. It would be instant noodles again; I was too tired to prepare anything else. I read one advertisement closely: *Would you like to work in Australia? We are seeking professionally qualified staff to work in the Children's Bureau in New South Wales. This is a welcoming community which hosts wonderful social events. We offer good employment conditions and training, with many leadership opportunities. In return we will offer a relocation allowance, extensive support with your transition and many attractive benefits. Please reply by email enclosing an up to date Curriculum Vitae.*

Wow! That would be nice. I visualized sunshine, sand, blue skies and clear blue water. Australia was such a long way from home, but maybe that would be a good thing. I would be able to leave all my troubles behind, and let's face it, I couldn't get further away from the boss from hell. I knew Kevin had already threatened to destroy my career if I ever left to work in this country, but surely he wouldn't have the same power to do that if my job was overseas.

I cut the advertisement out of the newspaper and carried it around in my handbag for a week. I mulled over the implications for ages. I always say you should never put off till tomorrow what you can avoid altogether. It was a huge leap, the other side of the world; I knew nothing about Australia apart from the awful soap operas which permeated the television channels here. Eventually after Kevin nearly drove me to drink, I applied for the post at one minute to the closing time on the date for submissions.

I didn't expect to hear anything for ages, so I was surprised when I received an email informing me that interviews would take place in Belfast the following week. They were certainly well organised, and I was grudgingly impressed. I decided to go along, more out of curiosity than anything else. Sure what had I got to lose? It would give me a chance to wear that nice suit I had bought for work last week. I wasn't completely convinced that I really wanted to move so far away from my home, but having this secret which Kevin knew nothing about thrilled me. It was like conducting some torrid affair, but obviously without the sneaking off during office hours, like John and Georgia.

I was determined that I wouldn't make a complete prat out of myself, so I studied relevant topics and prepared myself for a gruelling interview. I shouldn't have bothered. There were no hard questions at all. The interviewers concentrated on what life was like in Australia and the practicalities involved in securing a visa. I was given a brochure which outlined events which were currently taking place where my new employment would be located and a stack of forms to complete for the Immigration Department.

The following week I was woken at some ungodly hour of the morning by a woman called Kylie who told me that she was phoning from Australia to offer me the position. I was delighted. She explained the immigration process to me but I was too excited to take it all in, so she agreed to send me all the relevant papers in the post. I was going to have a new life. It would be fantastic, a new country, and the chance to put all the past behind me. But what if I was the oldest one there? What if I found it too difficult to adapt to a new country? I berated myself, what on earth was I doing thinking of going off on adventures at my time of life? The other recruits were probably about twenty years old with waists; I remembered vaguely having one of those. But on the plus side of things the determining factor in my argument for going was that there would be no more Kevin. It was going to be one of the greatest moments in my life when I told him that I was leaving.

CHAPTER 2

I knew it would take ages to process the immigration forms and I had to attend medical and x-ray examinations but I decided to tell Kevin, more out of courtesy than anything else. My parents had brought me up well. OK, there was an element of glee there too; well, wouldn't you milk it for all it was worth after all he had put me through?

After I delivered my news I could see that he was taken aback. 'I have contacts you know,' he scoffed. 'You can't work anywhere in this country without a reference from me.'

'Don't worry,' I retorted, 'I know that you must be too busy as I haven't had supervision from you for months, so I got a reference from the manager where I work part-time.'

'But you can't get a job without something in writing from me,' he snickered.

'That's where you are wrong, Kevin,' I said slowly.

'Do you think I am a fool?' he asked. 'I know about employment legislation in this country. I know you have to get references from your current employer.' I did think he was a fool, but then, what was my humble opinion against thousands of others?

'I have a reference, Kevin, I don't need one from you,' I insisted bravely. I glanced at him, daring him to challenge me, but he was a gutless wimp when it came to confrontation. He would give car accident victims new hope for recovery. He could walk, talk and perform rudimentary tasks, all without the benefit of a spine.

'Where is the job then?' he asked, clearly wondering what he could do to sabotage it.

'It's in New South Wales,' I replied.

'You are going to live in Wales?' His mouth opened in shock. I didn't feel like giving him a geography lesson. I had never made a fool of him; I just left him to display his natural talents himself.

'Whereabouts? Cardiff, I suppose? You know I have friends who live there too,' he sneered.

'That's nice for you,' I replied, 'but I'm not going there. I'm going to work in New South Wales; it's in Australia.' I could see the wheel was turning, but the hamster was dead. Gobshite. Dear God, he hadn't a clue.

'When do you think you are going then?' he demanded lifting his diary from the desk in order to make a note of the date.

'I don't know exactly,' I replied carefully. I was dreading this part. 'It takes a while to get a visa approved so I can't give you a definite date, but I expect to be going in a few months.'

'Well, I think you owe it to Family Services to give your notice immediately. If you are planning to leave you should just leave now,' he said firmly. He knew I had a mortgage to pay and that I couldn't leave one job unless I was starting another one immediately. 'Go on then,' he ordered, 'here's a piece of paper. You can write it now. I can help you if you like.' I'm sure you would, too, you horrible little man.

'I don't need to, Kevin,' I said patiently. 'I've already checked with the Personnel Department and they say that a month's leave is all I'm required to give so as soon as I get a visa I'll submit my notice then.' He glared at me. He was fuming and the muscles in his neck were stretched beyond snapping point. 'So if there's nothing else, I'll just let you get on with your work,' I said calmly and turned to leave his office, but not before noticing the look of outrage on his face. If looks could kill I'd have been exterminated on the spot.

My heart was racing but I'd said it. Now the words were out there I would have to follow through on the whole thing. I wondered what my new boss would be like. Please God, I prayed, don't let me run into another useless git like Kevin. But I knew Kevin would try to get back at me before I ever got there. He couldn't believe that I had defied him and planned my escape. In this organization to err was human, but to forgive was not company policy. He always needed a scapegoat to deflect from his incompetence, and as I had spent most of my time correcting his mistakes, I was usually it. My team slogan had become 'just undo it'.

I didn't have to wait long to see that Kevin had planned his revenge. He changed my caseload immediately and gave me the most challenging cases. 'Well, there's no point in you doing any long-term work is there?' he derided me. I felt sad that I didn't get a chance to explain to my clients that I was leaving, or to say goodbye to them. He wouldn't let me.

At every team meeting that followed he repeated the same mantra. He wanted it recorded that I was leaving. The other staff had begun to comment that he was trying to get rid of me. But Kevin was relentless. He openly criticized my work at every opportunity. He was so eager to find fault, you'd think there was some kind of a reward.

After an important case conference he called me into his office and shouted, 'Why do you habitually correct me in meetings?'

'Mainly because you're habitually wrong,' I answered piercingly.

'You know,' he said slithering across the room until he was standing in front of me. 'I can't have you here working from week to week and waiting around for you to leave. You can always be fired.' Yuck! Please breathe the other way. You're bleaching my hair.

'You can't fire me,' I retorted quickly, 'slaves have to be sold.' Like I said earlier, there was little point in reporting his unprofessional behaviour to his superiors. They had closed ranks when the previous allegations of bullying were made against him. Both staff members who complained had been sent to other offices with a proviso that they were not permitted to work with him again.

Just before he had to deliver his monthly report to Richard, his line manager, Kevin called the team into his office for what he called a brainstorming session. It would be more accurately described as blame storming as we sat around discussing why a deadline hadn't been reached, or a project failed, and who might be responsible. It was never him. Kevin always managed to keep his neck above water. I could tell by the colour of it.

We were trying to coordinate annual leave over the Christmas period and Kevin was kind enough to allow us to take a half day to be used for shopping. Though of course he made it sound as if it was coming out of his own allocation. He rarely used his full leave entitlement so each year he lost a lot of his allocated time. This said a lot about the fact that he didn't want to be in his own home. The rumours about his tyrannical wife were well founded; he must have learned his bullying tactics from the master. At least when he wasn't at home he could be in the office wreaking havoc and misery on us.

The team sat down and worked out all the different times and dates. I agreed to take the next morning off work to use mine then. Susan typed up the rota and put it in Kevin's tray. I heard her tell Kevin that I would be using my leave the next morning.

Next day I arrived at work at lunchtime. I had managed to get quite a lot of shopping done and I was feeling very pleased with myself. 'Here, you, get in here now,' Kevin screamed at me as I was walking up the corridor past his office. I scuttled into his room, fearing what was going to come next.

'Where the hell were you till this time?' he shouted into my face.

'I was on Christmas leave,' I stuttered, beginning to quake in my shoes. Kevin became extremely agitated and started to pace up and down the room.

'How dare you leave this office without my permission,' he screamed. I tried to interrupt him, to tell him that he had been given a copy of the leave rota but he wouldn't listen.

'I'm sick to death of you,' he howled. 'The sooner you leave this office the better.' His face was blazing; he could hardly contain himself. I thought he was going to thump me.

'I couldn't agree more,' I said slowly, 'so if you've finished shouting at me, I'll just go and get back to my work.' I left the office quietly. I bumped into Gladys as I stepped into the corridor; though this time she didn't need to be loitering outside his door. He could have been heard in the next town.

It was another busy morning and I was rushing into the office from court, my arms full of files. I saw Kevin get out of his car and move toward the entrance in front of me. He turned around, saw me coming and promptly slammed the door in my face. Great, don't have manners; don't bloody open the door for me. I might need to learn how to function as a paraplegic in future and opening doors is good training for me. Jesus, I sighed, my mother told me there would be days like this, she just didn't say there would be so many. I gritted my teeth; I fervently hoped that my visa would be approved soon so that I could finally leave the job and him behind for good.

Meanwhile Kylie, the relocation manager from Australia, sent me a letter which contained email addresses for the other people who were leaving from Ireland and the UK. There were about thirty people, five of whom were from Ireland. I noticed that they were all women but I didn't recognize any of the names. I was at home one night working on a report for court when I received a phone call from my friend, Bronagh.

'Hi, Louise,' she said brightly, 'I'm out tonight with people from work and a friend of one of the girls I know is going to Australia, to the same place as you. Do you want to talk to her?'

Before I had a chance to respond I heard a high-pitched squawk. 'Louise, Louise, I'm Maryann, I'm a friend of Bronagh's friend and I'm going to Australia too. I'm so excited, you know, tomorrow is the start of the rest of your life.'

Actually today is the last day of your life so far but that's neither here nor there. I quickly learned that Maryann talked in bumper stickers.

'Do you want to meet up sometime soon?' she asked breathlessly. I agreed. We arranged to meet after I had finished work the following Friday. I was very curious about meeting someone else who was foolhardy enough to leave behind everything that was familiar. But I was worried about meeting her as I assumed that I would definitely be one of the oldest people going.

When I finally met Maryann I realised that she had clocked up a few miles on the old clock herself. She was about five foot five in height, and the same width. She was so fat she could have had her own postcode. She was dressed from head to toe in pink, like some kind of Barbara Cartland impersonator. Velour tracksuit bottoms are not forgiving. If she pulled her pants down to her knees, her arse would still be in them. Her blonde hair was cut into a severe bob. She had stuck little pink clips with dragonflies attached to them in her hair. They spread all over her head like a fungus. Christ, maybe it wasn't an honour to be chosen for this job; maybe they were desperate.

Maryann explained that she worked for a local voluntary agency, but that she had been off work for a year with glandular fever. 'Do my glands look swollen?' she asked lifting her head. She had more chins than the Hong Kong telephone directory and her neck looked like a pair of hot dogs.

'Em, no, I don't think so,' I replied, unsure of what I was supposed to find under all those layers of fat.

Maryann lost no time in telling me her reasons for going to Australia. 'I understand that there are ten men for every one woman and that they really love Irish girls,' she giggled.

'But you aren't Irish.' I pointed out the blatantly obvious.

'But I've lived in Ireland for two years,' she explained.

And? 'You don't even have an Irish accent.' I again stated the obvious.

'Oh, they won't know the difference. I'll just say bejasus and begorrah. Did she think that Australians were thick? I hoped the Irish mafia existed in Australia and that they would tell her to wind her fat neck in. Irish? Most people wouldn't even understand that she was speaking English. Maryann bleated on, barely waiting to draw breath. Jesus! Didn't they ever shut up on her planet? She told me that she had contacted everyone on the email address list which had been sent from the office in Australia. 'This way I can get to know everyone a bit better before we leave,' she explained. I supposed she had a point. For the first time I began to realise that not only would I be in unfamiliar surroundings, but I would be leaving all of my friends behind. I never had any problems making friends, although I acknowledged that they would not be as nice as the ones I already had, I felt sure it would be easy to meet up with someone I could connect with.

Maryann informed me that she had contacted a woman called Colleen who was hoping to join us this evening.

'I hope you don't mind, but I want to gather round me as many new friends as I can. After all, you will probably be my new family.' Jesus, the cheek of her, she was no family of mine.

Colleen arrived and introduced herself. She, like Maryann, was in her late thirties. She had a short dark helmet of hair which framed a round face with brown eyes. She had lines and wrinkles around her mouth which I suspected had been acquired from her constant look of disapproval. She really should smile. It made people wonder what you were up to.

She was dressed like an unmade bed. She was wearing a pair of red and white striped trousers that look like a pair of pyjamas. She was so flat chested, if she looked down her blouse, the only bumps she would see would be her knees.

She opened a packet of cigarettes and offered me one. I declined. I used to smoke but now I just smouldered. Colleen immediately started to question how far everyone had got with the immigration process. Before we got a chance to reply she answered her own question.

'I've been waiting for a month without any word, so I just phoned Kylie and told her the date that I wanted to come out,' she said firmly.

'But surely it's up to the immigration department to process your visa, not the Children's Bureau,' I said.

'Well, I'm not waiting around. I've already handed in my notice at work and I leave there at the end of the month.'

'But what if the visa takes longer to come through?' I asked in surprise.

'Well, I'll just have to keep phoning the Children's Bureau so they process it quicker.' I could see that Colleen meant it; she was a bossy wee madam. I wondered who had died and made her Darth Vader? Colleen smugly informed us that she had already arranged to rent out her apartment and was going to move back to live with her parents for a while until her visa had been approved. I could see that Maryann was impressed.

'So why are you going out there?' I asked, curious to find out her reasons.

'Well, I just think I might have a better chance there, the lifestyle is so different and it would look good on my CV.' Good, at least she wasn't looking for a husband like Maryann. 'And of course I'm more likely to meet a man there than I am in this place,' she continued looking around the room which was predominately full of couples. Jesus! She was just as bad as that other one.

'Oh, you're right about the lifestyle,' said Maryann breathlessly. 'I'm going to make so many changes to my life. You know, there's so much fresh fruit and food there, and I'm going to go swimming and walking and bicycling and really make huge changes in my life. I'm going to be so fit and healthy. I've already talked it over with my nutritionist and she tells me that I have the opportunity to improve my health there. I hope my allergies will be cured; I suffer so badly with them all,' she sighed in a martyred way. I always ignored health food. I needed all the preservatives I could get.

We moved toward the restaurant and the waitress asked if we wanted smoking or non-smoking seating. I had always thought that having a smoking section in a restaurant was a little like having a peeing section in a pool. Maryann insisted that she had to be seated in a non-smoking section because of all her allergies. She spent the entire time talking about the treatments she had undergone, what she was and wasn't allowed to do in her life and how anything could trigger another bout of glandular fever.

I ordered steak and salad and she immediately started to complain that red meat was bad for me and that I should make another choice. 'Red meat is not bad for you,' I insisted. 'Now, blue-green meat, that's really really bad for you.' Colleen sniggered.

Maryann dominated the entire conversation. She had an opinion on everything, especially issues to do with her ill health. There wasn't much wrong with her mouth I noticed later as she devoured the biggest dessert in the place.

Maryann insisted on taking everyone's email address so she could keep in touch. She sent me an email that evening to say how much she had enjoyed herself and that she was delighted with her new 'family'. I noticed that her email address was floatfreeasadragonfly@hotmail.com. When I questioned her about her choice of name she said she was just like a dragonfly floating on a cloud. Cloud? Railway sleepers couldn't support her.

Colleen, Maryann and I met occasionally and discussed our plans for moving to Australia. The visas seemed to be taking ages to come through, and we couldn't begin work without them. Colleen had left her job, and rented out her apartment. She had gone to live with her parents. I envied her, I would have loved to tell Kevin to stick his job up his arse, but I had bills to pay and didn't have a choice.

Given the difficulties in work since I announced that I would be leaving, I had approached a local employment recruitment agency which was keen to offer me work, but Kevin refused to give me a reference, without which I couldn't work. It was the only power he had over me.

After a couple of weeks without work Colleen decided to go for a short holiday to Greece with her sister to take her mind off all the waiting. On her journey there she met a man called Owen who was sitting in the seat next to her on the plane. They saw quite a bit of each other when they were in Greece and had resumed the relationship when they returned.

'Maybe you won't leave at all now,' said Maryann smugly, 'maybe you'll stay here instead to be with him.'

'No, I'm going,' Colleen said adamantly.

'But how does poor Owen feel about that?' demanded Maryann. She was an information junkie and was always questioning people on the intimate details of their personal lives.

'He has just had to accept it. I've made plans to go there, and I'd sooner meet an Australian man than be stuck here with him and give up the chance of a lifetime. But sure, if it doesn't work out, I can always come back to him. Now,' she said determinedly, 'I'm starving. Has anyone ordered lunch?'

She accosted a waitress and asked for some menus and then ordered a huge meal. I ordered coffee, I wasn't particularly hungry. Maryann hummed and ha'd taking her time over the menu.

'Well,' she said when the waitress had stood over her for an inordinate amount of time. 'I don't want the bun on the burger as I'm allergic to white flour, you know, and I don't want onions as they give me dreadful heartburn, and I'm not so sure about the salad dressing, so I'll just have an undressed salad and a burger without the bap.'

'Would you like fries with that?' asked the waitress cautiously. 'Of course,' snapped Maryann, 'I haven't eaten a thing for hours.'

'I have to be so careful of what I eat,' she confided. 'The slightest thing at all could flare up my glandular fever and I suffer so badly from irritable bowel syndrome. You wouldn't believe the trouble I have had in that department. You know once I ...'

I interrupted her immediately. I didn't want to hear anything about her bloody bowels. 'Will you be going back to England before you leave for Australia?' Genius! It distracted her long enough to avoid the intimate details of her bodily functions.

She seemed to forget all her health problems when the dessert menu arrived. She ordered the largest slice of chocolate cake I had ever seen, which was topped with ice cream and fresh cream.

'Yum, yum,' she said as she tucked into it with gusto. It was the only time during the entire morning that she was quiet. So food was the plug that sealed her mouth. I must remember that in future.

CHAPTER 3

The following week Maryann phoned me at work in great excitement. 'My visa has come through, oh, I'm so excited. I was so worried I wouldn't pass the health examination, what with all my allergies and my glandular fever. I thought I might be turned down. I'm so relieved.' Yes, I'm sure she was relieved, but she wouldn't have given the slightest consideration to the fact that her BMI was probably larger than most people's bank balance.

'So what now? When will you be going?' I asked trying to hide my surprise.

'Oh, I think I might just take my time now that I've got the visa. I don't want to take too much out of myself and I would be so afraid that the journey might exacerbate my glands again.' Her and her bloody glands. Hypochondria was the only disease she hadn't got.

'But, Maryann, it sounds as if they are really short staffed and need people now.'

'Oh, I know, I know and of course I feel so bad about letting them all down, but you know I have to think of myself.' I'm sure that will be really difficult for you.

'When are you hoping to go over?' she continued. 'Maybe we could start our journey together.' She must be fecking joking. There was no way I was going to be stuck in an aircraft for two days with her whingeing and whining about her ailments and wittering away in the background. She never stopped to draw breath. I liked her in small doses, but already I had learned to be very careful about what I said. Not that I distrusted her, you understand, it was just that if I said anything even remotely funny she started to cackle loudly and the high pitched sound physically hurt my ears. She sounded like Orville the Duck on helium.

'And of course I have to rent out my house,' she continued. 'You know I've been looking into it and you have to have fire retardant furniture which means I have to buy new beds and a sofa as the furniture in my house isn't fire proof and I won't be able to rent it out unless I upgrade it.'

'That will cost you a fortune, won't it?' I asked.

'Oh, I've already contacted Australia and asked them for the money to buy the stuff out of my relocation expenses.'

'But your relocation money has to pay for your flights and accommodation and the removal of all your stuff,' I said in surprise. 'Can it be used for that?'

'Well, it's like this,' she said fervently. 'I wouldn't be renting out my house unless I was leaving so they will have to take responsibility for that themselves. I don't see why they shouldn't. If they are that desperate for staff to work for them, then they will just have to help me to be able to go out there.' Right, OK, sorry I asked.

'So what are you planning to do with your house?' she asked casually.

'Well, I figured I might as well sell it,' I replied slowly. 'I've arranged for someone to come out next week and value it and then put it on the market.' I might as well. If you were going to walk on thin ice you might as well dance.

'Oh, I see, so you will be taking all your stuff with you, then?' she asked.

'I probably won't be able to take the electrical stuff so I'll sell it or give it to some of my family and I'll have to get rid of a load of stuff.'

'Well, I've only got a couple of boxes of stuff, so I was wondering if I could put it in with yours as it might save me a bit of money. I mean, of course I'll pay what I have to but it might be cheaper if we put the stuff in together, don't you think?'

'I don't know, Maryann,' I said reluctantly. 'How much stuff do you have?' Was she always going to be such a skinflint?

'Well, I'm only bringing over a couple of boxes of personal stuff and the rest of my things are going into storage,' she reassured me.

'Oh, I suppose that's OK then,' I said reluctantly 'but you need to know that I won't be responsible if anything happens to it or if it gets lost or damaged.'

'OK, that's fair enough,' she said satisfied. She ended the telephone conversation quickly as she was keen to phone Colleen and tell her all about her good news.

After another couple of months when several people had viewed my house, but no offers had been made, I was becoming despondent. What if it never sold? Would I have to continue to pay for a mortgage at home and rent a property over there as well? I knew Colleen and Maryann had decided to rent out their properties, but to me that indicated that they weren't really serious about the whole thing. If I was prepared to move to the other side of the world, I might as well make the jump completely and start a new life. That meant selling my house and taking my chances completely out there.

I had a bit of a browse on the Internet and looked at loads of properties for sale in Australia. Some of the houses were gorgeous but others looked a bit rundown and seedy. They seemed to have a passion over there for net curtains, and I laughed when I read the details of one house, which indicated that the net curtains would be included in the sale. Big tickle. New South Wales seemed to be more expensive than other parts of the country. I hoped I would be able to make some profit from the sale of my own house and be able to put down a reasonable deposit on a new home there.

I had emailed some of the people on the list which the Children's Bureau had sent to me. Most of them were selling their houses and moving over to start afresh and I felt relieved that I was not the only one to take the plunge.

The following month Colleen left for Australia the day after her visa had been approved. She didn't even take the time to say goodbye to Maryann or me. She had promised to contact us both and tell us the truth about the place, what the office was like, and what the working conditions were like too.

I met Maryann several times while I waited for my visa to be processed. She didn't seem to be in any hurry to leave, even though she had tenants lined up to start renting her property.

'But where will you live?' I asked her.

'Oh, I'll just stay with friends for a while until I'm ready to go.'

So she was going to sponge off people for a while. I wondered if there was anything else that was keeping her here. Despite her excitement she seemed almost reluctant to leave.

We had met up for coffee at a venue which also sold ice cream. Maryann asked if I wanted to go and see a play at the local theatre.

'You'll just love it,' she enthused. 'It's all about some man who returns from Australia to a manor house which a relative has left him. It sounds like good fun and we might even pick up some information about our new country.'

I reluctantly agreed to go. Maryann took out her mobile phone and ordered the tickets; she paid immediately by credit card. I opened my purse to reimburse her.

'So that's eighteen pounds for the tickets then,' I said, handing her a twenty pound note. 'Here, just keep the change.'

'Right,' said Maryann, 'but of course because it's a credit card there's an administration charge. Just wait and I'll work it out for you.' I watched with total incredulity as she produced a large calculator from her even larger pink handbag. Her fat fingers prodded the keys; she then turned the calculator towards me.

'I think you'll find that this is a more accurate amount. It includes the price of the phone call too,' she said haughtily.

I had always felt uncomfortable with people who were so pedantic about money. You know what it's like, you go out for a meal and someone starts to complain that they haven't eaten bread so their contribution should be less. Don't tell me she was going to be the same? I diligently handed over the allocated amount without protest. She held the money in her chubby hands before transferring it to a pink purse.

'So what would you like?' I asked her, turning round so she could see the many varieties of ice cream on offer. Her face was pink with excitement; she looked like a child in a sweetshop.

'Go on,' I said indulgently, 'have whatever you like, my treat.' She clapped her podgy hands excitedly like a demented seal.

'Well, in that case I'll have a scoop of the strawberry and one of chocolate and a scoop of, em, let me see, oh, yes, that butterscotch one looks lovely and one of the mint.'

'Is it just for you, then?' Clearly the girl behind the counter was as surprised as me. I hoped she was on a commission.

'Yes,' continued Maryann, 'and of course I want some sprinkles and a wafer and a chocolate flake.'

'Right,' said the waitress, 'and for yourself then?'

'Oh, just a black coffee,' I said hastily. She looked at me in relief; I didn't want her to think I had suddenly joined Over Indulgers Anonymous. She reached for the biggest dish she could find. I swear it was a family-sized portion, and she began to pile on the ice cream and toppings; she had to push to get all the ice cream to fit into the bowl. She nearly staggered under the weight of the thing as she placed it on the counter. Before I could ask Maryann if there was anything else she wanted she was over at the table practically inhaling the food, her face only inches from the plate.

I paid for the desserts, yes, all of them. The price of it nearly made me spill my coffee. I could have bribed a bunch of gangsters for half that amount.

We duly went to see the play. Maryann tittered and guffawed from the front seat while I sat there in silence. It wasn't my type of thing at all, and I was bored. I'd had fun before, but this wasn't it.

During the interval I asked Maryann to order me a glass of wine while I went to the toilet. I knew there would be a queue for the toilets and that she would have to pay for my drink. I was right. When I returned she was staring at the change in her hand and mentally working out where her money had gone. I took a sip of wine and left the rest of it on the table when we were called for the second half.

'Aren't you going to drink that?' Maryann asked in dismay.

'No, I've gone off it now,' I said casually and moved towards the entrance to the theatre. I turned round to see her gulping it down her throat as quickly as she could, which was a miracle in itself as she didn't drink alcohol.

Afterwards we decided to go for a cup of coffee. I ordered a coffee while Maryann chose hot chocolate, with all the trimmings, cream, sprinkles and a chocolate flake. Well, here was a girl who didn't let her size affect her life choices. I paid for the drinks, observing that once again Maryann was studying the menu closely and had made no attempt to extract her purse from her handbag.

The waitress brought my coffee over and then returned with the largest hot chocolate I had ever seen. The mug was piled so high with sweetie stuff it would take two strapping farmers to lift it. Maryann didn't find this any problem at all. She got stuck in. As she ate greedily she looked at the receipt on the table in front of me where the waitress had left it.

'That can't be right,' she said.

'What?' Was there something else she could have shoved in there?

'Those extras, that can't be right.' Before I could question her further she had left the table and gone up to speak to the waitress. I heard her argue with the waitress about the price of the extra toppings she had ordered. The waitress pointed to the menu board which clearly indicated the price of each extra topping.

'Well, I've never had to pay so much for a hot chocolate,' Maryann protested huffily. I hung my head in embarrassment, conscious of the sidelong glances of the other diners who were clearly enjoying the fact that Maryann was making a total spectacle of herself. She waddled to the table still clutching the receipt.

'This is the most expensive place I've ever been in,' she complained loudly, lifting her spoon to dig out the remains of what was left of the disputed drink.

'I wouldn't worry about it, Maryann,' I said gently taking the receipt from her hand and putting it in my pocket. 'You didn't pay for it anyway.'

'Huh?' She obviously wasn't Irish as we always fight with each other over who gets to pay the bill. That would be the last time she ever humiliated me like this.

I gathered my bags and left the coffee shop with her following closely on my heels. I said goodbye and walked away. There are some people who cause happiness wherever they go and others whenever they go. I was relieved to get into my car welcoming the solitude and peace it offered.

I drove home asking myself what I had got involved in this time. If there was ever an idiot in the room they always seemed to gravitate toward me. I knew that leaving my home and family would be very difficult and that I might be dependent on Maryann and Colleen. It wasn't a thought that rested easily with me. I wondered if the whole relocation thing was not some big joke. You know, some kind of a social experiment where they put people together who would not normally have anything to do with each other. That's what it was, some type of scientific experiment, but with people instead of laboratory rats. I was determined to make as many new contacts as I could when I arrived in Australia so I wouldn't be stuck with either of them.

I wondered why Maryann was free during the day as she was always contactable at home. I had assumed that she worked antisocial hours but she told me that she had accused her line manager of bullying her and that she wasn't going back to work until it had all been resolved. Bullying? She wouldn't know what it meant if it bit her on her fat arse. She could have learned a few things about being bullied by Kevin who was still making my life a living hell.

From what I understood of the situation her employers had advised her that she had been on sick leave for a year, and that they couldn't afford to replace her but they needed to know if she was returning to work. She had contacted the union and made a huge fuss. As far as I could tell the bullying saga amounted to her team leader giving her an alleged dirty look one wet Wednesday afternoon.

Eventually she was awarded thirteen thousand pounds from her former employers when she agreed to resign. I was beginning to think that thirteen grand was money well spent if they ended up getting rid of her. Christ, I could learn a lot from this girl.

A few days later I was just leaving the house to go to work when the phone rang. It was Kylie. 'Your visa has been approved,' she informed me. 'So you can arrange to come over whenever you want now.' I was excited. This was it; this was my ticket out of hell.

I telephoned my family. I knew my mother would worry about me moving to the other side of the world. But I was a big girl now.

'And you won't be doing anything silly, now will you, Louise?' she asked me cautiously. Hmm, clearly this was a reference to the disaster of a husband I had chosen for myself. Isn't it funny that when you are with someone no one makes any comment but when you split up, they all tell you that they never liked him in the first place. Everyone who had ever met Patrick told me the same thing, but unfortunately only after it was all over so I was left feeling that I was the only one who had liked him. I should have known better because I realised from the start that I was always going to be second place in his life. I would always be following closely behind the real love of his life, his mammy. She was a cold hard interfering bitch of a woman who looked and dressed just like Margaret Thatcher and she had the social skills and compassion to match. While most Irish mammies were trying to marry their daughters off, after my disaster mine was begging me not to do it again.

'Don't worry, Mum.' I said, 'I'm not going out there to get a husband. I'm going for the work.' Mum knew that I had problems in my job with the boss but I didn't want to tell her just how bad it had become. I wasn't sleeping at night and when I did get to sleep I woke up early every morning, dreading the thought of going into the office. I had accumulated hours of flexitime which I hadn't able to use as Kevin had refused to let me take any. I would have to contact the Finance Department and make sure that I was reimbursed for this time with money before I left. I would be glad of it as I had to pay solicitors and estate agents for the sale of the house.

I phoned Sinead, my friend. She had suffered at the hands of Kevin too, but she had been lucky enough to be transferred to a different office. We supported each other as best we could through all the horrible behaviour he inflicted on us. Sinead knew that I was planning to leave because I could no longer tolerate working for Kevin but she thought it was terrible that I had to move so far away. She encouraged me to think about the consequences, but all I could see ahead was my exit route.

Once when I was at a meeting with the police and Kevin, we were waiting for another worker to join us. Alan, the police officer, started to talk about a case that he and I had dealt with a few months previously. A man in the Psychiatric Unit had alleged that another patient had sexually assaulted him.

'Of course by the time we arrived the patient had discharged himself,' explained Alan. Kevin sniggered.

'Yes, in more ways than one,' he chortled lecherously. I felt extremely uneasy; he should have won awards for creating a humiliating work environment.

Kevin called me into his office later that day. 'I've received a complaint about you,' he sneered menacingly.

'Oh, is it from the guy you sent over to the solicitor's office to make a complaint about me?' I asked casually. 'You do know that the solicitor rang me and told me all about it?' He visibly blanched.

'No,' he stuttered, 'Yvette has made a complaint about you, and I am upholding it. You have been encouraging staff to take sick leave.' What the hell was he wittering on about now? Seeing the look of confusion on my face, he continued. 'I know you told Yvette to stay at home and not come to work.' He primped himself up to his full height. 'That is a sackable offence, you know.'

'I don't know what you are talking about,' I confessed, racking my brains to think of anything I had said to Yvette which might have been misconstrued. Yvette had also faced the wrath of Kevin. He was never content having just one victim. While I became more withdrawn and anxious in the office her health had deteriorated significantly. She had been forced to take a few days on sick leave and I had phoned her to enquire how she was feeling and encouraged her not to come back until she was ready.

'I think you must have misunderstood just what I said to Yvette,' I said as calmly as I could, trying to quell the nerves which were knotting themselves like a rope in my stomach. 'I was trying to be sympathetic and to offer support.' Not that you'd know much about either, I thought silently.

'Well, Yvette is making a complaint about you,' he said gleefully, 'so once she does that you'll be sacked.' He smirked, pleased that he had finally found a way to get rid of me. I was devastated. I liked Yvette; we had tried to support each other as much as possible during Kevin's onslaughts. Had she turned traitor? Had she decided to bat for the other side? I left his office in a state of shock. Despite the offer of a new job in Australia my position here would be finished. He had always threatened to destroy my career and it looked like he had done it. I entered the office where Yvette was typing up a report. I could hardly bear to look at her.

'Is anything wrong?' she questioned gently. Judas! She knew bloody rightly what was wrong.

'Nothing much,' I sniffed. 'I know you've made a complaint about me, and I just wanted to say that I was only trying to offer you support. I wasn't trying to get you into trouble, or myself for that matter.' She looked at me as if I had two heads.

'I think you'd better explain what has happened,' she said slowly as she rose to close the office door. This would be a tasty titbit for Gladys. She was probably outside now. I told her all that Kevin had told me.

'But I didn't make a complaint,' she insisted. 'I was only relaying the conversation we had to Susan. I told her that you had told me to go back to the doctors to make sure I was well enough to return to work. I never for one minute even suggested that you had tried to encourage me to stay away from work. Jesus, Louise,' she sighed, 'you wouldn't need to do that. I have enough trouble trying to persuade myself to stay in this place as it is.'

'But then how? Was it Susan who suggested it to him?' I asked.

'No, I'll tell you who it was,' she sighed. 'It was Kevin. He came into the room as I was talking to Susan. He must have misheard what I said, or else he has twisted it around to suit his evil needs as usual. Yes,' she nodded, 'this would be his perfect excuse to get rid of you for good. Well, I'll sort this out now.' She left the office and returned a short time later. Her face was red and the tears glistened in her eyes.

'What happened?' I asked, though I could see on her face that it hadn't been a positive encounter.

'He basically told me that if I submitted a letter of complaint about you, then he would be nicer to me.'

'No!' The bastard. There really is a place in hell for people like him.

'Yes, I told him to shove it. I'm not going to start behaving like him.' I looked at her. It was on the tip of my tongue to say that she might have a quieter life, but I was relieved to learn that the woman had morals and values and I wasn't going to try to persuade her to cross over to the dark side, to him. I'd really need to watch my back though, as his harassment of me was escalating; now he was using whoever he came into contact with to get at me.

Yvette came into work the next day. She handed me a letter. 'I've copied this for Kevin and sent one to the Personnel Department as well,' she explained. I opened the envelope slowly. She had written that she was adamant that I had not actively forced her or encouraged her to remain on sick leave. She said that she was an adult and would made decisions about her own health in consultation with her GP and she protested that I had not influenced her in any manner.

'I know he's going to get back at me for this, Louise,' she said nervously, 'but I had to do what was right, though I think he's trying to divide and conquer.'

I hung my head, knowing that her words were prophetic. But at least I had planned my escape route. Yvette would be stuck here when I finally left. This would be an opportune time to tell him that I was going.

I took great pride in telling Kevin that I could at last give him a date when I would leave. I asked if I could use some of my eighty hours of flexitime I had accumulated to get packed up but he refused. He held on to the last little bit of power and control he had over me. Keep calm, I told myself, not all managers are annoying. Some are dead.

Kevin finally allowed me to leave work the day before I had planned, as he knew that the staff had organized a leaving party for me the next day. If I was not at work I wouldn't be able to go. He even took my security pass off me in case I tried to sneak back into the building. He had to be joking. I couldn't get far enough away from the place, though I would have loved to have the chance to deliver the goodbye speech I had prepared. That might have been what he was afraid of.

I spent the next two weeks saying goodbye to people who had been so significant in my life for so long. It was the strangest process; people felt the need to tell me things that they would not normally have voiced, as if I was dying. I knew just what the American wakes felt like now, when people emigrated, knowing they would never see their family again. This was the most painful thing I had ever done. I spent most of the time in tears, hugging people and promising that I would keep in touch. I knew even before I left that it would never be the same if I returned. My friends would get on with their own lives and I might never be able to fit back in again.

I was filled with fear and trepidation as I left for the airport early one Sunday morning in August. Sinead had agreed to drive me there. It would have been too painful to have my family say goodbye to me, but in leaving Sinead I know I was leaving one of the best friends I had ever had. She had been there for me in every crisis I had ever experienced and we had shared loads of adventures together. She was my sparring partner when it came to jokes and one-liners, and she knew the dialogue from all the old classic films. We had spent many a happy afternoon lolling around watching black and white movies and eating our weight in sweets.

I left her at the entrance to the departure lounge; I could hardly see the desk official in front of me through my tears. I turned round to wave a final goodbye to Sinead, to my life as I had known it, and to my country. I had a return ticket to use within a year, and I wondered how my life would have changed when I came back.

CHAPTER 4

I boarded the plane and strapped myself in. I tried to settle myself, but I was inconsolable. I stared out of the window and tried to hold on to every last glance of my country. I couldn't concentrate enough to read any of the papers or books I had brought with me. I sobbed continually from Belfast to London. People must have thought I was leaving home in a huff or going to London for an abortion.

Although my sense of direction is so bad I could be drawing maps for NATO, I managed to negotiate myself round Heathrow Airport. I followed the signs to the airport terminal which would take me to Sydney.

The tears flowed on and off throughout the entire two-day journey and while my fellow travellers were able to sleep, I couldn't. Every time I closed my eyes my mind filled with images of all that I was leaving behind. I was also frightened of what the future held in store for me. What if running away brought a different set of problems? What if I was making the biggest mistake of my life?

The plane finally landed at Sydney airport and I collected my luggage and joined the lengthy queue through Immigration.

'So what brings you to Australia?' The immigration officer was only being friendly and really, he didn't want the whole story, it was all too lengthy, too complicated anyway. What should I have said? That I was running away from the boss from hell? Everyone had told me how brave I was, exploring new territory at my age, but at this stage I was beginning to wonder if I was brave or stupid? After a thirty-six-hour journey it didn't seem such a clever idea after all. I looked a complete wreck and wearing the same clothes for two days didn't help my mood. While I had been in the air I had the irrational thought that if the plane crashed and I died I'd be stuck wearing the same clothes for all eternity.

I passed though immigration and followed the directions to the airport terminal which would leave me at my final destination. I hadn't seen much of the country so far and I wondered what this new city would look like. Despite all of Colleen's promises to keep in regular contact she hadn't done so. She had sent an odd text message and one email but she hadn't been particularly forthcoming about all the details of the place.

She was waiting for me in the airport lounge. I burst into tears when I saw her, the first and only person I was able to recognize in this new country. Kylie was there as a representative from the Children's Bureau to welcome me. We collected all my worldly possessions from the baggage carousel, and walked towards the car.

'I've booked you this car for the next three weeks,' said Kylie, 'but if you like Colleen can drive it now, as you are probably a bit disorientated.' She was right, I was exhausted. How could it be so tiring just sitting on my arse for two days?

As we drove to the apartment I would be staying in for the next three weeks I was struck by how clean the town was. There was no litter on the pavements and it seemed to be neat and orderly. Christ, it's Pleasantville, I thought, a bit unkindly, but the place looked a bit sterile. It really was suburbia: where they tore out the trees and then named streets after them.

We arrived at my accommodation. All I could see were blocks of apartments. There wasn't a person to be seen anywhere. We entered the apartment which was well decorated and neatly furnished. It had a double bed with built-in wardrobes, a small living room which had a two piece suite of furniture and a television set. There was a small kitchen and dining area. At least the bathroom was nice as it had a Jacuzzi, and a washing machine and dryer. My home for the next few weeks. I thought of the home I had left behind, a four-bedroom three-reception detached house and thought how the mighty had fallen. But I would have all of that again, in time. This was going to be a fresh start. I was going to rebuild my life.

After a cup of coffee Kylie and Colleen left. It was evident I was exhausted. I kept missing bits out of their sentences. Colleen arranged to take the car and return it to me the next day.

I woke in the middle of the night feeling totally disorientated, unsure of my surroundings. After two interrupted nights' sleep on the airplane and no sleep since the night before I left Ireland my body clock was out of sync. I got up and made a cup of coffee and looked out of the window. It was too cold on the terrace to sit outside. Was that because it was so early in the morning? Was it always this cold? I hadn't packed any winter clothing believing that Australia was one of the warmest countries on earth, and that I would only be wearing T-shirts and cool clothing from now on.

I counted out the time difference; it would be evening at home. I phoned my parents to let them know I had arrived safely and promised to keep in touch regularly. I couldn't maintain a conversation for any length of time with either of them; it was too painful as already I was missing them so much.

I took a sleeping pill and returned to bed. I pulled my coat over me as I couldn't find a spare blanket. I only woke when the cleaner came in to clean the room. She took pity on me and let me sleep on.

I had my first look at the town the next evening when Colleen drove over to bring me out to dinner. She had chosen a place near my apartment which was full of people eating and drinking outside while the sun was shining. I was finding it difficult to thaw out and suggested we eat inside.

I talked to Colleen about work; she had arrived in July, only two months before me. She encouraged me to take a few weeks to settle in before starting, but I knew that finances were going to be particularly tight and that I would have to start work as soon as possible. I still had a mortgage to pay at home while I waited for my house to sell. Colleen informed me that the apartment was only rented for three weeks, along with the car, and that I should start immediately to search for more permanent accommodation. She agreed to come with me and help me look for suitable properties at the weekend.

I spent the next couple of days driving round in the hired car, exploring my surroundings, trying to familiarize myself with my new home. I got lost more times than enough, and made a fool of myself turning on the wipers which were on the same side as the indicators at home.

I drove around New South Wales and stopped in a little place called Queanbeyan. But I felt more at home there as the town seemed to have a soul. I parked the car in an underground car park and snickered when I saw a sign which advertised the travelator to the fashion precinct. It was only an escalator to a shopping centre. The clothes were about twenty years behind anything I had seen at home. I kicked myself when I thought of all the clothes I had given away. I had thrown away better than what was on sale in the shops. I walked around the town for a while and discovered a second-hand bookshop where I bought a couple of books and then treated myself to a cup of coffee.

The accent was strange. Australians have an inflection; they go up at the end of their sentences, so everything sounds like a question. They have a habit of putting the word 'look' into a sentence which always made me jump. Back home we only said 'look' when we were trying to force a point, and usually by that stage the exchange would be a bit heated, and probably include fists. But here they used it before every question like, 'Look, do you want coffee? Look, do you have the time?'

Later Colleen and I went out for drinks to a local bar. A rock band was playing and the place was packed. This was more like it, a bit of night life. We sat at the bar and ordered drinks. At least Colleen wasn't like Maryann; she paid her way.

As the alcohol flowed Colleen began to tell me the truth about Australia and why she hadn't kept in touch as regularly as she had promised.

'It's not what they promised us,' she confided. 'The Aussies think we've come over and taken their jobs, and some of them are very resentful and hostile to us. They also seem to have given all the overseas workers all the worse clients.'

Hmm, I wasn't prepared for this. 'But what do you hope to get out of it all?' I asked.

'I'm hoping I might meet someone and then get married, get my citizenship and move somewhere else, maybe to Queensland or somewhere more exciting.'

'And have you been out with anyone since you came over?' I asked her casually.

'No, there doesn't seem to be anyone interested at this point,' she said sadly.

I looked around the bar. OK so maybe the Aussies weren't the bonniest race I'd ever seen; the gene pool could use a little chlorine. But there seemed to be some nice men here, like the one who was walking towards me this very minute.

'How ya going?' he asked me. 'Going? I've only just got here,' I explained while Colleen laughed and interpreted the Australian greeting for me.

He introduced himself. Richard asked if he could buy me a drink. I introduced him to Colleen who scowled at him. He signalled to his friend to join us and Richard introduced him to Colleen.

We began to chat; he seemed a nice bloke and he told me that he was really taken with my accent. This was more like it, a bit of attention and all I had to do was open my mouth. Why had Colleen said it was difficult?

At one point in the evening Richard excused himself to go to the toilets, and Colleen accosted me. 'Christ, you are only just off the plane and you have some guy eating out of your hand,' she gushed breathlessly.

'Ach, men, they're two a penny,' I replied, 'if you want one you can always find one.'

'But you make it look so easy,' she said in surprise. 'I should take flirting lessons from you.'

I changed the subject as quickly as I could. 'So do you like his friend?' I asked.

'Yes, he's gorgeous,' admitted Colleen, 'but I just can't do that flirting thing.'

'Just smile, Colleen,' I advised her. 'You're just the type, you have a pulse.'

Later on I heard her talking to Joe; she was practically interrogating the poor man. Next thing she would be asking him for his bank balance. What was wrong with the girl? Inevitably Joe made a lame excuse and went home alone, leaving Richard alone with Colleen and me. She got a cab back to her apartment and Richard walked me home. He was a lovely guy, but I was just not interested in a relationship with anyone. He asked for my phone number but I was a bit dishonest and gave him the wrong one. Maybe the fake number belonged to some nice girl who would turn out to be the love of his life. He kissed me goodbye and left.

Next morning I paid heavily for the cheap wine I had drunk the night before. A hangover was definitely the wrath of grapes. Why was I so thirsty when I had drunk so much last night? I spent a quiet day writing letters. I knew it was going to take a bit of effort on my part to maintain all my links with home but I was determined I wouldn't lose touch with anyone. Does that not give you an indication that I was trying to hold on to the past with both hands while being pushed into another life?

Colleen phoned. 'Hello, slut bag,' she said.

'Excuse me?' I said in horror.

'Well, you have only just arrived and you've men falling all over you. I've decided that I'm going to call you slut bag from now on.'

'And if you do that,' I said slowly, 'I will just have to kill you.' Silence. Jesus, what kind of an eejit was she? Did she think I was going to embrace that label? I could just visualize her introducing me to people. Oh Jane, how are you? Meet my friend, slut bag?? How not to win friends and influence people. I would nip this one in the bud once and for all. Just because some bloke walked me home didn't mean I was easy. The sad thing was she probably wanted to earn that particular label herself. Colleen told me that the overseas people had planned to meet up for drinks next day after work.

'Why don't you come along?' she encouraged me. 'You'll get a chance to meet people.' It sounded like it might be fun, and I was curious to see what the other overseas recruits were like.

I dressed in jeans and a nice top and waited outside the Children's Bureau for Colleen. This time next week I'd be getting out of the place myself. Colleen pulled heavily on a cigarette the moment she stepped outside the building and we walked towards a local bar. Colleen introduced me to some people and I began to chat. I felt comfortable enough; most of the people were very welcoming.

I sat down at a table with Mandy, one of the women I had e-mailed regularly. She was lovely. She had arrived the day before, and this was her first opportunity to meet up with people as well. We were soon exchanging stories about all that had happened since we had arrived when a woman approached us.

'Hiya, I'm Cheryl, so I am,' she said in the broadest Belfast accent I have ever heard. She sat down beside me. 'I'm from Belfast too, you know,' she said. I'd never have guessed.

'Oh, good, another Irish person. We're getting the numbers up rightly,' I smiled.

'I'm not Irish, so I'm not,' she snapped at me, the spittle forming on her bottom lip. 'I'm British, so I am.' Great, I'd come thousands of miles from home and I was faced with a diehard unionist.

'Have they taul ye who's gonna be your boss?' Cheryl asked as she gulped from a large pint of beer.

'I think I'm going to be in Tom's team,' I smiled.

'You're having me on. God, that's brilliant, so it is. Wait till I tell my wee chum. Here, Bianca c'm here till you hear this,' she shouted. She could have been heard in the next state. 'Wait till you hear, this wee doll here is after getting a job on Tom's team,' she bellowed across the room.

Bianca was another overseas recruit from England. She came tottering unsteadily towards us. She was wearing a short tight skirt, a striped sports top and white stilettos. She was wearing an excessive amount of gold jewellery including the hugest gold hoop earrings I had ever seen. Her nails, obviously false, were like talons. 'Here, Bianca, this here's Louise, so it is and Tom's getting her on his team, so he is.' I saw Cheryl and Bianca exchange a look. What? What was that look about? Was there something I was missing here?

'Well, it's shockin', so it is, but somebody has to tell you,' Cheryl gushed breathlessly. 'God love you, you'll soon find out for yourself, so you will. It's a disgrace, so it is, the way he makes you work all on your own. He niver gives you a bit of help at all, so he doesn't. He thinks he's one of them high-flyer thingamajigs. I know this all for miself, so I do, 'cos he's my boss too, but he's

46

fuckin' useless, so he is. He just makes you do all his work, so he does, and you will just have till work on your own, so you will.'

Well, I'd prefer that to having some manager breathing down my neck every five minutes like my last one. She continued without interruption. 'But it's just awful working for him, so it is, 'cos you won't get supervision or nothing. Honest to God, you should see the state of him, so you should.'

'Yeah, he's well useless, innit,' joined in Bianca taking a huge gulp from the bottle of Smirnoff ice that she was swinging in her hand.

'Oh, is he your manager too?' I asked cautiously.

'No,' she snorted, 'he's nuffin' to me but I fink Cheryl's right.' She looked at Cheryl in adoration. Sweet Jesus, what language was she speaking?

'What are the rest of the team like?' I asked nervously fearing that I wouldn't like whatever answer she gave me.

'Oh they really think they're somefink, so they do, but you'll find out just you wait and see. You'll be sorry you came out here, so you will,' said Cheryl threateningly.

I smiled patronisingly at her. 'Here I'm tellin ya,' shouted Cheryl aggressively 'I've had problems with them so I have 'cos I was here before Bianca so I just thought I should luk out for her. God love her, she's only a wee doll so she is. And now we sit together and everyfink, so we do.'

'Yeah,' drawled Bianca. 'Cheryl's been proper nice to me.' Cheryl preened.

Cheryl's husband Fred joined us and Cheryl introduced him to me. He shook my hand. He was pissed.

'What wus your name again luv?' he slurred.

I told him. He turned straight to Cheryl and gave her a knowing look. I knew that look. This was the look that I had seen a million times in the North of Ireland. It was a look that says, we know what you are. You are one of those. The others. The ones who are not like us. I expected him to wipe his hand after discovering he had touched a Taig, which is how a lot of Protestants refer to Catholics. But to be fair to the man, he didn't.

'You'll have to lose that there accent,' he scoffed at me.

'Pardon?' What the hell was he talking about? I spoke clearly and the Australians didn't seem to have any problem in understanding me.

'Yeah, you'll have to tone it down a bit so you will, now that you're in Australia.'

47

'Why?' I asked suspiciously.

'You don't want people to think you're from West Belfast,' he said snidely curling his top lip in distaste.

'What do you mean?' I was insulted, as I was probably supposed to be.

'You don't want to sound like somethin from some Catholic ghetto,' he sneered. The sectarian bastard. Jesus Christ, you take someone thousands of miles but scratch the surface and you will always find the bigot. I thought I had left all of that behind me.

'Actually,' I said getting up from the seat and standing up to my full five feet and one inch height, though I was probably a bit taller tonight as I was wearing heels. 'I am from West Belfast and I make no apologies for it and I didn't come here to change anything about me.'

I saw the anger flare in his eyes. He stood up unsteadily and glared at me. He looked as if he wanted to punch me. I didn't move. He swayed and shook his head then put his glass of beer down on the table noisily.

'This is the first time I've met anyone from the office so thanks for making a good impression on me,' I said. 'You've all reinforced my inherent distrust of strangers.' I turned to walk away. I was disgusted. Mandy was standing behind me.

'What a bastard,' she gasped.

'Did you hear all that?' I asked in disbelief.

'Yes, I did,' she replied. 'I thought he was going to hit you.' She shook her head worriedly. 'And as for those other two bitches, I can't get over the cheek of them trying to put you off your manager before you've even started. And you only just off the plane too.'

'I know. I'm supposed to start work on Monday but after hearing all that I'll have to think about it a bit more.'

'You aren't thinking of leaving and going home already are you?' asked Mandy in surprise.

'I don't know, Mandy. They've certainly given me a lot of things to think about.' I really didn't know what I was going to do next. Mandy gave me her telephone number.

'Look, take this, ring me anytime,' she said warmly.

'Thanks, Mandy,' I said. I could see that she was a decent woman. She was as shocked by their behaviour as I was. I walked away to find Colleen. I briefly told her what had happened. 'Oh, that Cheryl, she's really bigoted. She's always making horrible remarks about Irish people,' insisted Colleen.

'And they let her get away with it?'

'I don't think people in this country know much about what has been happening at home. Sure do you not remember when we got the list of email addresses from everyone who was coming over? Well, Cheryl was the only one from Ireland who didn't meet up with us. Did you not think that was a bit strange?' she questioned slyly.

'I did,' I replied. I had wondered what was happening there.

'Well,' Colleen gushed, 'she let it slip to Bianca that she didn't meet up with any of us because she could tell from our names that we were all Catholics.'

'And Bianca told you this?' I was shocked. Did Cheryl know that her best friend was blubbering all over the shop about her?

'Yes,' said Colleen determinedly, 'I share an apartment with Bianca and Fiona from home. Bianca has told me everything that Cheryl has said but I don't want to get into it all now.'

'OK, look, Colleen, I've had enough. I think I'll just go on home now,' I said wearily.

'Don't let her be putting you off,' she insisted. 'There are some nice people here.'

'I know but I'm still a bit jetlagged. I just want to go to bed.' I tried to sound convincing but I was exhausted and becoming increasingly worried that I had made the biggest mistake of my life.

'No problem,' she smiled, 'I'll stay here and wait for the men to come in. You never know what might happen tonight. She giggled. 'Sure I'll give you a ring in the morning and we can meet up for lunch, but only if I'm not busy,' she smirked. Hmm, she'd be lucky.

'Great, thanks, Colleen,' I smiled as I left the bar and walked towards a taxi rank. This day was a total waste of make-up. I needed time to think about the whole thing. If this was the way the staff acted on the first day I met them, was there any point in pursuing this? I had a return ticket; my house still hadn't sold at home. I could just get my bags and go to the airport and put this all behind me. If the team manager was as useless as they claimed he was, I really didn't want to be there. I had suffered enough last time due to my incompetent boss. I didn't want to go through all that again. Cheryl would be in my team too but so far I was not impressed with her. As for that other one who had legs as thin as an anorexic's toothpick, she was just hero worshipping Cheryl. She was just a social work groupie. I couldn't warm to her at all.

CHAPTER 5

I thought long and hard over the weekend as to whether I should even take up my position with the Children's Bureau. But Colleen argued that I shouldn't let a couple of bitches put me off what I came here to do. I decided to give it a try. If all else failed at least I had a return ticket in my bag. I carried it round with me like a security blanket.

I got up early. I had to; they started work at the Children's Bureau at 8.30am. The office was huge. Eight floors of a glass building in the city centre. It had two uniformed security guards at the front desk and a barrier system which prevented people from entering without the required security pass. I was very impressed; they must really care about the staff's personal safety here. I learned later that a director of child protection services had been shot, so the Children's Bureau was determined to protect the one they had. It had nothing to do with the safety and welfare of the plebs.

Kylie came down to the reception area to meet me. She chatted away as she escorted me into a lift and led me up to the sixth floor where I would be working. It was a cube farm and a cubicle is just a padded cell without a door. Each cubicle had four workstations which had state of the art computers. Everyone was sitting at a computer typing away on the keyboard for all they were worth.

I was introduced to the operations manager who seemed really nice. My co-workers seemed friendly enough. Lizzie, Laura and Janet shared my pod while Linda and Sally worked in the adjoining pod along with Cheryl. I greeted Cheryl and she said hello but quickly returned to her desk. Bianca was also rushing around as if she knew what she was doing. She didn't speak to me. Huh, she had been in a different frame of mind last week when she had plenty to say about my boss. Maybe she felt ashamed of her behaviour and was embarrassed to see me. She worked on the other side of the cubicle from me, and I could hear her voice generating out above all the others. She was a chav. I'm sorry, I'm not being a snob, but she looked like a pram face. Today she was wearing a pair of tracksuit bottoms, white trainers and her hair was pulled back in a tight ponytail, the typical housing estate facelift.

I met Tom, my team manager, who seemed like a lovely man. He was from England and he said he was glad that I would be bringing some experience with me. He was very welcoming and told me that I should just take a few days to settle in and find my feet, and that he wouldn't be giving me any work for a short while. He seemed very competent and at least he could communicate unlike Kevin. I wondered if Cheryl and Bianca were just being vindictive and nasty when they had warned me about him.

It took a bit of time to settle in; everything was done so differently from home. At first I felt deskilled, unsure of myself, trying hard to keep up with the new legislation which would guide my practice. I read case files and took part in a basic induction programme to familiarize myself with the work which the Children's Bureau did and what services the non government agencies provided.

I learned that Australians had a huge addiction to sweets though they called them lollies. At every meeting I attended there were always jars of sweets sitting on the table. They were also obsessed with morning and afternoon tea. They would nearly have a riot if they were deprived of these breaks. The first question they asked me when I started work was my birth date so they could plan for afternoon tea. They had parties for everyone, when the office stopped dead while someone blew out the candles on their cake. Have you ever noticed that birthday cake is the only food you can blow on and spit on and everybody rushes to get a piece?

The travel guides had warned that the majority of people who lived in this town were pubes. Public servants. It was true, they all raced through the town to be in time for work at 8.30am. Then at lunch time they would converge onto the streets, spilling out into cafes and restaurants for lunch. It was like a sea of suits. Then they would return to work before they raced out again on the 4.51pm express, which was when they finished their day. You could recognize the pubes as they all wore identification badges, either clipped onto waistbands or round their necks on coloured lanyards. I shuddered when I realised that I had become one of them too.

Everything was different. The ice lollies that I knew at home were called icy poles. I couldn't find Marmite. I missed the Sunday Times and Munchies. The chocolate here was disgusting. As well as all the normal daily things, I missed my family and friends more than I could ever admit. Every night I tried to come to terms with their absence in my life. I berated myself for making the move. I should have taken a job in Tesco's. Why did I let some bullying manager force me to leave my country where all my family and friends still remained? Everyone in work had their own friends and family to think about and they hadn't the time or energy to spare on some lonely immigrant.

I spent a lot of time crying at the most inappropriate times. Like at my desk. The slightest thing would set me off. Tom let me listen to the soundtrack of one of the bands from home and I burst into tears in front of the poor man. He put off having supervision with me for a while in case he had to ask me how I was feeling.

Colleen was very patient with my homesickness, but it was clear she hadn't had the strong friendships I had been lucky enough to have. When she had gone out socially at home it was always with her older sister who was married with a family. She didn't seem to have many friends. We met up after work for a drink. It was Monday night and the bar was deserted apart from two men, quite obviously public servants who were chatting together in between taking calls on their cell phones.

I had my head down doodling on the back of a newspaper when I looked up as one of them approached the table. His colleague had evidently left. He asked if he could sit down and Colleen, never missing an opportunity, agreed. I was a bit surprised; I wouldn't have thought he would have been her type. He was about fifty with a red flushed, shiny face and thinning hair. He was dressed in a dark navy suit, white shirt and tie. He had pink sapphire cufflinks and a matching tie pin. He had marinated himself in aftershave; I nearly choked when he sat down beside me. He began to chat, asking where we were from and where we worked. He asked Colleen for a cigarette and she gave him one. I smiled politely but continued to doodle, letting them get on with it. He pulled his chair closer to me until his knee was touching mine. I froze and moved my leg away swiftly. I waited for his apology but none was forthcoming. He started to press his right knee against my thigh while he continued to talk idly to Colleen. She was clearly interested. He talked about a boat he had recently acquired and he wondered if we would be interested in going for a sail with him. He moved his knee towards me again, never faltering in his eye contact with her. I felt as if a slug had just crawled along my leg. I subtly changed my position in the seat moving my body away from him and practically squashing myself into the wall. He widened his legs and continued to exert pressure on my knee and began to move it up and down, like a dog humping. He smiled lecherously at me, a snake in a suit.

'Do you mind?' I asked coldly and pulled my chair away. He didn't flinch, but after a few minutes began to slide his body toward mine again. The dirty bastard. I was repulsed. I stood up.

'Look, mister, I'm not interested in you so why don't you just fuck off.' Sometimes the only way to get rid of creeps like this is the direct approach. Colleen looked up mid-sentence, her mouth agape. I stood up expecting her to follow me, but she sat on. She looked annoyed; her mouth was pursed in displeasure. I grabbed my coat and left. Creep. If she wanted that type of man she was welcome to him.

Colleen phoned me next morning. She was still cross. She accused me of being a spoilsport. She argued that I should have been nice to Adrian; I might have got the opportunity to go sailing or stay over at his summer house at the coast. She argued that even if I didn't like him he would introduce her to other men.

'No thanks,' I said firmly. I wasn't going to prostitute myself; if I wanted to go to the coast I would go there myself, under my own steam. I didn't need some slime ball to take me there. If she was going to use men like him to get ahead then she must have been more desperate than I thought.

I went out on home visits with some of my co-workers where I found out what the reality of working in Australia was really like. I hadn't known that the town was the hard drug capital of the country. Behind the neat suburban houses lay an underworld, where drugs and prostitution were rife.

You'd have thought that I had seen the worst of it at home, but I had never had to walk over used syringes lying all over the place where kiddies could play with them. I even had to update my wardrobe with sensible closed-in shoes in case I got accidentally jabbed with a dirty needle. There had been several child deaths in the previous year, which explained why the Children's Bureau had actively sought to recruit experienced staff from overseas. It was a startling statistic, and one that the workers in the field were always left to consider every day.

Tom's intentions about letting me settle in didn't last; there was too much work to be done. When he allocated my cases I was shocked to learn that the Children's Bureau had had no contact with these families for months. And they expected me to be able to go in and explain that? It was going to be difficult enough to establish a relationship with people, but I was bound to experience a lot of hostility if they had been without support for this length of time. While a lot of clients we worked with resented the Children's Bureau intrusion, there were others, who had specifically requested help and assistance. They had been forced to cope without it. As I waded through the files I realised that there was every human misery contained there: abuse, neglect; abandonment; domestic violence; parental mental health problems; prostitution; alcoholism and drug dependency. And somewhere in the middle of this debris were children whose lives I hoped to improve. It would be tough going.

The Children's Bureau had four different teams. The intake service took telephone referrals from clients and professionals like teachers and doctors. In this country every professional had a mandatory responsibility to report suspected abuse or maltreatment. Failure to do so could result in a fine or imprisonment, or both. This generated a high volume of work as most people acted defensively because they were afraid of the consequences. Sometimes different mandatory reporters contacted the Children's Bureau with the same concerns, so the Children's Bureau could receive several reports on the same child. All of these had to be investigated.

The next department conducted an initial investigation and made an assessment on whether the case needed further intervention. If abuse was unsubstantiated then the case was closed. The majority of the work was of this nature. Families had been the victim of malicious reporters who sought to use the agency to inflict misery and grief on neighbours or other family members. If on the balance of probabilities abuse seemed likely, then further support was recommended. The case would be transferred to another team which undertook medium-term work with the family to identify and introduce supports, or in some cases to monitor a family more closely. This team, where I was based, worked extensively with the family to try and make effective changes, but if there was no improvement the Children's Bureau would apply to the Family Court for a variety of different care orders which, if awarded, placed responsibility for the child on the Children's Bureau. When a full care order had been secured then the case was transferred again to another team which worked with the family on a long-term basis.

I had studied the legislation. Good practice dictated that caseloads should be approximately twelve children per worker, but I was allocated twice that from the beginning. There were too many unallocated cases which were clearly causing embarrassment to the Children's Bureau. But there were discrepancies within the Children's Bureau when it came to measuring how much work was generated by a particular case. While the long-term team counted their cases in terms of how many children they had on their caseload, the medium-term team counted cases in terms of families, regardless of whether some of the children lived in separate placements, or how many children were in each of the families. One of the workers in my team had two families who had seven children each, but apparently that counted as only two cases.

By the end of my second week I realised that I would be forced to respond to emergencies only. This left little time for the real work which I had planned to do with families, the preventative work which should have assisted in reducing some of the pressures. While some of the work was subcontracted out to other agencies, the problem was that their waiting lists were so high that I was required to undertake whatever work I could do myself, watching and waiting while the pressures on the families increased. Most of the families were just people who seemed overwhelmed and bogged down by the pressures of life, but some had been guilty of abuse. These were the ones that required constant monitoring.

Initially I thought that the caseload I was allocated would be all that I would be dealing with – there was certainly enough work there – but I learned how wrong I could be. The initial assessment team were short staffed. Fifteen people had left within the previous six months because of the tyrannical behaviour of one of the managers. Several staff had divulged that this senior manager would call a different worker into the office daily. There she would criticize their performance repeatedly. Apparently she wouldn't stop until she had drawn tears. At least the Australians had a choice about leaving. The overseas people had a commitment to stay with the Children's Bureau for eighteen months; otherwise they would be forced to repay the relocation money that had been provided. As most of the overseas people like me had sold their houses at home and had made a commitment to adapting to a new country and starting a new life, they didn't have the same luxury. I felt like a prisoner. I was trapped here for at least eighteen months. I didn't have the money to reimburse the Children's Bureau for the relocation allowance I had been provided. I suspected they knew from the beginning just how difficult it would be for people to leave.

Because so many people had resigned there weren't enough staff left to carry out the initial work so the cases were transferred to our team. I had to rearrange my caseload to fit in the time to conduct the initial assessments. This was time consuming enough in itself; the problems arose when I completed the assessment and substantiated abuse or recommended further work. I was informed by management that there weren't enough staff to carry out this task. I was instructed that I would have to recommend a case closure. It felt like I was writing a child's death warrant and I refused. It didn't make any difference. As everything was recorded on the computer, the manager had the opportunity to type over any recommendations I had made, and to change them to something which suited the Children's Bureau.

The extra work interfered with the planned work I was supposed to undertake with my own clients. Most of them had to thrive on neglect themselves as far as I was concerned. Every time something erupted these vulnerable people would be left behind while I rushed around cancelling arranged appointments with them and racing out to another crisis. The problem wasn't just the time it took to undertake an assessment on whatever crisis had occurred, but in recording each and every report on the computer system. I had to start from scratch with every single report I received when I would have to insert the same information repetitively.

There were strict time frames which had to be adhered to in order to complete assessments, either twenty-four hours, seven days or twenty one days. Trying to keep up with that and whatever appointments and meetings I had already arranged was impossible.

On top of that there were the weekly team meetings which were compulsory. These seemed to be used as a bitching session where people complained about the fact that the Children's Bureau cars which we used were never replaced with petrol when the tank was empty. One fat lump of a manager, Muriel spent hours complaining that she didn't want to care for the goldfish which she had inherited from her predecessor who had become one of the disappeared. That was another strange occurrence. One minute someone was there, then the next minute they vanished without a trace. Rumours circulated that the person had been sent to 'special projects' which was a euphemism for being sacked.

Then there were the interminable complaints that no one cleaned up in the kitchen after themselves and a proper rota should be drawn up to make sure everyone had a turn. Can you imagine how ridiculous that was? I could be rushing in from court, or racing out to deal with a report and I would be expected to take time out, when a child had been assessed as being at risk, to wash a couple of cups. It was bloody ridiculous. I could just imagine saying to a client, look, will you just hold on a minute, don't be abusing your child until I deal with all my domestic chores. To think I went to university for years, and ended up becoming a tea lady.

Every morning we lined up like sheep for the daily nine o'clock meeting. We were asked if there were any emergency situations that needed to be recorded on the whiteboard in the team meeting room. Most of us lowered our heads. Clearly emergencies did not include caseloads which were increasing, or the fact that staff were struggling to manage their own caseloads as well as cases from their team members, who inevitably went on sick leave due to the enormous stress. I once disclosed that I had an emergency, a fashion emergency, the heel had just broken off my shoe. It got a laugh and lightened the atmosphere for a moment before the managers started, once again, to put undue pressure on us by telling us that there were a high number of unallocated cases and these were going to be shared out among us. They graciously permitted us to undertake some extra overtime in order to try and deal with the volume of paperwork which would slip every time a crisis arose. That was a joke; most of us were already doing that.

A crisis didn't even have to be with one of the families I was working with either. As it was policy to complete home visits with another worker, I might end up accompanying a worker who was trying to deal with a crisis in one of their cases. Then I would be expected to take notes during the visit. If your writing was eligible, which mine always was, as I wrote like a serial killer, then I would have to return to the office and type the notes up before I transferred them to the case worker. Management had tried out a pilot project where they gave us little hand-held computers, but they were so fiddly they made the task even more difficult for the technophobes like me.

At least my experience with the team I was in was more positive than my colleagues from overseas. Colleen had told me that some of them faced hostility from Australians who resented the fact they had taken what they perceived as their jobs.

CHAPTER 6

After a couple of weeks Tom took me to one side. 'Do me a favour Louise,' he asked, 'would you please take that student under your wing.' I frowned. I was aware of two students who were on placement with the Children's Bureau. One was a charming well-mannered man called Isaac who seemed eager to learn but I hadn't met the other one yet.

'Which one,' I asked hoping against hope that he would say Isaac.

'It's Lacey Bones,' he continued. 'Her practice teacher, Linda, is off sick at the moment and she needs someone to work with.'

'OK, but why me?' I asked. 'I've only just arrived off the boat.'

'Well,' said Tom in his most endearing way, laughing quietly as he said it, 'you've extensive experience, you are patient, you could teach her a lot, and... and, look, to tell you the truth, no one else will work with her!'

'Why?'

'Well,' replied Tom, 'it's because; she's loud, opinionated, crass and...she's from Arkansas.'

'I see,' I said, resigning myself to this new challenge. 'OK, I'll see what I can do.' I had considerable experience of working with students and knew how demanding they could be at times, but it might help me acclimatize to the environment more quickly if I spent a bit of time with one.

I walked up and introduced myself to Lacey; she squinted up at me disdainly. She was middle-aged and extremely overweight, with a badly done home perm and colour treatment. She was evidently unfamiliar with a professional dress code. She was wearing long shorts, socks and hiking boots and looked as if she should be digging a trench. I reminded myself that she was from Arkansas and this was as dressed up as she was going to get.

'I think you'll be coming out with me on some of my cases while your practice teacher is off sick,' I smiled.

'No, I don't think so,' she drawled in an American accent. Now I know why the most popular pick-up line in Arkansas is nice tooth. She squinted up at me through the thick lenses of her glasses. God love her, she wasn't the bonniest. Her face would not only stop a door, but also most clocks and a herd of charging buffalo. She looked like Rosemary West in a badly fitting nylon wig.

'Yes,' I asserted myself. 'Tom has just asked me to help you out until Linda returns.'

'But I don't wanna work with nobody else, I don't need to.' Christ, she was as ugly as a bulldog and half as smart. I tried again.

'I think Tom wants you to come out on a couple of home visits with me. You know, it can be interesting to go out with other people as their skills are all different.' Lacey sighed from the bottom of her feet.

'Gee, I'm really busy. What with all this work I have to do and all and I'm only here part-time, and I gotta go to Uni, and collect my boys from school, but I'll see what I can do for y'all.' She made it sound as if she was doing me a favour. I made a mental note to tell the boss I had tried, but that this woman clearly didn't want to benefit from my wisdom and experience.

During the rest of the week, I was forced to respond to a couple of emergency situations and needed another team mate to come out with me on some home visits and meetings. As Lacey was the only one available she reluctantly agreed to accompany me, displaying by her sighs that she was really too busy to be bothered by such trivial things as work.

On one of the visits the mother in question presented as irate. She criticized the Children's Bureau for annoying her, and said that she hadn't seen her boyfriend for months. The pregnant bump depicted otherwise. She started to cry and reiterated that her relationship with him was over and all she wanted was for us to get out of her life and leave her alone.

Lacey was sitting beside me on the sofa, and she interjected. 'That's terrible; poor you, you're probably trying your best to get over him. I know what it's like to end a relationship. Whenever I had to end my relationship with my husband everyone else was telling me that I should stay with him. Gee, it was real hard, you know, 'cos everyone thought he was brilliant. But I wanted to be with other men and my friends all turned against me so I can just imagine what's happening with you.'

The woman looked at Lacey in bewilderment through her tears. 'I thought I had friends then,' Lacey continued, 'but when it comes to the crunch you'll find that they always stick up for him. They'll always tell you that you're making the biggest mistake of your life by leaving him. But you can't listen to them, do you hear that, 'cos I didn't and I'm glad I didn't. If I had listened to them I would still be with him. Humph, I was just telling Louise here that I just couldn't bear having sex with the same man any more, you know what I mean? It just gets so routine, and there are so many men out there that I haven't slept with yet, I think they deserve to have a go, don't you?' The client was stunned. She nodded her head automatically.

'Don't you worry,' Lacey patted her hand sympathetically. 'I'll talk to the manager. I'll see to it that we just let you get on with your life. I know how hard it is when you just want to get on with things and people are complaining all the time about you, and the way you bring your children up. People are always complaining that I don't control my boys and that they are always fighting with each other, and trying to beat on me, but I'm their mom so I can do what I want with them and you should just do the same. So you do what I do, OK? You just ignore them and you do what you want to in your life. It's too short you know. You have to do what you want now, otherwise there's no point in it, is there?'

I could see the woman visibly recoil from Lacey's disclosures; I was feeling a bit flummoxed myself. 'Actually,' I said, trying to take control of the situation, 'I believe that there have been several reports to the police since the last day the Children's Bureau were here, so I'll need to follow this up. I'll call out with you next Tuesday at the same time to discuss the issues further.' I outlined the Children's Bureau position, and what my expectations were both for her, and myself as a worker.

When we left the house, I spoke quietly to Lacey in the car en route to the office. 'First of all, Lacey, this is not all about you, you can't just go telling people all your problems, they have enough of their own. Secondly you can't always take at face value what people are telling you, especially when there is concrete evidence to indicate otherwise.'

Lacey appeared dumbstruck 'Whadda mean?' she drawled.

'Look, Lacey, you really need to prepare yourself before you go out on an appraisal. You should always check to see what contact people have had with this Bureau. Most clients are decent people who are just trying their best to cope in very difficult circumstances but you get the odd one who lies through their teeth. There were numerous reports of domestic violence in that family and the children have been caught up in the middle of it.'

'But that woman said that she wasn't living with her boyfriend any more, so I don't see why we should be bothering her,' she said snippily. 'I know what it's like to try and get on with your life without all these people bothering you.' She sighed in martyrdom.

'Lacey, this isn't about you. You can't exchange personal information like that,' I said forcefully.

'Well, I don't see why not.' She shrugged her shoulders. 'I had to leave a relationship too so I can help her. I can give her my advice 'cos I know what I'm talking about.'

'It's not about you, Lacey,' I said firmly. 'She might have said she wasn't in a relationship with him any more but I take it you didn't notice the men's shoes that were sitting on the front porch before we went into the house?'

'Gee, no, I didn't see them.' Her blond frizz shook like a haystack in the wind.

'And the smell of cigarette smoke was really heavy in that living room, but she doesn't smoke. Didn't that give you another clue?' I asked carefully.

'I never noticed that either,' sighed Lacey.

'I'm only trying to teach you what sort of things to look out for, but you should be taught this at college,' I said patiently. She was not letting her education get in the way of her ignorance. This was her second placement and she didn't even know how to begin an assessment. I wondered what kind of training social workers received here.

'If you had read the file you would have known that that mother had one child who had to be removed from her,' I continued, 'and he's now in foster care. The abuse that child suffered was horrendous.'

'But she seems like she might be a good mom. She was knitting a blanket for the new baby. That's so sweet. Doesn't that show you that she is a real caring mom?'

'No, it doesn't I'm afraid,' I replied sadly. 'You know one of the biggest predictors of future behaviour is past behaviour. She might seem calm and contented now, but she will be a different person when she's faced with a squalling infant in the middle of the night, when she's tired and sore and just wanting to sleep.'

'So what happens then?' she drawled.

'As heartbreaking as it is for the mother, sometimes the only way to protect the child is to remove the baby and place the baby in foster care.'

'You're kidding me, aren't you?' she spat furiously. 'You mean you take babies away from their moms. Gee, that's awful. I can't do that.'

'You have to be objective, Lacey. You have to look at the bigger picture and think about what is in the best interests of the child.'

'Well, I won't be doing that. I'll just tell them I can't,' she said definitely.

'What did you think child protection was all about?' I smiled patronisingly at her.

'Well, see,' she became animated turning toward me in the passenger seat, 'I watched this programme on television called Judging Amy, about this judge and her mother is a social worker. She gets to figure out that kids have been abused and stuff and she does all sorts of neat things with the police. It looked like it might be fun.'

Fun? 'Sorry Lacey there's nothing fun about child protection. The decisions you make are crucial, they can mean the difference between life and death for a child.'

'Oh, you take things so seriously,' she laughed. 'The work I've been doing at the office is fun.'

'Well, I suppose as a student you get the chance to do individual work with kids, which is enjoyable, but once you start work you will be lucky if you set eyes on a child.' At home we did all the visits to the foster carer's home, and did individual work with the child. We also had to write reports for court and inform people of what services existed in their community which they could utilize. Here the work was farmed out to other agencies that did all that for us. Most of the workers I'd met so far had been excellent, they were really committed to the children, but some of them were just floating along, passing the buck back to us. You lost control of your cases when they were passed onto other agencies, and you had to have faith that they would work with you for the children.

'Maybe I'll go work for them then,' she said determinedly.

I explained as gently as I could what the implications for this particular woman would be if things did not change. I looked down and observed that Lacey was writing down what I was saying verbatim. Bloody students.

CHAPTER 7

In the meantime I needed somewhere more permanent to live. Colleen and I looked at houses and apartments all over the city. Some of them were gorgeous, but they had a queue of people lining up to view them and to submit an application form. Some of them were horrible, damp, dark and smelt of dead old ladies. I finally saw a gorgeous three bed roomed house. The rent was high, but with Maryann coming over shortly to share a place with me I would be able to manage. I submitted an application form and was interviewed on the phone by some harridan of a woman who asked me everything but what colour underwear I was wearing. She eventually informed me that the house was mine. Colleen and I decided to go out that night to celebrate.

'Let me go and change my clothes first,' she said 'I have to phone home and check that the family is all right.' I waited in her apartment while she changed and I heard her telephone her mother. She had only just said hello and I heard her immediately change her tone of voice.

'No, not yet, Mummy, no, no I haven't met anyone yet,' she entreated into the phone. She turned her back on me trying to speak quietly into the phone.

'Yes, I know that time is getting on,' she said in an exacerbated tone of voice.

'Yes, I know Nuala was married and had four children when she was my age, but you don't understand, it's really hard to meet people here. Yes, I am getting out. I know… I know they won't come knocking at my door.'

I moved to the living room to afford her some privacy. I sat on the sofa and selected a magazine to read. I was soon caught up with the latest gossip on Angelina and Brad when she returned.

'Sorry about that,' she said looking distinctly embarrassed, 'but you know what mothers are like.' She tried unsuccessfully to force a laugh.

'Does she always give you such a hard time?' I asked gently.

'Yes,' replied Colleen, 'It's the same every time I phone. She was the one who was so keen to get me to go to Australia. She told me that there were more men than women here and even I should be able to get myself a husband.'

'So that's what you came here for then?' I probed.

'Yes I suppose so, didn't you?'

'No, I bloody well did not,' I interjected. 'I wouldn't give a man house room.'

'But don't you think it would be so nice to get married and have children? You know, women my age don't always have children if they leave it to later in life.' She shrugged her shoulders.

So that explained why she was interrogating that poor fella in the bar. She wasn't interested in a potential date, but checking to see if he was husband material. She would have some fun doing that in this town as the majority of the population were professional women, most of whom worked in the public service, and the men could pick and choose between them.

'Well, what about Owen, that fella you met on your holidays?' I asked. 'Surely if you were that keen to get married you would have stayed behind and married him.'

She looked at me aghast. 'No, I don't think that would have worked out at all,' she stumbled.

'Did you introduce him to your family?'

'I did and they all seemed to like him well enough but I don't think it would have worked out between us, he had this em…problem.' She turned away silently.

I didn't want to start questioning her. She seemed reluctant to pursue the topic. 'Surely there must be a club for single people here where you get a chance to meet people.'

'There is,' she exclaimed. 'I joined it when I first arrived here, but there are loads of women in it, and only a few men and they weren't very nice. I don't know what I'm going to do, I'm not getting any younger and I really want to have children. My father has a field at home for me to build a house on, but I can't go back to live there without a husband.'

'Let's see if there are any personal advertisements in the local paper. There might be a load of men wanting to meet up with you, but they find it difficult here too. That might open up all sorts of possibilities for you.'

'You're joking, I couldn't do that, I couldn't meet up with someone I know nothing about. I don't like going for blind dates. My sister was always fixing me up with some men at home, and it always turned out to be a disaster.'

'I suppose it wouldn't do any harm to have a look,' she said reluctantly later as I emerged from the newsagent's with the paper in my hand. 'Let's go and order dinner first,' she pleaded. 'I'm starving.' It was becoming her mantra.

We walked to the restaurant and after we had ordered our food I rummaged around, separating out all the sections of the paper. I handed her the section which said Men Seeking Women. I was concentrating on the property section. The prices of some of the houses for sale here was astronomical.

'God how do you know who's nice and who's not?' Colleen frowned. 'They might try to make themselves sound as interesting as possible and turn out to be complete freaks.'

'You just have to read their adverts carefully,' I said. 'Let me see, you have to ring them and leave a message and if they like the sound of you they ring you back. You probably need to talk to them a while before you meet them and it says here you should meet them in a public place and make sure someone knows where you are.'

'Why?' She was as thick as champ.

'Well, they might turn out to be serial killers or rapists or something. They might use this type of thing to attract women just so they could attack them.'

'Christ,' sighed Colleen, 'you wouldn't really do this, would you?'

'No, Colleen, to tell you the truth I wouldn't,' I said slowly. 'But that's because I don't want a man. They are like parking spaces, the good ones are always taken and what's left is handicapped or extremely small.'

'But it's different for you; you don't have your family on your back all the time torturing you about getting married,' she said huffily.

'At least if you got a couple of dates from answering these ads then you are doing something. The next time your mother phones you can just tell her you are too busy to talk as you are going out on a date. You don't have to be telling other people about it either. If you hit it off with someone you could make up something about how you met. So what have you got to lose?'

'Do you think people tell the truth in these things? How do you know what to look for?'

'Well, why don't you read one that you might be interested in and we'll decipher it.'

'OK,' she said reluctantly and pulled the paper closer towards her. She examined it for a few minutes. 'Look, here's one, he sounds nice. It says he's financially secure and fun.'

'That means one paycheck from the street and annoying,' I advised her. 'Anyone else?'

'This one says he is open-minded. What does that mean?' She looked up at me questioningly.

'Desperate.'

'Well, what about this man? He says he wants a soul mate.'

'He's one step away from stalking,' I said caustically.

'This one is emotionally secure.'

'He's medicated.'

'Oh, I can't believe they are all that bad,' she sighed. 'What about this one? It says he considers himself special.'

'That just means he used to go to school in the wee yellow special bus. God's wee angels, my mother always called those children.'

'This one is spiritual,' she frowned.

'That probably means he's involved with a cult.'

'What does non-traditional mean?' she asked sceptically.

'His ex-wife lives in the basement.'

'Stable?'

'Boring.'

'This one is interesting. He says he's a poet.'

'He's a depressive schizophrenic.'

'Here's another one,' continued Colleen. 'He says he's commitment-minded. That must be a good thing, because you know how difficult it is for men to commit.'

'That means you should start picking out the curtains now.'

'Oh, it's all hopeless,' sighed Colleen throwing the paper down on the table. 'I can't do this without seeing them first.'

'Well, what about the Internet? That's how a lot of people meet nowadays. I'm sure they have sites for that in Australia. You might meet someone you like from somewhere else and you can get to travel to meet them. You don't want to be in this place for the rest of your life, do you?'

'No, it's dead,' she said adamantly. 'I thought coming to Australia was going to be so exciting. I used to watch Home and Away and see the beautiful beach and think, I'm going to be there. But this place is miles away from the ocean, the work is shite. By the time you have finished a day's work you are exhausted and fit for nothing. There are hardly any proper bars where you might meet people and if there are they are full of women all wanting the same thing. The men I've met are arrogant, they know they can pick and choose between us; it's definitely not what I thought it would be like.'

'Do you want to answer any of these?' I asked as I lifted the newspaper from the table and started to fold it away.

'No, I don't think that's for me,' she said sadly. 'Knowing my luck I'd end up with the serial killer.'

'But I like the look of that waiter over there,' she whispered. 'He might be the owner. There's money in this type of business. Why don't you see if you can talk to him a bit and find out if he is single?' She disappeared to the toilets. The waiter came to take the order and we chatted generally about the weather. He asked where I was from and I told him, making sure I asked him where he was from too. He told me he was from Queensland and was studying at the university. Colleen slunk back to the table and grinned inanely at the waiter. I introduced her to Christian. Christian smiled politely at her then went to the kitchen to give the order to the chef.

'You see,' Colleen said as she slid into her seat. 'I knew you would be able to do it, so tell me all about him,' she pleaded. I told her the little bit of information I had gleaned.

'I told you I wanted to go to Queensland,' she simpered. 'It must be fate. Do you think he's married?' she asked dreamily turning round and staring at him baldly. I didn't reply. 'Well, he's not wearing a ring, that must mean he's free. Look, here he comes again.' Christian placed fresh water and glasses on the table. Colleen smiled up at him in what she considered a flirtatious manner. He looked petrified; he left the table quickly and bolted across the room.

'We'll just have to keep coming in here until he asks me out,' she giggled as she poured herself a glass of water. 'Christian, hmmm, it's such a dreamy name, isn't it? I wonder if he owns the place.' Christian must have been running scared. He didn't return to the table again; he probably hid in the kitchen until we left.

CHAPTER 8

When we had finished dinner we went out to a bar for a couple of drinks. After a couple of glasses of wine Colleen began to talk more about the relationship she had with Owen. 'Well, he was really nice, and he had a good job, but there were problems with him.' She had alluded to this earlier on in the night.

'What do you mean?' I asked.

'Well, he used to get depressed and no matter what I did I couldn't shake him out of it.'

'Did he ever talk to someone about it?' I asked sympathetically.

'I made him go to the doctors and he got some antidepressant medication but it affected him. I mean that he had problems with, you know,' she looked embarrassed 'being able to do it. You know,' she stammered, 'he couldn't do it. He said that the medication affected him so he couldn't do it.' Oh, right, now I got it, sex.

'Did he go back to the doctor's again? I asked. 'You know, I read somewhere that it takes a while for medication to start working, but if it caused problems then he could have gone back to the doctors and changed it to something else.'

'It was hard enough getting him there in the first place,' she spurted. 'He refused to go back again, he just stopped taking the pills, but then he was too depressed to do anything, so it was all a vicious cycle. I mean,' she continued, 'he was a nice fella when he was in a good mood, but when he was depressed he changed. He wouldn't go anywhere, or do anything. He just wanted to sit in and watch DVDs and drink.'

'So how did he feel about you coming out to Australia?' I asked curiously.

'He knew that I was waiting for the visa to come through when I met him, but I think after we'd been together for a while he started to talk about coming out with me.'

'Oh, that's a huge leap,' I said in surprise. Was it not polite to wait until you were asked?

'Yes, I thought so too,' she confided. 'I wanted to come out and get settled in first and travel about a bit. I thought that if he got help then he might be able to come out at some time. But I assumed I would just meet someone else when I was here.' She looked around in dismay. The bar seemed to be full of couples 'I didn't realise how hard it was to meet anyone. Most of the men here are horrible, you wouldn't look at them. But, you know, Owen still emails me and texts me and I'm really tempted to either go back to him, or tell him to come out here. He would be better than nothing and at least my mother would leave me alone. She thinks he's nice. I think she knew his father and she went to school with his aunt. She says that his family are good people.'

'Do you love him, Colleen?' I asked gently.

'No, I mean, he's all right,' she confided. 'We weren't together for that long and I do like him. He's a really nice man and maybe I'd get to love him if we were together for longer. And, you know, maybe if we were married then he wouldn't have so many problems with sex and I'd have babies.'

'Or you might not be as interested in it?' She nodded. 'Well, scientists have discovered a food to diminish a woman's sex drive by ninety percent. It's called Wedding Cake.'

'Oh, you're just so cynical,' she chuckled.

'It's true, marriage changes passion...suddenly you're in bed with a relative.'

She smiled patronisingly at me 'But you don't know what it's like to go to all these family functions when you are always on your own. You don't know what it's like to have your mother apologise to her family because you haven't been married yet. And to make it worse my nineteen-year-old niece is in a steady relationship and is talking about getting engaged. I'm going to be standing there like a big pockel while everybody congratulates the bride. The longer I'm here the more I think that I should just ring Owen up and tell him to come out. At least we could travel about together and I wouldn't have to go to another nightclub again. I'm too old for all that nonsense.'

I couldn't believe what I was hearing. She was prepared to settle for half a relationship with someone she didn't really care about just so she wouldn't be alone and to make sure her family left her in peace. I knew what it was like to live in a marriage where it was the loneliest place on earth. Where I had a half relationship. I knew that it wouldn't work for her; I wished someone had been honest enough to tell me the same and save me from years of misery and heartache.

OK, I know I'm cynical, but I think being married has made me that way. I had clung desperately like a limpet to the excuse that I was only a wee girl and didn't know any better. It's the best one I can give for realising that I made the biggest mistake of my life.

In the beginning I had been flattered that Patrick chose me. To outsiders he was always charming, witty and kind. People didn't realise that the acts of generosity were only for public display. He took back everything he ever gave me, never to be seen again. He gave all my gifts to his mother. If I'm honest she was the other person in our marriage and she wasn't prepared to let him go. Despite the fact she had a perfectly good husband of her own she always called on Patrick, morning noon and night. The phone would never stop.

She still bought his clothes for him; she didn't trust me to do it. She dressed him like some village squire, including the checked jackets with the corduroy elbow patches. Eventually, with a lot of persuasion from his mother, he left me. He took up with another man. Apparently that was my fault; his mother claimed that I had made him gay.

I wouldn't be sharing that little story with many people, including Colleen. If I was honest maybe one of the other reasons for leaving the country, apart from Kevin, was to get away from Patrick. It was a bit too close for comfort when your ex-husband paraded his new boyfriend about the place.

I focused my attention back to Colleen. 'Look, Colleen,' I said. 'I know you are far away from everything that you know, and this place hasn't turned out to be what you expected. I've seen what it's like in the nightclubs here; it's like a cattle market. You're trying to compete with twenty-year-olds in tiny skirts. But you need to take your time, don't be rushing into anything. You know most relationships start when you aren't expecting it. Men can tell if you are desperate for a relationship. You may as well put a sticker on your forehead saying 'come get me'.'

Colleen laughed. I continued, 'When you meet the man of your dreams you are going to be with him for the rest of your life. That's a very long time. But in the meantime why don't you just relax and have some fun? Enjoy yourself; go out on dates with men even if you think they aren't marriage material.'

Colleen shook her head. 'It's all right for you, you're more confident than me. You aren't afraid to talk to them; you can tell jokes and make them laugh. I can't do that. And you don't want to get married. You've been married before.'

'Yes,' I replied. 'My husband and I were happy for twenty years and then we met. You know the trouble with some women is that they get all excited about nothing and then they marry him.'

'But it's true, Louise,' she insisted. 'You don't have the same pressure put on you as me. Someone actually asked you to marry them. You've had a wedding, even though you're now divorced.'

'You know,' I said confidentially 'there's stigma attached to divorce too Colleen. It's a public sign that you've failed at your marriage.'

'Why did you get divorced then?' she asked curiously. There was no way I was telling her the truth. I was too ashamed to admit it to myself.

'My husband and I divorced over religious differences. He thought he was God, and I didn't.'

'Oh, you never take anything seriously,' she laughed. Ummn I think it's called a defence mechanism.

'But it's true, Colleen,' I protested. 'I finally faced the fact that we were incompatible. I'm a Scorpio and he's an asshole. You know he told everyone that he will dance on my grave, so I've now arranged to be buried at sea.'

'But even if it didn't work out you've still been married but nobody has ever asked me. Nobody says you are on the shelf,' she said huffily.

'What about the rest of your family?' I tried to be sympathetic. 'Do they put you under the same pressure?'

Colleen frowned. 'My sister is always trying to fix me up on dates with men she knows, or friends of friends. She tells me that good things come to those who wait.'

'But aren't the good things just the leftovers from the people that got there first?'

Colleen sighed. 'I'm sorry to burden you with this; you must be finding it hard enough being away from home. I think I must be a bit drunk.'

'Nonsense,' I said confidently. 'You're not drunk if you can lie on the floor without hanging on.'

'Really, Louise, you've only just arrived here and you haven't moaned like I have.'

'Well, the way I look at it is, the more you complain, the longer God makes you live.'

72

Alice joined us. She was another overseas recruit. Colleen had spent the last couple of months in her company, but since I had come along I noticed that she seemed reluctant to do anything with Alice. I shrugged it off. Maybe they weren't such good friends after all.

'So have you found anywhere to live yet?' asked Alice.

'Yes, I've been lucky. I found a lovely house but it won't be ready for another two weeks and I can't afford to stay where I am until then.'

'You can stay with me until your house is ready,' offered Alice.

'Thanks, Alice, but I don't want to put you out.' I was touched that she had been generous enough to offer.

'It's no trouble,' she insisted. 'Sure it's only for a couple of weeks and at least it will cost you less than staying at the rented apartments.'

Alice had a point but I had reservations about moving in. There was something not quite right about her. I couldn't put my finger on it; one minute she was all over you and the next she ignored you completely. She had come over to Belfast to meet the rest of us who were going to work in the Children's Bureau and spent the entire time huffing and pouting with everyone. She had stayed in Maryann's house overnight. Maryann told me that when she went down the next morning Alice was sitting on her kitchen floor crying. Maryann couldn't get any sense out of her. She thought that maybe she was feeling a bit fragile as Alice had recently fallen out with her boyfriend. I hoped she wasn't going to be another looper; they seemed to have some attraction to me like moths to a flame.

I ignored my intuition and agreed to move in at the end of the week. I should have remembered that she who hesitates is probably right. I took my couple of suitcases and moved into her spare bedroom. Alice introduced me to Eloise her flat mate, who also worked for the Children's Bureau. She had relocated from Newcastle in Australia. She seemed really nice.

'It will be good for me to have a bit of company,' Alice explained conspiratorially, once I had unpacked the basics that I would need. 'That Eloise is a real weirdo.'

'What do you mean?' I asked carefully.

'She sits up in her room all the time and watches television; She doesn't come downstairs to talk to me. When I think of the effort I have gone to,' she complained. 'You know, I took her out all the time with me when she first started here, but what thanks do I get?' She shook her head. 'You know, she argues with me all the time about paying the bills and she has loads of money. I need somebody else to see what she's like. No one believes me when I tell them what it's really like living here. And to make things worse,' she rushed on, 'we share the same pod at work. I can't get away from her. I think she's spying on me,' she whispered.

Maybe because it was all going on in your head? Was she serious? Or was this just one more nutter I was going to encounter? Why hadn't she shared her outlandish fantasies before I agreed to move in?

I soon realised that what Alice had told me was true. When Alice was out Eloise chatted away to me but the minute Alice returned to the apartment Eloise fled to her room. After a couple of days I began to see why Eloise ran for cover when Alice appeared. Her moods went up and down like a fiddler's elbow. One minute she was happy, chatting away and laughing and the next she was scowling and bordering on suicidal. I couldn't keep up with her. The only thing that made her happy was food. On my way home I bought her chocolate or cake. It was like trying to placate a wild animal until you can get hold of a stick. I practically threw the food at her, hoping that it would put her in good humour so we could get through the night unscathed. After a week of living with her schizophrenic moods I was forced to go straight to my room when I came home from work and didn't emerge until the next morning. I didn't even have a television to watch so I caught up on some reading, and wrote letters home.

Alice tried to bring me onto her side of the war by complaining about Eloise, but to be honest Eloise had been more than pleasant and kind to me so I stayed out of it. It was easier said than done. From behind my closed door I could hear Alice roaring and shouting at Eloise. Alice was a tyrant, she bullied poor Eloise unmercifully. I considered referring Eloise to a support group for victims of domestic violence. Alice was always professional and helpful in work, but obviously she could only sustain the façade of sanity for a short while. I came home one day to see that she was still in her pyjamas and hadn't gone to work.

'Are you ill?' I asked her. 'Do you want me to do anything?'

'No, I just wanted to stay here today. That Eloise is spying on me you know. I think she's trying to take over my life.' Sorry, what? I missed your mad ramblings there for a minute.

'She is, I know she is,' Alice hissed. 'Her television is directly over my bed and I think she has a listening device in it. She's listening in to me; she's watching my every move.' Her eyes darted around the room suspiciously. Right, another fecking madwoman. Was this place full of them?

Next morning I met Colleen who had arranged a visit to a local psychic. 'Do you want to go too?' she asked. No thanks, unless she told me the winning lottery numbers so I could get out of this bloody place. I didn't want to know anything else. I went for a cup of coffee while Colleen had her appointment and read a couple of chapters of a book I had borrowed. The books for sale in the second-hand bookstores were so expensive I was glad I had joined the library as soon as I had arrived.

When Colleen returned she was flushed and seemed happy. She ordered a huge lunch and began to regale me with the tales which the psychic had told her. 'She told me that a relative called Patrick had passed over,' she whispered conspiratorially. Really, tell me any Irish person who doesn't have a Patrick in their family. 'And,' Colleen insisted, 'she talked about Mary, and that's my second name so she was really accurate about that too.'

'So did she say what was going to happen to you in Australia then?' I asked trying to hide the cynicism in my voice.

'Well apparently she said that I was married in a previous life to a man called Alfred and that he really loved me,' she smiled.

'So are you going to meet anyone here?' I asked eager to get to the point.

'Well,' she sighed, 'Barbara said that it's very difficult for Alfred to see me with someone else because he loved me so much, so that's why I'm not with someone now. You see, I just knew there had to be some reason, maybe I'm a bit psychic myself, you know.' Right, so the reason you aren't with anyone now isn't because you are a bossy moody cow, then?

'So this dead man, Alfred, is putting real live people off, you mean?' I asked incredulously.

'Exactly,' she nodded eagerly. 'He must have really loved me,' she sighed. Yes, but that won't be much comfort now when you are so desperate to get married and have children.

'Don't you see it's enough just to know that I have been married,' she insisted. 'If Alfred wants me to be with someone else, he will choose him for me. He will allow him to come to me,' she said mystically. Right, and if you don't ever get married at least you have a good excuse. Great, so no one loses out then. I could just imagine her trying to explain all that to her mother.

I came home and just as I turned my key in the door Alice leapt out at me with a knife in her hand. I nearly lost my life in fright. 'Oh, it's you,' she whispered looking suspiciously behind me. 'I thought it was Eloise.'

'And this is how you are going to greet her, is it?' I frowned.

'Oh, she's gone, she's run away,' she said dramatically, her eyes darting from side to side. 'She took all her things and left this morning, but I thought that it was her coming back to get my stuff now.'

'She hasn't run away, sure you told her to leave,' I said as evenly as I could. Aren't you supposed to speak quietly and calmly to mad lunatics?

'No, I didn't,' she insisted, spitting in my face with venom.

'You did, Alice.' I wiped the spittle away with the back of my hand. 'I heard you yesterday telling her to be out of the place before tomorrow.' Well, myself and most of the neighbours in the building would have heard her; she was screaming it at the top of her lungs. She shook her head from side to side.

'But I didn't,' she insisted. Well, maybe it happened in one of your lunatic moments which you obviously can't remember now. Just get me out of this place in one piece. Thanks be to God, I was moving out the next day. My nerves were in tatters tiptoeing round here, worrying that the slightest little thing was going to set her off. I walked slowly to my room; no sudden movements, just let her calm down. Was it safe? Was I going to be murdered in my bed? I lay awake all night, feeling relieved that I had an escape route from yet another disaster.

CHAPTER 9

I rose early. I had planned to do some last minute packing, but I just shoved what I could into my case and left as quickly and as quietly as I could. I didn't want to wake the beast. I drove frantically to the estate agent where I collected the keys to the house. When I got there I saw that it had been cleaned and it smelled of bleach and furniture polish. It had three bedrooms; the main one was just beside the front door. The en suite was beautifully tiled and the walk-in wardrobe could only have been planned by a woman. There were stacks of clothes rails, shelving and shoe racks built in.

I took a trip to the local shopping mall. Veni, Vedi, Visa: I came, I saw, I did a little shopping. Whoever said money can't buy happiness doesn't know where to shop. I bought pots and pans, a toaster, a kettle, towels and bedding. I arrived home with my bags full. My manager had loaned me a bed and someone else had loaned me a couple of old sofas which were doing the rounds of the new recruits' houses. I borrowed a couple of blankets to cover the sofas and Kylie had given me a TV cabinet. My first piece of proper furniture. I was excited; at last I would be able to have a place of my own, at least for a short while anyway.

The house overlooked a mountain and every night kangaroos came into the back garden. They made a noise like old men coughing. There were cockatoos and kookaburras outside my bedroom window. I cleaned and polished and went to garage sales at the weekend to pick up cheap pieces to add to it. I discovered this brilliant second-hand shop. It was basically a dump where people threw out all the things they no longer needed. The workers there sifted through it and sorted it out into categories: beds, wooden furniture, dishes, plates, electrical goods and the like. They had this special place called the best bits and you could find some really lovely stuff there. Some of it still had the price sticker on it from the shop, so you knew it hadn't even been used before. I bought two lamps for the lamp tables and with new shades they looked as if they had come straight out of a Laura Ashley store, and for a fraction of the price too. I even managed to get a lovely sisal rug which would be the exact colour of my sofa. I am a bit funny like that. Pernickety I suppose. I have to have things laid out symmetrically. Things have to balance, like pictures, or candlesticks, they all have to be paired up, as if they belonged together. Was that what I was trying to recreate? A bit of belonging for myself. Maybe if I had someone to match me, I'd feel more like I belonged to the world too.

I bought a television set and a DVD player. I knew that I might need some company in the evening. It would be months before Maryann arrived. She had asked if she could share the house with me, just until she found her feet and moved to independent accommodation. I sniggered when I considered that she probably hadn't seen her feet for years. I agreed. It would help to share the bills. She agreed to pay half the cost of the installation of electricity and the phone and gas. I borrowed a single bed for her and bought pink duvet covers and sheets, her signature colour. I found a lovely little dressing table on which I placed lots of nice soaps and nice smelly things. Over the following weeks I added pieces to her bedroom, hoping that she would be pleased with it when she eventually arrived.

'You know, you seem so happy here on your own,' Colleen remarked as she looked around the living room. We had just finished dinner which I had prepared in the house. It was the first meal I had cooked here and I was delighted with myself. Even if we had to eat it on our knees because I still hadn't got a table. My table was being sent over from home so there didn't seem any point in getting one here.

'I'm fed up with Bianca and Fiona,' grimaced Colleen. 'Those two are driving me mad. They are man mad, and that Fiona is really strange looking, her eyes are too close together and she has a face on her like a cat.' Meow! Who was being the catty one now? 'They are always coming in really late and making lots of noise,' she complained 'and I think there's something going on between them.'

'What do you mean?' I asked in surprise.

'They are always in the one bed, giggling and playing with each other. It's getting really embarrassing. I don't want to sound like a prude but I think they are lesbians. Not that I've anything against that,' she stiffened, 'but I think it's time I got a place of my own.'

'Well, you helped me find my place so I'll be happy to look at some apartments with you. What are you looking for?'

'Something small,' she explained, 'a one bedroom apartment would be fine. It would do until I get married and get a proper house.'

I ignored the last remark. 'Well, if you have any money left over from your relocation allowances then you can ask for it to buy furniture. It's really strange looking at rented properties in this place as they are all unfurnished.'

'OK,' she agreed 'I'll go on line and see what's available.'

'You still have some relocation leave left that you haven't used. You could take that to move in or go shopping to get stuff, or both. I'll be happy to help you out with moving stuff. I'm due to return the car this week but I could hold on to it for another week if you want.'

'That would be great,' she agreed. 'Thanks, I'll get a list of places and let you know. We could go after work tomorrow.'

Colleen met me after work. She had organised everything with military precision. 'I've got a list of places that we can see,' she said. I looked at the list. She had certainly done her homework. She had underlined a number of properties which seemed to have reasonable rents and which were close enough to work so that she could walk there every day.

'No problem, Colleen,' I said cheerfully. 'You're obviously still a bit fed up there and, you know, we are all too long in the tooth to be sharing with other people.'

'Yes, especially a pair of giggly lesbians.'

'What will you do about your lease though?' I questioned. 'You agreed to live with them for a year. Have you even talked to them about it?'

'No, I didn't want to tell them until I found somewhere else to live,' she explained. 'And I have been checking up on the homes site. I've already placed an advert asking if anyone is interested. I have also talked to Kylie and she says that I can get the new person to take over the bond for me. So I'm not responsible if any of them leaves the country. Plus I've asked work to help me out with a bond for a new place. I couldn't afford to do all that. It's only a loan and they will get it back when the year is up if I still stay here.'

'You've only been here a couple of months. Are you getting fed up with it already?' I looked at her curiously.

'It isn't what they told us it would be. I think they were very dishonest about the whole thing. They told us that our caseloads would be manageable. I thought it would be just like work back home, but it's more difficult to do, there are too many restrictions, and you can't leave the building before you get all the administrative stuff onto the computer. I still don't feel comfortable knowing that all my case notes for all my clients are on the computer system for everyone to read. Not that you would have the time to read other people's but still, anyone can check up to see what work you've done. I always feel like I have to keep shoving notes onto the system to make it look as if I have done something.'

I knew what she meant. Every single conversation or action had to be referenced and cross-referenced. Whenever the phone rang I had started to dread the phone ringing. No matter what it was, by answering it I was generating more work for myself. I noticed that the other staff had learned to type up the conversation they were having while on the phone, but I couldn't do that, I preferred to write notes in a notebook, but then I had to go to the trouble of translating them into a decipherable script and typing them on the system which was very time consuming.

We traipsed round the town looking at the apartments Colleen had identified which might be suitable. Some of them were grotty, some were nice, and some you wouldn't let your cat stay in. But no matter where we went, there was always a queue of people who wanted to get their applications in first.

The final one on our list looked promising. The kitchen and living room were open plan and there were huge windows which led onto a small patio. It had a mezzanine floor where the bedroom was located and an en suite. OK so you had to go through a built-in wardrobe to find the bathroom which didn't have a bath, only a shower, but it was lovely.

'It's perfect,' said Colleen, delighted. 'Just watch me, you have to get in with the estate manager. Be nice to them, they are more likely to remember you.' She simpered up to the estate manager.

'How are you? I'm Colleen,' she introduced herself. 'I won't waste any more of your time; I really like this one so I'll take it.' The estate agent handed her a form to complete and she tried to flirt with him. She had all the sexual allure of a fossilized trout. She completed the application form and was delighted when the agent phoned her a couple of days later to tell her that her application was successful and that she could move in the following week.

'It's brilliant news,' she said. 'All I need now is to find someone to take over my lease and my room. Do you want to go out tomorrow for something to eat to celebrate the fact that I've got a new place to live in.'

We met after work, and went to one of her favourite restaurants. But as far as I could see they were all her favourite. As long as they provided food, she loved them.

'I hope you don't mind if we go to the bar after this?' Colleen said during dinner.

'No, why?' I asked, sipping my wine. I didn't want to be leched by another public servant.

'Well, I've arranged to meet up with a guy called Simon who might be taking on the lease of the apartment with Fiona and Bianca. He's just lovely and he even flirted with me on the phone last night.' She simpered. By the smirks of her, she thought she was on to a good thing. I wondered if the poor fella knew what was in store for him.

We went to the bar, and I ordered a drink. I could see Colleen looking around. She had told me that she didn't know what Simon looked like. What if it was that creep who had been chasing me before? The one with the yacht which didn't seem to have materialized. After a short while a thin young man approached Colleen and asked her if she was called Colleen. She nodded dumbly.

'I thought you were, I recognised your accent,' he smiled. Simon was six foot tall with blond hair and blue eyes. He was charming and obviously keen to make a good impression. He asked us if we would like a drink and when he returned he said, 'You know, I don't usually carry cash around with me, so I just pay with my gold card.' He produced a tiny little card. It was the size of a cracker. He talked a bit about himself. All right, he talked incessantly about himself. He told us that his father was a diplomat but that he had got tired of living at home and wanted to live independently. His father had offered to buy him an apartment but he had decided that he would rather share with people first, before taking the next step of living alone. Colleen was smitten. He had looks, charm, and more importantly for her, good prospects.

'What do you think of him?' she simpered when he had gone to the bar again, insisting on buying us another drink.

'Gay,' I said slowly.

'Oh, you're so cynical, of course he isn't gay,' she said determinedly. 'How can he be gay when he's been flirting away with me?'

'He is, Colleen; he's gay, shallow and self-centred. He hasn't once even asked you what the apartment is like; he hasn't asked how much the rent is, what facilities you have. Do you not think that's all a bit strange?'

'Oh, just because you don't want a man doesn't mean that the rest of us don't,' Colleen chided me.

'Look, I'll prove it,' I said. I lifted my new handbag and placed it on the table. It had bamboo handles and a picture of Marilyn Monroe on the face which was surrounded with red sequins.

'What do you mean?' asked Colleen staring at the bag. 'What has a handbag got to do with anything?'

'Wait, watch and learn,' I said slowly as I saw Simon approach the table. He set the drinks down and immediately his eyes focused on the bag.

'Wow fabulous bag,' he said. I turned and smirked at Colleen. 'Gay,' I whispered to Colleen.

'That doesn't mean anything,' she hissed. 'It just means he has good taste.'

'You are really wasting your time there, Colleen, honestly. You'd be safer going for that cute barman who has been staring at you all night.' She didn't even turn round.

'I don't want a barman,' she spat. 'Sure there's no money in that at all, and I like Simon,' she said deliberately, 'I think we would be perfect together. He could open so many doors for me.'

'I think he's only interested in the back door, Colleen,' I said sarcastically.

'Oh, you are disgusting,' she derided. 'You just don't want to see anybody happy just because you don't want to get married.' I could see that we were going to be in for some night. I was bored. I had an early start tomorrow and I didn't want to listen to any more of Simon's self promotion record or watch Colleen's sycophantic simpering.

'Look, Colleen, would you mind if I just went home now?' I asked. 'I'm sure Simon will be able to look after you and make sure you get home safely. And I'm sure,' I said slowly looking directly at Simon, 'you will be the perfect gentleman.'

Simon grinned, clearly pleased with the responsibility I had placed on him. I was glad to leave them. Simon was getting on my tits and Colleen's simpering was getting on my nerves. She didn't flirt with Simon so much as leap across the room and throw herself into his arms. She was wasting her time there.

Next morning Colleen phoned me to tell me that she had had a lovely time with Simon and that he had walked her home. She told me that he looked as if he wanted to kiss her but that he had pulled away from her. I bet he did.

'You know you didn't do me any favours when you told him to be a gentleman,' she chided. 'I just wanted to drag him indoors and ravish him.'

'Don't worry, Colleen, I said acerbically. 'I'm sure he would have fought you all the way.' She rambled on, talking about how she had shown him the apartment, that he was delighted with the place and that he couldn't wait to move in.

'You know, I think he was afraid that he might lose out on the place if he pursued me, but just you wait. Once I move into that new apartment we'll be making up for lost time,' she said resolutely.

She was persistent. For the next week all I heard was Simon says this and Simon says that. It was worse than the bloody song, but without all the stupid movements. I bit my tongue. She would soon find out the making of him.

Colleen told me that she had arranged for Simon to come round to the apartment and meet Fiona and Bianca.

'They will just love him,' she gushed. 'You know, they are both so money hungry, they only hang around with people who are rich so they will try and snap him up. But I think he really likes me. You know his father has a summer house on the coast and he said we can use it any time we like.' Here we go again!

Colleen was right. Fiona and Bianca loved him, but I think they were more caught up with the fact that he had money than anything else. He didn't seem to work, he never talked about a job. He had arranged to move into the apartment the day after Colleen moved out. I helped her unpack and rearrange all her furniture in her new home. She had a small sofa and a bed with a chest of drawers and a bookcase. We went shopping and bought some nice accessories, some pictures, a few mirrors and a gorgeous faux fur throw which was so delicious, I bought one for my own bedroom.

Colleen loved her space. She was so relieved to get away from Fiona and Bianca who had been driving her mad. I gave her a couple of days to settle in and then I arranged to come to her apartment for a housewarming drink. When she opened the door I realised why she hadn't got a man. They would have suffocated from the smoke fumes. I felt like I was crawling through a haze of smoke into the depths of a pub ashtray. There was dirty laundry hanging over the back of the sofa and the floor was littered with half empty coffee cups. She was a skanky bitch.

As for the set up with Bianca and Fiona, it didn't take long for things to start to fall apart. Simon would come into the apartment in the middle of the night, usually drunk, and want the girls to get up and entertain him. He played his music loudly if they wouldn't get up. He didn't have to go to work next day, but they did.

We met Simon whenever we were out socially. He always seemed to be there. No matter where we went, he would always turn up. He was usually drunk or under the influence of something. He was always buying drinks with his gold card for everyone in his company. He seemed to throw a lot of his money around. I wondered if he was dealing in drugs. I couldn't believe that any father would let his son have free rein with a credit card. He was a bit of a nuisance. But Colleen still harboured hopes that Simon would lose the run of himself with her. She must have been really desperate. I went out with her, hoping that she might meet someone a bit nicer than him.

We were in a themed Irish bar, but as far as I could tell, we were the only Irish people there.

As I went to the bar to order drinks I noticed a man who was trying to catch Colleen's attentions. She was scowling into her drink. I brought the drinks over and pointed him out to her. She swivelled round and he smiled at her. She baulked and turned away. I could see the man was a bit taken aback, so I smiled at him and he came forward. He introduced himself to us and started to chat. I took that moment to go to the toilets. She would have to do this one on her own, I wasn't her pimp.

When I returned they were deep in conversation. I checked that she was all right, and felt safe with him, then I made my excuses and left to join some of the other people from work. She deserved a bit of happiness.

Next morning she phoned me, and told me that his name was Graham and that he had brought her home and stayed the night. I hoped she had given the place a good spring clean before she invited him in. She wasn't wasting much time. He was going to take her out to dinner tonight. She was very excited and I was pleased for her. I agreed to catch up with her the next day. I was happy to spend the night by myself as I wanted to telephone my family at home. Maybe all her mother's prayers would be answered now.

CHAPTER 10

Colleen saw Graham at least once a week. She complained that because he was in the police force he had to work antisocial hours and so he couldn't always get away to see her. He would phone her at odd hours, but she never complained; she was just so delighted to have any contact with him. Graham had a positive influence on her, she visibly changed, she looked younger, and she had more of a sparkle to her. She had phoned her mother immediately to tell her the good news. Her mother had complained that Colleen had better not mess this relationship up. She demanded that Colleen should make sure that he stated his intentions and put a ring on her finger soon. Colleen fervently hoped that this would happen too. She was really enamoured with Graham. His name littered every conversation we had. She thought he might be 'the one' and she raved about how her family would be so pleased when they finally met him.

But the romance didn't last long. Colleen had been bragging about her new boyfriend to one of her team mates, Olive, who seemed very interested in all of Graham's personal details. A short time later Colleen was at her desk when another worker, Julianne, asked to speak to her alone. It turned out that Graham was her boyfriend; they had been together for three years. Julianne had learned all about his liaison from Olive. The place was a village, nothing was secret there. Julianne acknowledged that Colleen hadn't known this information, but now that she did, she said that she should have no further contact with Graham.

Colleen was raging; she had had high hopes for this relationship. She rang and asked me to meet her after work, when she told me all about it. She was very distressed. 'Why should I give him up?' she ranted. 'Why should she get to keep him when he wants to be with me?' My heart broke for her. I knew that a relationship was the primary reason for her coming to Australia in the first place. Now what would she do?

'You're too good for him,' I protested as I handed her a paper tissue. But she wasn't going to let him go without a fight. She turned the whole saga into some contest between the two of them, with Graham as the main prize. She continued to see Graham, secretly. 'He'll soon get sick of her,' she explained, 'and then he'll be mine.' I wouldn't have bet the farm on it.

Eventually Colleen gave Graham an ultimatum; she demanded that he choose between her and Julianne. She lost. He probably realized she wasn't too capable in the old housekeeping department. Colleen was devastated. I spent a lot of time with her while she nursed her heartache and I worried about what she might do.

Colleen threw herself into her work, but she was embarrassed every time she met Julianne especially when Julianne informed the entire office that she had now become engaged and was getting married in a matter of months. Poor Colleen, that was another blow for her to deal with.

I took her out to restaurants as food was a source of comfort to her, and I tried to get her to go out to clubs but she wasn't interested. She hibernated, spending long hours mulling over everything that had happened. Eventually she seemed to pull herself out of the dark hole she had been in, but she seemed to have lost a bit of her soul. She became even more cynical, hard and bitter. Work was the only thing, apart from food, which distracted her.

I was up to my eyes in work when she rang me at my desk. I thought it was another of the many phone calls that she made when she needed a bit of support, but this one was different. 'You'll have to leave work now. I need someone to accompany me out of the office and it's not safe for me to go home,' she whispered conspiratorially.

'Sorry, what?' I stopped typing and concentrated. She had gained my undivided attention.

'Well, it's this case I've been working on. I was in court today with it and the mother isn't too happy. I'm worried about my personal safety. She might try and come to the office and attack me.'

'Has this woman threatened you?' I asked sceptically.

'Well, no, but she might,' she said hesitatingly.

'Has she a history of violence then?' I was worried.

'No, but you never know with these people. My team leader has organized for a taxi to meet me at the front door now, but I think I should go to your house where it's safer just in case she tries to follow me home. I don't want to go to Fiona and Bianca's house. They aren't speaking to me now because Simon is causing them so many problems so I've no one else to ask.' Great, I wasn't even second best choice, but paddy last.

'And has she specifically threatened you then?' I clarified.

'Well, not specifically but you can't be too careful with things like this.'

'Well, I'm up to my eyes in work here.' I looked around at the piles of papers which were toppling off my desk 'and I'll have to ask my team leader, we are short staffed here today again,' I said unenthusiastically. I had no intention of going anywhere with the volume of work I had to complete.

'Oh, he knows already Jack just talked to him. He's quite cute that Tom, isn't he?' she simpered. 'Is he married?' Even in the middle of a crisis, Colleen wouldn't lose out on the chance to meet a man.

'Yes, Colleen, he's married,' I protested.

'But is he happy with her? Does he talk about his wife? You never know what's going on behind closed doors,' she insisted 'and he would have loads of money if he's a team leader.' Yes, and most of it would be spent paying maintenance for his children. She hadn't a clue. I didn't respond. I wasn't getting into a discussion on something I knew nothing about.

'Anyway,' she sighed, 'Jack has already talked to him and told him all about it.' Damn, she'd covered every base. It looked like I would have to play along with it.

'Right, I'll just let Tom know I'm going then.'

'Don't forget to find out about the state of his marriage,' she hissed. 'He would be on really good money, you know.' I put the phone down in disgust. Tom was exactly like me, which is why I liked working for him. He never got annoyed about anything and he didn't get caught up in dramas but there was no way I was going to ask him for personal information about his life.

'Apparently I have to go home with Colleen who is afraid that some client type person might get her,' I said as I walked into his office.

'Yes, Jack's just off the phone, Are you OK with that?' he asked politely.

'Well, it doesn't look like I have any bloody choice seeing as she's making my home out to be some type of safe house. I'd hoped to work late tonight and finish that report for court, but I suppose I can do it tomorrow.'

'Tell me this,' asked Tom inquisitively, 'has she any child protection experience at all?' I sniggered.

'Apparently not. She worked with one of the voluntary agencies at home, so she probably wouldn't know a crisis situation if it bit her on the arse. Sorry to sound so disloyal as she's supposed to be a sort of friend.'

'Sort of?' he asked curiously.

'Well, it's like I keep saying, this Children's Bureau has assumed that just because we came from overseas we will be all one big happy family, and most of them you wouldn't go out in public with at all. I'm just not sure that her values are the same as mine.'

'What do you mean?' he asked warily.

'Well, I don't know about you, but I came here to do a job, but with her and some of the other ones I've met the work interferes with their social lives. They came out here to get a husband.' And they don't care if he's already attached, I thought bitterly.

'And you don't want one too?' he asked sardonically.

'You must be joking; I had one, who turned out to be worse than useless. I wouldn't go through that again. They don't realise that is what happens. First the engagement ring, then the wedding ring, and then the suffering.' Tom laughed.

'I don't agree with you about the marriage part, but I do about the rest. But you get off now and try and calm her down a bit, make her see sense.'

'So you mean I should just take her out and get her pissed?'

'Well, that might help,' he said. 'It certainly might help you to get through what is going to be a very long night.'

I met Colleen at her desk where she was flapping around, checking that her mobile phone was working in case she had to phone the police. She asked me to contact the security guards and see if the taxi had arrived.

'Sure they will phone you when it arrives,' I shrugged feeling embarrassed; I didn't want to get caught up in some soap opera. I felt used. I noticed the disdainful looks of Colleen's friend Debbie and I went over to say hello.

'It's a load of hype about nothing,' said Debbie firmly.

'Yes, you are absolutely right,' I said. 'I take it you've actually worked in child protection then?'

'Yes,' said Debbie 'isn't it bloody obvious?' We laughed.

I thought about what might have been considered a crisis in my old job. Threats made against me by a known criminal with a violent history didn't even warrant a report in a significant incident book there, but clearly the attitudes here were very different. I noticed Colleen's team leader, Jack, who was always friendly and courteous to me. He looked drained; no doubt if he had Colleen bashing his ear all day the poor man must be demented. No wonder he agreed to let her get home early. He obviously wanted her out of the way so he could have a bit of peace and quiet.

I brought Colleen home with me and ordered a takeaway. While she took a shower I organized the spare bedroom and put a couple of bottles of wine in the fridge. It looked like I might need them. It was a long night. Colleen expounded at length about the danger she had faced and the fact that she might need to take a few days off to recover.

'Recover from what?' I asked dubiously. She hadn't been injured or assaulted, so what was she yapping about? She talked about the stress of her job, the high profile caseload she had. I sat quietly wondering to myself if two bottles of wine would be enough to get me through the evening. I put on a DVD and encouraged her to relax and just unwind while I escaped to the bathroom for a long hot bath.

'But what if someone comes to the door?' she sniffed noisily.

'Just answer it,' I said laughing. She couldn't be serious. 'Sure none of your clients know I live here, and if anyone comes it will probably be Sandra next door. Just ask her in and I'll get out of the bath.' Her bottom lip trembled; she looked as if she was going to pout. 'I won't be long,' I assured her and hurried from the room. So much for a long luxurious bath. Jesus, could you cry under water?

I spent the rest of the evening tutting and aahing appropriately in all the right spaces while Colleen continued to complain about her excessive workload, her responsibilities and the stress she was under. She wouldn't know anything about it. Stress is when you wake up screaming and you realize you haven't fallen asleep yet. I feigned a headache and making sure she knew where everything was, I finally escaped to bed.

Next morning she was up and dressed when I went into the kitchen. 'I thought you might be taking today off?' I said in amazement.

'Oh, well, I thought about it but I've so much to do I can't take any more time off,' she sighed bravely. 'And you never know, maybe I will have to talk to the police and some of those officers might be cute.' She was starry eyed.

You mean you want to create a bit more drama and don't want to be left out of all the action. I sniggered when I thought of her team leader's face. Poor man, he must have thought he was going to have a day's grace. We travelled in to work together. I stopped at the shop to get a coffee; another late night tonight.

CHAPTER 11

Maryann had kept in touch with me by email. She had written that she had taken her couple of boxes over to my house where my sister had arranged to collect them. My sister was organizing the transportation of all my goods and worldly treasures. Maryann had also written that she had met a lovely man called Timothy through a local church pen pal group. He was thirty-six, and as he was one year younger than her, she claimed he was her toy boy. He lived at home with his mother and he was a Eucharistic minister of the church. She had written that the relationship was serious but that she still intended coming over to Australia. She told me that she had been dieting and running regularly and that she was determined to look fit and healthy when she arrived.

When Maryann finally arrived she was carrying an enormous pink flowered bag which banged into everyone within a two mile radius. She was puffing and wheezing as she waddled towards us at the arrivals lounge. She hadn't lost an ounce of weight, just three months of time by the look of it.

'I thought you said she had been jogging,' whispered Colleen.

'She had to give it up because her thighs kept rubbing together and setting her knickers on fire,' I hissed.

Maryann grabbed me and clutched me to her huge bosom. I was smothered in layers of fat. I hugged her back knowing how frightened and alone I had felt when I had first arrived.

'You both have a tan?' She glared at Colleen and me. 'You both look great.' She seemed surprised. We chatted as we waited at the luggage carousel to collect her bags.

'Oh I'm so excited,' she gushed. 'I can't wait to see everything. What is the house like? What about work, do you know yet which team I will be on? Who is my team leader? Will I be working with either of you? You'll have to tell me all about it,' she stated as she launched from one question to another, never giving us time to reply to any of them.

I drove her to the house and she twittered beside me through the entire journey. Colleen sat quietly in the back of the car. Just be patient, Louise, I told myself, she's been on an airplane for the last two days, she probably hasn't had a chance to talk in all that time, and for her talking is as natural as breathing.

We entered the house and I showed her the bedroom I had prepared for her. The bed was second-hand and it had already done the rounds of the other overseas recruits but I had bought fresh sheets and a new quilt with a lovely pink cover, which I thought she would appreciate. She seemed a bit put out by the room. What was she expecting, the Ritz Carlton? She asked to look at my bedroom. I showed it to her.

'But you have the en suite in yours,' she whined.

'Yes, but I've been here for three months paying the rent by myself, as well as my mortgage at home, but if you want to swap I'm sure we can come to some arrangement.'

'So I will be paying less for having the smaller room then?' she asked confidently.

'No, Maryann,' I replied as forcefully as I could. I was determined to nip her miserliness in the bud. 'The rent is shared in half. You have the large bathroom and the bedrooms are the same size.'

'But you have a double bed and I've only got a single one,' she moaned.

'Look, Maryann,' I was beginning to lose patience, 'the bed actually belongs to my boss at work who has been kind enough to let me borrow it. When my furniture arrives you can have my king-sized bed if you want, but at the minute we have to make do with what we have.'

Seeing Maryann start to purse her lips in a disapproving fashion Colleen reinforced my sentiments. 'I was sharing with two girls from work and I had the biggest room but we shared the rent equally and all the bills. I know you are used to living by yourself and it's a bit like taking a step back, but the rent is so high in this place you couldn't afford it on your own.'

Maryann still seemed dissatisfied with this response. 'So these sofas aren't yours,' she asked moving into the living room and touching them.

'No, Maryann, practically everything in this place belongs to someone else. They have all been kind enough to let me borrow them and they will all have to be returned.'

'So when your furniture arrives, this stuff all goes back to people,' she said cautiously.

'Yes, Maryann it does,' I said firmly. But I could see where this was leading.

'Oh,' she replied shaking her head. 'I thought that I might want to get somewhere of my own some day, and I could use this stuff. I mean, if they can do without it, then they mustn't really want it.' Jesus, she was causing complications already and she was only through the door.

'Well, you can talk about it when my stuff comes,' I sighed.

'And when is that? You've got some of my boxes, you know!' she said accusingly.

Jesus, to hear her you'd think I'd hijacked her stuff. 'I don't know, I haven't heard anything yet, but as soon as I do I'll let you know. Look,' I tried to divert her, 'you must be tired. I've made some lunch for you but if you want to have a lie down we can do something later on. What about a nice cup of coffee and a biscuit?' If she had something in her mouth it would at least keep her quiet.

'It was nice of you to collect me,' she conceded as we moved toward the kitchen. 'Did work give you the money for the petrol?'

'No, Maryann, they didn't,' interjected Colleen. 'Louise paid for it, and I'm sure she's not going to be charging you for the ride. But usually the Children's Bureau gives a hamper of food and stuff when you arrive so they gave me some vouchers for Woolworth's instead. There's some here for you and Louise.'

Maryann's fat fingers reached out and grabbed them from Colleen before I could make a move. 'These are for both of you, you know,' interrupted Colleen, looking at me in dismay.

'Oh, I know, I know,' Maryann sighed, 'sure we can use them when we go shopping.'

We moved towards the kitchen and I pointed out the pantry. 'Just help yourself to whatever you want,' I said. 'I wasn't sure what you liked, but we can do some proper shopping later on when you have had a bit of a rest.'

Her eyes lit on a packet of chocolate biscuits; obviously chocolate was her favourite colour. I laughed. 'You see, I knew you would like those. I'll make a cup of coffee and you can have some.'

Before I had filled the kettle with water she had scoffed half the packet. Pieces of biscuit were flying out of her mouth, all down the front of her top and landing on the kitchen floor. 'Yum yum,' she mumbled between bites, the crumbs falling out of her mouth as she talked. The things you see when you haven't got a gun. She then opened the fridge which was filled to capacity. I had spent a fortune on food in readiness for her arrival. She poked around and saw a chocolate cake. She took it out of the fridge and hugged it to her, her eyes wide in delight. Some do Jenny Craig, some do Richard Simmons but she does Sara Lee. As she stood up she noticed a carton of beer. She pointed to it and grimaced.

'I don't like alcohol in my house,' she said crossly.

'It's our house now,' I said quickly, 'and beer is not just for breakfast anymore.' She glared at me.

'Look, don't annoy yourself about it. To some it's a six-pack but to me it's a support group.' I noticed that she had ignored the fruit and yoghurts which I had bought because she had told me that she was on a diet. Thank goodness I decided to buy junk as well. 'I'm always careful to get something every day from the four basic food groups,' I told her. 'Canned, frozen, fast and takeout.' She ignored me. She pulled the cake out of the box and scrabbling in the drawer for a fork she got stuck in. Colleen and I watched in fascination as she hogged down the entire cake in one sitting.

'Oh, sorry,' she looked up as she was licking the chocolate from the paper plate, 'did you want some?'

'No, thanks, I'm on a diet,' I stuttered. A successful diet is the triumph of mind over platter. Colleen turned away in disgust and went outside to smoke a cigarette. She rolled her eyes at me and nodded her head in the direction of Maryann who was now licking the cardboard plate. I could see I was going to have great times ahead.

'So tell me all about Timothy?' I asked politely that evening when we were alone. Colleen was collecting us later to take us to dinner.

She hesitated. 'Well, he's six foot two and he's really nice,' she said finally.

'What does he do?' I asked as I moved her case from the sofa so I could sit down.

'He's a joiner,' she said flatly.

'Did he live near you?'

'Well no, he lives with his mammy,' she said slowly.

'And do you think he might come out here at some point?'

'Well I don't know, you never know who else I might meet here. There's bound to be loads of nice Christian men,' she stammered. Huh! She was in for a rude awakening.

'Forgive me for speaking frankly, Maryann,' I said as gently as I could, 'but there doesn't seem to be an awful lot of passion in this relationship.'

93

'Well, I came here for a new life and like I said, you never know who you might meet.'

'That's true,' I agreed. 'Just don't rush into anything. You have the rest of your life to figure out what's right for you.' Jesus, I had become some type of agony aunt.

'Thanks, Louise,' she replied solemnly. 'Now where is the nearest chapel? I need to light a candle to God to thank him for getting me here safely.'

'I'll show you where the nearest one is when we go out for dinner later,' I said.

'I hope you are going to mass every week!' she said firmly. Now she was the religious police. It's hard to be religious when certain people are never incinerated by bolts of lightning.

I returned home from work next day to find she had unpacked all her belongings which were spilling all over her bedroom, into the living room and kitchen. Clothes and papers littered every spare space. She was hunkered down in the living room; there wasn't even a spare inch for me to put down my handbag.

'Here, I have something for you,' she said as she hunted through the debris.

She pulled out a scrap of paper and gave it to me. It was Bronagh's email address. I had left my address book behind and wouldn't be getting it until my furniture and stuff came out, and I had been anxious about maintaining contact with friends from home. At last I would have contact with the outside world. I knew that regular contact with Bronagh would keep me sane. She was the kindest woman I'd ever met, and she had a droll Belfast humour which always made me laugh. Bronagh never got into a flap about anything. She was the kind of woman I wanted to be around if there was ever a calamity. Her shoulders were soggy from all the tears I had cried there as I had assailed her with every crisis in my life.

I went into my bedroom to have a shower and to get changed out of my work clothes. My bed was littered with clothing, all of it mine. Had we been broken into? Had anything important been stolen? I noticed that my CD player was missing. Most of my toiletries had disappeared from the en suite. My good Jo Malone products which I wouldn't be able to get here. What kind of a vain robber would do that? I rushed into the living room.

'Did you go out, Maryann? I mean, were you here when it happened? Are you all right? Did they take anything of yours?' I asked frantically. She looked up at me.

'Wha?' she asked dumbly.

'My stuff is all over the place, we'll have to phone the police, there's been a robbery,' I said hysterically.

'But I haven't left the house all day,' she protested. Bastards, they had the cheek to sneak into someone's house when they were still there.

'But my CD player, my cosmetics, everything's all over the place.'

'Oh, that,' she sighed, 'I borrowed it to listen to some music.'

'Right,' I said slowly. 'I'm sure that's all right but you should have asked me first. But what happened with my clothes?'

'Oh, I was just trying some stuff on, you know, you have some lovely things there, I hadn't realised you liked fashion so much. I can't wait to borrow some of those lovely skirts and tops?' Borrow? She wouldn't get one of those huge tree trunk thighs into the waistband of one of my skirts. Did she really think we were the same size? Was she totally blind? What was the reverse of anorexia where you look in the mirror and think you are thin?

'I'd appreciate it if you wouldn't touch my stuff, Maryann,' I said resolutely.

'Suit yourself,' she said shrugging her shoulders and continuing to sort through the papers in her hand.

'What about my toiletries? Where are they?' I asked as I looked around the mess she had created all over the living and dining area. Were they under that lot?

'Oh, I just thought since we were sharing a house we may as well share the other stuff.' I sighed. I've always hated conflict, I would run a mile from it, but when she started to mess around with the few things that were precious to me in this country, this meant business.

'I don't think so, Maryann. Anything that is in my bedroom, wardrobe or en suite is mine and I don't want you touching my stuff again,' I said steadily. Her lip trembled; she looked as if she was going to cry. Just like that horrid spoiled brat out of the Just William stories I had read as a child.

'I didn't mean any harm,' she simpered. 'I just thought it would save a bit of money if we shared household things.'

'Listen, Maryann,' I said as calmly as I could, 'Jo Malone is not some household item. I'm going to put the stuff back in my bathroom, and I don't want you touching them again.'

She hung her head, clearly huffing. At least I'd get a bit of peace and quiet tonight. I went into her bathroom. The Egyptian cotton towels I had purchased, just for display, were lying damp and sodden on the bathroom floor. Tubes and bottles were scattered all over the vanity unit, all of them had their lids off, and my bottles of shampoo and conditioner rested on the shower floor, their lids open, dripping down the plug hole. My shower gel, which had cost me the price of a new liver, was empty. I knew, all things being equal, that fat people use more soap, but I had only used it once as it was so expensive. I grabbed my stuff and stormed back to my bedroom. I sat on the bed with the sodden towels in my hand and sobbed. I don't want to be mean, but I really didn't think that living with this woman was going to work out at all.

I got up next morning determined to try and make the best of a difficult situation. When I reached the office I contacted Bronagh by email.

I told Bronagh that Maryann had arrived safely, but that already she was beginning to get on my nerves. I filled her in on all the problems I had experienced with her already. Bronagh was quick to reply that Maryann was no friend of hers and that she had met her through an acquaintance. Clearly she knew what she was like and she didn't even have to live with her. 'Has she divided up the bill and paid less because she only had one bite out of the bread?' Bronagh questioned. 'Yes,' I replied but unfortunately with her greed she usually ate her own share and other people's as well so she wouldn't be trying that one here.

CHAPTER 12

During the following weeks Maryann plodded her way round the town. She had informed the department that she needed some essential items until her stuff arrived in Australia and demanded that the Children's Bureau pay for these out of her relocation allowance. The essential items included a pink CD player, pink curling tongs and some posters for her room, pink dragonflies with glittery bits and spangles all over them. Her bedroom was a shrine to her signature colour, pink and a testimony to poor taste. It would have been wonderful for a little girl of about six, but the pink net canopy which hung over the pink quilt covers adorned with dragonflies was a bit much for a thirty-six-year-old woman.

'I'll need these when I move out on my own anyway,' she insisted.

'Why, are you going somewhere?' I asked, shocked as I had only agreed to take the leasehold on for a year because she had agreed to share the expenses with me. Was I going to be left paying for the rent on my own as well as my mortgage at home.

'Well, when Timothy comes over we will need to get our own place,' she protested.

Maryann insisted on creating her personal space before she could consider starting work, but sticking up a few posters would have taken all of ten minutes. When I asked when she intended to start work she complained that the journey to Australia might start to trigger a bout of glandular fever so she had to look after her health. Yes, and the thirteen grand she received from her former employers would cushion the blow of having no salary. The fact that she was making money out of renting her property at home and that she hadn't contributed to any household finances here helped too. It was clear that the Children's Bureau hadn't been aware that she had been on sick leave for a year before she came over. What if she needed sick leave in this job? I began to realise that if there was a way to financially benefit from any situation, then Maryann would be in the middle of it all.

Every day for the next few weeks Maryann was waiting when I came home from work, ready to pounce and demanding to know where we were going out for dinner. But that had turned into a minefield. She was obsessed with the calorific value of each and every morsel both on her plate and everyone else's. She talked about vitamins and proteins and of course all of the allergies which her naturopath had diagnosed her with. There was the gluten, and the dairy products and of course the citrus fruits. She just couldn't absorb them properly, she explained. She asked both Colleen and me what we weighed so she could work out our body mass index.

'It's actually none of your business,' I said through gritted teeth, 'but I've always believed that you shouldn't weigh more than your refrigerator.'

She was looking forward to the office Christmas parties which would take place next month. To her, food eaten at Christmas parties had no calories, courtesy of Santa.

She complained, when we had red meat, about the suffering which the animals must experience before they die.

'Well, if God didn't want us to eat animals he shouldn't have made them taste like meat,' I explained before returning to the menu. 'And,' I continued, 'if God is inside us, then I hope he likes fajitas, because that's what he's getting tonight.'

'But they are only defenceless animals,' she exclaimed.

'Good, I love defenceless animals, especially in a good gravy.' Colleen sniggered quietly. Now there was a girl who loved her dinner. No matter what Maryann told her it wouldn't put her off her food. If we are what we eat then Colleen was cheap, fast, and easy.

Maryann obviously lost all memory of her allergies and her diet when the dessert menu was produced. Here she believed that if she ate equal amounts of dark chocolate and white chocolate, it was a balanced diet. She also thought that if she ate a chocolate bar before each meal it would take the edge off her appetite and she would eat less. Some chance, she gobbled everything down greedily. For her a calorie was a basic measure of the amount of rationalization offered prior to taking a second helping of food. Then came the customary dividing of the bill, with her bickering over every penny she had to spend. She would suddenly realise what she had shovelled into her mouth, and more importantly, how much it was going to cost her. Every day it was the same litany.

'I shouldn't be paying as much because I didn't have a starter,' she said defiantly. That's right, you didn't, but you had two desserts instead. She was so mean she would steal a dead fly from a blind spider.

She was always eating chocolate or sweets. She thought chocolate covered raisins, cherries, orange slices and strawberries all counted as fruit, so she could eat as many as she wanted. She believed that movie-related foods did not have calories because they were part of the entertainment package.

She had let me borrow her hired car to go into town once but I could hardly get into it with all the empty sweet and pie wrappers that were scattered all over it. I could see that being overweight just sort of snacked up on her. I had to stop at the nearest bin and get rid of all the rubbish in case anyone thought I was a sloppy pig. I bought fresh bread in the bakery and left it on the kitchen bench to cool while I called in next door to deliver some mail to my neighbours. When I returned she had scoffed the lot, there was nothing left but a pile of crumbs. She clearly believed that if you ate something, and no one else saw you eat it, it had no calories.

I never had a minute to myself. Each morning I could hear her rattling around in the kitchen before I left for work. She would accost me as I tried to sneak into the kitchen to grab an apple or piece of fruit for my lunch.

'Do you think my glands are swollen today?' she would ask. I knew the routine by heart.

'What about my arms. Do they look a bit swollen?' I didn't know whether that was water or fat. If she was diagnosed with a flesh-eating disease the doctor would give her about thirteen years to live.

She never stopped, it was inexorable. She could join a support group. Actually did you hear about the self-help group for compulsive talkers? It's called On and On Anon.

I came into the kitchen. She was standing in the middle of the floor wearing a huge pink nightdress with a dragonfly motif pasted on the front. She was lucky to get so much material but it was still very short. I noticed she had flabby thighs, but fortunately her stomach covered them.

'You know, I'm a bit worried about you,' she said as she scoffed a box of sugar puffs from the packet, the cereal falling at her feet on the floor. 'You seem very quiet; you were much more fun when you were at home. Is something worrying you?'

Where did I start? How did I begin to say that she was irritating the living daylights out of me? She was messy, and never picked up after herself. She left her bedroom door open and all I could see were soiled clothes lying on the floor and wrappers from biscuits and sweets littering the room. When she was in a bad mood, which was frequent, she would hole up there with essential supplies of sweets and cakes. The cupboards were bare as she had eaten everything in the house. She had the use of a hired car, and would use it to go for drives during the day while I was at work, but while she had explored most of New South Wales she still hadn't managed to find a grocery shop where she could start to replace all the food she had scoffed. There wasn't a tea bag left in the place.

I had decided to wait this out as long as possible and I usually bought lunch every day on my way to work. She couldn't have everything her own way. She had been living with me for three weeks now and not once had she put her hand in her pocket to pay for rent or any of the other bills. Where did I start though? Sorry, Maryann, but you are really getting on my tits? Sorry, Maryann, but if I hear one more complaint about your health I'll give you something to moan about? How important did a person have to be before they are considered assassinated instead of just murdered?

'What about going up to that high tower today to see the town properly?' she screeched one Sunday morning as she came into my bedroom where I was trying to hide.

'No, thanks, Maryann, I don't see the point of paying to go up a tall building and then putting money in binoculars to look at things on the ground.'

'Oh, well, what about a nice drive, go on, it will do you good,' she entreated.

I hadn't anything else planned that day, apart from hiding from her, and as Colleen was working overtime and I hadn't anyone else to palm her onto I agreed.

'I'll just go and change my clothes,' she squeaked.

Yes, why don't you slip into something nicer, like unconsciousness? She returned in a pink pair of velour tracksuit pants and a yellow shirt which had yet another dragonfly motif plastered all over the front. She was carrying an enormous pink straw bag with a green peaked cap plonked on her huge head. It looked like she had thrown the clothes on her from across the room. Whatever kind of look she was going for, she had missed.

She drove to the local markets; I was exhausted by the time we got there, listening to her incessant chatter. She waddled round the markets and bought some Hopi candles. 'So when we get back you can do my ears for me,' she declared putting them into her voluminous bag.

What? Ears? 'No way, Maryann, sorry, but I have a thing about ears. I can't touch anybody else's.' I recoiled.

'But I need these for my health, Louise,' she whinged like a spoiled child. 'You don't want me to get worse.' Worse? Could there be any bloody worse? People like her were the reason that people like me needed medication.

'No, I'm sorry, Maryann,' I said with as much conviction as I could muster. 'I am not touching your ears under any circumstances.'

She grabbed her large pink handbag and clutched it to her chest in affront as if I had attempted to assault her.

'I suppose I could always get Colleen to do them for me,' she sighed in martyrdom. 'She's a real friend.'

She spent the rest of the morning huffing. I was planning to leave her there and get a taxi home by myself when she came up to me.

'I bought you a present,' she simpered as she handed me a little picture frame with the $1 dollar price tag still attached. Yeah, great, thanks, Maryann, this will make up for everything.

'You're very quiet,' she said. 'Are you due your period?' Dear God, now she thought I was premenstrual. I resisted the urge to punch her. No, I don't have PMS, I just really hate you!

She accosted me the next morning when I was sitting outside having a much needed cup of coffee.

'Oh, there you are,' she exclaimed. Yes, I'm out of bed and dressed what more do you want? 'I was just looking for you. You know, I was reading a bit out of one of my prayer books this morning and I really think you should read it.' She thrust the book in my face.

'No, thanks, Maryann.' I stood up and walked past her into the kitchen pouring the rest of my coffee down the sink. I wouldn't get any peace to drink it now.

'No, really you should,' she followed me. 'It's from one of the gospels and I think you might get a bit of strength from it.'

'No thanks.' I didn't need strength; all I needed was a bit of patience to get through this. What the hell had I done? I had left a sod off home to live in a…a bed sit with some hypochondriac religious fanatic. Was I right in the head? Even Kevin was beginning to look more attractive the longer I stayed here.

'You really should find Jesus and let him into your heart,' she said solemnly.

'I did find him. He was behind the sofa the whole time.' She hadn't listened to a word I said.

'You really should read it,' she said as she shoved the book into my face again.

'Listen, to tell the truth, Maryann, I'm really not interested. I think religion is a very personal thing and…' She interjected immediately talking over everything I tried to say. Have you noticed that people who want to share their religious view with you almost never want you to share yours with them?

I walked away while she was still talking and left the house to go to work. I was early but at least I would generate a bit of overtime by trying to get away from her. Did I leave the womb for this?

I met Colleen after work as I was on my way home. 'I found this place in the shopping centre which sells all these new age things,' she said excitedly 'so I bought a pack of angel oracle cards today. Why don't I do a reading for us and see what lies ahead. Maybe it will tell me that I'm going to meet some hunky man. You can both come round to the apartment if you like.'

'Why don't you come round to our house?' I suggested. I couldn't bear the thought of sitting in her apartment and trying hard to breathe through my mouth and I knew that Maryann would complain the whole time about how her asthma would be affected. She agreed. She and Maryann went for something to eat while I went home and had a bath; all I wanted was to just chill out after a busy day.

'I'll do one for you, just to get it out of the way,' Colleen sighed when she arrived at the house and settled herself on the living room floor dramatically. She produced the pack of angel oracle cards from her handbag. Yes, and obviously we'll get to the most important part of the evening – yourself. Maryann curled her fat feet under her, settling herself in for the night. Colleen shuffled the cards and told me to ask a question.

'I don't need to hear the question,' she said bossily. 'The angels will guide me through the reading. Just think about a question and hold it in your head and I will ask the angels for an answer.' Right, just humour her, Louise. Hmm, what to ask? I know, what was the purpose of coming to this place in the first place? That was the one question that I really wanted to know, what karmic forces had been in place to get me here.

'Right I'm concentrating,' Colleen said dramatically as she continued to shuffle the cards. 'Ooooh,' sighed Maryann clearly impressed with Colleen's psychic abilities.

'Now, I'm just going to pick a card from the pack and your answer lies within,' she said mysteriously. I stifled a giggle. Colleen pulled a card from the pack in her hand and placed it down slowly and deliberately on the floor. We all stared at it. *Marriage*. Shit! I didn't want that card; there must have been some mistake. Maybe it was a reference to the fact that I had left my country to get away from a marriage. Yes, that was it; it didn't mean marriage in the literal sense. I looked over at Colleen waiting for her to consult the guide book and interpret the reading for me. Her lips pursed, she snatched the card from the table.

'You can't have that one,' she insisted. 'That's the one I want.' Oh, sorry. Jesus, you'd think I did it on purpose. 'You mustn't have been concentrating,' she scolded, 'you'll just have to do it again.' She returned the offending card to the pack and shuffled the cards roughly. 'This time just concentrate harder,' she scolded. I thought of the same question again, trying to hold it in my mind like she had suggested. Colleen eventually drew another card from the pack and placed it face up on the table again. *Marriage*. Clearly the angels were having a bit of a laugh. 'Oh, it's just not working with you, you must be hostile,' she snapped as she snatched the card and returned it to its pack. 'I'll just have to do a reading for Maryann, you're useless at this.' Hello! She was the one who was doing the bloody readings.

They could just get on with it themselves. I went into my bedroom and picked up the leaflet which was face down on my bed. The instructions for installing the DVD player, this was more like it. It would be far more interesting than some useless card reading where I couldn't do anything right.

Meanwhile Timothy continued to text Maryann and she usually returned his calls though I often saw her sigh dramatically when she looked down at the caller display on her mobile and discovered it was him.

One Saturday morning Colleen, Maryann and I were on our way to lunch. There seemed little else to do in this place. Maryann still hadn't started work. Timothy had sent her a text message as she was driving. She should have known it was time to go on a diet, she couldn't feel the vibration from her mobile.

When she parked the car she opened her phone and read it aloud to us. "Marry me," he had written. 'Christ,' she said. She looked stunned.

'Call him back, say yes, quickly, say yes,' screamed Colleen.

'Think about this carefully,' I pleaded, trying to be the voice of reason in all the madness. What kind of man texted a proposal?

'Call him, call him,' squealed Colleen like a demented parrot. 'You can't afford to lose him.' I knew Maryann wasn't the bonniest but Colleen was as subtle as a well-thrown brick.

'Look, why don't we go on and you can meet us in the restaurant when you are ready. Take your time,' I said kindly. God, all she needed was Colleen pushing her into a marriage just because it was her own favourite fantasy.

'I think Maryann needs a bit of time to digest what has happened,' I said when we had been seated.

'Why?' Colleen said dismissively. 'It's not like she has men queueing up for her, is it? She doesn't seem to have had a boyfriend for years and now this one is looking to marry her so what more could she want?'

'Look, Colleen, you have two choices in life, you can stay single and be miserable, or get married and wish you were dead. Which do you want for her? She hasn't once said that she loves him. She might not even want to marry him.'

'Nonsense, he's asked her. She could have the chance to go home and get married and have children instead of hanging round this bloody place. Sure it's what she came over for anyway,' she said bitterly.

Maryann joined us about half an hour later. She seemed to be forcing a smile. 'So will we order champagne now?' asked Colleen, again with the sensitivity of a tumble dryer.

'Well, I've told him that I'm a bit surprised but that I'll think about it,' replied Maryann hesitatingly.

'Think about it? Think about it?' roared Colleen. 'If you don't say yes now you might never get another chance. Do you want to be on the shelf for the rest of your life? Text him right back and say you will, go on,' she commanded. Maryann resigned herself to doing as Colleen had asked.

'There now, you nearly lost him. If it hadn't been for me you might still be on your own.' Colleen smiled smugly, clearly pleased with her own actions in the endeavour. If only it was so easy to get her married off.

Colleen spent the rest of the time talking about the weddings where it should be held, and who would be invited. She became more and more excited as the day went on and swept Maryann along in a tide of cakes, frocks and flowers.

'You don't have a sister so I'll be your bridesmaid; I've done it before so I know exactly what to do.' She reached down and produced a notebook from her handbag.

'Right, we need a list. Have you thought about a colour for the bridesmaids and the flowers? Hmm, I quite like blue, but you can't have that as my dresses are blue.'

'Your dresses?' I interjected.

'Yes, well, I just fell in love with them when I saw them at that bridal fair I went to, so I bought one for my sister and one for my niece, but, you know, if I don't get married soon they will never fit,' she giggled hysterically. She really had bought bridesmaid dresses. She was serious about this whole wedding thing. 'Oh, this is just so exciting,' she gushed. 'I have the headdresses and the cummerbunds made to match them and of course,' she said smugly, 'I already have my own dress. Oh, you should see it, it's just gorgeous. It has loads of frills at the bottom and sequins sewn all over the skirt and it has a long train with a beautiful bow just at the back. It's the loveliest dress I have ever seen and I knew as soon as I tried it on that it was the one.' She sighed happily. 'I just couldn't resist it. All I need now is a groom,' she giggled. Maryann looked as if she had been run over by a bus, her mouth was agape. I tried to stifle my laughter, thinking of Colleen prancing around like Miss Havisham in her wedding dress waiting for some bloke to appear.

'What about cream?' She sucked on the end of the pen. 'Yes,' she scribbled, 'you are probably too old for white at your age. I know, what about cream and brown? The bridesmaid's dress would match my eyes then.' She began to jot down other ideas. She was running away with herself like a bullet out of a gun. 'Now we need a location, you know, some of the venues are booked up years in advance. You need to get on the ball and organize a church and somewhere nice for the reception. I have a printout for the venues in Northern Ireland but I don't know anything about England. I'll have to get on the Internet and find out some more information. I take it you will get married in Bradford?' She pointed her pen at Maryann. 'That's good, and then all your family could come too. Hmm Bradford might be nice, I haven't been there before and I'm sure Timothy's family would be happy to travel there for the wedding. When is it going to be? Have you thought about a theme? You can either have traditional or contemporary. I think something simple would suit you better. You will have to get the invitations out quickly. I did a course in calligraphy you know, so I could write out the invitation cards for you. That would be one less thing for you to worry about.' She jotted this down on her notepad which was filling up with details.

'You'll need to book cars well in advance too. It's not as if we could get you into a side car.' She laughed heartily at her own joke. Maryann looked as if she was about to be sick, though she would probably recover by the time the dessert menu arrived.

'What about an engagement ring?' Colleen asked. 'You can't be engaged without a ring,' she went on in consternation.

'Well,' confessed Maryann, 'Timothy said he might come over in July so we'll see what happens. We can always get one then.'

'Nonsense, sure I can go with you and we can have a look at the jewellers here. Then he can just send you the money. You would suit something plain and simple with the size of your hands. What about a solitaire? I know, let's go to the jewellers in town when we've had lunch. We could have a look and see what might suit you. Sure I could always try on a few myself. You never know what's round the corner, and at least I'd have a ring picked for when I meet a nice man. I have always fancied a cluster myself, but you never know until it's on your finger what you might suit,' she laughed to herself. 'And then we will have to get a dress for you. You won't be wearing a veil of course; I think we can safely say that you are a bit too old for that. And you might find it hard to get a dress to fit you in the shops as you're so large, so we might have to look at patterns and get it made by a dressmaker. But we could go and have a look at what's fashionable at the minute. I think you are making the right decision, going for cream, it's much more appropriate,' she gushed on.

'So you are engaged?' She put her pen down on the table and gazed at Maryann in wonder. 'I'm so excited for you. You have only just arrived and you have got yourself a husband, and at least you haven't got an Australian one, so that leaves one for the rest of us. You know, you should phone your family now and let them know. They won't mind being woken up in the night to hear that you are getting married.'

'No, Colleen,' Maryann exclaimed vehemently. 'I'm not waking anybody at this time, it's the middle of the night over there.'

'You are right,' sighed Colleen, 'of course, what was I thinking? It's Timothy who should be phoning your father and asking for your hand in marriage.' Maryann looked traumatized.

'My father?' she spluttered. 'Well, no, not yet, I'd rather tell him myself. I haven't known Timothy that long after all and I don't want him to be surprised. They haven't even met him yet.'

'But you are engaged. I can't wait to tell everyone in work, it's, so exciting. You are the first one of us to get engaged, so who knows whose turn it might be next,' she smiled coyly.

'Actually I'd prefer it if you didn't tell anyone,' pleaded Maryann.

'Why, are you ashamed of him?' snapped Colleen.

'No, of course not,' Maryann put her head down. 'But I think for the minute it would be best if it's all kept as a secret.'

'Don't worry,' I smiled patronizingly at Maryann. 'Your secret is safe with me and all my friends.' Colleen ignored my remark.

'Oh, that's so romantic, a secret engagement. I hope this means he's really going to marry you though; you can't afford to be wasting your time on someone who is only messing you about,' she said huffily.

'No, I don't think Timothy is like that,' Maryann frowned. 'I think he's serious.'

'Well, I'm sure you will change your mind about telling people when you get a ring. I know, let's go after lunch. Oh, all this excitement has made me so hungry, I think I'll have steak and chips, and I might even persuade myself to have some dessert too. Don't worry,' she patted Maryann's arm, 'I'll try and put on a bit of weight to make you look a bit slimmer before the big day.'

'I think you are rushing things a wee bit,' Maryann said slowly, her bottom lip trembling.

'Oh, come here you, you big eejit,' said Colleen, reaching up and struggling to give her a hug as she couldn't get her arms to reach round her. 'Sure it's all right to be a bit emotional; this is the most important time in your life.'

'But I'd rather take things a bit slower if you don't mind,' sniffed Maryann. Hmm I knew what that meant, she obviously hoped she would be able to extricate herself from this business but knew that it was pointless trying when Colleen was around. It also left her open to other possibilities, which I had begun to suspect was what she really wanted.

CHAPTER 13

If I thought my problems were bad while Maryann was at home they were worse once she eventually started work. She was assigned to a different floor of the Children's Bureau but she repeatedly phoned to clarify things with me. I encouraged her to speak to her team leader and to identity any training she thought she might need. But she was insistent. 'What does this mean? How are you supposed to work this? How do you change the password on the computer? How do you leave voicemail?' Let me drop everything and work on your problem. She was worse than a demanding child. She wanted to meet me for lunch every day, but I didn't have the time or, to be truthful, the energy. Some days I was so busy I was lucky to have an early morning coffee, never mind lunch.

'But I don't know anyone else,' she whined.

'Ask Colleen,' I suggested hoping that she would just leave me alone.

A new girl had started work in my team called Katie who seemed to be very quiet and withdrawn. She was from England and had arrived in Australia as part of the overseas recruitment drive. Because we were new to the office we seemed to spend a lot of time together. One day we arranged to go together to see a display of cars and computers which you could purchase through salary sacrificing scheme. This basically meant that you could rent them out, and pay the difference later.

When we arrived Maryann was already there. She came up to me repeatedly to ask me what the organizer had just said. She poked her head in between Katie and me, reaching out to prod at the computers, and hitting everyone within range with her enormous pink bag.

'Do you know her?' asked Katie who looked exasperated by Maryann's constant interruptions.

'Unfortunately, yes,' I replied and went on to explain that she was currently sharing a house with me. I confided in Katie that the morning routine included a run down of her health, the position of her glands, and how many times she had gone to the toilet in the night.

'I see there's nothing wrong with her legs then?' said Katie slowly.

'Well, she has complained about her hands being swollen but she hasn't mentioned her legs yet. Why what do you mean?' I asked.

'I mean she can walk to the chip shop, fat bastard.' I stared at Katie in surprise and then burst into gales of laughter. From that moment on we become inseparable.

Next morning Katie approached me while I was sitting at my desk. 'Did you hear that Maryann got run over last night?' she asked.

'What?' I spluttered.

'Yes apparently the driver said he had enough room to get around her, but he didn't know if he had enough petrol.' We both burst out laughing. From then on we tried to outdo each other in poking fun at the poor unsuspecting Maryann. Katie could get away with murder. She looked as if butter wouldn't melt in her mouth but alone with me on our way to meetings or at lunch break she was so funny, and swore like a sailor. Katie made everything bearable and the doubts I had about coming in the first place started to diminish over time.

Bianca arrived for work. She was due to appear in court for an important case, and she had obviously made an effort with her dress. She was wearing a tight white suit. The material was so cheap and thin you could see right through it. Everyone in the office stopped and stared. The red g-string she was wearing was not only visible through her trousers; it was hanging out of the back of them. Katie looked at me in horror.

'Did you see the state of that slapper?' she asked incredulously.

'Wot u lokin at?' I replied. 'You is just jealous cos she is a fit bird. You fink she's well thick, innit, but she luvs er ats and her bling and her crew dey are all mint.' Katie and I burst out laughing. We spent the rest of day emailing each other in chavspeak.

One busy morning my computer crashed. I asked Gareth, who worked in the pod next to me, if he could help me.

'Sorry,' I apologised, 'I don't want to take you away from your work.'

'No, that's all right,' he smiled, 'I can't get any work done with all the men that keep coming into this pod.'

'To see you?' Gareth was gorgeous, but as gay as a row of pink tents.

'No, not me,' he laughed.

'Well, who do you mean?' I asked curiously.

'All the men come up here to chat up Bianca. Surely you've seen them all hanging around.'

'Well, it won't do them any good,' I said diplomatically.

'Why?' he asked, clearly puzzled.

'Bianca has been having a relationship with that wee girl, Fiona, for months,' I explained.

'You're joking.' He was astounded.

'No honestly. You know that girl, Colleen, from the other floor?'

'Yes, what about her?' He nodded.

'Well, she shared an apartment with them for months. She said that they slept together, and were always going into the bedroom and giggling and carrying on.'

'Hmm, I wondered why she wasn't interested in having a relation with anyone,' said Gareth. 'So that explains it.'

'Maybe Colleen was mistaken or she's just being bitchy. I don't know. I just know what she told me.'

'Well, I suppose she would know more than most if she lived with them,' he conceded.

Bianca must have got wind of the conversation, or else Colleen's gossip had finally reached her ears. She was determined to convince the world that she was straight. It was a Monday morning and Bianca was regaling Cheryl with tales of all the antics she had got up to on the weekend. They were both speaking loudly and laughing out loud.

'Ow many lads is too many?' I heard her asking Cheryl.

'Could you keep the noise down, please?' the operations manager asked them. She had obviously picked up on the unsavoury content of the conversation.

'Sorry,' said Bianca, 'we wus only avin a laff.'

I had arranged to go out on a home visit with Katie when a report came in on a new case. I hadn't even met the family yet. The other workers all complained that they had something else arranged. Katie had too, but as she knew I was not allowed to go out alone she rearranged one of her visits. We would have to call there afterwards. As we travelled to the house I updated Kate on the case. The mother had already come to the attention of the office because of a number of incidents of domestic violence. The older child had been injured during one of them. The mother had assured the office that she was not having any further contact with her boyfriend. However he had called at the house, assaulted the mother and lifted the older child, threatening to throw her through the window. A neighbour who had heard the commotion had alerted the police. The police arrived and had managed to negotiate with the man who had eventually handed the child back to her mother.

By the time we got there a volunteer who offered support to families had arrived for the mother. She let us into the house. There was a pram in the hall; in it a young baby lay asleep. She had obviously cried herself to sleep. She continued to hiccup loudly which wrenched through her little body. The older child, a little girl of two, was walking around the room wearing her mother's high heels and a black g-string over her pyjamas. She was singing quietly to herself and talking to her dolls. The mother started shouting as soon as Katie and I entered the room.

'I can't cope. Get them fucking kids away from me, I don't want them, it's all their fault.' She became hysterical despite the efforts of the support worker to calm her. The little girl didn't flinch. We agreed to take the children under a voluntary agreement for a short period of time; it seemed to be the best solution for the moment. She signed the relevant forms and we gathered up what clothing we thought might fit and put them in the car. When I lifted the two-year-old up into my arms and carried her out to the car she smiled up at me and put her arms round my neck. The infant jolted awake and began to cry loudly. Katie soothed her as she carried her out to the car and placed her in the child seat. As we were preparing to drive off the mother came out to the door and shouted, 'Don't bring those bastards back; they have ruined my fuckin' life.'

'Charming,' said Katie. She phoned the office and asked the secretary to find a foster placement for the children. We would have to take them back to the office with us until one had been secured. It was going to be another long night.

It was Saturday afternoon. Colleen and Maryann had gone into town for lunch. I had declined their invitation; I just wanted to spend some time alone, glad of some peace and quiet. They returned to the house while I was sitting outside in the garden.

'Do you want some?' asked Maryann as she scoffed down the biggest ice cream cone I had ever seen.

'No, no thanks. I ate yesterday.'

'Ha ha,' she chortled running her tongue up the side of the cone before it had a chance to drip. I made coffee and Colleen joined me outside where she smoked a cigarette. 'So when does the stuff come over?' asked Maryann as she waddled toward the back porch. 'I was just telling Colleen that I'm so excited. There are things I need for my health,' she said conspiratorially. 'You know it hasn't been the same since I came here.' She droned on and on citing illness after illness which she suffered from and all the time the ice cream disappeared into the vast cavernous hole that was her mouth.

I continued to read my book until she had finished. 'Well, the stuff hasn't left my house yet but the shipping company hopes to collect everything next week.'

'How much stuff have you sent over?' Colleen asked Maryann.

'Oh, nothing much, I took all my personal stuff that I didn't want lost to my dad's house. This is just a couple of boxes of clothes and vitamins and things for my health.'

'And have you arranged to give Louise money for this?' Colleen asked carefully looking at me. I turned away so I wouldn't be seen smirking.

'Well, of course I'll be only too glad to pay, but Louise says that the bill won't come in until the stuff has gone through immigration. Isn't that right, Louise?'

'Yes, that's right,' I replied.

'But whatever it costs me it should still be cheaper than what it would have cost if I had sent it over myself.' Maryann smiled smugly, delighted that she had saved yet another sum. Every penny was a prisoner with her.

'Well, if that's the case I have a couple of boxes too that I could send over if that would be all right,' said Colleen.

'How much stuff do you have?' I asked becoming worried. I didn't want them to take advantage of me.

'Well, I can get my mother to bring over the stuff in her attic that I left behind. It's only a couple of small boxes of my winter clothes which I thought I wouldn't need but I'd be really glad of it now. Naturally I'd be glad to cover whatever it costs and as Maryann says it would still be cheaper than sending it over myself. Sure I sent a case of clothes over here at the airport and it cost me three hundred pounds. It's really expensive. You know Maryann.' Her words fell on deaf ears; Maryann was hunting around in the larder.

'OK, well, I'll give you my sister's number and you can get your mother to phone her and arrange to have it delivered. If it's only a couple of small boxes then it shouldn't make much difference.'

Colleen and Maryann had arranged to go out for drinks one Sunday afternoon. They were meeting up with Rory, a man we had met who came from Ireland. I reluctantly agreed to go along. Rory was all foam and no beer, but he had a good sense of humour and he appreciated my wit. Colleen wasn't physically attracted to him. She said he was a slap head who was grossly overweight. But he came from the same neck of the woods as her so she thought he might be potential husband material.

Rory and I usually tried to outdo each other with jokes and one-liners. When we arrived it was clear that the festivities had been underway for some time. Rory was stocious. As the evening progressed the jokes became more and more lethal. Rory was in some form, and it seemed as if I was the brunt of his humour. I tried to lighten the mood and started to tell a few racy jokes which Rory responded to. I looked up and noticed that Maryann looked as if she was chewing a live wasp. She pursed her lips in disapproval. She tut-tutted in censure when Colleen and I ordered another drink, our second one. It was the only time in my life when the designated driver actually drove me to drink.

'Are you sure you should be having that?' she asked huffily.

'Oh, wise up, Maryann,' I said. 'I'd rather have a bottle in front of me than a frontal lobotomy.' I was grateful to get out of the house and to be in other people's company. She didn't get the chance to whinge about her health when she was in company and I knew that Rory wouldn't tolerate her hypochondria. Maryann sat in silence, clearly peeved. When Rory bought another drink she started again.

'Look, just enjoy yourself,' pleaded Colleen. But Maryann was having none of it.

'Why do you need another one?' she asked contemptuously. 'Surely one would have been sufficient.'

'I don't know about you, Colleen, but I drink to make other people interesting,' I said. 'We never ask Maryann why she has so many desserts or why she eats so much junk. If this was a sweet shop there would be no restraining her.' Maryann turned away, folded her dinner lady arms and huffed for the rest of the evening.

Colleen tried to flirt with Rory who looked petrified. I wasn't surprised. She had all the sex appeal of a wet paper bag. But at least it diverted him from poking fun at me. When we left the bar to go home Maryann's mood hadn't improved at all. As we walked towards the car she started on me.

'You know, you should really think about what people will say about you if you are going to share jokes in mixed company.'

What? 'What the hell are you talking about, Maryann?' I was sick to death of her moodiness and her slovenliness and I was not going to let her get away this time. I turned to face her.

'I was really disgusted when you started telling jokes,' she spat, 'and, you know, if my boyfriend was here he would have been disgusted too.'

'Well quite frankly I don't give a rat's arse what your boyfriend thinks of me,' I stated indignantly, 'and to tell the truth, Maryann, since we are being so honest, you might need to ask yourself a few questions about your relationship with him yourself. He obviously isn't what or who you want and yet you've agreed to some type of secret engagement with him. Maybe you need to look at your own behaviour before you start making comments about other people's.' I was proud of myself for standing up to her. She looked aghast.

'Here, hold on a minute, that's not fair,' interjected Colleen. 'She can marry whoever she wants.'

'I'm not saying she can't, Colleen,' I insisted, 'but it seems that you are putting more effort into the wedding arrangements than she is.'

'Well, the trouble with you is you are against people getting married just because it didn't work out for you,' she said bitterly her mouth pursing in disapproval.

'I'm not against marriage at all,' I argued. 'I just think that it's difficult enough if you aren't that keen on the guy. She's just setting herself up to fail if she goes ahead with this.'

'Well, I think Maryann has a point you know,' said Colleen sourly. 'You were telling all sorts of jokes with Rory, and flirting with him. I was disgusted with you too, you practically threw yourself at him.' What? She was the one who had repeatedly asked for flirting lessons and she was accusing me of behaving inappropriately.

'Wise up, Colleen,' I protested, 'I was only being civil to the bloke but I wouldn't take him to a dog show on a lead.

'Oh you, you're just a whore bag, so you are,' she screamed. I was appalled. How bloody dare she suggest that? I marched towards her.

'Don't call me a whore bag. You are the one who was running around with another woman's boyfriend.' Maryann struggled for breath. She obviously hadn't known about that little gem. She might have to add Colleen to her list of

114

inappropriate people. She'd be getting out the holy water and blessing her with it next. 'Listen,' I continued 'I don't care what your whiny-assed opinion of me is, but I can tell you one thing, I won't embarrass either of you again with my company, you can just count me out of your lives for good.' I stormed off.

What the hell had happened? I was really surprised by what had happened to Colleen. She might as well have been taken over by aliens; she had completely turned around. She was siding with Maryann, forgetting that she was the one who wanted me to teach her flirting techniques so that she could catch the attentions of men. She had come over all Mother Theresa. As for Maryann, what would you expect from a pig but a grunt? She was a sanctimonious bitch who could do with a good hand up her skirt. I vowed there and then that I would never go out in public with either of them again. I should have listened to the advice that you should love your enemies, just in case your friends turn out to be a bunch of bastards. I took a taxi home and went straight to bed. That would be the last time I spent any time with them.

CHAPTER 14

I left the house earlier than normal and made my own way into work. I didn't wake Maryann or wait for her to get ready to join me. She needn't think I was going to spend any more time in her company. She had certainly showed her true colours the previous night. Her and Colleen's behaviour had really upset me. I realised, not for the first time, that they weren't the type of people I would have ever chosen to be friends with if we had been at home. My real friends were those who, when you think you've made a fool of yourself, don't feel you've done a permanent job. And, I asked myself, why should I be stuck with them just because I have moved to a new country? I knew that Colleen would soon get fed up with Maryann's incessant talking and she would not have anyone to go with her to nightclubs in her quest to find a man. Maryann didn't like going to clubs as the noise hurt her ears and of course she needed her sleep with all the ailments she had. Well, let the pair of them get on with it. I had come over here to work, and that was what I was going to concentrate on completely now.

I was a bit quieter than usual. Katie was training all day and wouldn't be in the office so Lacey was the only one to notice. She asked me what was wrong.

'Oh, nothing, it's just that I found out some friends weren't as nice as I had thought they were.' I shrugged.

'You mean those horrible women, Maryann and Colleen?'

'Um, yes,' I replied reluctantly. I briefly explained what had happened with them the previous night.

'You know, my whole life people have judged me and said I was mad,' interjected Lacey, 'but I never listened to them and you shouldn't let those bad girls do that to you.'

'I know, I guess you are right,' I agreed. 'It's just difficult to come to terms with yet another mistake I've made. I'm hopeless with people; I think I'm too trusting. And then I'm usually let down.'

'Huh, you think that's bad,' complained Lacey. 'Sure it happened in my own family. You know, my brothers used to hold me down while my mom beat me. It happened regularly. She used to say I was a slut, she was always fighting with me, but I never listened to her. You shouldn't take any notice of those stupid women. That Colleen looks like she needs to smile, and as for that other one, does she have no idea of what her excess weight is doing to her body? You know, maybe I should talk to her about nutrition and help her along the right path.'

I laughed. Lacey had taken over again; she was off devising plans to rectify the problems in other people's lives, even though by the sound of it, she had more problems at home with her children than any of the families we worked with.

I returned home from work. My head was splitting. I was hunting around in the kitchen cupboards for some aspirin when Maryann appeared.

'Oh, there you are, are you all right? I was wondering where you wanted to go for dinner.' Again? Was that the only question she was going to ask for ever?

'No thanks, I've got a headache.' She had clearly forgotten that I had told her I wouldn't be in her company again.

'Oh, are you not well then? Funny, I don't feel too well myself. I really must book myself an appointment with a naturopath and an aromatherapist. I haven't been quite myself since I came here. Haven't you noticed that my skin is a bit blotchier and my tongue is a bit discoloured?' she questioned, poking it out in my face. I nearly threw up over her shoes.

'I'll be all right, it's probably just an aneurism,' I replied. She screeched with laughter. It was like having a conversation with a chainsaw. Every time she opened her mouth I winced and I knew it had nothing to do with the headache.

'Oh, I have a wonderful recipe for headaches from Delia Smith,' she gushed. 'You take a piece of lime and rub it on your forehead. You will soon find that the pain disappears.'

'I've got a good one too,' I replied shortly. 'You take a piece of lime, drop it in a glass of ice and add about eight oz of vodka then you drink the whole lot. You might still have a headache but you won't give a shit.' I looked up. Her mouth was wide open. I know that a diplomat thinks twice before saying nothing but in this case I couldn't resist.

'If you have anything to say about that you can just put your hand over your mouth,' I said and left the room.

I went to work each morning, and although we were supposed to finish at 4.51pm, which was public servant finishing time, I was usually so busy that I worked until 6pm. Sometimes in a crisis I had to work later and didn't get home until eight or nine o clock, when I was fit only to eat a snack and crash into bed.

Sometimes Katie and I went to the local shopping centre at lunch time, just for a dander around; we needed to get out of the office. Normally I sought refuge in a shoe shop – there was nothing like the smell of fresh leather – and happiness always came with a heel, but in this place, forget it. The shoes were the ugliest I had ever seen. The fashion for sale in the shops was all stuff I had gone through about two years previously at home. You wouldn't be seen dead in it. As for the jewellery, think bling, of the cheap and nasty variety. Bianca probably had a field day. I normally only bought a sandwich. I had to say that about the Aussies, they had a great selection of bread.

If I was at work when a crisis erupted I could end up having to deal with it as well, so I needed to escape. I ended up most days hiding in the library which was just around the corner from work. On Friday, if we were lucky enough to get time for lunch, Katie and I ordered chips and made chip butties which we ate outside in the warm weather. We tried to recreate the experiences from home, but without success.

The days passed quickly enough. When I wasn't at work I visited Katie and her partner Geoff who always welcomed me. I felt at ease with both of them. Geoff was a bit quiet to begin with but I discovered that he had a wicked sense of humour and he made the most sarcastic remarks, which make me laugh. Sometimes I went out after work on a Friday for a couple of drinks with some of the women from my team. I had stuck to my promise about not going out with Maryann and Colleen again. While Maryann still shared my house, I hadn't spoken to her in weeks; she got mad if I interrupted her. She went out for dinner after work each evening. The last time she cornered me she had asked if I wanted to go out for dinner with Colleen and her.

'No thanks, Maryann,' I said, 'I have a computer, a vibrator, and pizza delivery. Why should I leave the house?' Her mouth opened in shock. I left the room. Christ I could have bitten my tongue off. There was no call for vulgar remarks. I was beginning to sound just as bad as Lacey.

If I was at home alone I usually cooked for myself, had a long quiet bath and went to bed with a good book. I just savoured the silence and I had learned that the best way to get rid of a telemarketer was to ask them what they are wearing. I always heard Maryann come in to the house, but she had stopped coming into my bedroom, as I always pretended to be asleep.

One day Colleen phoned me at work and asked if we could meet up as she wanted to talk to me. We arranged to meet for a cup of coffee at lunchtime. I was curious; I wondered what she had to say to me. Was she fed up with Maryann already?

'Thanks for coming,' she greeted me. I was a bit nervous; I hadn't been alone with her for weeks.

'You know, I really wanted to call you before this. I think this has gone on for long enough.' I looked at her sceptically. 'You, not going out with us. You know, Louise, we were friends before we came out here, and I think we should stick together. I know you seem to be really irritated by Maryann, and to tell the truth she's really getting on my nerves a bit too, so I was thinking that maybe you and I should go out for drinks together. She's not interested in going to nightclubs or bars or anything like that, so I don't think she would mind.'

'What exactly are you suggesting?' I asked guardedly.

'Well, I just thought that Saturday night's are lonely enough in this place, and that we could go to one of the bars in the city centre. We had great fun together when we went before, and to tell you the truth I do miss going out with you. You really made me laugh.'

'So it's not as much fun going out with Maryann?' She didn't notice I was being snide.

'No,' she admitted. 'She doesn't have the same sense of humour as us and she's not interested in talking to men.'

'So you haven't met anyone yet? I thought you would have been snapped up by now,' I said breathlessly. I was being sarcastic, the lowest form of wit, I know, forgive me. Colleen beamed at me.

'No, it's hard trying to talk to anyone with Maryann there I think she puts people off.'

'You mean none of the fellas wants to talk to the fat friend?' Colleen sniggered.

'You see,' she beamed at me. 'I've really missed your sense of humour and I'm lost without your flirting techniques, you know how hopeless I am at all that. What about going out this Saturday night?' So this was the real reason why she had contacted me. She wanted to use me as bait to hook men for her. Well, she could bloody well think again.

'I don't think so,' I said slowly. 'I've already made plans. I'm going out for dinner that night.'

'What about Friday then?' she queried, not even bothering to find out whom I had arranged to have dinner with.

'I'm going out for drinks with Katie then,' I explained.

119

'Oh, well what about next week? I'm sure it's driving you mad living with Maryann,' she laughed. 'I'm sure you would be glad of the chance to get away from her for a few hours.'

'Actually,' I said slowly, 'I don't see much of her at all. She comes into the house, eats my food, uses my phone and goes to her room to watch television.'

'Look, what about going for a drink after work today?' she implored. 'We can talk some more then.'

'I don't think so, Colleen.' I said deliberately. 'I'm starting to get a bit picky about my friends. I only want to be with people who accept me as I am and don't expect me to change so there's little point in going out with you.'

'Oh, you're overreacting,' she laughed. 'I was only mad at you because Rory was spending so much time talking to you.'

'Well, you probably said it without thinking, the way you do most things, but men like Rory are two a penny. There's nothing between him and me, and there never will be. God love his wee cotton socks, but I deserve better than him and I deserve better friends too. None of my friends at home would ever speak to me the way you and Maryann did and you know why?' She didn't answer. 'Because they love me and they accept me, and to tell the truth, Colleen, life's too short. I don't want to be around anyone who doesn't accept me for who I am.'

'Of course I accept you. I think I just got a bit carried away because Maryann was giving out to you.'

'So you thought you'd jump on the bandwagon? That's even worse; you have no loyalty at all. It's funny you know,' I continued, 'the way you never complained about the way I dressed or spoke before Maryann came along.'

'Oh, you know, I was only joking about you wearing skirts,' she simpered.

'It's not just about the clothes, though, is it, Colleen?' I said sardonically.

'What do you mean?' she asked suspiciously.

'I've been giving it some thought,' I said slowly, 'and it seems to me that when you first arrived here you were friendly with Fiona and when Alice arrived you dumped Fiona and took up with her. Then when I came along you picked a big fight with Alice and spent all your time with me. Then as soon as Maryann arrives, I'm toast. I don't want to be with anyone as fickle as you, I think you are just a user.'

'Here, just hold on a minute, we're supposed to be friends,' bristled Colleen.

'We were, Colleen, until Maryann came along. She'll be your friend until the next one arrives.'

'That's not fair,' said Colleen quietly, putting her coffee cup down forcefully on the table.

'It is, Colleen. The one thing all the new people have in common is the use of a hired car, and you came here to travel. So now Maryann has bought a car you'll stick with her for good. But you've realised now that the one thing you won't have is someone to go and chase men with. But I'm not interested. I told you before I didn't want a relationship with anyone and I'm not going to be used by you to get one for yourself.'

Colleen's mouth opened in shock. I stood up and walked away, leaving her sitting there in the coffee shop. I was visibly shaking. I usually walked away from any potential situation where there was going to be any dispute. But I had spoken my piece. I'd stood up for myself. I'd rather spend the rest of my days alone than with people I couldn't trust people, who couldn't appreciate me for what I was.

Colleen was right. This town was a strange place to meet people. While I was adamant that I didn't want a relationship with some man, I would have liked to have a friend who I could go to the movies with, or out for lunch. Katie spent most of her free time with Geoff and while I enjoyed their company I didn't want to be in their way. I hadn't realised how important all of these things were to me until I lost them. Well, I didn't so much lose them as give them all away. My friends at home were just getting on with their lives without me. I knew they missed me, they had phoned and written and emailed me since I left. But I knew it would be hard to maintain a relationship at such a huge distance. For the umpteenth time I asked myself what on earth I had been thinking, coming out here in the first place.

CHAPTER 15

I was due to go out on a home visit with Lacey. I was forced to spend a lot of time with her as office visits were always conducted in pairs and no one else would go out with her. I soon understood why. I had to set the boundaries very tightly with her; for a middle aged woman, she was very naive. After some negotiation with her I had to make her agree that she would leave all the talking to me when we visited clients and that she would just take notes. She reluctantly agreed to do so.

Lacey was quick to criticize the town, and the lack of social life here. She told me that she had had an exciting social life when she lived in Brisbane but that people weren't friendly here at all. She particularly vented at length at the fact that there were no eligible men. My God, another Colleen who had also believed that she would be living the sex in the city life here.

Lacey told me that she moved to Australia years ago from America and that she had met a man in Brisbane. They had been together for years and had been married and had two children.

'What are your children's names?' I asked politely.

'The oldest one is called Ashley and the younger one is Shirley,' she beamed. She had boys? Wait a minute, were these not girls' names? No wonder the poor children had problems. Were they not the laugh of the entire school? She might as well have painted targets on their foreheads to make it easier for the playground bullies to find them.

Lacey told me that she hadn't been happy in Australia and had wanted to return to America. They had eventually moved to Arkansas where they had lived in her home town for four years, but after they were divorced the family returned to Australia.

'I'm sorry, Lacey,' I said sympathetically. 'I know divorce isn't an easy thing to go through.'

'Nah, don't be,' she drawled. 'I was the one who divorced him. He really irked me.' Irked? What the hell did that mean? 'You know,' she continued conspiratorially, 'all my friends in America used to tell me all the time that he was so wonderful and I was lucky to have him and all. But I just got so sick of hearing it.'

'Sorry, I don't understand, you divorced your husband because he was nice?' I asked disbelievingly.

'Well, I wanted to have sex with other men, but he wouldn't agree to it, so I divorced him,' she stated baldly.

'But you had children together?' I gasped.

'James and I share the kids right down the line so I can go to college and work if I want to.'

Lacey told me that she had two part-time jobs which brought in a bit of money for her. One was at a restaurant where she worked as a waitress and the other was working as a nude model.

'A nude model?' I was shocked.

'Oh, yes, I've done that for years,' she said calmly. 'It's really hard work, you know. People just think it's about taking your clothes off but you have to pose in the same place for ages and sometimes you get a cramp but you just can't move.'

'But Lacey, you mean people are just looking at you naked. Don't you feel a bit uncomfortable?' I might be a bit judgmental but I imagined that any models I had seen, nude or otherwise, were young, pretty and, well, slim. Why is it that most nudists are people you don't want to see naked? Didn't she know that clothes make the man? Naked people have little or no influence on society.

'No, it doesn't bother me at all, even with the scars,' she said casually.

'Scars?' I was afraid to ask.

'Yeah, see I had this breast reduction one time and I have these scars all over my chest, but I don't see why I should hide them,' she prickled.

'So how did you get into that?' I gulped.

'Well I thought it might be a good way to meet guys,' she said. 'But I've only been with a couple from there, but, see, being naked doesn't bother me. I don't usually wear any clothes when I'm in the house, and it's so lovely just lying out in the garden with the sun shining on your body, it's real neat.'

'But you have children? I mean, you have adolescent boys?' I stumbled choosing my words carefully.

'Oh they're only babies, they don't mind. Gee I was like that from the first, when I was pregnant with Ashley, yes, ma'am,' she shook her head firmly. 'See, I had this thing when I was pregnant when I just got so irritated when I wore any clothes so I just took them all off and after a while I just got used to it.'

'So you couldn't wear clothes? That must have been awful.' I had heard of pregnant women having cravings during pregnancy but I'd never heard of this one.

'Yeah,' Lacey nodded. 'My mom used to be cross but she's been horrible to me my whole life so that doesn't matter.'

'What about if visitors came to the house though?' I was dying to know.

'Well, people used to stare a bit when they came to the house, but it was my house, I didn't care what they thought,' she said categorically. Yes, I had already learned that she didn't care about the impact her behaviour would have on other people.

During the following weeks Lacey told me all about her two sons. She complained that they really hated each other, how she couldn't get them to do anything and how they were rude and abusive towards her and each other. She had already repeated the same litany to anyone else in the office who would listen.

'I think it was the divorce that did it, you know,' she said sagely. 'They might have been all right if they were in a family with two parents.' Yes, but you instigated the divorce, so surely you must accept some responsibility here. Or was she going to try and blame someone else for it? Wait for it? Yes, here it came.

'But it was all James's fault,' she continued just as I had predicted. 'He just irked me; I didn't want to live with him anymore. If he had just agreed to let me have sex with other guys it might have been different.'

'But I think the vows of marriage might just mention something about fidelity. That's usually what you promise when you love someone and want to spend the rest of your life with them.'

'But I didn't love him,' she continued. 'I only married him because of Amanda.' Amanda, who the hell was Amanda? I was becoming hugely confused. 'Well,' she sighed and started to speak slowly as if she was talking to someone who is mentally subnormal, 'my brother's girlfriend got pregnant and had this child, see, called Amanda but her mother was real mad, I mean like real mental. She left Amanda with him but he couldn't look after her 'cos he lived in a car and he had no job. My mom always fed him and gave him money for liquor and stuff but he couldn't afford to look after no child. So Child Protection Services wanted

Amanda to go to a foster home but I thought if we were married we would get to keep her and we could just adopt her. So we got married, but they wouldn't let us keep her 'cos Amanda didn't want to come. And then her mom turned up out of the blue and took her to live with her anyway.'

'So what happened to her?' I was aghast.

'Oh, she went into foster care again, but 'cos she said she didn't want to live with me at the start I didn't want her back,' she said bitterly.

'So you got married to have a child.' It was an age old story.

'Well, see, this is the thing, I was pregnant at the time anyway; I knew I wanted to have a baby then. I thought it would be fun and I always said I'd have one before I was forty.'

'So you were pregnant with Ashley then?' I clarified.

'Yes, it took me ages to get pregnant you know,' she said conspiratorially. 'I thought there might be something wrong with me and I was really trying all the time. I mean, James wasn't the only one, you can't rely on just one guy to get you pregnant.'

'Excuse me?' I was scandalized.

'Well, I was dating some guys and just waiting to see who would get me pregnant first.' I shook my head in despair.

'Lacey, if you don't mind me asking, have you ever thought that Ashley might not be your husband's son?'

'Well, yeah, of course I've thought about it, I'm not dumb,' she sighed and looked at me as if she was speaking to someone who is retarded. 'But, see, Ashley has dark hair like James so when he was born I was glad I'd gotten married 'cos he must have been James's.' She smiled smugly, clearly pleased with herself.

'And if he hadn't looked like James, could he have been someone else's?' I questioned.

'Yeah, I guess,' she said reluctantly. 'But, see, Tommy wasn't working, and I think Jimmy ended up in prison and I don't know what happened to the other ones, but James had a good job. See, here's the thing, James really wanted to be a dad, so I just thought it was better the way it happened.' I was stunned. Had the woman no values at all?

'At least you didn't have that worry when Shirley was born,' I said when I had rediscovered the power of speech. A look of fear crossed her face. I remained

125

silent. I knew she would tell me eventually. She was just so eager to spill the beans on all the murky layers of her life. Nothing was sacred with her.

'Well, I always said I wanted to have two kids by the same father,' she said slowly. Right, nice life ambition there, Lacey! Very classy! 'Well, he probably is,' she said hesitatingly, 'I mean, the boys look a bit like brothers.' That might be because they have the same mother. Had she never thought of that? If electricity came from electrons did morality come from morons?

'Does Shirley look like your ex-husband then?' I asked nervously.

'No, he doesn't look anything like him, but he's probably his. It's too late to do anything about it now, anyway, and anyway,' she continued, 'I couldn't do without the child support James gives me.'

So poor James might be walking around thinking he had two sons when in fact he might not have any at all? I couldn't believe that women like this really existed in the world. But Lacey never failed to shock me, but always in some horrible way. It was like not being able to take your eyes of a road traffic accident even though there is blood and gore splattered in front of you and you feel sick to your stomach.

'So you haven't met anyone you like since you came to this place then?' I asked Lacey.

'Oh, there was this one guy, Wayne, from Western Australia but that was ages ago. I met him on the Internet. We emailed each other for a while and then he came down and stayed with me for a week. It was just wonderful; you know I think he's my soul mate. We had a great time together. There's just something about him, he isn't as tall as I would usually like, but he's got a really big one,' she giggled girlishly, 'and he was so easy to be with. But his teeth are a bit bad, he could do with some cosmetic surgery but that can soon be arranged.' She brightened as she talked about him. 'When he came down I told the boys that this was their new dad. I just wanted them to get on so well. I told them to call James by his first name as it was only going to get confusing for them with Wayne getting to be called dad now. But he doesn't like kids,' she stated matter-of-factly. 'And we were trying to have sex all the time and they kept coming in to play on the computer and they were annoying him, so I sent them to their dad's.'

'Where is Wayne now?' I asked reluctantly.

'Oh, he had to go to work in Africa but when he comes back I'm going to move to Western Australia to be with him.'

'What about the children?' If he didn't like children, was she still going to take them with her anyway?

'I told you Wayne doesn't like kids so they can stay with their dad. They stayed with him when I left to go and live in Western Australia.' She had left the children? 'You know it's really great up there, and Wayne has a boat, and his friends are so sweet.'

'So you've met them too.' She didn't waste much time.

'Yeah, I met them all when I went up and stayed with him for a while, but it was all a bit much for him, he just didn't know how good it was. I was the best thing that ever happened to him, but he was a bit stressed 'cos he had been working real hard and he was just exhausted.' Hmm, there was clearly something she wasn't telling me here. I remained silent, knowing that this woman couldn't keep quiet long enough to hold back on anything.

'And then he got annoyed with me 'cos I rearranged the furniture in his house when he was out one day,' she continued. 'But you should have seen it, it looked so neat when I had finished. And his cupboards were all messed up; I know how to organize a good larder. I took ages doing it all but it was worth it, it just made life so much easier for him. You know, some men are just useless at that type of thing. But then he said it wasn't working, but I knew that he just had so much to think about with me coming to live with him full time and all, and he needed to sort things out there. So he left me at the airport and I came back, but it's only for a while until he comes back from Africa and then we'll get together again,' she protested. 'He's such a hottie, you should see him. I have his photo somewhere here in my purse. I took it out of his house, and, do you know, he hasn't even missed it. That's men for you,' she smiled indulgently. 'I'll just show it to ya.'

She began to rummage around in her handbag. 'That's great, Lacey,' I said trying to keep my eyes on the traffic ahead, but fighting the urge not to crash the car with all the shocking tales she was telling.

'So he doesn't mind that you are going out with someone else now?' I probed.

'Well, I guess he can't say anything 'cos he's dating someone in Africa anyway,' she admitted bitterly.

'And you don't mind?' She was obviously much more liberal than me.

'Well, he can't help it; he's changed a bit since I last saw him because of the medication.' Medication? Dear God, there was more?

'You know,' she continued earnestly, 'I've been reading up on the Internet about all the side effects with malaria medication. They say that it can change your personality; there have been stories of people changing completely once they take it and their family not recognizing them. I think that's what has happened to him 'cos he keeps on saying that it's over and that he doesn't want to be with me. But I know he doesn't mean it, he's just afraid that it's all so real, and he must be a bit nervous about it all.'

'Is it possible that he doesn't want to be in a relationship with you, Lacey?' I asked gently.

'No, of course not,' she said dismissively. 'The sex was brilliant; I know that we're meant to be together. He was up for everything. I know it's only because of the medication; it must have affected his brain.'

'Oh, here it is,' she exclaimed. As she went to remove the photo from her purse another one slipped out. 'Ooops, wrong one,' she said as it dropped on to the seat beside me. 'I had forgotten I had that photo there.' She gazed at it longingly. 'Do you want to see one of my other boyfriends? That's Dwayne,' she informed me as she shoved it in my face before I could reply.

The photograph depicted a man who was about forty. He was standing outside a mobile home, naked and with an erection. This was real trailer trash. I dropped it as if I had been burned. I was grateful that I had the hand brake on as we were stopped at a red light. If we'd been driving I would have rear ended the car in front.

She returned the photograph to her purse. 'I met Dwayne when I first came to Australia and I was with him for a few weeks. See, he had this friend who was in the police and Dwayne got him to pretend that we'd been together for a couple of years so I got permanent residency.' She grinned. 'But then I got thinking that there were other men who might be better for me so I left him. Gee, I really broke his heart,' she said smugly. I wasn't surprised. The woman was nothing but a mercenary bitch. She moved through life picking people off like a sniper.

'Here's Wayne,' she said grinning inanely as she looked at the photo before holding it up to me. I was afraid to look. At least this one was clothed. He was a middle-aged man dressed in a suit with a flower pinned on the lapel of his jacket. It had obviously been taken at his daughter's wedding. He was holding her arm and smiling into the camera. His teeth were badly shaped and discoloured and his hair line had receded so much it was difficult to see if it had ever been there. I couldn't see the Adonis which she had portrayed, but I watched her as she smiled lovingly at the photograph and tucked it back into her purse. I noticed she didn't have any photographs of her children there; it was easy to guess where her priorities lay.

CHAPTER 16

I saw Lacey coming toward my desk. Damn, she had spotted me; it was too late to climb under it. Today she was a vision in khaki, T-shirt, shorts and obligatory hiking boots. Didn't people have a dress code around here?

'Hello, Lacey,' I said politely.

'I'm worried about Ian, this guy I met on the Internet,' she began before she had even sat down on the chair which she pulled up beside me. 'He came round last night and we were playing around on the sofa and I put my hands down his trousers. He has the smallest dick I've ever seen.' Laura and Lizzie, who were pretending to be busy working, both visibly blanched while I nearly fell off my chair.

'I mean he wouldn't even let me give him a blow job. I don't know what is wrong with him,' she moaned.

'Lacey!!' I was visibly shocked, and judging by the reaction of my colleagues they were too. She had a mouth dirtier than a wicker toilet seat. 'There are some things you should really keep to yourself. Confession might be good for the soul but it's bad for your career.' She seemed unperturbed.

'Sure, come over for dinner on Saturday and you can see for yourself whether you think he's interested in me.' After her outburst in front of the team there was no way I wanted to go out socially with this woman. Things between Colleen, Maryann and I had deteriorated beyond repair but I would rather be alone than go with her. Was there something wrong with me? I had such good friends at home: decent, caring people. I hadn't realized how important they were to me until I left them, bloody typical!

'That's very kind of you,' I finally muttered, 'but I've other plans for the weekend.'

'You aren't going out with those horrible women, Maryann and Colleen?' I didn't answer. 'You shouldn't let them dictate to you. I've been told my whole life that I should change but I didn't. No siree.' She shook her head firmly. 'Even though I lost all my friends I still wouldn't let them dictate to me.'

'Are you coming out with me now to this meeting?' I asked her trying to change the subject as quickly as possible.

'Yes, I'll just get my purse.' She marched off like a sergeant major.

As we left the building I let a few people pass in front of the car. There were two kinds of pedestrians, the quick and the dead. Honestly, you know, in some parts of the world, people still prayed in the streets, in this country they were called pedestrians. I was about to drive across the intersection in the car when a large truck came flying toward me and hit the side of the car. I would like to say my life flashed in front of me, but I didn't even get that far. All I heard was a loud bang and then instant pain in my back and neck. At least I was alive, thank God. If I'd died I would have been trapped forever with Lacey. I glanced over at her; she appeared to be fine and took over with all the grace of a sergeant major. She ran to the office and ordered someone to call an ambulance. I was reluctantly impressed by her organizational skills. I was transported to hospital with Lacey in the ambulance and admitted for tests.

'Where are my shoes?' I asked as I looked down at my bare feet.

'Don't worry, I've got the purse,' she said carrying my new briefcase in her hand, 'and I've got the Barbie shoes.' She looked down at the pink high heels I had been wearing.

'Well, as long as the shoes aren't damaged I'll be grand. They probably cost more than you will ever earn.' She laughed.

I was discharged after a few hours, but I felt stiff and sore for a few days afterwards. I had been advised to take some time off from work on sick leave.

A couple of days later Lacey phoned. 'I know it can't be easy for you when you are ill and so far away from your family so I wondered what you were doing this Saturday?'

'Well, I hadn't planned anything as I didn't think I would be up to it,' I said.

'Gee, that's great, then you can come to my house for Thanksgiving dinner. I'll pick ya up, as I know you can't drive yet, it will do you good to get out of the house.' Her kindness touched me but I was hesitant especially when she said that her new boyfriend, Ian, would be there as well as her two sons.

'But I don't want to get in the way of your relationship, especially since you say it's so hard to find a man in this place.'

'Don't worry about him. I think he's too caught up in his ex-wife for me. It's been nearly two weeks now,' she replied sullenly.

'Well, maybe he just wants to get to know you first, Lacey. That can only be a good thing,' I explained. 'Aren't you glad that he's not going to just use you and discard you afterwards?'

'Gee, I never thought of that,' she replied earnestly. 'I'll collect you at your house at about five o clock.' I was very apprehensive; maybe it would be good to have a new friend. I knew that she couldn't compare with my friends at home, but it was surely better than nothing, and certainly better than going out with Sister Maryann and her sidekick Colleen and facing another character assassination.

I waited for Lacey to collect me from my house. I decided to wear my jeans and a blue top and I had plaited my hair. She arrived in a beat up old banger. The door handle was held together with a piece of string. The door wouldn't open properly. I managed with a bit of aerobics to squeeze myself into the front seat, but only after I had removed a pile of sweet wrappers and empty soda cans which were scattered all over it. I put them in the back to add to the debris that was already there. It was even worse than Maryann's car.

En route to her house she told me that she had to call at the swimming centre to collect her oldest son. Would there be room for him with all the rubbish lying around the back seat and the floor? When we arrived she couldn't find him. A huge thunder and lightning storm had erupted, and already trees had fallen and the debris had been blown across the main roads.

'He must have gone to his dad's,' she rationalized as she returned to the car and drove off. The skies erupted as she pulled into the driveway of a detached house.

'Do you want to come in?' she asked casually. Did I want to meet someone's ex-husband? No thanks, I had one of them myself and I wouldn't want to inflict him on another poor woman. Did all ex-husbands not come from the same circle of hell?

I waited in the car. The rain was sleeting down and the thunder was roaring overhead. Suddenly a huge flash of lightning streaked the sky, hitting the fence directly in front of the car. Brilliant, I'd survived a war at home only to come over here to be fried.

Feeling frightened and nervous of being zapped in the car I grabbed my bag and ran towards the house. I threw myself through the front door as a large dog came bounding toward me; it jumped up and began to lick my neck. I turned my back against the dog, and faced the wall.

'Get it off me, get it off me,' I cried in alarm.

Lacey screamed at the dog to get down and called her son, Ashley, who came into the room. He was dressed from head to toe in black. He came toward me. 'Oh, Fifi, you naughty little girl,' he lisped. 'Get down, you'll ruin her fabulous bag. Is it European?' he asked as he eyed my leather handbag, one hand on the collar of the dog. I nodded. 'I just thought so,' he smiled smugly. 'Down, Fifi, you'll ruin my good pants.' He dragged the dog out of the room.

I turned round to make sure that it was safe to enter the room and noticed a book lying on its side on the floor. There were two bookcases in the room which were crammed full of books. This was the first house in Australia where I had seen any books. There were beautiful wall hangings and art work on the walls. For a man, I admitted, the house was tastefully decorated, and there wasn't a dirty sock or plate to be seen.

At this point a man entered the room. My head was lowered as I saw that water was dripping off me from the rain, my T-shirt was soaked and my jeans were sticking to me. I tugged my wet clothing away from my body and lifted my head. I looked up into the eyes of an Adonis. The thunder crashed outside, but I felt as if I had been hit with a bolt of lightning. I was immobilized. I stared at him, my mouth agape. There was something about him, something so familiar I couldn't put my finger on it. He looked almost Celtic with his dark hair and striking blue eyes. I was struck for words, and I heard Lacey say, 'Louise, this is James.'

'Hi, James,' I stuttered as I began to grasp the fact that this man was her ex-husband. This man! He couldn't possibly be. He was gorgeous. She was at least fifteen years older than him, and couldn't compare with him in the beauty stakes. No wonder she couldn't find any decent men if she was comparing them to him.

James politely asked if I would like a drink and I managed to shake my head, no. I twittered on inanely and he mentioned the recent car accident. 'I'm sorry I nearly killed your wife,' I eventually mumbled.

'Ex-wife,' he corrected me politely, smiling at me.

Lacey stood up and told Ashley to go out to the car. I turned to follow her, feeling that I should say something witty, or clever, something for him to remember me by. Nothing. I was practically mute.

'I like your accent,' he said.

'Thanks.' I stumbled and hesitated only long enough to turn and run out of the house. Great. Very mature, Louise, the first decent bloke I had met and I had to do the adult thing and run away. Was this a tactic that was going to carry me through life? Why couldn't I have said something witty, like what about the rest of me? That would have clinched it, but for the first time I was lost for words. I was to learn that it wouldn't be the last time that evening.

I got into the car beside Lacey who was trying to placate Ashley. She had made him sit in the back and he wasn't happy. He started whingeing. 'I wanna sit in the front, Mom, I don't wanna sit here.' He started blubbering. Lacey glared at me as if I had done something wrong.

'Don't worry,' I said politely 'I'll get in the back.' Lacey nodded. She had clearly been expecting this. I got out and Ashley clambered from the back seat. He brushed past me as he slid into the front seat. For a child who had been at a swimming pool he was very smelly. Did they not have water in it? Was this another downside of the drought that they were facing?

I pushed a pile of rubble over in the back seat and climbed in. From my vantage point I could see the back of Ashley's head. I had initially thought his hair was damp from the pool but I could see clearly now that it was thick with grease. He started whingeing again

'You didn't come when I wanted you too; you're such a lazy bitch, mom. I had to wait there by myself and then I had to walk all the way to my dad's.' He made it sound as if he had conquered Mount Everest in his bare feet and with only a bag of chips to sustain him; his father's house was only across the road from the swimming complex, for God's sake. He continued complaining that she hadn't picked him up from the swimming pool when he wanted her to.

I sat in silence, my thoughts reeling around in my head. I had been bowled over by James. What the hell had he been doing with someone like her? He was gorgeous. And he had the loveliest manners. He certainly wasn't what I had expected. Why did she really leave him? There must be some awful secret she hadn't yet told me.

We arrived at Lacey's house and I immediately recognised this area as I had clients who lived in this street. Katie and I had often wondered aloud as we had driven past, who lived in this particular house. The front garden was littered with rubbish. An old shopping trolley lay abandoned on its side beneath the steps to the front door. There were black plastic bags of rubbish lying in a heap in the drive. I tried to hide my alarm. If this was the image she presented to the world what would it be like inside?

I didn't have to wait long to find out. It was even worse, the place was a tip. You would have thought I would be prepared for this considering all the skanky houses I'd been in since I came to this country. This one defied belief. Had she not been expecting visitors? She must have watched Little House on the Prairie for decorating tips; it was all so basic. The biggest table I'd ever seen was placed at an angle in the dining room. It filled the entire area. Judging by the surface she must have believed that dust protected furniture. It was surrounded by a mix-match of different chairs, none of which were high enough to reach the table. Great, so now I'd have to eat dinner with my chin in my plate.

The kitchen was cluttered with jars and bowls; there wasn't an empty space of bench space to be seen. Photographs lined the shelves beside pots and pans, each one dustier and dirtier than the one before. I would be lucky to get out of this place with only a dose of botulism.

Ashley stood in the middle of the kitchen stuffing cake into his mouth and glugging from the neck of a family sized bottle of lemonade. He set it down and belched loudly. Very attractive.

Lacey proudly displayed the rest of the house, which became increasingly worse with every glance into each room. The boys each had their own bedroom. When Lacey opened Shirley's door, I reeled back on my heels. The smell was cloying and sour. The floors were littered with soiled clothing, sweet wrappers and empty lemonade cans. Shirley had graffitied his walls in red paint. 'Die scumsucker! I am a child of Satan!' I was horrified. I glanced at Lacey but she seemed unperturbed by what she was displaying. There must be something seriously wrong with that child. Was he only showing off, or were these his intentions?

What kind of woman let her children live like this? It was nothing but pure unadulterated squalor. The house looked like a warehouse for some charity shop. Mismatched pieces of furniture were lined up against every wall and sitting in the middle of the rooms. In the living room a huge television was precariously balanced on top of a piano. Above the fireplace there was an enormous painting of a naked woman reclining on a sofa. I didn't have to move closer to realise that the model was Lacey herself, in all her glory. It was not a pretty sight. I turned away in embarrassment.

Lacey entered her bedroom. The room contained a double bed which was unmade; a heap of grimy clothing lay on top of it. In the corner of the room was a set of drawers, the top was cluttered with dirty crockery and clothing spilled out from the open drawers onto the floor. A desk had been placed behind the door which held a computer.

Lacey was met by an avalanche of abuse which came from a small child who was sitting there. He started to scream at Lacey while still continuing to keep his eyes fixed on his computer game.

'I'm hungry, get me something now,' he demanded.

'This is Shirley,' she said proudly patting him on the head.

'Get your hands off me, you mother fucker,' he screamed. I nearly jumped out of my skin. What a horrible little boy. He had a face on him like a scalped arse, though maybe that was just what he needed if he was cheeky enough to speak to his mother like that. He frowned at the computer screen through a long dark greasy fringe; his hair was shoulder length and looked as if it had never been brushed, ever. But Lacey was blind to the bad manners of her offspring.

'Get me something now, I'm starving,' he screamed as he continued to batter the life out of the keyboard. I know what I would give you to eat if you were mine, you little brat. A bit of hot tongue and cold shoulder wouldn't do you any harm, you ill-reared tinker. But Lacey seemed oblivious to it all. Christ, now I knew why animals eat their young.

'All right, honey, I'll just get you something now,' she said ingratiatingly as she hurried to the kitchen and began to frantically take down pots and pans, questioning loudly what Shirley would like to eat. She rushed in to him with a pan in her hand.

'Would you like some beans, honey? What about a nice sandwich? Eggs? Grilled cheese on toast? I know, hot dogs, I know you love them.'

She hurried back to the kitchen and began to frantically search in the huge fridge which was filled to capacity. Well, at least she didn't neglect them in that area. I felt as if I was conducting a risk assessment on a client. I hadn't expected to be working today.

I moved towards the dining area, wondering which chair looked reasonably clean to sit in. A large black cat sprang out from the cushion I lifted up and I nearly lost my life in fright. It snarled at me and ran out of the dining room into Lacey's bedroom. Oh, cats! That explained the putrid stench.

I cleared the clothes and underwear from a chair with my elbow and tried to clean it as inconspicuously as I could with a tea towel which had been lying on the table. Big mistake. I realised this as soon as I touched it. It was rancid. I pulled my hand away and hesitatingly held it up to my nose. It smelled of germs, old socks and smelly damp coats on packed buses. I nearly threw up on the floor, though I doubt if it would have been noticed. I held my hand as far away as I could from my body letting it dangle there uselessly, as if it belonged to somebody else.

'Would you mind if I used your bathroom?' I asked Lacey who was by now stirring food in a saucepan.

'Yeah, just help yourself,' she said cheerfully.

I went into the toilet which was separate. The stink of urine nearly floored me. I felt like heaving. I quickly left it and entered the bathroom next door. I have to say I am really really choosy about bathrooms, and I have been known to leave restaurants and cafes if their toilet facilities were not up to scratch. This one would fail every test designed by the hygiene police. The vanity unit was cracked and lined with dirt. Half opened and used tubes of toothpaste were lying all over the surface beside ancient worn toothbrushes. The floor was covered in empty toilet roll tubes; the bath was thick with grime and a stained shower curtain hung precariously by one ring from the shower rod.

There was a small wooden unit beside the bath which might once have been white, but which was now more of dysentery beige. The surface was filled with all sorts of bottles and jars, each of them dustier than its neighbour. There was no soap to be seen. I checked behind the shower curtain, pushing it with my elbow so I wouldn't have to actually touch it. I was afraid I would get a disease if I did. This was going to be a great evening. Now I would have to contend with dysentery as well.

As I peered behind the curtain I realised that there was no shower gel or any type of cleaning product to be seen. Did these people never wash themselves? Instead there on the side of the bath sat a huge, pink vibrator. It was the strangest thing I had ever seen; I was horrified and fascinated at the same time. It had what looked like little plastic rabbit ears which were attached to the main piece and on the other side there was some type of appendage. What the hell did you do with that? I wondered frantically, searching my brain for all sorts of possibilities. Nope, sorry, I gave up; it was all beyond me. You would need a doctorate in gynaecology to figure out where that bit was supposed to go.

I ran the hot tap, and washed my hand as best I could, wiping it on my jeans. There was no way I was going to touch the old, grey mouldy towel that had been dumped on the floor. It smelled of... I moved closer. Dear God, it smelled of cat's piss. Lacey obviously went to a finishing school which taught that housework completed properly could kill you.

As I left the bathroom I admonished myself, you're a grown up now, Louise, you don't have to do anything you don't want to. If you don't want to stay here, then don't. There, that was pretty simple, brain, thanks. I would just make my excuses and leave. I had seen enough by now and eating food here? It was just too risky. I could always say I felt unwell, yes, that would do, well, it wouldn't be a lie, and I couldn't go to hell for saying that.

CHAPTER 17

I returned to the kitchen just as screams erupted in the adjoining hallway. Lacey ran past me into the hall where I could see that Shirley and Ashley were wrestling on the ground, punching each other.

'Get off me, you cocksucker,' screamed Shirley.

'Not until you let go first, you faggot,' wailed Ashley as he tried to pull his brother's hair and scratch at his face. He was wearing red nail polish.

Lacey tried to intervene. She pleaded with the boys to let go of each other. In utter shock I sat down on a chair at the dining table. I was drained. I had heard Lacey tell me and the entire office how much her two sons despised each other but this wasn't just a case of sibling rivalry. This was pathological hatred. Having quit smoking ten years earlier I felt the greatest desire for a cigarette.

Lacey screamed at Ashley to let go, and he removed himself from his brother's reach. 'It's not fair,' he whined. 'You always blame me for everything.' He tossed his head dramatically and sashayed off to his bedroom.

'Now let's get you something to eat, honey. Your blood sugar level must be low,' Lacey said cajolingly to Shirley who stared at her defiantly.

He stormed towards the kitchen and threw open the pantry door. The woman was clearly preparing for the holocaust; there was more food in one place than I had ever seen.

'There's nothing to eat in this goddamn house,' he announced.

'But I've got your lovely hot dogs here for you, sugar,' she said. 'They're right here for y'all, but they're a little hot for you now, baby, you just have to let them cool down.'

He ignored her. Lacey ran toward him and proffered him the bowl of hotdogs, which he pushed out of her hand. The food fell to the floor, where of course the cat appeared in an instant and started to eat it.

'Don't you want these, honey?' asked Lacey as she wrestled a hotdog from the cat's,' paw. 'Gee, I guess you don't,' she sighed as she placed the bowl of food on the counter top where the cat jumped up and resumed where he had left off.

Lacey moved toward the larder and started to select different items. 'What about baked beans? Soup? Spaghetti? Do you want eggs? What about grilled cheese? A sandwich? I could do you some bacon and eggs while y'all waiting for dinner.'

Every suggestion she made was met with a loud Yuck!! 'It's his blood sugar,' she whispered to me conspiratorially.

'Why, is he diabetic?' I asked feeling that I might have misjudged the boy for his rude behaviour, when the poor child had some genuine medical condition.

'No, he just needs to eat regularly otherwise he gets a bit upset,' she explained carefully. I shook my head in dismay; it looked like I was going to be in for some evening of fun with this kid.

Shirley selected a packet of biscuits and began to gorge himself greedily. Meanwhile Lacey had opened a can of beans and was heating them on the stove. She poured them into a bowl, which looked none too clean, and placed them on the countertop beside Shirley. Even the cat who sniffed at them turned away in disgust.

Shirley walked away, ignoring both her and the beans and returned to his computer game. Lacey sighed loudly and carried the bowl of beans into the bedroom and sat them down beside him. He marched into the kitchen like a sergeant major and returned the untouched bowl of food to the kitchen bench where his mother picked it up again and returned it to him. This game of chase the beans lasted throughout the entire evening until he eventually threw them in the sink untouched.

'I told you I didn't want them, you ugly fat bitch,' he screamed as he slammed her up against the sink.

My decision to leave had disappeared; I think I was suffering from some type of post-traumatic stress disorder. I mechanically helped Lacey prepare the food for dinner, making sure that I scrubbed and peeled the vegetables carefully. I had imagined Thanksgiving dinner as a family celebration, a quiet time to reflect, to count your blessings and enjoy the company of family and friends; I couldn't have been further from the truth. I was stuck here with the Antichrist.

Lacey and I didn't have much of a chance to talk due to the continued interruptions of Shirley, which with hindsight was probably a good thing.

'Mom, Mom,' he shrieked at the top of his lungs. Lacey dropped her food preparations and dashed toward him.

'Mom, Ashley won't let me stay on the computer,' he complained sulkily.

'Well, baby,' I heard her say, 'it's, time for Ashley to have a turn now.'

'But I don't want him to,' he yelled. 'I want to finish my game.'

'Well, you can have more time later when Ashley goes to his dad's.'

'But I want to go now,' he roared.

'Come and eat your beans honey, you've got yourself all wound up,' she pleaded.

'I don't want no fucking beans.' He moved towards her and screeched into her face. 'If you don't leave me alone I'll kill you. I'll stab you and chop you up and drink all the blood.' Christ! I knew by her lack of reaction that this was not a new way of relating to her.

He stomped off to his cave or bedroom or whatever lair or den half-socialized kids reside in, slamming the door behind him. A moment later the house was surrounded by the deafening roar of some alien type thing he was trying to kill on his play station. Lacey smiled indulgently at the closed bedroom door.

'He just gets so excited to see new people,' she grinned inanely.

'Can you ask him to turn it down a little,' I begged. The noise was giving me a massive headache, though hopefully it would be an aneurism and I could use the excuse to leave. I wondered if I would be able to feign my own death.

'Sure,' she replied indulgently and patted me patronizingly on the arm as she left. 'Gee, I forget you're not used to being around kids.' Kids? These weren't kids, they were unsocialized animals.

'Is there anything I can get you?' she asked when she returned, suddenly remembering her manners.

'A drink,' I replied, 'a large drink. Don't worry, I'll get the glasses,' I offered as I reached to take two from the open shelf. I could see the dust piled on the bottom of them. 'I hope you don't mind but I like my glasses really cold, it really makes the wine taste much nicer,' I said as I reached to run them under the taps.

'Oops,' I said, 'sorry, that must have been the hot tap.' I hoped that the blast of hot water would at least dilute some of the germs I was inevitably going to pour down my throat. Lacey didn't seem to notice as she opened the bottle of wine I had brought and poured some into my outstretched glass.

'Now you just sit right there and tell me all about y'all,' she said calmly.

I'd have loved to, but where? I perched on the edge of a bar stool which was sitting beside the counter. This would have to do; I hoped that the bloody cat hadn't been sitting on it before my arse got a chance, or some of her unwashed boys. Ugh! The pair of them looked like they could do with a good steep in bleach. Before I could open my mouth the screaming started again.

'Mom, Mom, I wanna hot dog. I wanna hot dog,' he bellowed.

'See, I told you he was hungry,' she smirked as if she had just won a prize.

'Mom, Mom,' he roared again, 'I wanna hot dog right now, goddamn it.'

'Don't be hollering, I'm getting to you now, honey.' I shook my head in quiet disgust as she raced to meet the little despot's needs.

'I'd rather hear about you,' I said when she had brought his horribleness the food he desired. 'What happened between you and James? He's not what I expected, you know.'

'What do you mean?' she asked sharply.

'Lacey! Are you blind? He's gorgeous.'

'Humph,' mumbled Lacey, obviously not agreeing with my assessment. 'He irked me; I just didn't wanna have sex with him no more.'

'Right, so how long have you been separated?'

'Well, I left him four years ago. Like I told you, I wanted to have sex with other people so we got divorced, and obviously I got divorced in America so he would have to give me alimony.' She saw the look of surprise on my face. 'Yep, he sure does,' she said proudly. 'He has to pay me up until next Christmas. But I should get more money from my welfare then to make up for what I'll miss out on.' Clearly this woman had all her financial needs sorted out.

'Why did you ask about James?' she enquired looking at me quizzically.

'Well, it's just you keep telling me that there are no eligible men here, so I wondered what had happened and why you weren't together.'

'I wanted to have sex with other guys but James wouldn't agree to it so I had to divorce him. Then I met this gorgeous guy; he used to come visit at a friend's house. He was only twenty-two; he was the hottest thing I had ever seen.' She smiled sentimentally. 'He was called Billy and you know he had the cutest butt, and I was just so into him,' she laughed gaily.

'What did he do?' I tried to change the subject.

'Do?'

140

'Yes, what did he work at?' What did she think I meant?

'He didn't do anything,' she replied as if she was speaking to a complete moron. 'We hung out together, and sometimes we would get high. He was so much fun.'

'You took drugs?'

'It was only pot,' she said snippily.

'Where were the children?' I was losing track here.

'They were with their dad. I left him with the kids to be with Billy. But he was real drunk one time and he set this barn on fire. So I thought maybe he wasn't so good.' She smiled sadly. 'But, anyway, he was real hard to get hold off 'cos he had all these demands on him.'

'Demands?' I realised I was beginning to sound like a parrot, repeating almost every word she said, but I was so fascinated by this conversation. People at home didn't have conversations like this.

'...and I knew he had kids to all these women and it got to be such a pain, they just wouldn't leave him alone.'

'Children? How many children?' I gulped.

'Four, I think, anyway the women were always ringing him up or calling round to the house; we never had any peace. They always wanted money for the kids, but,' she said disdainly, 'I told Billy they got enough from welfare and that he was only indulging them. And he was a lovely father; you know, he was building a toy chest for his little girl to put her little teddies in.' She sighed as if reliving a fond memory.

'But didn't he pay maintenance for the children?'

'He didn't work so he didn't have to,' she said proudly 'but these women kept calling round, they really harassed him; sometimes he would have sex with them just to shut them up.'

'When he was with you?' I swallowed.

'Well, I didn't mind, he did what he had do, and it never affected us anyway.' I sat in stunned silence, trying to comprehend what made a woman leave what looked like a perfectly good husband to go chasing after some guy who sounded pretty low life to me.

'What happened?' I eventually asked, worried that I might not like the answer.

'Oh, he went back to one of his old girlfriends, so I just went home to James and the boys.' And he let you? What kind of a saint was this man? '…And I told him I still wasn't going to have sex with him and I still wanted a divorce.'

'And you lived in the same house?' I couldn't believe what I was hearing.

'Only in Arkansas, but I agreed to come back to Australia with him and the boys. I thought it might be fun and I was so sick of all my friends saying how wonderful James was all the time.' But shouldn't people be saying things like that about your husband? Would you rather they said he was a bastard? Like mine, I thought silently.

'I'm not saying he wasn't a good man,' she continued, 'but he just started to irk me. Then I went to live with a friend of his when I got to Australia until I got a place for me and the boys. James lived with his parents; of course, they wanted me to stay with them but I didn't think I could stick being with him a moment longer.' Yes, I thought. There was also the small matter of you wanting to shag half the town and country which probably wouldn't put you on a good footing with your in-laws. I didn't envy these people whoever they were.

'And James has never been in another relationship' I asked carefully, expecting her to tell me that he had fallen in love with someone the minute he landed on Australian soil.

'No, I don't know what's wrong with him; he's too fussy and he has loads of women looking at him on RSVP.'

'What's that, Lacey?'

'It's an Internet dating site. Haven't you used one before? They are great. I met Wayne on one. I made James come round here one night and I helped him post his information on the site; he got loads of hits. I think he was in the top one hundred guys for ages once I posted his photograph. Why, do you think you might like him?' she asked looking up at me carefully.

'I think he seems nice,' I admitted. 'But it would be too weird, Lacey, after all he's your ex-husband.'

'I don't want him y'all; it would be good for him to meet someone nice. I could introduce you both properly. What about dinner? You could both come over here for dinner.' I would rather stick needles in my eyes.

'No, Lacey, thanks, but that's too weird for me and what about you?' I tried to sidetrack her again. 'You didn't feel like you wanted to get back together after it went wrong with Billy?'

'No, never, I told you he irked me, and I wanted to have sex with other people. Once I met Wayne I knew I didn't wanna be with no one else but him.'

'But Wayne's not here, Lacey; it doesn't look like it might work out between you two now and sure you have Ian now.'

'Humph, he's no match for Wayne. I knew the minute I looked at Wayne that the sex would be great and it was, he was into everything, and I mean everything,' she laughed coyly. 'I thought we would get married. I wanted to have a child with him and you know if he had stayed here any longer it probably would have happened. I don't approve of contraception.' She shook her head firmly in distaste.

'But you don't seriously mean that you would deliberately get pregnant just to keep a man?'

'Well, the child maintenance for Ashley will soon end, and my alimony will be ending soon too. A girl has to look at all her options,' she said sagely.

'Please tell me you are joking me?' Jesus, Lacey, whatever you do, don't let your sense of morals prevent you from doing what is right.

'Oh, don't be so naive,' she protested. 'It's the oldest trick in the book, honey. But, you know, it doesn't always work. See, I got pregnant to this boy in Arkansas one time; he was the cutest thing. His family was real rich, they owned half the town. I thought they would probably give us a house for a wedding gift when we got married. I couldn't wait to live on that side of town. He was the only child so he was going to get it all when they died.' Jesus, she thought she could marry more money in ten minutes than she could earn in a lifetime. She wasn't going to let schooling get in the way of her education.

'What happened?' I asked, afraid of the answer I might hear.

'Oh, it turned out that they didn't approve.' She pursed her lips in disdain 'They sent him away to school and gave me money for an abortion.' School? He was sent away to school?

'What age was he?'

'He was fifteen at the time, no wait, sixteen; yes, definitely I remember he had just turned sixteen 'cos they couldn't get the police onto me then. I taught him everything I knew,' she laughed.

'So you had an abortion?' I stammered.

'Yes, it didn't look like there was any point in keeping the kid so his family gave me the money and I just went and got it done.'

143

'God, Lacey, that must have been a terrible thing for a wee girl to go through. Were you only the same age as him then?'

'No,' she looked at me in amazement 'I was about thirty-six then.' I almost fainted. Weren't there laws against this type of thing? A thirty-six-year-old woman and a sixteen-year-old boy? She had deliberately fallen pregnant. She had used this boy hoping she would be able to get rich quick. Did Wayne know how close he had come to becoming another meal ticket for her? She was so low she could milk a pregnant snake! It was evident that James had fulfilled the purpose she had planned for him too. He seemed to have worked hard to be able to provide her and her children with a comfortable living. She was able to pick and choose part-time jobs and to study if she wanted to. I wondered if James ever considered that he was just a tool that she had used to get what she wanted.

'So,' Lacey continued as she gulped from her glass of wine, 'I had the abortion and there was a whole pile of money left so I bought a ticket to Australia. So it's all worked out in the end, you see, it always does.'

I sat in silence. Even in the most horrendous stories I had encountered I had never heard anything as blatant as this. I was shell-shocked. What kind of a woman bared her soul so openly? She didn't know me very well. She didn't know what I might do with the information. I could go into the office on Monday and relay everything that she had said. I knew I wouldn't, but how did she know that? I was trying not to judge her, she had obviously had a hard life, but to publicly admit that you had used someone just to get ahead in life, was that not abusive in itself? I realised that Lacey and I didn't share the same values; we didn't seem to have anything in common and I didn't think after all she had told me that I wanted to pursue a friendship with her. Wouldn't I be guilty by association? People might ostracize me the way they did her if I continued to have contact with her.

CHAPTER 18

I looked over, Lacey hadn't flinched during the relaying of the tale she had told me. She didn't seem embarrassed by her own behaviour. I knew women who had had abortions and in all of these cases the decision always came with a lot of pain, guilt and recriminations. This woman deliberately became pregnant in order to move up the social ladder and she discarded the baby when it looked as if things hadn't worked out to her advantage. I had never met anyone who was so blatant about their decision. She made it sound as if she was throwing out an old pair of shoes.

Lacey didn't seem to notice or care that what she had disclosed had impacted on me. She gushed on, talking nineteen to the dozen, trying to update me on all the events in her life. I knew that getting to know someone and building a friendship requires some sharing of personal information, but this was beyond that. I was sick. My stomach was in knots and I was finding it difficult to breathe normally. I realised that Lacey didn't care how I felt about her actions. Her only concern was in telling the tale and more importantly, by doing that to talk about herself. She continued unabashed.

'So, you see, it was a good thing I had the abortion 'cos if they hadn't given me the money I wouldn't have been able to come out here and I wouldn't have met Wayne. Course,' she said dismissively, 'I had to be with James first, but anyway,' she brightened, 'Wayne was worth waiting for.'

'So you said you met Wayne on an Internet site then?' I asked when I eventually remembered how to speak. 'Is that the same one that you signed James up for?'

'No, I met Wayne on the site for herpes people.' What??????? Dear God, no, not more. I didn't know how much more of this I could listen to.

'Oh, yeah, didn't I tell you? I caught herpes when I was nineteen and Wayne has it too so we both knew what we were getting into before we even met. It never stopped him,' she giggled.

I turned away in disgust. I didn't want to hear any more but her next remark nearly made me lose the run of myself. 'Don't you just love anal sex?' she drawled. I practically swallowed my tongue.

Dear Lord, once again I was too stunned for words. What type of a question was that to be asking anyone? She rambled on about Wayne and clearly wasn't interested in any response I might care to make. I tried to divert her from the subject of Wayne; I didn't want to hear any more lurid tales of their time together. The house was so small; the children could probably hear everything their mother said.

'So you had to have a caesarean when you had the baby then?' I tried to divert her. 'That must have been difficult for you?' I said sympathetically. You see I wasn't a complete idiot. I knew all about herpes as I had seen a documentary on it once on television. I watched it one evening while I was waiting to go out on a date with some man. The documentary proved to be more interesting than him as it turned out, and I'd regretted that I had missed the end of the programme. But I had learned that you can't give birth through the normal channels as it were, in case the baby ends up being born blind.

'I didn't tell them about the herpes but it was a real long labour and I had to go to hospital with him. Then they found sores and said I had to have a caesarean. I refused but they made me do it. I wouldn't sign the papers and they made James do it. He was so weak that he signed them,' she said in disgust. 'He didn't listen to what I wanted.' She sighed. 'He never did. Is it any wonder I divorced him? He never put me first. He's a weak and dysfunctional man.'

'But, Lacey, I don't think he had a choice,' I stumbled. 'The doctors wouldn't let you give birth normally.'

'Humph, well, they should have, it's my body, and I can do what I like with it. It was none of his business if I had herpes.' She clearly didn't care that Ashley could have been born blind. She was prepared to lie and cheat to get what she wanted regardless of all the pain and suffering she might inflict on other people, in this case an innocent baby. At that point my drink ended up in my lap.

'Sorry, Lacey, I'll just go and clean up,' I uttered and rushed to the bathroom for a minute to sponge my jeans down with the water I scooped into my hand. I was not going to touch anything else there; God knows where it had been. I stayed in the bathroom for as long as I could bear it, all the while trying not to let my eyes turn towards that, that…thing behind the shower curtain. I felt like it was looking at me, like some kind of one-eyed monster, snickering at me. Suddenly I realised what the extra appendage was for. It was obviously to be inserted rectally. Sweet Jesus, I was going to vomit. I was out of my depth here. What the hell kind of situation had I got myself into now? It was like something you would see on the Jerry Springer show.

'So now, ladies and gentlemen, my next guest is Lacey Bones all the way from good old Arkansas where there are five million people and only fifteen last names. Her hobbies are sodomy, slovenliness and sleeping around. Let her tell us all about the time she left a relationship with a good guy to try sleeping with half the county. Yep, folks, come on down, Lacey.' Well, actually, he probably wouldn't be wise to say that to a woman like her, she would have taken it as a personal invitation. Any minute now some relative of hers was going to appear on the scene and accuse Lacey of sleeping with her son, who was Lacey's cousin or brother or uncle. Then they would all scream and shout at each other and throw furniture around the room. I was interrupted in this fantasy by Lacey who was droning on in the background drowning out the shouts of Jerry, Jerry!!!

Let's think about this for a minute, Louise, I reprimanded myself. Here was a woman who clearly wasn't popular at work, and I was the eejit to go and offer her the hand of friendship. Didn't I think there might be reasons why everyone else despised her? She had left her husband so she could sleep with some low life, and she gave birth to a child without being honest about a highly contagious disease. Was that what was wrong with Shirley? Could herpes affect your behaviour, make you antisocial? I gathered myself as best I could and prepared to go back to Lacey who seemed completely unruffled by the entire conversation. I knew instinctively that the fact she was sharing stuff so openly with me wasn't because she thought I was the greatest friend she had ever met. It was because she clearly had no boundaries at all. What was I going to hear next?

I entered the kitchen to be greeted by the dulcet tones of Shirley. 'Mom, Mom, I want to go on the computer,' he bawled. 'It's not fair, why don't I have my own computer? All the other kids have a computer; they don't have to share with their gay, faggot brother.' Gay? So the oldest one was gay? Why was I not surprised? I looked quizzically at Lacey who seemed unperturbed by the tone of the conversation. It must be common knowledge, but should twelve-year-olds know about sexuality?

Shirley was screaming into her face. He was agitated and shaking with rage. 'I wanna have my own computer now,' he shrieked.

'Well, honey,' she said patiently, 'I don't have the money, I'll just have to see if we can get Ian to get one for you.' She was planning ahead.

'I want it now, I want it now,' he yelled throwing himself to the floor and thrashing around, punching the air with his fists and kicking his heels on the ground. Lacey walked round him to continue with her dinner preparations.

147

Eventually he picked himself up from the floor and started squirming and hopping from one front to another.

'Do you haveda go potty, baby?' Lacey asked him tenderly. She gently pushed him towards the bathroom. 'Just holler when you're done, honey, and I'll come in and wipe your bottom.' I felt nauseous. He was twelve years old for Christ's sake. When she eventually finished cleaning him up she pleaded with Ashley to let Shirley return to the computer by bribing him with a family-sized bag of crisps. He took them into the living room and lay down on the sofa shoving handfuls into his mouth. I was relieved, it was the only thing which seemed to quiet the Shirley beast.

While we prepared the food Lacey drank heartily from her wine glass and I asked her about her relationship with Ian. 'I think he's still too caught up with his ex-wife, and he isn't ready to have a relationship with me. But tell me what you think when he comes, oh, here he comes now,' she turned in response to a knock on the front door.

Ian entered the room with his teenage daughter, Tina. He was well dressed, articulate and charming and most importantly, clean. What the hell was a man like this doing with such a slovenly woman? He had brought wine, cheese and chocolates for his host. A considerate man. Well done, Ian, I was very impressed. Ian told me that he was originally from England but that he had been living in Australia for twenty years. His accent hadn't mellowed in time and it felt good to talk to someone who obviously understood my sense of humour. We chatted about our experiences of trying to adjust to a new country. His daughter was really sweet; she sat beside her father, and didn't venture into the bedroom where the computer was, and where Shirley was still frantically playing a game.

'So have you already met Shirley and Ashley?' I asked her.

'Yes, I have,' she said. She moved closer to her father and looked nervously toward the bedroom door. A girl after my own heart.

Lacey invited everyone to the table for dinner. Ashley ran into the dining area at speed shoving Tina out of the way in his haste to grab a seat. Ian and Tina sat down beside each other. Shirley refused to leave the computer. He kept shouting, 'My time's not up yet.' We waited for ages before Lacey eventually persuaded or bribed him to join us. I was sorry she had as he sat in the seat beside me. Up close he seemed to have the same aversion to soap and water as his brother. He refused to eat any of the food Lacey had prepared. He demanded sausages.

'But look what your mum has made for you. There's lovely chicken. Why don't you try some of that?' Ian tried to entice him into eating.

'Nah!!!'

'Oh go on, you'll like it once you taste it,' Ian encouraged him.

'It's shit,' he shrieked. I recoiled in shock; Ian's hand was caught midway across the table with a plate of chicken in his hand. He looked like he had been punched.

'I want sausages, Mom, Mom,' he started to scream at the top of his lungs. I nearly fell off my chair, so much noise from such a small boy. My ears felt like they were melting from the high-pitched decibels he had emitted.

'Right, honey. Gee, don't be fussin'. I made some already for y'all.' His mother rushed to the kitchen and returned with a bowl of sausages. I recognised the dirty bowl; these were the same ones that the cat had been eating earlier. She set the bowl down in front of him and he started picking them up with his fingers, screaming and squirming in his seat because they were hot. He should practise safe eating and use utensils.

'Well, use your fork,' encouraged Ian patiently. This request was ignored.

Lacey asked if anyone would like to say grace. Silence. 'Well maybe we should give thanks for one thing in our lives today.' She intoned. Everyone bowed their heads except Lacey's children. Ashley continued to shovel the food into his mouth. His plate was piled high; there was certainly nothing wrong with his appetite. We were distracted only by the sound of the slurping and slobbering of Shirley who was munching his way through the bowl of sausages. He should have been at a trough; my appetite disappeared further with every slop and snort he made. It obviously had the same effect on Ian who started to pick at his food while his daughter stared at Shirley in obvious disgust.

Dinner conversation didn't focus on politics or world events; instead Lacey talked at length about her ex-husband's vasectomy. 'He had to be readmitted to hospital as his testicles had swollen and become engorged with blood,' she said matter-of-factly as she gnawed at the meat from a chicken leg which she waved around in her hand.

If there was any chance of recovering my appetite, then that subject killed it off stone dead. What kind of a family was this? I looked over at Ian who looked pale. Tina visibly squirmed in her seat at the talk of blood and engorged body parts. 'Course I still didn't have sex with him anyway,' she laughed.

'Yeah, we know, we've heard it all before,' complained Ashley, his mouth full.

'Yeah, Mom, you got a new vibrator,' interjected Shirley. 'They are in her room,' he said firmly. I looked at him in bewilderment. 'Her vibrators, she keeps them in the computer drawer,' Shirley reported smugly, 'or in the bathroom.' Yes, I had already encountered that one. Ian and I exchanged looks of embarrassment. I bet Tina would have a few questions for her father later.

After dinner I started to help clear up the dishes. I lifted the chocolate pudding that Lacey had baked from the table and asked where I should put it.

'Just leave it on the table. Mum will eat it later,' grumbled Ashley who was now eating the leftovers from other people's plates.

'What?' I said, looking at Ashley in puzzlement.

'She gets up at night and eats everything in the fridge,' he whined.

'No, I don't,' protested Lacey, clearly looking a bit embarrassed for the first time all evening. The confessions of a trailer trash mother hadn't ruffled her, neither had her disclosures of abortions, sex toys or sexually transmitted diseases. But this one had finally hit a nerve.

'Yes you do,' chorused Ashley and Shirley in unison.

'I think I'll have to be going,' said Ian. 'I have to get Tina home to bed, and she has an early start in the morning.' Tina still sat in stunned silence at the table, unmoving.

At that moment a man named Robert called at the house. He had just moved into the street and he wondered if Lacey might have a torch he could borrow. Lacey invited Robert into the house and offered him coffee. He declined but stood for a few minutes chatting with her. Ian took advantage of the situation.

'Can I give you a lift home?' he asked.

Ian didn't know where I lived but I was damn sure I was not going to stay here for one minute longer; it had been the most painful evening of my entire life.

'Of course you can,' I smiled at Ian. I wasn't sure which of us raced to the door first.

Lacey called out, 'Y'all come back now,' as we clambered into the car. I turned round to see the two boys pulling each other round the front hall while Tina looked on, her mouth a round O of horror. They were kicking and biting at each other while Lacey chatted nonchalantly to Robert on the doorstep.

'Drive, drive,' I whispered through clenched teeth, 'and don't look back, they might be gaining on you.' Tina sat in the back seat of the car. She still hadn't uttered one syllable since dinner. Once we were safely out of earshot Ian and I looked at each other and laughed. Our laughter quickly became hysterical. I laughed until the tears started to roll down my cheeks.

'So have you known Lacey long?' asked Ian.

'Obviously not long enough,' I said. 'I'm sorry, I know she's your girlfriend but I won't be extending that friendship.'

'No, no we're only friends,' intoned Ian. 'We aren't having a relationship.'

'But I thought she said…'

'No, we're only friends,' Ian said firmly, 'I can assure you of that. I don't think we are compatible at all.'

Ian drove me to my apartment and I said goodnight. I hoped despite all that had happened this evening that I would see him again. I was not physically attracted to him, but it would be nice to have a new friend. At least he had manners and, of course, the all important boundaries which were clearly missing in Lacey's life.

CHAPTER 19

I arrived at work early the following Monday. 'So how was your Thanksgiving dinner?' Laura asked as she started to remove her coat. Naturally Lacey had already told everyone that I was going to her house for dinner. That woman couldn't keep her trap shut about anything.

'Do you want me to be polite or honest?'

'Hmm honest I think,' said Laura curiously, moving her chair closer to me.

'Someone should have warned me,' I sighed. 'It was an unmitigated disaster.' I told Laura all about it, but I declined to reveal all of Lacey's personal disclosures. 'If I ever see that woman again, it will be too soon.'

'I wanted to warn you about her,' said Laura slowly, 'and I'm really sorry that I didn't. I just didn't know you well enough. You know there have been complaints made about her because of her inappropriate behaviour?'

'You mean at work?'

'Yes,' revealed Laura, 'she talks about sex all the time when she's not talking about her two dysfunctional children. That's why no one else will work with her. She'll be lucky to pass her placement with her behaviour.'

I wasn't surprised. So that was why everyone avoided her like the plague. Speaking of the devil, here she came, a vision in burgundy velour, but the grey socks kind of ruined the whole look. They were pulled up to her knees making her look like some overgrown boy scout.

'Hey, woman, guess what happened?' Never in a million years would I ever be able to imagine what was likely to happen in her world.

'You know that guy, Robert?'

'No, who's Robert,' I asked cautiously.

'Oh, you know, that new neighbour,' she said exasperated.

Oh yes, I remembered Lacey had monopolized him on the doorstep. 'He asked me to go for a drive,' she beamed. 'He said he likes to go up to the mountains sometimes and he wants to take me with him next time. You know, he called back to my house next day after dinner to say thanks. Gee, don't you love nice manners?' I was surprised she even knew what manners were.

'And then what happened?' I asked.

'Well, I asked him in for coffee and I had some of that black bottomed pie left. He said I was a brilliant cook, and we got chatting and, you know, he seems really nice.'

'Does Robert not have a wife?' I asked suspiciously.

'Yes he does,' she said dismissively, 'but they don't really get along any more. She doesn't like going for drives and he knew that I would. You see, he knows me already. Gee, it might be fun, get me out a bit, and he's right, I love being up in the cool air of the mountains,' she grinned. Was she retarded?

'And what do you think you will be doing in the mountains with Robert?' I asked as calmly as I could.

'Well, he wants to go for a drive in his four by four and I suppose he wants me to look at trees and nature and stuff.'

'Yes, Lacey, and what kind of nature do you think he might be interested in?'

'Whadda mean?'

'Lacey, married men don't generally ask single women to go for mountain drives unless they are expecting something to happen.'

'Oh,' she flustered. 'Well, he's kind of cute and he seems nice and he told me he doesn't sleep with his wife so what's the harm?' I shook my head. I would get repetitive strain injury in my neck if I spent any more time with her. The woman had the morals of an alley cat and the smell in her house to match it.

I turned back to the computer; there was no point in trying to reason with the woman. She walked away huffily.

Katie arrived. She had rented a property which was about ten miles out of town. 'Bloody buses,' she said taking off her coat. 'I can't rely on them to get me here on time. I'll have to get another car because we usually have to work overtime and I don't want to end up stranded or have Geoff coming to collect me all the time.'

'Have you talked to Kylie about it?' She looked puzzled. 'Maryann had a few thousand dollars left from the money they had allocated to her. Because she's

153

only sending a couple of boxes over with me, it won't cost her as much so she asked the Children's Bureau to give her the rest of it to buy a car.'

'You're joking.' Katie stopped in surprise.

'I'm not. She told them that she needed a car so she could travel around Australia. She told them that it was the only way she could de-stress from all the pressures of work. But knowing her, she probably tortured them and they paid her the money to go away.'

'But I thought they said that the money could only be used for relocation expenses. A new car wasn't part of the deal.'

'Neither is buying furniture,' I said.

'What do you mean?' she asked, clearly puzzled.

'I think most people got the rest of their money to buy electrical things and stuff for their new houses. But Maryann got money for that as well as money to buy furniture before she even got here.' I saw the look of astonishment on Katie's face. 'Didn't you know? She told them that she couldn't rent out her house as she needed to buy fire retardant furniture so they gave her money for sofas and beds and whatever else she asked for.'

'I didn't know that at all. Well, if they are going to give us all of it, I could use it to help buy a car; otherwise I can't get to work in the first place. I think I'll just go and see Kylie now. You know, we didn't stay at the apartments they provided for us either, so we saved some money there. But, you know, Louise, I wish we had known that you were taking in lodgers for free. We could have sponged off you for ages like Maryann.'

'Don't remind me, Katie. I think I made a complete fool of myself there. Once my shipment finally gets here and I hand over their stuff I hope that will be the last I ever see of the pair of them.'

Katie returned a short time later. She looked deflated. 'Kylie says there's no chance. She says that the money has only to be used for relocation purposes and not for anything else.'

'So there are rules for some but not for others. That fat fucker got sofas, beds and a car, and all you are asking for is the rest of your allowance to get a car so you can get into feckin work. I don't know, Katie; it seems that the only way you get anything in this place is to cry up their faces all day long.'

'I know but, I wouldn't demean myself by doing that,' she avowed, 'and I didn't want to argue with Kylie with that Colleen loitering outside Greg's office making a show out of herself. I swear the man hides in the toilets all day to avoid her.'

'Colleen gets obsessed about people,' I explained. 'You should have seen the state of her when she met this waiter called Christian. She dragged me to the restaurant about six times before I refused to go anymore. I could see the poor man hiding behind the pots and pans, afraid to come out.'

We didn't have time to complain as Katie and I had to go out on a home visit then. Katie drove the car while I navigated. When we reached the address on the form we noticed that the front garden of the house was overgrown with weeds and littered with rubbish and bits of broken bicycles. It was still a step up from Lacey's house. I knew even before I confirmed the address that this was the house we were seeking.

I knocked at the door, which was covered in greasy fingerprints. A woman appeared. She was dishevelled and pale. I showed her my identification card, and asked her if we could come in to talk to her about a report. She shrugged her shoulders, the ash from her cigarette falling at her feet. She turned and walked into the house and we followed.

The front hall opened onto a living room which contained a sofa which was piled high with pillows and blankets. We looked down at our feet; we had to step over piles of excrement as we made our way into the living room. A huge television set was placed in front of the window, blocking out any natural light. Old sheets had been nailed above the window as makeshift curtains.

A large dog rushed in and began to bark loudly. She yelled at it to be quiet, and when it ignored this command she led it outside. 'Don't worry, doll,' she assured me. 'She's afraid you're going to go near her pups. She only had them yesterday,' she explained, the cigarette still hanging from her bottom lip. She perched on the arm of a chair but we continued to stand. There was no way I was setting my bottom down anywhere. I tried not to look at Katie. I could feel her revulsion from across the room.

'I'm afraid someone has made a report to us that the house isn't suitable for children,' I explained as tactfully as I could. She looked up surprised. 'Who's been dobbing on me? Was it that fucker...?' She named someone I didn't know. Judging by what I could see already, whoever had reported her had done the children a favour.

'Look, maybe it would just be quicker if you just showed me around.' She shrugged again, leading us into the kitchen. The dining area contained a small sofa which was piled high with unwashed clothes, and more dirty clothing lay strewn all over the floor. The kitchen benches were littered with dirty dishes, empty beer cans and wine bottles. Unfinished food lay congealing on the benches and the floor. Maggots squirmed about greedily in a plate of food. Fat blue bottles flew around the room, hitting their heavy bodies against the windowpane as they fought to get outdoors. I knew how they felt!

The kitchen sink was piled high with dirty dishes which were lying in greasy water; the fat had solidified on the surface in big yellow lumps. In the utility area the dog had given birth to six little pups which were mewing on top of a pile of soiled washing. I nearly lost my life when I saw cockroaches scuttling around the place. I had a real aversion to them; they literally made my stomach heave. I held my breath, trying not to vomit. The smell was rancid. Katie had paled.

I asked weakly to see upstairs. The landing and walls of the stairway had huge holes punched in them. The main bedroom contained a broken double bed which lay turned over on its side; a torn soiled mattress was discarded beside it. Dirty underwear was piled in a heap in a corner of the room.

The older child's room contained three television sets, each set piled on top of the other, a broken chair, which had the arms ripped off, and a single bed. The blankets were rumpled and grey with grime. Tatty net curtains heavy with dust had been nailed onto the window frames.

The younger children's room had graffiti all over the walls; the carpet was littered with dog excrement. Broken toys were discarded on the filthy carpet. One of the beds was broken and had been placed up against the wall; the other bed had a filthy mattress and a pillow. On top of it two little girls lay sleeping, coiled up together. They were naked. The sheet had been pushed down, perhaps in sleep. I could see how grubby they were. The soles of their feet were black. We had seen enough.

The older child was staying with a friend, but was due to return today. I negotiated with the mother to take the children to stay with their grandmother until I could get a professional company to clean up the house and fumigate it. I wiped my feet on the doormat on my way out; Katie and I were silent as we returned to the office. All I could smell was the putrid stench of the woman's house; it had permeated through my clothes. I knew that I wouldn't have time to go home and have a shower with all the work this report had generated, so I continued on until the evening. It took that length of time to coordinate all the services the woman needed and to start the time consuming task of recording my assessment on the computer system.

I managed to get home by eight o clock. I stripped off most of my clothes in the garage, placing it all in a black plastic bag which was kept for this purpose. I sealed it tightly. It had to be unopened for about two weeks. I had learned that this was the only way to kill the fleas. I shivered as I ran up the stairs into the house in my underwear and immediately went to the en suite and had a long hot shower. I scrubbed myself red, trying to get rid of the stench of neglect.

There was no substitute for soap and water my mother always said, but in some of the houses they had just given up. Can you imagine getting up in the morning and not washing yourself and falling into the same dirty bed at the end of the day? What amazed me most was the most slovenly women never seemed to be without a boyfriend, while I knew lots of lovely clean single women who couldn't get a dog to bark at them.

Often when we arrived at the clients' houses we knew even before they opened the door that it was going to be bad. We braced ourselves for the moment that they would open the door. Sometimes the stench nearly floored you. The women would be slouching around in short nighties, lolling about exposing themselves all over the place while you perched on their dirty sofas and tried to talk to them about hygiene and the fact that kids need to be washed every day.

When I emerged from the bathroom I was too tired for dinner. I walked into the kitchen for a drink of water only to find Maryann who was obviously trying to maintain a balanced diet; she had a cookie in each hand. She was standing there in a voluminous pink nightie. She was getting even bigger if that was possible. She was like some big pink blob.

'You're late home,' she said between a mouthful of biscuit, her jowls wobbling as she spoke. 'I was just about to say the rosary. Do you want to join me?'

Sweet Jesus, spare me from your followers. 'No thanks, Maryann,' I mumbled. 'If I want a taste of religion, I'll bite a priest.' I turned and went into my bedroom and collapsed into bed. I was too tired to blow-dry my hair. I brushed it and wrapped it up again in a clean towel. I could always stick it up in a clip tomorrow. I would have to get up earlier in the morning to finish all the other work that I hadn't had a chance to touch today.

Next morning I was struggling with the mechanics of the photocopier when Lacey cornered me. 'Hey, woman, there you are. I was looking all over for you.'

'Hi, Lacey,' I replied lamely. Damn, I really must find a new place to hide.

'Ian was talking to me at the weekend about you,' she leered. What the hell had she said to him about me? 'Yeah, he seems to really like you,' she simpered.

'But Lacey, he's your boyfriend, and I would never dip my fingers into another woman's rice bowl. Honestly, Lacey, I'm not interested in Ian, I hope you don't think I did anything to make him think I was,' I stammered.

'No, no, it's just I saw the way he looked at you, and he obviously likes girly girls. That's why he's not interested in me,' she sighed dismissively. 'I'll have to get myself a pair of high heels at the weekend like you wear, but you know I only wear men's shoes as my feet are so wide.' I looked down. The only place she would be able to get any high heels would be in a sex shop where they sell clothes for transvestites.

'Are you sure you aren't really interested in him?' she continued. 'He's a real nice guy, and he would be really good to you.'

'No, Lacey, honestly, I don't want a relationship with Ian or anyone for that matter.' I laughed gently.

'What about James?' she persisted. I shook my head as I gathered the papers from the machine and started to staple them together into a report.

'Yeah, I've been thinking, you seem ideal for him; he reads all the time like you and he's nice and polite like you and he has a master's degree as well so you two would be perfect for each other.'

'Well, Lacey, James might not think so, and to tell the truth he might think it all a bit awkward too, with you being his ex-wife and working with me.' I was not going to admit to myself that I considered myself to be her friend. After the weekend's antics of her children and her disclosures I had decided to just behave like everyone else and stay away from her.

'It's not like he's pining over me,' Lacey retorted sharply. 'He needs someone in his life, and I think it should be you. How about if I fix up dinner for you and James at my house?' she pleaded.

She must be bloody joking if she thought I was going to expose myself to salmonella and her horrible children again. I would rather remove my own feet and microwave them. I played for time. 'Lacey, this is rushing things a bit much for me, I don't know anything about him and I'm not sure if I even want to go out with anyone now. It hasn't been that long since I got here. I'm not sure I'm ready for a relationship.'

'Nonsense, it would be good for you to have someone in your life. Most women want to be in a relationship. What's wrong with you?' she asked suspiciously.

Pardon? All this from a woman who had left her relationship because she wanted to be with other men? 'I haven't time to talk about it now, Lacey,' I uttered. 'I'm due in court in ten minutes.' She moved away from my desk reluctantly. I hoped this would be the end of the matter.

I spent the rest of the week trying hard to avoid Lacey. What did I hope to achieve from a friendship with her? Did I really want to be friends with someone who had no boundaries? There was no doubt that she was open and honest, which was a refreshing change from the ice maidens I had spent the last few months with, but we didn't seem to have anything in common, and to tell the truth if I never saw her children again it would be too soon.

Lacey tried to corner me at every opportunity at work but I skilfully managed to avoid her. Well I hid a lot, and in all sorts of strange and unusual places. She was coming to the end of her placement. The staff at work had provided afternoon tea and everyone had donated money for a present for one of the other students from Lacey's course who had been with us at the same time. I asked one of the reception staff if they would be organizing the same for Lacey when she left at the end of the week.

'Em, no,' Jenny hesitated, looking nervous. She knew that I had worked with Lacey more than any other staff member. 'I did ask,' said Jenny slowly, 'but no one wants to donate for her, and everyone said they wouldn't go to afternoon tea for that woman.'

'Oh, I see,' I said. 'Sorry I'm not trying to cause trouble, I just thought that no one had asked me to contribute to a leaving gift for her, and I thought I might have been overlooked.'

'No, no, I don't think anyone will be donating for a leaving gift for her. To be honest,' she whispered conspiratorially, 'most of the staff will be glad to get rid of that woman; she has caused so much trouble and dissent since she came here. Well, you weren't here when she started in this office, but she caused problems from the beginning because she demanded that the secretarial staff type up all her notes.' She shook her head sadly. 'We don't even have the time to do that for the staff here, but she must have thought she had tickets on herself, giving out orders and demanding this that and the other. We had to get one of the managers to talk to her about it as we were all going to leave.'

She saw the look of surprise on my face. 'Honestly,' she sighed, 'you don't know what it's been like with that woman. And don't tell me you've missed all the complaining she does about those boys of hers, and how they are always beating up on each other? I even overheard one of the team leaders discussing whether it should be assessed as a child protection report. And she has no limits at all. We were sitting here one day in the break room having a cup of coffee and she came in and started to tell everyone about her ex-husband's vasectomy. I mean, that's not the type of thing you want to hear, is it?'

'No,' I answered. Having been subjected to the same story I knew how uncomfortable I had felt having that information inflicted on me. But surely she only told me that story because I had met James; don't tell me she was telling complete strangers all about it? Most people would think that it was none of their business and wouldn't be interested in even hearing it.

'And as for all that talk about sex,' Jenny continued. 'She has really offended a lot of people. Do you know she's always asking us if we know of any single men so she can get together with them? She never leaves us alone.'

'But why doesn't anybody say something?' I was irritated; did people here just like to whinge about things?

'It's not up to us; we're just the secretarial staff. It should be up to the managers. They are aware of it all themselves.' Jenny sniffed.

'But, do you know, she's leaving this week and she thinks she's been the best student that the Children's Bureau has ever had. She doesn't think that she's done anything wrong. In fact she thinks she's going to be offered a job here immediately when she finishes her training.'

'Well, I'll tell you one thing,' said Jenny frowning, 'if she comes to work here I'll be asking for an immediate transfer, and I think that all the other staff will do the same.'

'That's terrible, Jenny. I'm sorry you have had to deal with it all.'

'Well, you've only just arrived. You wouldn't know the half of it but I have to say that I felt sorry for you when you had to work with her. Nobody else would, you know.'

'I thought Tom was only joking when he said that to me.' The cheeky fecker, he had set me up.

'No, he was serious. We even brought it up in a union meeting and the case managers all said they would refuse to work with her because she was so unprofessional.'

'That's terrible, Jenny,' I agreed. 'I know that a complaint had been made about her because of all the filthy talk she engages in but I hadn't known that things were as bad as that. Why don't they inform the college and let them know about their concerns? Surely if they don't then she will just continue to behave the way she's been doing?'

'Well, one of the workers, Sheila, she had to sit near her and listen to her every day, she asked the same question but the managers told her it was none of her business. But I noticed that they moved Lacey to another desk away from her.

I think they are just so desperate for staff, they are hoping she will come and join the Children's Bureau, but they don't realise that if she gets a position here, half the staff will leave. I hope you don't mind me saying this,' she whispered tentatively, 'but haven't you noticed that people are a bit distant with you?'

'Well, I did notice that,' I agreed, 'but I thought it was because I was from overseas. I heard that a lot of the overseas recruits had a hard time here as people resent them.'

'Oh, we don't resent you,' Jenny said firmly. 'I would say that everyone here really likes you, you are a brilliant worker, they are always talking about how much overtime you and that Katie always do, but as long as you are with that Lacey woman then they won't have anything to do with you.'

'I see, Jenny, thanks for explaining that for me, I really hadn't realised.'

'Well, she'll be gone in a couple of days, and hopefully that will be the end of it.' Jenny returned to her work station. So what Laura had told me about the complaint about Lacey was true, but it seemed she hadn't told me the half of it.

CHAPTER 20

I picked up the phone. 'Hey, woman.' It was Lacey. I was at home trying to get through some paperwork for work. 'You're really hard to get a hold of at work, you know,' she said accusingly 'I thought I would get to see you before I left.'

Not if I could help it. 'Well, you know, we have been just run off our feet,' I said slowly, 'I haven't had a minute to bless myself.' I work hard because millions on welfare depend on me.

'Well, you'll be glad to know that I've been talking to James about you,' she said haughtily. 'I told him that I thought you liked him and that he should go out with you.'

'Lacey, you can't make people go out with other people; he might not even be interested,' I said in exasperation. I was horrified, how dare she try and match-make when she hadn't been given permission to do so. What would the man think of me? I hope he didn't think I had put her up to this. I hope he didn't think I was like her, accosting people and demanding to know if they had any single friends who might be interested in dating me. I was mortified at the thought.

'Oh, he is, he is interested. I already asked him, and he said he liked you, but he said that it might be a bit weird with you being my friend and all.'

Your friend???? First I heard of it. The only reason you are alive is because it's illegal to kill you. 'Well, at least you tried,' I said relieved that at least the episode would be all over. Now I would have no need to see or speak to Lacey again.

'But,' she continued, 'I told him that that was stupid, that it didn't matter how you met, if you like someone you should just go for it, but you know, he's just as shy as you. So I've decided to have dinner for you both next week at my house. That way it won't be awkward for either of you.'

Awkward? Could it get any more bloody awkward than that? She wanted a relationship between her ex-husband and her 'friend' to be played out in her dining room? What will we do for an encore? A bit of afternoon delight on the dining room table? No, don't answer that. With her lack of boundaries it was probably expected.

'And Ian can come too, of course,' she said smugly. So Ian gets to watch another circus act at her house, with me as the main performer? I was distinctly uncomfortable about the whole thing. If James was interested in me why couldn't he just phone me and we could arrange something ourselves? Why does she have to be stuck centre stage in the middle of the whole thing? Was it not a bit strange that he let her arrange this? What kind of relationship do they really have? Surely you couldn't be that friendly with an ex spouse? Were you not supposed to think badly of an ex and tell everyone you meet what a bastard they were and how you were lucky to have escaped from their clutches? Is it not in the break up rule book?

I knew that they had children between them, well, allegedly, according to Lacey, but was this normal practice for the pair of them? Were they liberated or was I just being a provincial prude? What the hell was she thinking? I couldn't imagine anything more awkward. How would I even begin to have a conversation with James when Lacey would be sitting there, taking notes?

'I'll make chicken and gravy and biscuits with corn bread and then black bottomed pie, no sweet potato pie, I think,' Lacey droned on. 'Do you eat red meat? What about fish?' She was off, working out recipes, and planning a menu, oblivious to the fact I was cringing with embarrassment. Not that I didn't feel some level of excitement. James was an attractive man after all, and at least he could read which was more than could be said for the guys who aspired to be Neanderthals that I had met since I came to this country. It would be good to talk to someone about literature; I wondered if he liked eighteenth century poetry? I had to admit there was something so familiar about him; would it be too cheesy to say we must have met in a former life? Yes, it bloody would, I scolded myself. If I continued anymore with this romantic twaddle I was going to make myself sick.

I was anxious about the thought of returning to Lacey's house. I had dodged salmonella the last time, but now that I knew what was in store for me I was even more reluctant to go. Her children would be there for a start. Would they behave any differently when their father was there? What would they think of it all? Their mother and father would be making small talk while their father's potential date looked on. Had this happened before in their house? Was I just another victim? What kind of people were they? Was this one of those Rosemary and Fred West scenarios where they found playmates for each other? Would my family read about my demise in lurid details in some down at heel newspaper?

I wondered what James felt about the whole thing. We hadn't spoken since the day I met him so I had no idea how he felt about the situation. I might have felt happier if we had the opportunity to talk about it ourselves. It would have reduced my anxiety, but Lacey had raced ahead, organizing everything and bullying me into attending. Had she done the same with James? Or might he be just as nervous as me?

What about Ian? He had told me that he wasn't interested in a relationship with Lacey and that they were only friends so why was he coming? Did Lacey think that if she fixed me up with James then Ian would start to take more of an interest in her? I tried to consider the whole business as just another dinner, and at least if I went out I would have a legitimate reason for leaving the house. Things at home were decidedly frosty with Maryann who either tried unsuccessfully to get me to pray with her or continually tried to get me to join her for dinner.

I debated with myself for days, deciding one minute that I would go, and the next that I would just make some excuse and stay at home. I was sick to my stomach that day in work. Now that I had learned how all the other staff felt about Lacey was I not putting myself in a vulnerable position by meeting with her after work? Would they hold this against me?

Katie was the only one I had talked to about the imminent dinner. She made no bones about the fact that she didn't like Lacey. 'Skanky dirty bitch,' was how she referred to her. But she said that as my initial impression of James was positive I owed it to myself and to him to see if it would go anywhere.

I arranged for Lacey to collect me at the house on her way home from her part-time job. I didn't want her collecting me outside the office in case anyone saw us together. Already I felt ashamed of being in this woman's company and yet I had agreed to go to her house. Again! I felt as if I was conducting some furtive affair as I left the office and made my way home.

I showered and stood in front of the mirror to apply my make-up. They said time was a great healer, but it was a lousy beautician. I was anxious about what I should wear. Obviously I wanted to wear something nice, but I didn't want to wear anything too good as it would be destroyed in that house. I settled on a black patterned skirt and a black top with a little black cardigan. They were all washable. I poured myself a gin and tonic to take the edge of my nervousness. My stomach was in knots.

Lacey arrived and let out a loud wolf whistle when she saw me, which made me feel even more uncomfortable. I wanted to turn back inside and not leave the house. But Lacey wouldn't take no for an answer and she practically bundled me into the car. I was being kidnapped. As we drove to her house I noticed that she seemed a bit anxious too.

'I'm sorry I was late to collect you,' she exhaled noisily. 'I've been so busy. I just hope I get everything done before Ian and James arrive.'

I sat in the car beside her dreading every moment and wondering what was in store for me. I didn't expect it to be pleasant, after the nightmare meal I had been subjected to on Thanksgiving Day. I had practically doused myself with bleach before leaving the house, trying to germproof my body. I tried to tell myself that countless numbers of people had eaten in her kitchen and gone on to lead relatively normal lives, but my powers of persuasion were running low.

I could see when I entered the house that she hadn't made any changes. The place was as bad as ever, if not worse. Her idea of housework was to sweep the room with a glance. If a messy kitchen was a happy kitchen, then her kitchen was delirious!

Shirley was playing a game on the computer and Ashley was in the kitchen eating his way through a litre of ice cream. I gave Ashley a box of chocolates and told him he was to share them with his brother. He opened them up immediately and started gorging himself. Chocolate dribbled down his chin in brown rivers as he fumbled with the wrappers of the sweets, stuffing them into his mouth at an alarming rate. Maybe the chocolates were a bad idea; I had naively believed that he would eat them after his dinner.

Lacey ignored him. She raced around trying to prepare the food for cooking. I walked towards the kitchen, took a large breath and got stuck in. She opened a bottle of wine and started to drink huge gulps of it. 'Oh, I really needed that,' she said as she burped loudly. 'Go and see what's on television,' she instructed Ashley who was still standing there munching away at the sweets. God, that was an easy one. Dust!

I asked how I could help her and she allowed me to prepare the vegetables. There wasn't a skin left on a carrot or potato by the time I had finished. I also managed to give a couple of the saucepans she would be using a good scrub when she went to the bathroom. My wine was still untouched while she moved onto her second glass as she set the table. She had called both of her sons and asked them to do it, but they had ignored her. Each one was clearly more useless than the one before. The timer on the cooker was clicking away, but not to measure the cooking time of food. It was used to measure how much time each boy had on the computer. I watched as the dial moved around to sixty minutes, knowing that the trouble was going to start when Shirley's turn was over. I was right. As soon as the timer emitted a loud ring he started.

'Why do I have to get off? Why can't I have my own computer? Why does that queer have to have a go on it?' he screamed at the top of his lungs.

A scuffle broke out between Shirley and Ashley and I could hear them push and pull each other round the room. Lacey ran to intervene and Shirley stormed into the kitchen, clearly the loser. He glared at me from under his grimy fringe, looking like the terminator. He spotted the half empty box of sweets on the kitchen counter and grabbed them, tearing the paper from them with his teeth. He continued to glower at me. He reminded me of some animal in a zoo, locked in a cage, filled with pent-up rage and frustration. He, too, like his brother before him, began to shove chocolates into his mouth. When he saw his mother coming into the kitchen he grabbed the box of sweets and stormed off to his bedroom slamming the door behind him. My nerves were in tatters, I felt as if I had just dealt with a terrible conflict situation. That child really scared me, he was just so angry; it was so tangible you could feel it across the room. It felt like... evil.

I reached for my glass of wine, taking a large gulp. Jesus, it was no wonder the poor woman drank. If I had to live with these horrible children I'd never be sober. Lacey continued preparing food and I helped her as best I could wishing that I had the courage to just leave. Regardless of whether I thought James seemed like a nice man, I didn't want to be here, not in her smelly house, and not near her ill reared children.

The night had started badly and by the time Ian arrived Lacey was squiffy. Things tumbled downhill from there. When James arrived he came over to say hello to me while I was in the kitchen, trying furtively to clean up. He looked gorgeous in a dark blue shirt which matched his eyes perfectly. I could feel my heart jump in my chest whenever he looked at me. He seemed a bit uncomfortable and I was relieved. At least this proved he didn't do this type of thing on a regular basis. James went to say hello to the boys.

Ian was much more relaxed now that Tina was not with him. He was entertaining and charming and we shared jokes. I could sense that he was interested in me, but there was no way I was going there. It was bad enough to even consider having a relationship with Lacey's ex-husband, never mind her current boyfriend.

James returned to the kitchen where Lacey handed him a bottle of wine and a bottle opener. I realised she had finished the first bottle of wine herself. My glass was still sitting by the kitchen sink. Lacey talked away to Ian but almost ignored James. James was polite but he seemed a bit distant. He was clearly as uncomfortable with the situation as me. I was reassured. I didn't want to think that he let his ex-wife fix him up on dates with women.

Ian, James and I sat down at the dining table and Lacey fluttered between us, putting things on the table and stirring things in pots on the stove. She did most of the talking; in fact it was difficult to get a word in edgeways. At least when the attention was focused on her, James and I might have some peace.

When dinner was ready she yelled at the boys and told them to come into the dining room. Ashley raced in and grabbed what looked like the only comfortable chair in the place; he pushed Ian out of the way to get to it. I looked up and noticed Ian's face start to grimace.

Shirley refused to come for his dinner and James had to practically carry him to the table where he sulked, glaring at anyone who attempted to speak to him. No one said grace. Ian, James and I commented on the lovely food which Lacey had prepared. Given the limited amount of time she had, she had produced a wonderful array of food. We didn't get time to admire it though as Ashley reached over everyone, grabbing what he could and shovelling it onto his plate.

Lacey took Shirley's plate and placed some food on it. He sat in brooding silence, picking through his food as if looking for forensic evidence. As we started to eat Shirley grabbed his glass of lemonade and began to take huge gulps. When he finished he burped loudly. Like mother like son. I caught Ian's eye and I knew he was thinking exactly the same as me – brat! I was sure Ian wouldn't tolerate that type of behaviour from his own children.

James told Shirley to excuse himself and he did in a whiny singsong voice. He then returned to exploring his food, but didn't eat it. He squirmed in his chair and then began to pass wind, loudly. Ashley began to snigger, his long lank greasy hair falling into his plate as he scooped the food into his mouth. Ashley's sniggers encouraged Shirley to continue to pass wind. Ian nearly fell off the chair. I put my fork down, I couldn't eat another bite. Ian and I exchanged glances. Oh God, it was like déjà vu all over again. I wondered if I should just stand up and ask Ian if he was ready to leave. I knew that he would leave with me, I just knew it. Like a coward I let the moment pass and waited to see what would happen next.

'Stop that immediately,' ordered James, 'have some manners while you are at the table.'

'I don't have to do what you say,' chanted Shirley. 'It's not your turn to look after me, and you're not my dad.'

'Don't be ridiculous Shirley,' insisted James.

'You're not my dad; Satan is,' he shrieked. He picked up a forkful of potato and pinged it at Ashley who retaliated by throwing his meat across the table at his brother. Ian's mouth was open in shock, as was mine. I looked at Lacey to see that she was staring out the window, oblivious to the behaviour of her children. She was practically inhaling the wine in her glass.

James ordered the boys to go to their rooms; I could see that he was mortified. He spoke slowly and deliberately and the boys eventually left the table giggling and sniggering as they raced to Lacey's bedroom where they resumed their fighting over the computer.

James got up from the table and walked into the room after them. He took Shirley by the arm and dragged him to his bedroom where I could hear him trying to negotiate with him. He eventually kept him quiet by putting a game on the play station. We could all hear the noise of the game emanating from Shirley's bedroom. Ian and I sat in silence; I was too stunned to move. James returned to the table.

'Anyone for dessert?' asked Lacey casually as she stumbled to her feet and moved unsteadily to the kitchen. She returned with a Black Forest chocolate cake and some cream. She started hacking it into slices and placed a plate full of cake in front of each of us. It looked like an autopsy. Ian and I were too stunned to refuse, we began to automatically eat. After we had eaten dessert she put her feet up on the table and began to drink the wine straight from the neck of the bottle. Classy! Bacteria was the only culture she had.

As the night progressed Lacey got drunker and drunker and her behaviour became more and more outrageous. Lacey took James outside and left Ian and me alone. We sat in silence, too stunned to even communicate. James told me later that she told him that if he didn't make a move on me soon, 'no dick Ian' would get in there first.

When James returned, Lacey dragged Ian outside and James and I were left alone at the dining table. We chatted easily, but I was very nervous. I felt exposed. It was like being on one of those dating shows which recorded every move you made. I felt self-conscious and awkward though James was polite and charming and he tried to put me at my ease. I had been right about his love of literature. I also discovered that his grandparents had come from Ireland. So that explained his Celtic looks.

By the time Lacey and Ian returned James and I had started to clear the table and were putting the dirty dishes into the sink. I also tried to throw in as many others as I could which were within reach. Lacey stumbled towards me.

'You know I wouldn't ever let another woman in my kitchen except for her,' she drooled. 'I think she's going to make a brilliant stepmother.'

My face went red with embarrassment. I was mortified. Imagine saying a thing like that in front of James. She was practically giving him permission to marry me. Even Ian looked aghast. I poured hot water into the sink and began to scrub the dishes trying to hide my face so they wouldn't see how embarrassed I was. I worked diligently. By the time I had finished those dishes were cleaner than they had ever been in that house.

James was silent. He hunted around in cupboards and drawers until he eventually found a reasonably clean dishcloth and began to dry the dishes. Lacey sat with her feet on the table chatting away to Ian, a bottle of wine in her hand, while her cat walked through the leftovers which Ashley hadn't managed to finish.

At the end of the evening, James offered to drive me home. At least we would have some time alone without the pressure of Lacey and Ian watching every move between us. But my hopes for quality time were dashed when I realised that Ashley would be coming too as he had planned to spend the night with his dad.

James asked Ashley if he wanted him to drop him off at his house first, which was on the way, but Ashley refused. The boy had no shame. He sat up in the back seat of the car, leaning forward and listening intently to every word we said. What kind of self-respecting adolescent boy would put himself in that position?

When James left me at my apartment he told me he would phone me the following week and he bent over to kiss me gently on the lips. I waved goodbye as he drove away. That would probably be the last I would ever see of him. Even I could see that it would be difficult for him to have a relationship with anyone who was even remotely connected with his ex-wife. I fervently hoped that he didn't think I was like her in any way. I was grateful only that Lacey had finished her placement. I could just imagine the gossip she would provide to all the other staff about tonight and my date with James.

I went into the house and threw my clothes into the washing machine; I didn't care if a boil wash shrank them. I took a hot shower then lay in bed and thought of all that had happened that evening. I liked James, I really did, but where would Lacey fit into it all? Was there not something a bit distasteful and unsavoury about the whole thing? I had been most impressed to discover that James was nothing like Lacey. He was well mannered and polite and he seemed to have values which she didn't share. It wasn't fair to assume that just because she was foul mouthed and manipulative he would be as well. Lacey had admitted that he had been a good husband to her, and he was certainly an improvement on my own husband. Not that I was lining him up to be next, you understand, but as I had made such a catastrophic choice in my life then, the fear was always there that I might do it again.

CHAPTER 21

I was in the bath reading a book. Maryann had gone out on another feeding frenzy and I was enjoying the time by myself. The phone rang. Christ, I can't get a minute's peace in this place, it would be quieter in Beirut, I muttered as I grabbed a towel. It was Lacey. 'So how are you and James getting on?' she asked. 'Has he asked you out on a date yet?'

'Hmm, no,' I replied dripping water all over the hall floor. 'He said he'd phone me next week, but you know how busy I am.' I felt like I had to justify the fact that James hadn't phoned.

'Oh, don't worry, I'll speak to him. Honestly, you two; you will never get anywhere without me,' she laughed uproariously.

'No, please, Lacey, don't. I'd rather James phoned me himself without you making him,' I implored.

'Oh, you know what men are like, they just don't think like us.' She tutted. She started to talk about Ian and berated the fact that he still didn't seem interested in pursuing a relationship with her. I still felt drained from the previous evening. I had begun to seriously question whether I wanted a relationship with a man who had such obnoxious children. If they behaved like that in their own home what would it be like if James and I ever got together? I wouldn't tolerate their horrible behaviour but Lacey was oblivious to it. It would be difficult to try to impose some boundaries with her children when the woman had none. I managed to get Lacey off the phone and stepped back into the bath, but it was cold. I pulled the plug, dried myself and went to bed where I settled down to read.

James phoned me later that evening and asked me to go to his house for dinner the following week. I hoped that he had used his initiative to phone me and that he hadn't been bullied into it by Lacey, but I felt too nervous to ask. I agreed to go. It would be interesting to see him on his own territory, and hopefully we would both feel more comfortable away from Lacey and the children.

I thought about James over the next few days. My track record of relationships hadn't been positive to date and I wondered if once again I was choosing to get involved in something that any other woman would run a mile from. I had great difficulty in accepting that the monsters I had met were James's children. He was so polite and well mannered, but it was clear that this hadn't rubbed off on the boys. Maybe they were brats because of her poor influences. I hoped they would be better behaved when they were with their father.

I returned home from work. I was loaded down with stuff that I needed to finish that night. It was a hot evening and I was looking forward to having a cool shower. I opened the door and went into the living room. Maryann was lying sprawled all over the sofa snorting her way through a litre of ice cream.

'I've been thinking,' she said, 'you were the one who said that you didn't want to get married so I don't see why you are going out with that man. You're only wasting his time, and there are other girls who would love somebody like him.'

'What are you on about, Maryann?' I sighed as I bent down to unbuckle my shoes.

'I just think that maybe you should let Colleen go out with him. He sounds like a nice man and it would be just what she needs after all that nonsense with Graham.'

I couldn't believe what I was hearing. 'I'm not playing pass the parcel with James,' I spat. 'Colleen is big enough and ugly enough to find somebody of her own.'

'I just knew that you would say that,' she said gleefully. 'You are just so selfish. Poor Colleen hasn't been out with anyone in ages.'

'Save it for Oprah,' I retorted. 'I don't give a rat's ass what happens to Colleen so stop nagging me.'

'Oh, I can't do anything right with you,' she sighed. 'I think it's time that I moved into a place of my own.' Thank you, Jesus! Given that she hadn't given me one penny since she arrived I thought it was a wonderful idea. She had started work now and was getting paid nearly as much as me. There was no reason why she shouldn't be contributing.

'I've been out looking for places with Colleen,' she continued, 'and I've found a place round the corner so I'm thinking of moving out on Friday.'

'That's good,' I said casually as I walked into the kitchen. The fridge was empty. She had eaten everything in sight. 'So you'll be paying up all the rent money you owe me?' I asked her as I returned to the living room empty handed. Her mouth gaped open. It wasn't a pretty sight.

'Well I was just thinking I haven't really been here very long and you have probably been glad of the company,' she simpered. 'You would have been all alone if it wasn't for me. And really, you know, I have to give my new landlady a bond and I have to pay a month's rent in advance. So I don't really have a lot left after that.'

'Do you know that if you had moved into the rented apartment which work provided you would have had to pay $1000 a week?' I reminded her.

'Yes, Colleen told me she had to pay that amount too. I think it's disgraceful.'

'Well, I had to pay it, we all did, except you. The only reason why you moved in with me was to save money and you've done it. But you owe me three months' rent, Maryann. I can't afford to be carrying you. You also agreed to pay towards the setting up of the electricity and the phone. You haven't done that either. I haven't got a phone bill yet, but when I do you will have to contribute to it.'

'But I won't be here by then,' she replied indignantly.

'Maybe not, but you have been, you are never off that phone, calling England and Ireland. I'm not paying for your calls.'

'Well, I think that's a bit rich,' she exclaimed struggling to move her girth into a sitting position. 'I've been more than good to you since I moved here. Sure didn't I take you to restaurants.'

'I paid my own way there, Maryann, and the only reason we went to a restaurant was because you and Colleen wanted to eat out all the time. I would have been happy enough with a bowl of cereal. You know I hate cooking so much, I don't even butter my bread.'

'Well, I don't have it, I can't give you anything.' She folded her arms firmly. Her chins were resting on her neck. All of them.

'So you are just going to leave here on Friday without contributing in any way to the bills that have accumulated over the past three months?' I queried. She had to be bloody joking if she thought she was going to pull that stunt on me.

'Well, like I said,' she sniffed, 'I'm really struggling having to pay for a bond and a month's rent in advance. I don't know where I'm going to get the money to buy food. And of course I need to buy sheets and towels and kitchenware. I don't have any of that.'

'Neither did I when I arrived here,' I said slowly 'But I had to put my hand in my pocket and pay for it all. And you needn't pull a fast one with the bond.

You know the Children's Bureau will pay for it like they have done for everybody else.'

'But you don't know how hard it is for me,' she whined. I have to pay my mortgage at home, and it's going to be so hard to pay for rent as well.'

'If you're looking for sympathy, you'll find it in the dictionary between shit and syphilis,' I snapped. 'What do you think I've been doing this last five months? I've been paying both, and at least you have a tenant in your house contributing to the rent. I don't have anybody doing that.'

'Well, I can't afford to give you money as well as buying all the stuff I need for my new place. I haven't any food in my new place. I will have to go shopping and stock up. It will cost a fortune.'

'Well, here's a life lesson, Maryann. It has cost me a fortune keeping you this last three months.' I moved closer. 'I assumed, foolishly, that you would be decent enough to pay your share of the bills, but you have no honour or decency in you. You are just a greedy, money grabbing fool. You have eaten everything in this house. You have run up my phone bill, and used up all the toiletries I had without once putting your hand in your pocket. You are lying there on your fat arse eating the last of my ice cream. You know, I said furiously, 'looking back over the time that we've been together, I can't help but wonder: What the fuck was I thinking?'

'Oh, there's no need to start using obscenities,' she said, her mouth pursed in disgust.

'Well, I will tell you what, Maryann,' I said forcefully, 'It's my house, I pay for it so I can do what I like and I tell you what you can do. You can just fuck off. Don't be waiting until Friday to leave. Just go now.'

'What do you mean? You mean you are throwing me out in the street?' Her mouth gaped open in surprise.

'Don't be so bloody melodramatic,' I sighed. 'You can go and stay in Colleen's. It's only for a couple of days anyway. And to tell you the truth now that you've shown your true colours I don't want you about the place any more. I'm only sorry I didn't do this months ago.'

'But, but,' she stammered.

'I mean it, Maryann; you have a car in the drive there, pack your stuff and go. I'll be back in an hour and if you aren't out of this place by then I'll be phoning the police. You can leave your key on the kitchen bench.'

I went into my bedroom and fumbled in the drawer for my jewellery case. There was no way I was leaving that behind. God knows what she would do. I left the house. I knew that my reputation would be mud in work by tomorrow, but I couldn't imagine anyone there tolerating her freeloading for months. I knew that she wouldn't be on the street like she had suggested. Colleen would let her stay with her. Let her have a couple of days sponging off her. The pair of them deserved each other.

I drove around for ages before I started to feel guilty. I had been really mean to Maryann. As usual I regretted my speech, never my silence. I sometimes wished my mouth had a backspace key. I decided to return to the apartment to see if I could salvage something out of the bloody mess.

She had gone. She had stripped the bed of the sheets, my sheets, and had taken all the towels and tea towels out of the hotpress. I moved around the apartment mentally noting what else was missing. She had emptied the freezer and removed every single item from the larder, it was completely bare. She had taken some of the dishes and cutlery and half the pots and pans. As if that wasn't bad enough, before she left she dragged a chest of drawers across the floor and damaged it. I would have to pay for the cost of repairs to the floor before I would be able to terminate my rental agreement.

I ran into my bedroom. I knew it. She had taken all my Jo Malone products from the en suite and my hairdryer. My CD player was also missing from my bedroom. The robbing bitch. It was bad enough that she had lounged around here using me for three months. Now she had to add theft to her list of accomplishments.

I lifted the phone to call the police, but I stopped, what was the point? I'd rather just get on with my life without her. If the price of getting rid of her was three months' rent, electrical items and a load of groceries, then it was worth it. I didn't know what I had been thinking letting everything slide for so long. I reasoned that I had been too exhausted at the end of the day to protest about all the problems I had experienced with her. Hopefully I'd never have to see her again.

I drove over to James's house at the agreed time the following week. I was very apprehensive. I was a bit put out when James welcomed me into the house and I discovered that Ashley was there too. I had thought that we would be able to spend some time alone. James made Ashley come out of the bedroom to say hello and then he slunk off to his computer game. Would we ever have time together or did James feel so uncomfortable with me that he needed back up in the form of his adolescent son? Still, at least the monster wasn't there; I had something to be grateful for.

175

I looked around the living room. It was spotless. James went into the kitchen to finish preparing dinner. You could have eaten your dinner off the floor. How on earth had he coped with Lacey's slovenly ways? Or had he done all the cleaning in the house before they separated.

'Would you like to see some photographs of my trip to Japan while I'm preparing dinner?' James asked. I accepted them politely. There was usually nothing as boring as looking at other people's photos, but it was clear he was keen to display the images of his recent trip overseas. I looked at them closely. Some of the photography was stunning. James told me that he had studied photography at university. He had a real eye for detail.

When I had finished he said, 'Here are some photos of the boys when they were little,' and he placed a large album on the table in front of me. I was curious. What rock did they crawl from under? I was surprised. The children looked clean. But there was something about Shirley's eyes. In every single pose he stared defiantly, with an evil stare. He looked like Damien out of The Omen.

I looked carefully and noticed that the houses in the photographs were all tidy and clean. So there must have been some standards then. Had these been maintained only by James?

I turned a page and was immediately confronted by a picture of a very large naked woman who was heavily pregnant. The photograph was taken on the beach and I could see passers-by with their mouths open in shock. I knew exactly how they felt. 'Jesus Christ, James,' I stumbled. I was not prepared for this. 'It's naked pictures of Lacey,' I said dropping the album as if I had been scorched.

'Oh, that's Lacey when she was pregnant with Ashley,' James said calmly. 'She couldn't wear clothes when she was pregnant so she took them off that day and ran down the beach.' She had told me that she couldn't wear clothes but I thought that it was just in the house. I didn't know it was in public.

'Christ, weren't you mortified with embarrassment?' I asked in surprise.

'Em, no, it was her body,' he stated matter-of-factly. He was more open-minded than me. I must have sound like some puritan, but hadn't he ever heard of decency?

'And she did this regularly?' I asked incredulously.

'Oh, all the time,' he nodded.

'Didn't people ever complain?'

'Well, there was that one time when Lacey was naked when her friends were all at our house and the next door neighbours complained that she wasn't decent.'

'Well, I have to say I would probably agree with the neighbour too, James.'

'Oh, it was nothing to her; she was used to taking her clothes off because she was working as a nude model.' That's right, she had told me that one day, but the visual image was a bit different when you were confronted with it.

James looked at the photographs of the children when they were younger. 'They were so sweet then,' he sighed. 'I don't know what has happened to them. Within the past couple of years they seem to be becoming more and more unmanageable.'

'Do they always fight with each other?' I asked, curious to see if his account of the children's behaviour conflicted with what Lacey had told everyone in the office.

'All the time, but to tell the truth they are worse when they come here from their mother's house. It takes a couple of days for them to settle down and behave themselves. I think she gives them a lot of sugary drinks over there and they don't get that in this house.'

'So you notice a big change then?'

'Yes. I mean, Lacey is a good mother and she has made a lot of sacrifices for the children, but she gives in too easily. When they start complaining and demanding candy she goes out and gets them. I think she's very lenient on Shirley too when he misbehaves and Ashley gets the brunt of it as he's older which is unfair. I think we both expect him to behave better, because we know that he can.'

'But Shirley can't?' What was wrong with him? Was he not just an ill-reared brat?

'He's a strange child. He has had huge temper tantrums since he was about two years old. He would throw himself on the floor and scream and scream until he got what he wanted. He won't eat particular foods and he won't eat food that has touched other food on the plate.'

'Does he have any problems changing from one routine to another?' I asked curiously.

'Yes, he does, you know,' he agreed. 'He has to know in advance that he's going somewhere. If I tell him that we will be leaving at a certain time and I get delayed he gets so frustrated, he will ask every minute when he's going home.'

'Hmm, he sounds just like this little boy that I worked with at home. He couldn't adjust to any change in routine and he wouldn't eat the same food as the rest of the family. I've seen his temper tantrums and they were horrific. He was diagnosed with Asperger's Syndrome. But when I spoke to the child psychologist he told me that these children usually have really poor social skills and they are usually addicted to something, like a particular subject or the computer.'

'Oh, well, that's Shirley then, isn't it?' James conceded. 'He throws a tantrum every time he has to finish his turn on the computer.'

'How many hours of computer time do they get a day?' I wondered aloud.

'In their mother's house they get to use it for an hour at a time and then they have to change over, so it goes on all day and night. But Shirley always gets up early in the morning so he usually has a few hours under his belt before Ashley even gets out of bed.'

'And what time do the children usually go to bed?' Was I working here? I felt as if I was conducting a parenting assessment, but I was struggling to make sense of this.

'They go to bed late in their mother's house, but here I insist that they go to bed at a reasonable time as Ashley is so hard to get up in the morning.'

I heard heavy breathing outside the door, which was ajar. I moved quickly to open it. It was Ashley. He had been snooping around, and listening to everything we said. The nosey bollocks. He looked a bit shamefaced that I had caught him.

'You are just in time. We are going to serve dinner,' said James. 'Do you want to set the table, Ashley?' Ashley set the table without complaining. I was very impressed; he hadn't done it when his mother asked him to do it in her house. Maybe James had better control over the children. I was relieved. Maybe it wasn't as bad as I thought it was going to be. Maybe all my fears about the impact of the children's behaviour on me were unfounded.

As we were eating dinner James asked me if I would like to go to a party at his older brother Joseph's house the following week. He told me that he had only one brother, Joseph, and they had a very close relationship. James told me that Joseph and his wife would be there with their son, Brendan, who was the same age as Ashley. Would this be another ill reared brat? I dreaded to think that there was another person in the world who behaved like these children.

James's mother and father had also been invited. I was pleased that he had invited me and proud that he seemed so pleased to introduce me to his family. After dinner when I left to go home, James gave me a hug and a quick kiss on the lips, but I was so anxious in case Ashley suddenly appeared, and I think James felt the same.

CHAPTER 22

I was rushing about in work trying to get ready for court when Lacey phoned. I had my headphones on and I was poking around in my briefcase, trying to make sure I had all the relevant reports I needed. 'So have you two had sex yet?' she asked.

'Jesus, Lacey, you shouldn't be asking people questions like that,' I said steadily though her question had thrown me. Imagine anyone asking you that.

'So that must mean you haven't,' she sighed. 'I phoned James's house this morning 'cos I thought you'd be there. I thought you wudda stayed over with him last night.'

'Oh, why, did you want something?' I asked trying hard to divert her away from the details of my relationship with James as I continued to check the contents of my briefcase.

'No, I just wondered if you had done the deed yet.' Done the deed? Was it any of her bloody business if we had? Why was it so important to her? She really was the nosiest woman I had ever met. I wondered how difficult it was going to be to keep my relationship with James separate and private from her. She might be comfortable with revealing all sorts of intimate details of her life but I wasn't and I didn't believe James would feel comfortable with me broadcasting details of our lives together either.

'Listen, I can't talk now,' I protested. 'I'm really busy. Speak to you later.' I put the phone down firmly.

I eventually managed to get home from work. It was eight o'clock and I was exhausted and hungry. The phone was ringing as I put my key in the door. I picked it up. It was Lacey. Again. Dear God, was she going to question me twice a day? She sounded very irritated. 'I hear you were saying that Shirley has some kind of mental illness,' she snarled.

'What are you talking about, Lacey?' I asked hesitatingly.

'Ashley said he heard you telling James that Shirley had Asperger's Syndrome or something like that.' So Ashley really had been listening to our conversation. 'There's nothing wrong with my son,' she continued, 'and I don't want you saying that kinda stuff about him.'

'Look, Lacey,' I said firmly. 'I think Ashley must have misheard. I wasn't talking about Shirley. I was talking about a child I worked with at home who was diagnosed with Asperger's Syndrome. I didn't say that Shirley had it. I'm not a clinician, I can't diagnose anything like that and I wouldn't presume to do so.'

'Well as long as you know I'm totally opposed to drugs for kids,' she sighed. 'You know half of the kids in America are on Ritalin and I don't believe in giving drugs to children.'

I'm not trying to give drugs to your children, Lacey,' I insisted. 'I don't know where you have got that information from, but I can tell you now that it's wrong.'

'You know,' she continued, 'I think that doctors are just too quick to diagnose people and say that they have mental illness even when they haven't. Sure my mom tried to get me admitted to an institution because the doctor said I had schizophrenia. I had to run away from home, you know,' she said adamantly. 'You know,' she was on a roll, 'she did the same with my brother Davy. One time he took acid and he had this real bad trip. He drove home from two states away and he was really paranoid when he got there. So Mom had to put him in an institution and he got electro-convulsive therapy there. He was there for ages before they let him out again. Then one day he slammed the door at my mom's house and my mom told him that if he ever did that again she would put him back in an institution. Do you know what he did?' She shrieked. 'He went and shot himself, in his bedroom. And I had to clean up all his brains and stuff 'cos no one else would do it.'

'Lacey, that's just horrible.' I was going to throw up right in the hall, the graphic description was horrific. Was it any wonder the woman was a couple of sandwiches short of a picnic? She had suffered a horrific childhood.

'Look I gotta go,' she said distractedly. 'The kids are here and I'm gonna hang out with them. I just wanted to check what you said about my Shirley. See you later,' and she put down the phone. She had just passed on the most horrible information to me which I was still reeling from and she had gone to hang out with the boys. To her it was just like swatting a fly. Didn't she realise that these sordid confessions had an impact on people? I couldn't get the vision of what she had described out of my head all night. I skipped dinner, again.

The following day I returned to the office from court again with a notebook full of instructions which had to be acted on immediately. The phone rang. It was the owner of a day care centre where two of the children in my care had been placed. The mother of the children had arrived at the centre and was trying to remove them.

'You have a copy of the court order,' I said firmly to the worker. 'You know that she's not allowed to take them, so just call the police.'

'Can you come down as well,' she pleaded. 'She's refusing to leave without her kids and is making a scene; some of the babies are getting really upset.'

'All right,' I said, 'I'll see what I can do.' I sighed. There couldn't be a crisis today, my schedule was already full. I had spent all morning in court on this case, and had a million other things I needed to do. I approached Katie. She was the only one who was prepared to work overtime if needed, and I knew that we wouldn't be able to get this all sorted and get back into the office for 4.51pm when we were supposed to quit.

'Katie, pet, sweetheart,' I asked as I walked over to her desk, 'are you free for a while? That case I was in court with this morning is starting to go pear-shaped. I have to go to a day care centre; the police are on their way. That mother is trying to remove the kids.'

Katie glanced at her diary. 'Just let me cancel something and I'll be right with you but I'll need to phone Geoff. He won't be too happy if I'm late again.'

'I'm sorry,' I said to Katie, 'there is literally no one else to ask.'

'It's not your fault that they haven't got the staff here,' she replied. 'Or at least, many staff that know what they are doing.'

'Thanks, Katie, I'll just go and see if there's a car available.' I was lucky, there was a free car that afternoon. I signed my name in the book and collected the car keys; I briefly told Tom where I was going while Katie signed the white board which was there so the staff could keep an eye on our whereabouts and what time we were expected to return.

As Katie drove towards the day care centre I briefed her on the concerns for the children, and why the court had granted an order that morning to prevent the parents from having unsupervised contact with the children. We arrived to find the police were already there. I showed the officers a copy of the order and they agreed to go inside and appraise the situation. The mother was in the waiting area, clearly under the influence of something. Her eyes were glazed and she was speaking rapidly. She lurched towards me when she saw me. 'You bitch,' she screamed, 'they're my kids; I can take them if I want. You can't stop me.'

One of the police officers had entered the door behind me; he moved forward and warned the mother to step away from me. Katie and I went into the office and spoke to the day care manager. We reiterated that the children were not to be removed from the centre by their mother or father.

'I wonder how she got here.' Katie said as we left.

'I was just thinking the same thing,' I replied.

'Doesn't it seem a bit stupid to just turn up out of the blue and try and take the children away? How did she think she was going to get away?' asked Katie.

'She probably thought she could just run down the road trying to push a couple of buggies. You know, that woman is thick. I have shoes that are smarter than her.'

The police were still negotiating with the mother and trying to encourage her to leave the premises. We left them to it. What a bloody waste of time. As we were leaving the centre I noticed a car parked directly in front of it. I saw the driver duck his head when he saw our car approach. The government registration plates probably gave us away.

'Katie,' I asked, 'will you do me a favour? Will you just drive up the road a bit and come back again so I can see who the driver of that car is.'

'No problem,' she replied and moved out onto the main road.

'It couldn't be the father,' I explained. 'He swore in court this morning that he wouldn't have any further contact with her. He wouldn't be that stupid would he?'

Katie drove past the car; I looked in through the driver's window. I could see the outline of a man; he had ducked his body towards the passenger seat when he saw our car approach. Katie drove a hundred yards up the road and turned and came back. She drove slowly as we approached the car. I looked in and saw the father of the children. I looked directly into his face. He looked shocked.

'Jesus, Katie, that's how she got here. I wondered what she was going to do with the children if she got them. I didn't think she was taking a bus. He's involved in this whole thing with her. You'd better go back to the centre, and let's hope the police are still there.'

We arrived just as the police officers were about to get into their car. I explained to them that the father of the children had obviously brought the mother to the centre, and that the chances of abduction of the children were therefore more serious than we had originally anticipated. We all turned round as the car we had seen raced into the car park of the childcare centre at high speed. When it stopped the mother rushed out of the centre and ran towards it. She clambered into the passenger seat and the car drove off.

'No worries, I've got a note of the registration. I'll run it through the system to see who the driver of that vehicle is,' the officer said. I already knew his name, address and date of birth. I supplied them to the officer. I'd have to follow this up when we go back to the office. The father was obviously involved in this attempted abduction. I shuddered when I thought of what he might do if he was alone with the children. We returned to the centre and reiterated that the children were to be kept under close supervision.

'I don't think it's safe for the children to continue their placement here,' I told the manager. 'It might be better if the children stay with their foster carers tomorrow until I secure another placement for them.' This was another piece of work I didn't need. As we drove towards the office I began to make notes. It was important that I accurately recorded the sequence of events, as the matter would have to be brought to the attention of the courts. We had only driven about a mile when Katie gasped. 'What?' I asked looking over at her carefully.

'I've just looked in the rear view mirror,' she said slowly. 'That client is following us.' I turned around. It was true. His car was right behind ours, he was following us. He was driving so close I could see his bald spot. Where was the button that says in case of emergency, break glass? Scream. Bleed to death? It was after five o clock. Katie and I had to return the car to the office and then go to the nearest car park to collect our own cars and then drive home. If he followed us to the office, he could easily follow one of us home.

'You'd better phone Tom and tell him what's happened,' said Katie.

I phoned Tom and explained the situation. 'If you come back to the office we can get the police to escort you to the car park, or you can just take the car you have home,' he said. But that was the point; the man knew which car we were driving. We would only be making it easy for him if we followed this advice.

'Look, I'll try and lose him,' said Katie stepping into police detective mode. She took off down a side street, and started to weave in and out of different streets. The car followed us for a while but she eventually lost it.

'Not so fast,' I pleaded. You should never drive faster than your Guardian Angel can fly.

'It's okay,' I said to Tom as I continued to update him on what was happening. 'Katie has saved the day. She's managed to lose the tail we had. But I'm going to phone the foster care agency and make sure they tell the foster carers to be careful. They could just as easily follow their car home, and find out where they live.'

'Good idea. Give me a ring when you come back to the office and don't worry,' reassured Tom. I phoned the foster care agency, but as it was after five o'clock the office was closed and the answer machine came on. I made a note of the emergency number which was provided and dialled it. There was no answer. I left a message asking someone to call me immediately and explained briefly what my concerns were.

'Jesus, that was a close one,' I said. 'I'm shaking. Honestly, Katie, I don't know how you've kept your calm in all of this. I couldn't live with myself if that man got his hands on those children.'

'Has he done anything like this before?' Katie asked.

'I don't know if he can add kidnapping to his repertoire,' I said. 'It's bad enough that he fiddled with his own daughter who was only a baby.'

'And the mother was going to snatch the kids and let him have contact with them?' she asked incredulously.

'No, you've got it all wrong, Katie. She's a perfect mother who's always right. She reminds me of someone we both know with an attitude like that.'

'I know, I could just see Lacey stuck in the middle of a scene like that. Only she'd be begging the paedophile to bugger her instead of the child.'

'Oh, God, that's disgusting.' Katie gagged.

'I know, but it's probably the truth.'

'That client is just a stupid skanky bitch,' said Katie. 'She'd be better off going home and having a good wash.'

'I think she needs more than washing, she needs a good steep. And him, the bloody pervy bastard, the cheek of him going with her to take the kids. And he swore blind in court this morning that he wouldn't have contact with her again, that his children were too important to him.'

'Did he start to cry again?' she asked laughing. Katie had dealt with this man before too.

'Oh, of course he did, it was tears and snot all over the place. He has put the waterworks on too much around me; I just tell him that I can't talk to him when he's in that state.'

'Bloody scroats, they make me…' said Katie. A voice interrupted her.

'You have come to the end of the message bank,' it said mechanically.

'Shit,' said Katie 'the bloody mobile is still on. We've been talking about clients and now we've fucking recorded it.' I reached for the mobile phone and pulled it out of its holder making sure it was now turned off. I was stunned. We looked at each other in horror.

'Christ we'll lose our jobs now. We'll be bloody deported.'

'Well, at least that will save us the plane journey.' We started to laugh, but it was more hysterical laughter than anything else. 'Do you think they'll tell Tom?' I asked.

'They'll fucking tell the big bosses,' Katie protested.

'Oh, Christ, I'll be homeless and jobless.' I was saying it through my tears. The mobile phone rang in my hand and I nearly jumped out of my skin. It was one of the workers from the foster care agency. I immediately launched into numerous apologies. I tried to explain that we were only debriefing when we were talking about the clients. The worker listened silently.

'You know, Louise,' she said, 'I didn't listen to what you left on the end of the message I was only concerned with the bit that affected the carers.'

'So will you please delete the message? Will you promise you won't send it to the suits?' She laughed.

'No, don't worry,' she said. 'I'll delete it. I promise no one will hear it, except me, because now I'm so intrigued to hear what you had to say.' Phew! That was a relief. I updated her on events and offered a caution to the foster carers.

'Don't worry, I'll tell them to phone the police if they see anything suspicious,' she said. 'I really appreciate you letting us know about your concerns.'

'Well, where we come from we all work together. It's called multi agency working. We all have the children's interests at heart. And we really appreciate you not squealing on us, you will be top of our Christmas card list.' The worker laughed.

'No worries,' she said. 'I'll catch up with you tomorrow.'

We returned to the office. None of the line managers had waited behind. 'Bloody typical,' said Katie as I returned the car keys and the office mobile phone.

'I know, we could be dead and buried for all they care about us in this place.'

'They promised us all sorts of support but I don't see it here do you?' she asked.'

'No,' I agreed grimly as I looked around the deserted office. 'Once they got us here they didn't give a damn anymore, their job was done.'

At least Katie and I had a way out. Most of the other recruits had come to New South Wales intending to work for two years there in order to acquire citizenship, and then they planned to move elsewhere. But they had found out that while they were qualified social workers they were not eligible to join the Australian Association of Social Workers without an academic degree. There had been a meeting about this issue with representatives from the AASW. Katie and I were the only ones who weren't aware of the meeting. Like two bad fairies, we hadn't been invited. But ironically we were two of the very few people who were eligible to join.

'Do you think it would be any better elsewhere?' Katie asked as we walked towards the car park to retrieve our cars. I was looking furtively over my shoulder; I still expected to see the client lurking around somewhere, ready to pounce.

'I don't know,' I sighed. 'I thought we were coming over to teach the Aussies how to do proper social work, but the minute you step out of line and try and suggest anything which will improve your practice they jump on you.' I know we've both been giving out because they don't have pre-birth case conferences. Even though some of these mothers have had their other children removed. Is that not the stupidest thing you have ever heard?' I asked. Katie agreed.

'Imagine just letting some scroat out of hospital with a new baby, and just waiting around for a report to come in about them. By then it could be too bloody late. I hadn't realised we would be working with such high risk cases, and that we would be left on our own.'

'I know I can't remember the last time I had supervision. I don't think Tom even knows which cases I have now.'

'Well I'm going to book a time for supervision before I go back home. I'm not taking the chance of having everything blowing up when I'm away.'

Katie intended to return home for three weeks. I dreaded her going. Not only would I miss a good friend, but she was a hard worker. She didn't mind putting in the extra hours required. While the other staff ran for the 4.51pm express at the end of the day Katie and I were still out in the field. I knew that I would probably have to complete visits on my own when she wasn't here. They weren't permitted, but it was the only way I could manage to do the work required.

CHAPTER 23

I met Katie in the car park next morning and we walked to the office together. 'Geoff was raging I was late again,' she confided.

'I'm not surprised. It must feel as if we never leave this bloody place.'

'You're right. By the time the weekend comes round you are too knackered to do anything. I can just about cope with one drink on a Friday after work. If I had any more I'd be lying snoring in the corner. We have no life.'

'I know it's like that time I was mugged,' I said, 'and the mugger demanded my money or my life. I had to tell him, sorry, mister, I'm a social worker, so I have no money and no life. Did you sleep all right last night after all our adventures?' Katie had huge dark rings under her eyes, and I was becoming really worried about her.

'No, it's becoming a real problem,' she confided. 'I just lie there at night thinking of all that I have to do in work, and panicking that I won't get it all finished in time. And then in the middle of it if something blows up on one of your cases you are back to square one, trying to play catch up. It's just exhausting. Maybe I'll feel differently about it when I go home,' she said hopefully. 'I might feel more positive about this place when I've had a bit of a break from it.' I knew what she meant, but I didn't want to achieve immortality through my work; I wanted to achieve immortality through not dying. I was just working here till a good fast-food job opened up.

We entered the office. Tom approached us. 'Oh, look, it's Cagney and Lacey,' he smiled.

'Feck off,' I said jovially. 'Neither of us wants to be Lacey. We're good girls we are.'

Tom laughed. 'Did you enjoy your adventures last night?' he asked.

The rest of the team gathered round to hear what had occurred. I updated him on everything that had happened and eventually settled down to try and record all the events. This was the most time-consuming part of this job. We would all be stuck in front of computer screens for hours at a time, chained by the administrative duties we had to perform, which impacted on the time we had available to actually do direct work with families. We were personal assistants, glorified typists instead of social workers. We weren't even allowed to use that title as it might offend the other workers who didn't have a social work qualification. Christ, at home they wouldn't have been able to get through the door if they didn't have their social work qualification. Here you could have a degree in ethno-musicality and you would still be snapped up.

Lacey phoned while I was still trying to record the details of the evening before. 'Have you and James had sex yet?'

'Oh, for God's sake, Lacey. I'm up to my eyes here. I've to be in court this afternoon and I haven't even finished this affidavit. I told you before not to ask me that. I don't think that's any of your business.' I sighed. 'And there's no point asking me because you know I won't discuss it with you.'

'Well, don't worry,' she mocked. 'James tells me everything.' Everything? Does he indeed? What was she trying to say? Was he leaving me and telling her all sorts of intimate details about our relationship? Were they comparing notes? He couldn't be. I knew I hadn't known him for very long, but I trusted James. I couldn't believe that he would do anything like that. She was just being malicious.

'I know that you are going to Joseph's house tonight,' she said snidely. 'Well, you know, there's something wrong with him, he never liked me. He's just a thug. As for his dad, just you watch, he'll spend the entire time looking down the front of your dress and his mother is no better, she thinks she is something, she thinks she is so high and mighty but she's not. They never liked me,' she spat, 'they were always so horrible to me. Just you watch out. They will be the same with you.'

'Sorry, Lacey, I can't talk about it now. I'm too busy,' I said firmly and put the phone down. I was devastated. How did she know that I was going to Joseph's house? Had James really told her? What about James's family? Were they as difficult as she had suggested? My own marriage had ended due to the constant interference of my mother-in-law. She had always told her son he could be what he wanted to be, so he became an asshole. I couldn't cope with going through the same thing again. And how was I to know the truth? It wasn't the type of question I could ask James. Can you imagine sitting down with a cup of coffee and saying, excuse me, James, but are your family a right shower of bastards?

I tried to ignore everything that Lacey had told me about them. After all, I had given her a chance in the beginning, so why shouldn't I do the same with these people.

I made a special effort with my appearance that evening and I was wearing a lovely red and white sun dress with red patent leather shoes. When James collected me from my house he looked at me appreciatively.

'You look gorgeous,' he said as he hugged me. I smiled and got into the front seat of the car. Ashley was sitting in the back seat. He hadn't made an effort as usual, he was minging. I wouldn't get a chance to speak to James properly without big ears listening in. I would have to try and speak to him alone later. I was determined to ask him just what he had told Lacey about me.

Joseph met me at the front door; he immediately gave me a hug and was very welcoming. I felt relaxed in his company; the ogres that Lacey had conjured up didn't materialise. I met Joseph's wife, Carmella, who was a glamorous Italian. She was so welcoming that I felt immediately at home there. She brought me to meet her son Brendan; this was the moment I had dreaded. Please God, I prayed don't let him be another monster. God must have been listening. I was taken aback. Brendan was stunning. He was tall, with the face of an angel; you could brush the floor with his eyelashes, they were so long. He had the most beautiful manners and sunny nature to match his good looks. He hugged me warmly and all through the evening he made a determined effort to make sure I was comfortable and he constantly checked that I had a drink. Now why couldn't James's sons be like this? I looked over; Ashley sat at the far end of the table, guzzling everything in sight. He had deliberately not spoken to anyone who had addressed him; he was too interested in stuffing his face. I looked at him as he gorged himself and then turned again to Brendan who was now serving drinks and food to guests and being sociable and pleasant. What was more he was spotless; you could have eaten your dinner on his shirt. Chalk and cheese, the pair of them.

I was introduced to friends of the family. At one stage James brought his father over to meet me. He was a charming man. Henry talked about his Irish background. He was interesting and had a wonderful sense of humour and I felt instantly at ease with him. James had to leave the party as Ashley had demanded a hamburger because he was hungry. Was greed not a sin? Henry talked easily to me, and I felt comfortable in his company. I was enjoying myself. A short while later I was introduced to James's mother. She was not the monster that Lacey had portrayed. She was glamorous and warm and funny.

'I hope you don't mind,' Susan said, 'but I really wanted to meet the woman who has put a smile on my son's face.' I was touched, what a lovely thing to say.

She left to speak to the other guests but later came back. 'I could listen to your accent for ages,' she confided as she sat down beside me. We talked openly. She was clearly well read and well travelled and she thought the world of both her sons. I fervently hoped that I would see more of James's family again; I had never felt so welcomed in all my life. Thank God I hadn't listened to Lacey who had tried to dissuade me from meeting them. Susan invited me to Christmas lunch with the family but I had to decline as I had already arranged to work on that day.

'We'll do come on Boxing Day, we would be delighted to see you,' she said holding my hand warmly.' I enthusiastically agreed.

James brought me back to my apartment. 'Have you got a minute?' I asked.

'Sure,' he replied. 'I'll just be a minute,' he told Ashley who had started to undo his seat belt to get out of the car. I looked at James in horror. 'Just stay there a minute,' he said firmly to Ashley and closed the car door. Ashley was fuming; he wouldn't be able to report back to his mother about what we had talked about.

'Is anything wrong?' James asked me when we went inside 'Didn't you have a good time?' He looked anxious.

'I had a lovely time,' I reassured him, 'that's not it. I need to know how Lacey knew that I was going with you to Joseph's house tonight.'

'Ashley told her,' James replied quickly. 'Joseph thought it might be good for him to spend a bit of time with his cousin Brendan.' Well, that was a waste of time; he had ignored everyone including Brendan. He was only interested in shovelling food into his face or becoming engrossed in other people's conversations.

'So you didn't tell her then?'

'No, it's none of her business what we do,' he said, sounding surprised.

'James, I need to ask you this, it's really important.' I hesitated for a moment but finally blurted out, 'She says that you tell her everything.' James stiffened. The colour rose in his cheeks and moved down towards his neck, disappearing under his shirt. He was livid.

'I can assure you,' he said steadily 'that I don't tell her anything about us even though she's always asking. If she has said that I do, then she's a bloody liar. What we have is special, Louise. I don't want that contaminated by her. She has nothing to contribute to us.' I was comforted. He pulled me close to him and kissed me.

'Please, Louise, don't let her try and come between us. She's not worth it.' I believed him. I trusted him. I didn't know what Lacey hoped to achieve with her interference, but I was not having any more of it. James was right. What we had was special and I didn't want her to pollute it.

'Look, why don't we spend some time together at the weekend,' James suggested. 'Would you like to go out to dinner?'

'On one condition,' I replied softly. James looked at me curiously. 'I want you to leave the five foot contraceptive at home.'

James smiled. 'That will be easy,' he said hugging me tightly and kissing me again before he left.

But Lacey didn't give up. She was relentless. If she wasn't phoning me at home or at work she was trying to reach me by email. She sent them on a daily basis but she was lucky if she got a one sentence answer in return. I just couldn't keep up with her. The latest one made me suspect that she was delusional.

'I wanna be invited for Christmas at James's folks with my kids and my partner,' she wrote. 'I wanna have a Christmas party at my house and invite them and James's family and my in-laws and you. Can you see that happening? We can all be just one big happy family. I think we can build a community of great people and extend it to include lots of friends and extended family, and help community and family groups and write papers on it. Maybe I will do my PhD on it and show that it will lower drug use, crime and suicide. I want to be able to work towards making this world a better place.'

In-laws? She was going to find some man and get married within a fortnight? As for the doctorate, she had been to university for the last thirty years and she hadn't even achieved a qualification yet. I ignored it.

Lacey phoned my work daily. No matter how many times I told her I was busy, she still persisted. Any other person would have taken the hint that I didn't want her in my life. I knew she probably believed that once I had met James I had dumped her, but what she wouldn't see was that I only really got to know her properly then and that was when I had realised she was not the kind of friend I wanted. I felt sorry for her, she didn't seem to have any other friends, but maybe there was a reason for that. Lacey and I didn't have a reciprocal relationship. I was just an audience for her. All she wanted to talk about was herself. I wasn't her therapist, though frankly that was what she needed, psychological help. I started to distance myself more and more from her. It wasn't just because I preferred James's company; she was a liability.

James was with the boys, and I was looking forward to a quiet weekend. I was sitting in the garden having a cup of coffee when Lacey called round unexpectedly. She seemed to be under the influence of something and she had been drinking. I could smell it as soon as I opened the door to her. She helped herself to a beer from the fridge and we went out to sit in the garden, where I had been reading. She seemed a bit agitated.

'I don't know if James is good enough for you,' she stated boldly. 'I mean, he's all right now, but you'll see, he will just start irking you too and you won't want to be with him either.'

'What's brought all this on, Lacey?' I asked, my heart racing. What the hell was she on about now?

'I've been thinking maybe we should all move to Ireland and I could get a job. The kids would love that. There's nothing in this place, it really sucks. I've always wanted to see what Ireland was like. So how about it, sister girl?' Christ, the woman was a bigger nutcase than I had previously thought. I wouldn't introduce her to anyone I knew at home, I would feel too ashamed. And my family would think I had lost the run of myself if I had anything to do with someone like her.

'Well, Lacey, to tell the truth I've only just got here and I don't want to be moving back just yet,' I said gently.

'But you and I could have such fun over there,' she laughed. 'And you could introduce me to all your friends. We could travel around. I've seen photographs and it looks gorgeous. We would be real happy together, and it would be better than this place, don't y'all think?'

Her eyes were glazed, she was speaking rapidly. I'd never seen her acting quite so frantically before. 'But what about the boys? Wouldn't they miss their dad?' I hoped to distract her.

'Well, they could stay with him if they wanna. I'm just so sick of this place. It's not what I thought it would be.' Jesus, she and Colleen should start a support group; they both had the same lament.

'But what about James?' I said trying to be the voice of reason. 'I'd really miss him, you know, Lacey.'

'Huh, you will soon get sick of him. He's a weak and dysfunctional man.' she sputtered.

'What? Lacey, that's a terrible thing to say and I don't think it's fair at all.'

'Oh just you wait,' she said threateningly, 'you'll find out for yourself and as for that family of his, they are all mad.'

'What do you mean? I think they are wonderful people.' I bristled. I wasn't going to have her attack James or his family.

'Look,' she simpered, 'I'm sure if you moved back to Ireland you would meet someone else, someone better for you. Maybe I could meet someone else there too.' She was speaking faster than a speeding ticket. 'This place really sucks. You know that guy Malcolm I met on RSVP? Well, he emailed me and said he was gonna call and I waited and waited and he didn't. I think he's gonna go away next week to be with his grandchildren, but I thought he might come down and see me, or I could go up there. I mean, it's only eight hours' drive to Melbourne and it wouldn't cost me nothin' if I went to stay with him. This place sucks,' she repeated. She started to pace up and down the back porch and went back into the kitchen to get another beer. I was uncomfortable. She was behaving strangely. When she returned she hovered around me like a fly.

'So you're not going to go to Ireland then?' she demanded.

'No,' I said firmly.

'Well, I suppose James could come too then,' she relented. 'He could get a job there. Yeah, that might be better, and then he could take the kids if we wanted to travel around.'

'I'll not be moving to Ireland anytime soon, and I'm not sure if James would even want to go there.'

'Sure he'll just go wherever you want. He's so into you, you know. I think he really loves you. I've never seen him like this before.' She sat down and began drinking her beer.

'I'm sick of Ian,' she finally blurted out. 'I don't know what he wants. I think he only wants me for a friend. You know, he comes round for dinner and I think he might just be coming over when he hasn't got his kids. He talks about his ex-wife all the time, and I think he's still hung up on her. We haven't had sex yet, and he says he's not into anal sex. But see, he's building this big house and it has four bedrooms and a rumpus room. I haven't seen it yet but it sounds really great and I think that it would be good for my kids to have somewhere nice like that to live, but I don't know if that's what he wants. I can't figure out what to do. Should I just hang on till he moves in and then we'll move in together? Or do I just tell him that we're gonna be just friends?'

'You probably need to talk to him about this one, Lacey,' I replied coldly. 'Ask him what he wants from you or where he thinks things are going.'

'Oh, I have asked him,' she sighed. 'He says he just wants to be friends with me. But what's the point of seeing him then?' I was becoming exasperated. I was sick to death of hearing this lament.

'Lacey, have you never just had a friend where you could just enjoy each other's company?' I questioned.

'Yeah, I had this friend one time,' she explained. 'He was called Brad but he was gay and he wouldn't have sex with me no matter how much I begged him.' She got up from her chair and started to pace up and down the porch again. She seemed really agitated.

'I don't know what to do about Shirley,' she said eventually, coming back to sit down again. At last, for once she was going to be honest and admit that there was a problem here.

'Why, what's wrong?' I asked sympathetically.

'Well, see, I went to see this counsellor once and I told her all about Shirley. The counsellor said she thought he was oppositional but I don't know about that.'

'Well he does seem to like arguing with people,' I conceded.

'Yeah, I know that, but I was like that when I was a kid and they tried to say I was mentally unwell for years. You know, my mom tried to have me committed to this institution once but I think Shirley's just like me and he'll grow out of it too. Gee he's just so impulsive he doesn't think about things. I think that very soon he's gonna be easily led into using drugs. You know how easy it is to get them round here, and then he's gonna end up in the local kiddie jail. You know, I've been thinking about it,' she said deliberately. 'You'd better be real careful in case he tries to steal all your stuff and sells it to buy drugs.'

'But he's never been in this house Lacey.' I was affronted.

'Oh, he could soon get the key off his dad. I know you've given him one. Shirley could soon find it if he wanted to. He's real smart about things like that.'

'So you're telling me that he might rob me?' I was horrified. I knew his behaviour was deplorable, but I hadn't known anything like this.

'Well, I guess he could, you just need to be real careful when he's around.' If his defiant behaviour hadn't concerned me already this confession from his mother really alarmed me. She was basically saying that her son was a sociopath.

When Lacey eventually left, I spent a lot of time reflecting on what she had said. Usually Lacey's confessions involved herself; this was the first time that she had extended her repertoire to involve her son. I hadn't realised that she harboured such deep-rooted negative feelings towards him. Surely this would be damaging to his self-esteem? While I felt sorry for the child I was determined that he would never set foot over my door. But was that enough? I had given James a house key. He had used it once to wait in the house while I was at work when my bed was being delivered. Was he careful with it?

Was there any point in continuing a relationship with James when Shirley would always be part of his life? I realised that I might have become involved in something which was too big for me to handle. I was already feeling out of my depth. I was to learn quickly just how deep in the mire I was caught.

CHAPTER 24

James called for me at the apartment as we had planned to go out for dinner and a movie. 'While you're here, James, I need to ask you if you told Lacey that I'd given you a key,' I said gently.

'Yes, I did,' he said calmly.

'Why did you tell her that?' I pouted.

'Well, she called at my house last week and she wanted a cup of coffee but I told her that I was going over to your house as you were getting that bed delivered. Why, did I do something wrong?' he asked cautiously.

'No, James, of course not. It's just she has been saying that you tell her everything. It makes me feel really uncomfortable. I wondered how she knew about the key. She made it sound as if you tell her everything off your own bat.'

'I don't, Louise. I've already told you, I tell her as little as possible, and certainly nothing about us.'

'You know,' I confided, 'I've been thinking about things and I feel a bit like a child of divorced parents stuck in the middle of the pair of you, and I've been wondering if it's all worth it. Honestly, I worry that if I spend more time with you she's going to get annoyed. I think if there's any chance of you two reconciling you should just get on with it. I'm only going to complicate the whole thing.'

'Reconcile? With her?' James looked appalled. 'Louise, if she was the last woman on the planet I wouldn't go near her. She caused me too much grief when I was married to her, I would never go there again.'

'Well, to tell you the truth, James, I've begun to have doubts about us,' I said sadly.

'Is it because you don't think I love you enough?' he asked. I could see the pain on his face. I knew this was killing him.

'No, God, no, the worst part of it is it's not even you. You're practically perfect,' I explained. 'It's just Lacey and the children, especially Shirley. Lacey told me all this stuff about him at the weekend, and because of that I'm afraid that

I can't continue a relationship with you any more.' James looked devastated but spoke calmly. 'What exactly did she say?' he asked.

'You'd better sit down,' I informed him. I repeated what Lacey had told me about Shirley and told him my concern that he was likely to steal from me. 'I'm not judging the wee boy here, James,' I insisted, 'but if his own mother tells me that, what else can I do? I don't ever want to get to the stage of moving in with you, when I'm so afraid that it will happen. I know how endemic drugs are in this place, and if his mother thinks he's going to be a junkie, then it must be true.'

'I can't believe she said that about Shirley.' James was disgusted. 'That's the most dysfunctional thing she has ever said. But I can tell you now that he won't be stealing from you or anyone else.'

'But how can you know this? You know, if she had said it about Ashley I would have just laughed at her, but with Shirley it might just come true. He's a strange child, and I think he needs help. She usually ignores his behaviour; at least this time she had the grace to admit that there is a problem.'

'So you want to end this relationship because of my child?' he asked stiffly. I could see that he was wounded.

'It's not because of your child, it's her as well. I just feel like I'm suffocating here. I can't get any space from her at all, and when she tells me that you tell her everything I feel like you are both comparing notes, that I can't trust either of you. I mean, how did she know that I got on well with your family?'

'Ashley told her. Sure he was there too.' The big girl's blouse, he was always sneaking round corners and carrying tales, the big Ginny Ann. Any other normal self-respecting teenager would be out with his mates, not indulging in gossip.

'She has asked, though,' James continued. 'She comes over for coffee all the time now. I don't know what's going on. If I saw her half a dozen times in the four years since we moved here it would probably be the height of it, and now she never seems to be off my doorstep. I've had to tell her that I don't have time to talk. As soon as I see her I just grab the car keys and tell her I'm just on my way out.'

'Maybe she does want to reconcile with you, and maybe you owe it to the boys to try and make a go of things with her,' I said dejectedly. James baulked.

'I won't do that,' he said adamantly. 'If we break up, it won't be because I have any intention of returning to her. That's final. But I don't want to lose you over some stupid remark that she made. Have you thought that she might just be trying to put you off being with me?'

'What do you mean?' I shifted uncomfortably.

'Well, she might think that it was the only way to break us up. You know, Shirley said the other day that I had taken away his mother's only friend. He didn't think that up himself, she told him that. She might be trying to get you back in her life as a friend. It's probably more important to her than us being together.' I hadn't thought of that.

'She keeps on asking me if we have had sex. I swear, James, I don't want her to know anything about our relationship at all. God knows what she's doing with the information she's fishing for, but knowing how selfish Lacey is, it can't be for anybody's best interests, only her own.'

'Look, just give us a chance,' he pleaded. 'Once she realizes that we are going to get on with our lives without her she will back off and leave us alone. As for Shirley, I wouldn't tolerate the behaviour she does; in my house he has to treat people with respect.'

James was very convincing, and I knew that my feelings for him had grown significantly. I loved being with him; he brought sunshine into every day. We would face this together, that's what partners were for. Even though we had only started our relationship I suspected we would be together forever. He loved me, and I loved him, it was as simple as that.

Even though I never returned her calls and wouldn't answer the phone when I saw her number show up, Lacey was persistent. She phoned one evening and immediately launched into her latest woe.

'I really need to get another job, 'cos I wanna leave that waitressing job. They really take advantage of me there, making me do all the work, while all the cuties get to do table work and get all the tips. There's no money in it and I've only had sex with one guy who had dinner there. It really sucks for meeting guys.'

'Oh,' I said. Clearly no other response was required. I could have left the phone down and gone about my business and she would still keep talking.

'I have an interview at the kiddie jail next week; maybe I'll get some work there.' Oh yes, I remembered her talking about that place. That's where she said Shirley was going to end up for criminal behaviour. That would be handy. At least she would get to see him every day.

'I gotta go and hang out with the boys now. Talk to you soon.'

'So how did the interview go?' I asked her politely the following week when she phoned.

'Gee, it went really well, they really liked me. I could make some real changes there. It's mostly weekend work, but James can look after the boys. And I might be able to do some nights as well, you get more money for that. Some of those boys there just need a bit of discipline.' This from a woman who couldn't manage her own children?

'So what type of questions did they ask you?' I asked trying to feign interest.

'Well, they asked me stuff about the children's laws, but I don't know nothing about that. Then they asked what I would do if some of the boys got into conflict and got into a fight.'

'Oh, that seems like a sensible question. What did you say?'

'Gee, I told them that I would just hose them down.' Em, yes, I can see that working, and would you not think that might be considered some type of child abuse? It was clearly time to stop and let the air out of her brain.

Thankfully this was one job she didn't get. If she had been offered the job after that interview I would have left the country immediately in disgust. But she continued to apply for other posts. She phoned to tell me she had an interview in a hostel for homeless men. She was quite excited. She called me later that evening to tell me all about the interview.

'Well, they were really nice and easy to talk to, and I just told them all about my herpes.'

'Christ, Lacey,' I said as I tried to wipe my face after spilling half my coffee down my chin. 'Why did you need to say that?'

'Well, I thought that the men were probably feeling a bit left out, you know, like people didn't wanna go near them. So I thought it would help them see that I was feeling a bit like that too, and I could understand what place they were in.'

'How did they react to that information?' I asked incredulously.

'Well they were probably glad that I told them. I mean, now they know that I can feel sorry for the men who live there.'

At least she didn't start talking about sex; surely she wouldn't start to do that around vulnerable men? But who could tell what this woman would come out with next. We had nothing in common other than a shared gender. I would have avoided someone like her like the plague at home, but in this country I was too easy to find.

'And when will you hear about the outcome?' I asked politely. To be truthful I didn't give a damn. Any agency that employed her deserved all they got.

200

'They said they will phone me tomorrow. You know, that place could do with a good spruce up. It would take someone like me to make the place a bit more homely. The waiting room is a bit grotty, and it could do with some new curtains. I was thinking I could get some material and run up some cushion covers as well, make the place a bit brighter. I'm sure they would let me paint the reception. It's just so dark and horrible. Hey, maybe I could get some of the men to help me, yeah that would be like a project for them, they would get something out of it too. They will be so glad when I start there, I can make such a good difference… And there's this big kitchen, and I could bake brownies for them for afternoon tea, and I could maybe teach some of the men to cook as well. They probably eat junk food all the time, no wonder they look like they have malnutrition. Most people don't know enough about nutrition, and the importance of good food. And, you know, there's a piece of ground outside which would make a great garden and it would help the clients to do something useful.'

'Maybe they aren't into homes and gardens,' I said when I managed to get a word in edgeways.

'Well, I could soon persuade them,' she said determinedly. I bet she could.

The following day she phoned me again. 'Hey, woman, guess what? I got the job.'

'Really?' I tried to hide the surprise in my voice. 'That's great Lacey. When do you start?'

'Well, they said they would need to talk to me about boundaries and stuff first. It's probably about not letting the men take advantage of me or something?' Yes, right, Lacey, you wouldn't be thinking that maybe it has something to do with inappropriate self-disclosure perhaps?

'You know a lot of those guys probably haven't seen a real woman in a long time. God knows what I'm going to do to them,' she giggled uproariously. 'Well, anyway,' she said when she had composed herself, 'they said that I can start next week.'

'That's great,' I said wondering what kind of an agency would accept someone who had such obvious difficulties with personal disclosure. I knew that she liked to shock people, but I could see that the biggest part of her really didn't care how other people reacted to what she said. She wasn't sensitive enough to see that people sometimes reeled from her confessions, which were all so sordid and distasteful.

Later, when I was at work, Laura told me that Lacey had bumped into her in the shops and asked her to go to a movie with her and some of her colleagues from her new job. Laura begged me to join them. 'I don't really think I should,' I said, 'it's just getting so confusing with me going out with James now.'

'Oh, please,' implored Laura. 'Lacey kind of bullied me into going to see this movie and I don't want to go out with her on my own.' I considered it. I was older and probably more streetwise than Laura, so if I was shocked by what Lacey said, then poor Laura would be worse. I reluctantly agreed to go and Laura made all the arrangements.

A few days later Lacey entered the office floor where I was working and walked over to speak to Margaret who always saw the good in everyone. The fact that she was a nun didn't have anything to do with that either.

'So how are you doing at your course?' I heard Margaret ask her.

'I'm doing real well,' replied Lacey.

'So have you come to see your practice teacher?' asked Margaret.

'No, I'm meeting Laura and Louise; we're going to the movies. Louise is sleeping with the enemy you know.' Margaret let out a loud laugh. I was on the telephone; I hoped that the psychologist I was speaking to hadn't overheard that remark. Had the woman no bloody boundaries? I ended the telephone call as quickly as I could, determined to get her out of the building before she caused any more embarrassment, both to her and myself.

As we were leaving the office she said loudly, 'You know, I'm so over him, I don't care how many blow jobs she gives him.'

'Shhh,' said Sheila harshly, trying to communicate with someone on the phone. I approached her and began to apologise profusely but Sheila shook her head, and returned to her telephone conversation. Lacey had embarrassed me yet again. This was the last time I would ever be seen in public with that woman.

We met up with Lacey's manager, Gerard, from the hostel where she had been recently employed. He looked normal enough. Lacey introduced me to him as the woman who stole her husband. I was horrified, and quick to point out the truth. Lacey laughed. Both Gerard and I looked deeply uncomfortable. He probably deserved all he got; if she couldn't behave herself on an interview did he really expect anything better at a social occasion?

Lacey flirted outrageously with him, but it was clear to everyone that the man wasn't interested. He kept trying to include Laura and me in the conversation and worked hard to stop Lacey from monopolizing everything.

His girlfriend, Isobel, joined him, but still Lacey continued to flirt with Gerard. Isobel looked as if she was ready to strangle her, but it was clear Lacey was no threat. Isobel was twenty years younger, and she had a waist. After a drink we went to the movies. At least she had to be quiet during the screening of the film.

Afterwards Lacey said that she wanted to go for a drink with Gerard and Isobel. There was no way I was going to observe that. I was not that starved for entertainment. Laura and I made our excuses and left, well, actually we ran away, at high speed. We giggled together the whole way home about Lacey's obvious flirting and Gerard's continued attempts to ignore her.

'I will have to apologise to Sheila in work on Monday,' I confided to Laura 'All that talk about oral sex was totally inappropriate, especially when people were on the phone and trying to work.'

'It's not your fault, she should be the one who apologizes,' replied Laura firmly.

'I know, but she doesn't ever think she's done anything wrong.' I was beginning to realise that she interpreted things the way she wanted to, instead of looking at the reality of the situation.

CHAPTER 25

Lacey phoned me in great excitement. 'You'll never guess what happened but I met this really really cute guy.'

'Oh, where?' I asked curiously. Was this another experiment on the Internet herpes dating site?

'At work. He's just gorgeous, he has the cutest butt I have ever seen and he's only about thirty but I get the feeling he really likes me.'

'That's great, Lacey, I'm really pleased for you,' I said tightly, 'but does work not frown on workplace romance.'

'No, that's the good thing, he doesn't work here.'

'No, so what does he do then?' I asked casually.

'Do? I don't know, he's sort of like a client.' Sweet Jesus give me strength. What next?

'Let me get this right? He's a client and you met him through your work and you fancy him and you want to have a relationship with him?'

'Mmm, yes I guess so,' she agreed.

'But is that not ethically wrong? Jesus, Lacey, you really need to construct some boundaries for yourself.' I knew I sounded like some tight arsed old biddy, but this was serious. God knows who the woman was getting mixed up with now. 'So he stays at the hostel?' I asked.

'Well not really.'

'What do you mean?' This was really confusing me. It was like twenty questions. What was he – animal, vegetable or mineral?

'Well, he lives in a tent in the grounds of this place, so I don't really think he's like a resident, you know. He comes in sometimes for something to eat, or to get a shower and stuff, but he's not like all the other ones here. He's just so cute and he has the most amazing brown eyes. You know I always wanted to have a kid with brown eyes?' She sighed pensively. Sweet Jesus, she had now selected the father of her new child.

'Lacey, hold on a minute,' I rushed on 'You can't be serious about having a relationship with some client-type person. What if there's something wrong with him. Is that hostel not for men who are homeless? I'm not trying to judge the poor fella, whoever he is, but having a relationship with a worker mightn't be a good idea for him either. What if he is some type of an axe wielding murderer?'

'Well, he didn't actually kill anyone,' she said deliberately.

'What?????'

'Well, I read his file,' she exhaled loudly. 'Gee, this stuff is so interesting. The stuff you learn about people, it's just so much better than RSVP. You know, people don't always tell you the truth on the net.' Dear God, the crazy woman was using her position to secure a potential date. She continued 'They tell you all sorts of things and then you meet them and you find out that it was all lies. This is different, the reports are from psychiatrists and social workers and stuff, so like they have to tell the truth, it's, like, their job.' She paused to draw breath 'I've been reading a couple of files this morning in the office, and it's all fascinating reading about their history, what happened to them before they even got here. You know it might just make you feel sorry for some of them the way they have been treated. And Brian's story is really sad, you know, I just want to go out and hug him and tell him it's going to be all right, and anyway,' she said huffily, 'he's single.'

'Lacey.' I struggled to compose myself and not scream down the phone 'Get it into your head right now; this is not some kind of dating agency. Don't tell me you only went to work there because you might meet men?' Was there no end to the woman's desperation? She was silent. Clearly I had hit the nail on the head. Dear God, no, don't tell me she was hoping to take advantage of some poor guy who was down on his luck. She was supposed to be helping people there, not making further complications for them.

'Well,' she continued huffily. 'It's all right for you, you've met James, but I haven't had a proper relationship with anybody since Wayne, and you have to explore every avenue. You don't know what it's like to be on your own. And the boys need a stepfather; it would be so much easier to bring them up if I had someone else to share my life with.'

'Yes, I can appreciate that Lacey,' I said in exasperation. 'But a client? Have you no standards at all?' I could hear her rustling papers in the background, reading the poor man's life story, exposed for her titillation.

'I'm not dumb,' she said snippily 'I'm not going to date someone bad.'

'But you said he didn't kill anyone like you were making some kind of recommendation for him.'

'I told you, he didn't kill anyone… he just kinda hit her.' Domestic violence then? Very classy yet again, Lacey.

'So you would consider associating with a man who obviously has major issues with self control and who thinks it's all right to hit women. Jesus, Lacey, have they not taught you anything at all on that social work course you're on? Did you not learn about the damage violence does to families when you were on placement?'

'Oh you're such a worry wort,' she snorted in derision. 'He didn't exactly hit her, he tried to hit her. There's a big difference,' she stated matter-of-factly. 'It says here that he found her sleeping with someone else. And it's only natural to get angry, but I always told my boys if Wayne cheated on me, I wouldn't care, I would still love him. But I guess he didn't love her as much as I loved Wayne.' She sighed. 'But maybe she wasn't right for him; maybe he hasn't met someone to love properly, someone like me. I could be so good to him,' she gushed. 'I could cook for him and clean for him, and, like I say, he's got such a cute butt, I bet he would be into just everything.' She giggled.

'There is the small matter of some man raising his hand to a woman, Lacey,' I said slowly and deliberately. 'You can't tell me that that is a selection criterion for a potential boyfriend.'

'Well, he didn't, like, batter her or anything like that,' she retorted. 'He just em… tried to hit her… em, with an axe.'

'What?' I nearly passed out on the floor.

'Well, like it says, he told the police that he found her sleeping with some guy and it turns out it's his best friend, so you can't really blame him for that, can you? He must have been so embarrassed and hurt; he probably didn't even know what he was doing, the poor guy.'

'Yes, actually I can,' I said in disgust. 'Have you even thought for one minute about where this is going? Next thing you know you'll be saying you've invited him over for dinner to meet your boys.'

'Hmm, well, I guess you won't be coming then?' she said finally.

'Lacey!!! Tell me the truth, you didn't ask him to go to your house for dinner, did you?'

206

'Well, he looks like he could do with some nourishing food and like I said, he's so cute, you should see the way he looks at me,' she simpered.

'Sizing up his next victim maybe?' Christ, this woman wasn't going to take no for an answer.

'No, he's not like that,' she insisted.

'But he is, he's done it before, Lacey.' I pleaded. 'And you can't say he doesn't live at the hostel because technically he lives in a tent in the back garden.'

'But there's nothing wrong with that,' she said indignantly. 'I lived in a tent in James's garden when I didn't have anywhere else to live.' I nearly dropped the phone. In a moment of total clarity I realised that the woman was mad. Really and truly mental, stark staring radio rental. I had heard enough. I just couldn't listen to this anymore, it was too damaging for me. There was no point trying to reason with someone who was deranged. I put the phone down. I wondered for the first time if her madness would ever damage me.

She phoned me the following week at work; I was up to my eyes and didn't even want to talk to her. But I knew she would continue to phone until I did. 'I just wanted to let you know that I didn't get it on with Brian,' she said churlishly.

'I'm relieved to hear that,' I granted. 'I'm glad you came to your senses, it would only have led to tears.'

'Well, it's only 'cos he went away,' she said huffily. 'I mean, I was only getting to know him, and he was helping me out in the garden and stuff. I don't know if he will be back.'

'Where has he gone?' I enquired.

'Oh, they came and took him to some psychiatric unit 'cos he had an episode.'

'Episode?' I sighed. Wait for it.

'Well, I wasn't here. It happened last night, and one of the other guys is in hospital,' she whispered conspiratorially into the phone.

'Lacey, have you ever thought you might have dodged a bullet there?'

'Humph,' she retorted. 'I really liked him, and I think he would be a good guy with the right woman but if I'd gotten with him you would have just told James on me, wouldn't you?' she said spitefully.

'I think I would probably have gone a bit further than that,' I said truthfully. Clearly this was not the time to talk to her about the instability which accompanied mental health.

'Well they'll just give him shock treatment and then he'll be back again. I could make a welcome home package for him, you know, for when he gets out, or I could go and visit him. You know, I don't think he has any family round here at all, poor baby.'

I put the phone down. There was clearly no arguing with her. The way she disclosed all this personal stuff, it felt like she had vomited all over me. She just wanted an audience, and I didn't want to go to the show.

I had already started to screen my calls and never phoned her of my own volition. I knew the time was coming when I needed to say to her, openly and honestly, that I didn't want anything more to do with her. I suspected this might make it difficult for James and me; she would have the opportunity to try and poison the boys against us, or more particularly against me. But if I had to choose between her or James, then James would win hands down.

CHAPTER 26

Katie and I were having a cup of coffee together. It was only ten o'clock in the morning but already I felt as if I had completed an entire day's work. Laura joined us.

'You look really worried,' she said. 'Is that woman still stalking you?' Laura shared a pod with me. She knew that Lacey phoned me constantly at work. 'Louise has got a girlfriend,' chanted Laura. I glared at her, it wasn't bloody funny. I was never interested in batting for the other side. I'd never seen the point of going to bed with someone who had the same bits as yourself.

'Yes,' I agreed. 'I haven't received my full quota of ten phone calls to the office today from her.' I spent more time on her, trying to get rid of her than I did with clients.

'I'm not flattered that I've all this social work experience and qualifications behind me when they let something like that in here,' Katie said. 'In fact, I'm becoming a bit embarrassed having to tell people where I work.' I knew exactly what she meant. Some of the staff were hopeless. Like one woman, Linda, who was mercifully free of the ravages of intelligence. She was always off work either on sick leave or carer's leave. She had the whiniest voice I had ever heard. 'Why do I have to do it?' she would whinge constantly. I was tempted to ask her if she would like some cheese and crackers to go with that whine. She was one step up from an x-ray. Honestly she was like a bunch of bones with the person scraped off.

'I've passed bigger than that,' laughed Katie.

'I know, so how many times do I have to flush before she goes away?' I asked. Linda never ate but she was always away from her desk on a break.

'How many children does she have?' I asked Laura expecting her to answer that it was at least twelve.

'She only has one child.'

'Well the child must be sick all the time as she's never here.'

'I'm not surprised,' confided Laura in a whisper. 'I've heard from different staff that her house is disgusting. One of them had to pull a pair of knickers from her shoe which got stuck when she walked in through the front door. Apparently there are soiled clothes and old food lying everywhere. Someone should make a report on her.'

Well, no wonder she and Lacey had got on so well. They both had the same hygiene standards. Linda couldn't be bothered cleaning her house and when she was here she found ways to try and pass her work on to other people. She had tried that trick with both Katie and me when we had first started, but we weren't having any of it, and told her so. I wasn't saying she was lazy, but she should try out for Australian Idle. She was about as useful as a windshield wiper on a goat's ass.

Despite this, Linda had been promoted to the post of senior practitioner, which was a bit of a joke in itself. No one knew how many cases senior practitioners held. They were supposed to hold complex cases, but as far as I could see, her caseload hadn't been increased or altered since her promotion. If anything arose which might make her feel in the least bit stressed, she just took sick leave.

Due to the fact she always seemed to be on sick leave or carer's leave, Laura, Katie and I had started to note in our diaries the days she was actually there because we were the one's who had to try and pick up the pieces. Even Tom strained to manage the caseloads he had been left with as well as his managerial responsibilities. The complex cases were the most difficult, and were supposed to be passed on to senior practitioners but it never happened. I had to work with people who were hostile to intervention. I was verbally assaulted and threatened on a regular basis, but there was no support offered. I felt devalued, that I wasn't worth anything. Even a word of sympathy or an acknowledgement of our difficult working conditions might have helped in conveying to us that what we did mattered. But it never happened.

'Is Lacey not going out with anyone at the minute?' asked Laura casually.

'No, who the hell would take her?' I put my cup down and looked at her inquisitively 'Why? Do you know someone that might be interested? Please Laura, I beg you, get some man to take her off my hands. I'll give you money, I'll do your work, anything, just please take her away.'

Laura laughed. 'Well, I was just thinking there's this guy I know. I'm not interested in him, he's too old for me, but he might be Lacey's type.'

'Who is it?'

210

'It's Pete,' she confided. Pete worked in a different department I had met him once and thought he might be Lacey's type. He had a pulse. Laura agreed to talk to him about Lacey. When we returned to the office she rang him and talked to him for a short while then put the phone down as she chortled. 'He thought that it was you I was setting him up with, and he got all excited, Louise.'

'Me? No, please, I hope you told him that I was taken,' I insisted.

'I did, he was very disappointed, it seems you must have made a great impression on him when he met you.' I think I just said hello and smiled, it was hardly a riveting introduction. 'Well, I've talked to him about Lacey,' she continued 'and he's willing to give it a go.'

'Really?' Was this going to be my ticket out of this mess? Please God, let them hit it off; let him deal with her from now on.

'Yes, he says to give him her phone number and he will give her a ring. Do you think she will agree to it?'

'Well, if she's considering dating clients she'll take anyone,' said Katie sharply.

'You're kidding?' said Laura aghast. 'Clients? It's worse than I thought.'

'I'll just ring her now; if she talks to him today she'll maybe leave me alone.' I turned round to dial her number when the phone rang. Of course it was Lacey.

'Oh hello, Lacey,' I smiled. 'I was just going to phone you. I have a bit of news for you.'

'Oh, what is it?' she asked curiously. She probably thought I was going to spill the beans on my relationship with James. She hadn't a chance in hell.

'Well, there's this guy at work, he's really lovely and he's on his own and is really interested in going out with a lovely woman so I thought of you.' Katie stood beside me making faces. I put my hand over the receiver so I wouldn't burst out laughing.

'Oh, what's he like?'

'Well, he's about six foot tall and he has brown hair, and brown eyes. He's a fine handsome man.' Laura sniggered beside me and I nearly lost it again. 'He's fifty,' I continued, 'and he has a good job and a nice car and a lovely house. The only thing missing in his life is someone special like you.' I tried to stop the giggles which were rising up inside me.

'Gee really?' She became excited. 'What's his name?'

211

'His name is Pete. I don't know if you met him when you were on your placement, but he made a good impression on everyone else.' For all the wrong reasons. He couldn't tell what any woman in the place looked like because his eyes never travelled above their cleavage.

'Gee that would be great; you know there aren't enough nice guys in this place. It might be good to get on with someone like that. What's his house like?'

'I don't know myself but it's in a nice area. I think he's been divorced about the same time as you so you will have loads to talk about.'

'Does he earn more money than James?' she asked nosily. The mercenary bitch, she always had to get things down to the lowest common denominator, especially if it came to cash.

'I think he probably does.'

'Good,' she said firmly. 'Does he have kids?'

'Kids?' I didn't know. I looked at Laura who nodded and held up her fingers to indicate that he had two. She made a waving signal. 'He does, but they're grown up. God love him, he would probably love a ready-made family like you and your boys. He seems real sporty and active. Maybe he could take the boys to football or rugby or something. I can just see you, Lacey, standing on the side lines cheering them all on.' Katie clamped her hand over her mouth and tried to stifle a giggle.

'Well, I was a soccer coach in America,' she said proudly.

'Well, there you go; maybe on some level I knew that you two would be perfect together. I'm not usually wrong about these things. So is it OK if I give your number to him?'

'Yeah, that would be great.' She was hooked.

'Good, I'll catch up with you later, bye now.' I put the phone down. Laura and Katie were practically rolling on the floor laughing.

'You are one bad bitch,' said Katie, 'feeding that poor woman all that stuff. She's probably running off now to look for wedding dresses.'

'I know, I wish I could say I feel bad, but I don't. I'll do whatever it takes to get that woman out of my life. Did you not notice she was so excited she forgot to tell me why she was calling?'

'She was probably just giving you the daily instalment of life according to Lacey. Maybe she will have something a bit more interesting to talk about now.' I gave Laura Lacey's phone number and she passed it on to Pete. He agreed he would phone her that day. We didn't have long to wait.

'Hi, Lacey,' I said as I answered the phone. I had seen her number show up on the caller display. Laura and Katie were trying to sort out papers for filing. They both dropped what they were doing and rushed over to my desk. I put my finger to my lips to motion them to be quiet and then I turned on the loudspeaker button on the phone. '…so he said he liked that too, and he's gonna take me out for dinner tomorrow night.'

'That's great, Lacey,' I said.

'Yeah,' she continued 'he seems like a nice regular guy.'

'I'm sure he is and you know it will be good for you to get out. You do far too much for those boys; you need something in life that is just for you,' I said ingratiatingly.

'You're right, you know, I'm always running after them and with my school work and my job I'm kept really busy.'

'You are just marvellous,' I said and turned round to see Katie trying to gag Laura who was struggling not to laugh. 'Sure you can let me know how you get on. Talk to you later.' I put the phone down.

'You couldn't bloody make it up, could you?' asked Laura. 'You were being a sarcastic bitch to her and she thought you were being all compassionate and caring.'

'You catch more flies with honey than you do with vinegar,' I said. We went back to work, but every time one of them looked at me I sniggered and went into a fit of giggles. I was practically hysterical with happiness; at last the number one problem in my life would be gone.

A couple of days later Lacey phoned me at home but I saw her number and ignored it. She knew that James would be with me and I wanted to spend time alone with him. She eventually tracked me down at work. She was dying to tell me all about her date.

'Pete took me out for dinner and then afterwards we went back to his place. Then we had sex,' she burbled. 'Gee, his house is lovely. It would be perfect for the boys and me. He has a rumpus room downstairs which the kids used to hang out. He has a cleaner too, who comes in to help him. But I told him he didn't need one any more 'cos I was a brilliant cleaner.' Jesus, I'd never seen any evidence of that in her own house. 'Then we had sex again. He said he gave the best oral sex in the world but I didn't think he was that good,' she said reluctantly. 'You should have heard him groaning, baby, I'm going to blow, I'm going to blow. I didn't know what that meant. But he's so like me, he's just into everything. Don't you just love anal sex?'

'Lacey, please don't tell me any more, that's your private businesses,' I said scandalized.

'It's OK,' she said.

'No, really, Lacey,' I insisted, 'I don't want to know about it.'

'Why not? Just because you don't tell me nuthin' about you and James doesn't mean I can't talk about me and Pete.'

'Lacey,' I said as firmly as I could. 'You might like to talk about it, but not everyone likes to listen.'

'Anyway,' she continued as if I hadn't spoken. 'I think Pete really likes me 'cos he phoned me the next evening when I was at home and he said, 'Guess what I've got in my hand?' And you know what it was?' She screeched. Let me guess. 'It was his dick and he started to masturbate while talking to me over the phone. Then he said that he wanted to come over so we could have sex in the garage. And, I mean, I really wanted to but the boys were in the house. He must think I'm so hot, he just couldn't wait. You know,' she gushed 'it reminds me of when Wayne was here. We used to have sex in the garage all the time 'cos the boys wouldn't let us do it in my room when they were on the computer.'

Dear God she wasn't really saying that she had tried to have sex in front of the children. I didn't want to hear any more of her sordid tales and her squalid life. I felt distinctly uncomfortable, and as for Pete, I had to face this man at work. All I could visualise was him screaming, give it to me baby, let me hold those puppies. I tried a different tactic. 'Lacey, I have to work with Pete. I'm sure he wouldn't be too pleased to know that you are telling me all this.'

'Why not? People are gonna know we're, like, together as a couple anyway if I get pregnant.'

'Lacey,' I asked as calmly as I could, though my heart was racing. 'You did use a condom, didn't you?'

'No, I don't believe in contraception,' she said resolutely. 'All those hormones. You should read what they do to people.' I was stunned. I didn't know where to start. My mind was reeling with all the possibilities which could arise. How do you start to explain to a woman in her fifties that she might have caught HIV or God knows what else? What was the bloody point? She had already caught herpes, she should have had enough common sense to protect herself but she chose not to. She didn't seem to have made any protest, she was only thinking about herself as usual. It was all instant gratification and sod the consequences.

214

And pregnancy? At her age? Was that possible? This was getting worse. A child would have no quality of life in that house. Can you just imagine what it would be like growing up with those two dysfunctional boys as brothers? The thought was unbearable. She had been on just one date with this man, but she had obviously decided that he would be next in line to provide the Lacey Bones's meal ticket for another eighteen years. What kind of man put himself in this position? He didn't seem to be too worried about boundaries either if he was going to have sex while her sons were in the house. Did he have no respect for himself?

I didn't want to hear any more. I felt physically sick. I realised that this time Lacey had crossed the line. I had to reluctantly admit that I had colluded with her on some level; I had listened while she relayed all her experiences. She never regulated them in her own mind first. She never gave any thought to the devastating impact this information had on me. She was too busy churning it out. She was an emotional vampire. She literally sucked the life force out of me.

The truth was she didn't care. She gloried in it. It was all Lacey and there was no room for anyone or anything else. She expected me to be her conscience but I had my own conscience to live with, and this time I had heard more than enough.

'Look Lacey,' I said, 'I really don't want to hear any more. I have to go now. I'm sorry, goodbye.' I put down the phone. I wondered why I had put up with Lacey for so long. I think at some level I had believed that she had some power over James and I didn't want that relationship to be destroyed. It was the most important relationship I had ever had. But while neither of us had invited Lacey into our lives she still continued to pursue me relentlessly. She seemed to be obsessed with me and with my life with James. Has she said this? Has she done that? She would ask him. But my relationship with James was completely different from the one he had shared with her. For a start I loved him. She had always protested that she didn't. James had told me that he felt more love from me in months than he had ever experienced with her in a twelve-year marriage. But I didn't want this to be a competition with James as the first prize. I just wanted to get on with my life with him without her interference. I just wanted her to leave me alone.

CHAPTER 27

I realised the screw-up fairy had visited me again when I received a letter from the immigration department asking me to complete a form to allow my stuff to go through quarantine. They needed to know if there was any food or drugs in my shipment and if I needed to pay tax on anything that was new.

I phoned Maryann but her line was engaged. The office telephone bill must have trebled since she joined the Children's Bureau. I knew that Colleen was training so I sent them both an email telling them the good news that the shipment was due to arrive in Sydney soon but that I needed details of what was in their couple of boxes in order to complete the form. Colleen replied and compiled a list of things which she had sent over. I looked at the list; she couldn't possibly have crammed all that into two boxes, could she?

But Maryann was a bit vague. 'Is there anything there that shouldn't be?' I asked her, realizing for the first time that I had trusted this woman whom I hardly knew. Hadn't living with her proved that? She could be a major drugs baron trying to import kilos of the stuff. The fantasy immediately started to play out in my mind of being hauled off to jail and imprisoned because quarantine had discovered a major haul of her drugs. But I was the one who would be convicted. And I was too far away for my family and friends to even visit.

'Look, you'd better tell me what is in those boxes; it can't be hard to remember sure there was only a couple, wasn't there? Wasn't there?' I asked as she avoided my gaze and looked a bit shamefaced.

'Right then, I'll just have to contact my sister and see what exactly you sent over.' Maryann stormed off huffily.

I rang my sister Maria who told me that she was surprised at the volume of stuff that Maryann had brought to my house. 'Did you know that she came back again with more boxes of stuff later on?' asked Maria.

'No, no, I didn't.'

'Well, she said that you told her it was all right. I'm sorry I didn't check with you, but she told me she had come to some financial arrangement with you.'

'But she said she only had a couple of boxes,' I argued feebly.

'Well as far as I can remember, I think there were about eleven of hers and about eight belonging to that other girl.' Nineteen boxes? When I thought of all the stuff I had given away or discarded in order to reduce the cost of removal I nearly fell over. They had both lied to me. And of course I hadn't been there to stop them. Did they think I wouldn't ever find out? Did they think that nineteen boxes would not be noticed among my furniture and personal belongings?

'But don't worry,' said Maria, 'the shipping company gave me a quote for your stuff before they brought their stuff over, so all you have to do is add theirs to it.'

'Oh good,' I said relieved. 'OK, send me it and I'll also contact the shipping company to confirm it so they don't think I'm trying to cheat them or make anything out of it.' While I was concerned about the high volume of goods which Maryann and Colleen had submitted I was reassured by the verbal agreement we had made that they would pay for the relocation of their items when they arrived in Australia.

I contacted the shipping company and asked them to send a quote for eight small boxes for Maryann and four for Colleen. I deliberately asked for a quote for a smaller number of boxes, just in case the boxes might be very small. I wanted to prove that I was not seeking to financially benefit from the agreement we had made. The shipping company duly obliged and they advised me that including taxes and shipping the cost would be eight thousand dollars. I was shocked. I hadn't received the bill from the shipping company yet for my own stuff as it still had to include fees at immigration. I began to fear that if I couldn't pay this amount I wouldn't be able to retrieve my own stuff. I knew that we had all been awarded the same relocation allowance, but as mine had been used for the flight, the apartment and the hire of a car, there wasn't much left to use for relocation.

I filled in the forms for the immigration department as well as I could, even though Maryann still hadn't told me what was in hers. For the first time since I had met her she had been really stuck for words. I spoke to Kylie, the relocation manager, about my predicament; she agreed that Maryann and Colleen both had an obligation to pay towards the shipment of their stuff and that they should be asked to contribute to it. I forwarded each of them a copy of the quote I had received from the shipping company. They wouldn't be getting their stuff until they paid what they owed. But I had to pay the full amount before my own stuff could be released. Thankfully I had finally sold my house so I could use the proceeds from the sale to pay for my stuff.

Maryann immediately replied and said she didn't have the money to give me. Yes, because her allowance had been used to buy furniture and a new car when she came to Australia. Colleen emailed me and said that she was prepared to offer me $100 but that she hadn't wanted the stuff to be sent over in the first place, and that I had forced her to send it. Jesus, no one could force that woman to do anything she didn't want to do.

Maryann approached my desk as I was trying to compile a report for an imminent meeting. 'I want to talk about my boxes,' she shrieked. I saw she had set aside this special time to humiliate herself in public.

'Look, I don't have time for this, I'm busy,' I protested. I had no intention of discussing my personal business in front of my colleagues. Who did she think I was, Lacey? She stormed off but I immediately received an email from her saying that she wanted to know the date when the stuff would arrive so she could arrange to pick it up. I replied that she would only get her stuff when she had paid what she owed me.

She bombarded me with countless emails demanding to know when the stuff would arrive, all of which I ignored. I had made it plain enough to the pair of them what they needed to do. I was not trying to cheat them; I only wanted what was fair.

The next email from Maryann informed me that she was prepared to pay me $100 for the return of her boxes. She wrote that this was all she could afford to give me at this time and that she had already given me her car which was worth a thousand pounds. A thousand pounds? She had to be bloody joking. She had placed an advert for the sale of her car in the local papers at home offering it to anyone for one hundred pounds but no one would buy it. She had then offered it to me in lieu of rent. Given that she owed me at least ten times that amount and had made no effort to repay it, I was grateful for anything she offered. I had contacted my brother and asked if he wanted the car for my niece who had just passed her driving test. My brother had said he would make sure the car was safe to drive on the road before he let my niece anywhere near it. He arranged to collect the car, and later phoned me to say that it was useless. He said that the suspension had gone completely on the driver's side; the seat was practically sitting on the floor. Hardly surprising with the weight of Maryann. The brakes didn't work and everything that could go wrong with a car had already happened. In the end it had cost him a hundred pounds to get the thing towed away. I had told Maryann all this.

Maryann contacted me again by email. *I know that your stuff is arriving at your house next Thursday* she wrote, *so I will call there about 7pm to collect my things. If you don't want to see me that's OK, you can just leave the stuff outside and I can pick it up myself.*

How on earth did she know that? I went round to speak to Kylie who said that Maryann had told her that she had found out the date when the stuff was being delivered because she had called the shipping company herself. I walked off, but not before I saw Colleen slinking around. She had the hots for Kylie's secretary, Greg, who was already going out with a nice girl from the department. It was evident to everyone in the entire building that the feeling wasn't reciprocated, but not a girl to give up without a fight, Colleen hovered around outside Kylie's office all day in the hopes that she would bump into him. She was the laughing stock of the office.

I emailed the shipping company to complain about the lack of confidentiality and said that I was very unhappy that they had given out information to another person. John from the shipping company rang me immediately. He explained that a woman had called claiming to be my sister and that she had asked when it was being delivered.

'But my sister doesn't live in Australia,' I insisted.

'Well, she had an Irish accent, and she sounded just like you,' he protested. It must have been Colleen! 'I'm sorry, but I thought it was one of your family calling. We wouldn't have told her otherwise.' I acknowledged that John couldn't be faulted; he hadn't known that Colleen would be so underhand and sneaky. That was it; I decided the pair of them could get stuffed.

Maryann wouldn't give in so easily. She plonked herself in front of my desk and demanded that I talk to her about my boxes. I was sick of it. I marched into Tom's office. I was going to deal with this once and for all.

'Look, Tom, I said, 'I don't want to sound like some whingeing bastard, but I need you to get that bitch Maryann off my back. It's interfering with my work.' He nodded and left to speak to the operations manager. Later that day I got an email inviting me to attend for mediation that seemed to be the Children's Bureau response to everything.

I met up with Lionel, the mediation officer. I told him all that had happened and he explained the mediation process. He told me that Colleen had refused to participate in mediation but that Maryann was keen. That was because she had more to lose. He asked me if I could attend the following week but I advised him that I was taking a week's leave.

Maryann arrived later that day when I was trying to pack up. She started yapping about her bloody boxes. I was sick of hearing about it. I marched up to the operation manager's office. 'I'm telling Patricia about you,' I stated like a petulant child before marching into her room. The fact that the room was in darkness and I had to clap my hands to trigger the lights didn't deter me. Maryann had moved on by then.

Next morning I received an email from the human resources department which stated that as the mediation service had pulled out if there was any more disruption in regard to personal matters, then disciplinary action would be taken. I was relieved. That should get the bitch off my back for a while.

CHAPTER 28

I drove over to James's house where he had arranged to cook dinner again. He was a fantastic cook and he clearly enjoyed doing so. I was a bit nervous. I knew I would have to broach the subject of Lacey, but I didn't know how to start the conversation. I had already told him that she had been asking all sorts of questions about our relationship but that I wouldn't tell her anything. But this was different. What was I going to say? I couldn't just blurt out, excuse me, James, but do you know that your ex-wife is going behind your back and undermining you at every opportunity?

When I arrived I could see that James seemed a bit anxious too. After dinner, while we were enjoying a glass of wine, he finally opened up.

'I think there's something we need to talk about Louise,' he said.

'Thank God.' I exhaled in relief 'I was so anxious about the whole thing. I didn't know what you would think of me if I said anything negative about Lacey, but it's clear to me she's trying her best to put me off you. I think she wants you back.'

'Lacey?' He looked at me in total surprise.

'Well, isn't that what you wanted to talk to me about?' I asked hesitatingly.

'Well, no, actually I wanted to talk about us, but maybe before we do that you had better tell me what Lacey has been saying.'

'Well, she's been telling me that I'm too good for you, and that you are weak. She said that you would never protect me if anything bad was going to happen to me.'

'Are you joking, Louise? I'd give my life for you,' he said steadfastly.

'Well, she told me one night some psychopath tried to climb into her bedroom and that when she screamed for help you phoned the police but locked your bedroom door and wouldn't come and rescue her.' James looked furious.

'Look, I'll tell you what really happened. There was a time when we were first separated, when Lacey had run off after some man who had let her down. I was living in our house and looking after the boys and I agreed she could stay there for one night. Some guy climbed onto the roof of the house and was trying to get into my house through the window. She was screaming at me that he had a knife, but to tell you the truth I thought it was all a big set up. I actually thought she had set the whole thing up so that I would be killed. She was acting really strangely then, and I didn't trust her at all. I phoned the police like she said, and I went into the room where the boys were sleeping and locked the door so that they wouldn't be harmed.

'So the truth of the matter is that you were trying to protect the children?'

'Yes,' James said. 'The police came and caught the man. He was high as a kite and had taken all sorts of anti-psychotic medication at the time, and he was taken to the nearest mental hospital where he was admitted.'

'I see,' I said slowly, feeling like a complete fool. 'Lacey forgot to tell me the children were in the house at the time. She was trying to make out that you were some kind of frightened weak man who wouldn't come and save her.' James laughed.

'I think it would be fair to say that Lacey can look after herself.' I nodded in agreement.

'What else did she say?' he asked.

'Well,' I continued feeling ever so embarrassed, 'she said that when you split up you cried and cried because you were worried that no one would ever have sex with you again. She said you were pitiful at the time, that you couldn't live without her and that if she asked you to, you would go back to her in a heartbeat.'

'She said that?' James's face was red with fury. 'How dare she say that? Listen Louise,' he said catching hold of my hand, 'I wouldn't take Lacey back if she begged me to, in fact,' he continued, 'after we arrived in Australia I think she realised what she had done, splitting the family up and she finally realized that the sex and the city lifestyle she had envisioned hadn't materialized. She phoned me up, she was in tears. I was living with my parents with the boys, and I had arranged to move into my own house the following week. She told me that she had made the biggest mistake of her life, that she missed us, and the family we had, and she begged and pleaded for me to give her another chance and take her back. I told her in no uncertain terms that she had made her decision before we left America and that she would just have to live with it. There was no way in God's earth that I was going to reconcile with that woman.' 'In fact,' James continued, 'I think I found out more about her in the latter end of our marriage, and when it was over, than I ever knew about her while we were together. If she

222

was the last woman on earth I swear to you, I wouldn't go near her. Every time I think of her all I can do is cringe with embarrassment. I could tell you all this horrible stuff about her but what would it achieve? Let's just say that I was very naive when I met her, she was much older than me, you know, and I trusted her. I learned later on that I had made the biggest mistake of my life and I will have to live with that knowledge every day of my life.'

I was speechless, I looked at James. In all the time I had known him he had always been open and honest with me and I trusted him. I knew by his reaction that he was telling me the truth.

'I love you, Louise,' he said looking into my eyes as he held my hand. 'You have taught me what real love is. I would trust you with my life, and I'm not acting like a naive young man when I say that now. I feel sorry for Lacey; I don't think she can love anyone other than herself. She's the one who has lost out on so much joy and happiness but she will never see that. She destroys anything good that is offered to her, she crushes it and kills it completely. She's now trying to destroy your relationship with me, but I know her from old. One of these days she will turn on you. When she realizes that you have seen through her, that you aren't going to listen to all her stories about me, she will turn against you and believe me, I've seen her when she is vengeful and malicious. She has told so many lies, and caused so much pain to people over the years, but it will all come out.

'What lies?'

'Do you know that she emailed all our friends and told them that I had left her? Every one of them knew the truth, that she had ended our marriage so she could run off with some low life guy who was only twenty. But she couldn't admit it to herself; she had to cast me in the role of the villain. She lost all her friends in Arkansas then. They all emailed me and said I was better off without her. At the time I was so devastated that my marriage had ended that I couldn't see it, but I know now that they were all right. I was better off without her, and I think you will be too.'

'She told me that you might try and drive a wedge between her and me, because you would want to control me,' I admitted reluctantly. James laughed.

'Look, Louise do you think that I'm the kind to be controlling anyone? I'd prefer it if you made your own mind up about Lacey but I get the feeling that your relationship with her has run its course. You are not the same type of people; you have a good and loving heart. You are honest and hardworking and you come from a decent family who care about you. Lacey didn't have any of that. I can't blame her for the way she turned out, her childhood was horrendous. I've seen her when she's with her family and they are all so nasty to each other, but especially to her. But what concerns me the most here is that while she was carrying out a character assassination of me with you, she was coming here and doing the same with you.'

'What?' I was incredulous.

'It's true, Louise, I wanted to talk to you about it, but I thought it would be better that you found out what she was like for yourself. I didn't want to influence you.'

'Found what out, James?'

'You know every time that she spent time with you she left you and went straight to my house.'

'But why, James? Was she comparing notes?' I asked quizzically.

'Well, I don't know what she was up to, but she came round one day when I was just getting ready to meet you for dinner. I knew she had just been to your house. She said, "Be careful, we don't know her very well."'

We? Where was the 'we' in a divorced couple? 'So you usually let your ex-wife pick your new partners do you?' I said snidely.

'Never. It was only because it was you that I agreed to go for dinner that night at all. I didn't want to because I thought she had the chance to poison it if anything developed.'

I was enraged. The two-faced cow, what the hell was she up to? A true friend stabs you in the front. I wondered aloud, 'Do you think she might be jealous that if we are serious I might be spending time with your children, time that is spent away from her time with them?' Didn't she realise that her children were the worst behaved brats I had ever encountered and that if James and I ever got really serious it would be despite the boys and all the problems they had caused and not because of them.

'I can't begin to fathom what she's up to, Louise,' he disclosed.

'Look, it's like this, James, I haven't felt comfortable with Lacey for weeks. Apart from the fact that she tries to embarrass me when we go out in public, I just can't see me having a friendship with her. No offence, but she seems a bit unstable at times and she keeps asking me all these questions about our life together. I think she's trying to live her life vicariously through us. I mean, there are times when she has been kind to me. She knew it was hard for me after all that nonsense with the bitches; I thought at the start that she might turn out to be a decent woman. I tried hard not to judge her at the start. I think naively I thought that all the other people at work were being too hard on her and that she deserved a chance, but I have to admit that they were right and I was wrong.'

'You weren't to know that at the time,' said James pulling me towards him. 'You are a decent woman and you were kind to her, too. But you didn't think that she would do anything like this.'

'It's hard to admit when you have made mistakes about people but since I came to this country my bullshit radar must have stopped working.' It was true, Colleen and Maryann had both turned out to be mercenary, lying bitches and Lacey had turned out to be a two faced cow who had been trying her best to undermine this relationship. What was I? Flypaper for freaks!?

'You have met some decent people too,' James insisted. 'Katie has turned out to be a wonderful friend to you.'

'That's true; the only decent people I have met in the middle of all of this are you and Katie. She's not like them, I know that. She's a decent girl who would go out of her way to help people, not try and take advantage of them and I know you wouldn't either.'

'What are you going to do now?' asked James slowly.

'I think I will just tell Lacey that I don't want to see her anymore. I know she will probably tell me that you have won, that you have manipulated me and made me choose between you two but it's not true. I don't want to waste my time with anyone who is undermining me.'

I knew that I couldn't say what I wanted to say when Lacey phoned me at work. I didn't want everyone listening in to the conversation. I knew, too, that if she phoned me at home she would talk over me like she had done so many times before. The only thing to do was to tell her in person.

I arrived home after work to find James in the back garden cutting my grass. I had resigned myself to writing a report, but I preferred to do it in the comfort of my home than in the office. I spent more time there than I wanted to. If I stayed there any longer the boss would soon be charging me rent.

'Well, this is a surprise.' I smiled at him and he beamed back. 'I thought I would just make life a bit easier for you,' he said. We moved towards each other and kissed and hugged.

'Do you want a drink?' I asked. It was a hot day.

'A cold beer would be lovely but not until I finish this.'

'OK, I'm just going to have a shower. I'll be out shortly.' I turned and walked inside. This was really thoughtful of him to come over and cut the grass I smiled. I had struggled to maintain the lawn, as taking care of the garden was part of the tenancy agreement I had no other choice.

I had just emerged from the shower when I heard James calling me. I opened the bedroom window to see what he wanted. 'There's some woman coming up your path,' he informed me. 'I think it might be Maryann.'

'Tell her to go away, please, James,' I pleaded. I didn't have the energy to deal with her right now. I closed the bedroom door, which was adjacent to the front door and went into the walk-in wardrobe to choose something suitable to wear. James opened the wardrobe door and stuck his head in.

'She says she's here to see you.'

'I told you to tell her I wasn't here,' I hissed.

'Oh, I thought you said let her in.' Was my accent that difficult to understand?

'Don't you let that bitch into my house,' I beseeched.

'Look, come out and talk to her,' said James, clearly perturbed to find that I had reduced myself to some melodramatic teenager who was literally hiding in the closet. 'Be an adult, come out and tell her what she needs to hear.' James obviously didn't know that I avoided conflict whenever possible.

Maybe he was right. I couldn't go around trying to avoid her for my whole life; she was the one who should be ashamed to approach me. I put on a bath robe and went to the door.

'I've come for my boxes,' Maryann shrieked as she stood in the front porch. She threw what looked like a bundled up rag at me. I looked down. It was one of my Egyptian cotton sheets which she had 'borrowed'. I threw it behind the door. The last time I had seen it, it had still had the gift wrap attached. It certainly didn't look like that now. And where were all the other things she had stolen?

'Look, Maryann, it's simple, you pay up what you owe me for all the shipping and taxes and fees for the immigration department and then you can have your boxes.'

'But I don't have that kind of money,' she whined.

'Well, that's funny, neither do I, but you got the same amount as I did which was to be used for relocating all your stuff. You thought you were onto a good one, trying to slip in a whole pile of other stuff. Did you think I wouldn't notice?' I asked snidely.

'Well, I know that the stuff is coming next week so I want to go to Sydney and collect my boxes,' she protested. Her face flushed. Climbing the steps to the house must have exhausted her.

'I think you will find that if you go to the immigration department they will probably ask you for ID and as you haven't been involved in shipping the stuff over they won't give it to you.'

'Well, why don't you come with me?' she wheedled. 'Look, I think it would be good for us both, we can have a lovely chat on the drive there and maybe stop somewhere nice for lunch.'

'You must be bloody joking.' How dare she patronize me. 'I told you even before I found out that you had lied to me. I don't want anything more to do with you.'

'Well, I need my things,' she persisted. 'There's stuff there that I need for my health and sentimental things as well. I know you wouldn't want me to be annoyed because I don't have them,' she said coyly.

'That's where you are wrong, Maryann. I don't care if you never get them. If you and that other one don't pay what the shipping company have informed me is the amount you have to pay, then I will burn the lot of it.'

'But you can't. That's not your stuff, you can't do that,' she screamed at me.

'Watch me. The goods are in my possession, and the immigration department, which is an official department, recognizes that they belong to me, so I can do what I want with them.'

'Look, this has gone far enough,' she bristled, coming closer to me menacingly. 'I want my stuff and I want it by next week.'

'If you even come near this place next week I'll call the police,' I barked. 'Now do yourself a favour, Maryann, and just fuck off.' I closed the door in her face. I was shaking. I didn't know what she hoped to achieve by coming to my house but it was futile. If she wanted her stuff she would have to pay for it. Why should I be forced to pay thousands of pounds for their stuff? It was no good to me. God knows what they had sent over.

Maryann stood outside the door and screamed like a fishwife. 'Louise, Louise, you come out here right now, do you hear me? I want my boxes!' Eventually she skulked up the driveway to her car and drove away.

CHAPTER 29

It was a busy morning, the removal men were at the house unloading all my furniture. James was helping them. The phone rang; it was Lacey. I hadn't spoken to her for a few weeks and to be truthful I liked it that way.

'Can I speak to my husband?' she demanded. Husband?

'I didn't know you had one, Lacey,' I replied immediately. She wasn't going to score points over me.

'I need to speak to James,' she sighed dramatically.

'Oh, James, you mean *my* boyfriend? OK, just a minute and I'll get him,' I said patronisingly. I handed the phone to James.

'It's your ex-wife,' I said loudly, causing the removal men to turn round and stare at me. James spoke to Lacey on the phone for a short while and then returned the phone to me.

'I'm really sorry but I have to go now, Louise,' he explained. 'Lacey has to go to work, so I said the kids could come round to my house.'

'But you told her you would be here all day with me. She already knew that.'

'Yes, she did, but she's been offered work.'

'So you just drop everything and run to her when she calls?' I realised I sounded like a spoiled brat. But I wasn't used to being in the middle of a situation like this, and I didn't like it. I felt like stomping my feet and screaming until I was sick. I didn't want him to have any other demands. If the children needed him that was different, I wouldn't deprive them of their father, but I didn't want to play second fiddle to her whims.

I watched resignedly as James left, he agreed to call round later. If they were halfway normal children I could have asked him to bring them over, but I wasn't in any mood to deal with their dreadful behaviour today.

The removal men struggled on. There seemed to be an awful lot of stuff. All the boxes I had packed at home had been repacked and relabelled. What was going on here? I didn't recognise any of the stuff, apart from my large pieces of furniture. Surely there wasn't as much stuff as this to be brought over. Where did it all come from? Had it been mixed up with someone else's personal belongings?

I was about to go down to the garage to explain my concern to the removal men when I noticed my dinner set. This was more like it. I put my hand in the box to pull out the plates when I unearthed the biggest pair of knickers I had ever seen. Was this a packing material? They were enormous. White cotton long-legged bloomers with elastic, which obviously went round the knee. What the hell was this? They weren't mine. I was right; the removal company must have got my stuff mixed up with someone else's. Christ, I hoped they wouldn't think I wore anything as disgusting at this. Yes, that had to be it. Surely only old ladies would wear this type of thing. I thought of some poor old woman sitting in front of a packing case and being shocked when she unpacked my skimpy knickers. She would be just as shocked as me; the heart attack which would ensue would probably finish her off. I threw the big pants back into the empty box. I would have to check all the boxes to see what else I had been given by mistake.

As I continued to unpack I found other huge garments. Size 30, I read on the label. Gosh I didn't know clothes were made as large as that. I looked at some type of pink top which had a dragonfly appliqué on the front. It would cover a mattress, it was enormous. I recognised the dragonfly motif. Wait a minute, it was pink, it must belong to Maryann. Uuugh! I felt contaminated. Her stuff was all mixed up with my personal belongings. I was going to have to go through every single box and separate them all out. I cringed with embarrassment. The old lady in the nursing home vanished from my mind as I realised that the removal men had probably found them in my house, where Maryann had left them.

The knickers were hers. All the memories which I had tried to suppress for years about Patrick's mother came reeling back. I remembered the humiliation that I faced every time she gave me one of her parcels full of her old soiled clothing. This was no different. I felt violated. I wanted to go into a corner and cry. But I had to be strong; I didn't want to break down in front of the removal men. I would save this for later.

I busied myself sorting through the contents of the box. Imagine transporting a pair of knickers to the other side of the world? I thought Maryann told me that it was only essential items she had sent over, but judging from the size of the things I realised that they were probably essential for her. I unearthed lots of grubby, saggy-balled long-lined bras which could have been used as double hammocks. I'd never seen the like of them in my life before. These were instruments which my granny would have called foundation garments. Good sensible items which looked as if they had been constructed by some shipping builder. The clothes and shoes were either worn or soiled and some of my stuff would have to be destroyed due to cross contamination.

When I plugged in my computer it wouldn't work, there seemed to be some kind of sticky stuff on it. I rang my sister to find out what had happened. She told me that Maryann had brought over a huge box of snacks, drinks and foodstuffs which she wanted to send to Australia but the removal men had disposed of them because they were illegal to transport. She had put this box on top of my box containing my computer. One of the cans of coke had exploded and the liquid had leaked all over the box below. I was disgusted. What kind of a person transported crisps and minerals to the other side of the world. Did she think she was going to die of starvation?

I made coffee for the removal men and continued to unpack the boxes of clothes which they had brought upstairs. It took ages going through every box. It was exciting in parts, like discovering old friends, but unsettling as I continued to find things which obviously didn't belong to me. One box contained several pairs of old flannelette pyjamas which were old and frayed and worn thin. These weren't mine either. I pushed the garments away from me with distaste. I was mortified thinking that people would even consider that I would wear something as skanky as these. They weren't fit to be used as floor cloths. They were too small to fit Maryann's girth so they must be Colleen's.

The rest of Colleen's boxes contained half burned candles, old clothes and a coat which probably once claimed to be white. It was trimmed in some smelly fur fabric. It smelt of damp, sweat and stale cigarette smoke. Please God, don't let the removal men think I would even house something as disgusting as this. I threw it back into the box and kicked the box to the corner of the room. I would get the removal men to carry the box back down to the garage; I didn't want it in the house.

Maryann must have packed every item she had ever owned. There were tatty school jotters, diaries and photographs interspersed with half-used tubes of toothpaste, half-empty packets of sanitary towels and half-empty tins of baby powder. Baby powder? Sure she didn't have a child, what would she want with that? Though wait, I suddenly realised what she probably used it for. To put on her crevices to avoid chaffing because of her excess weight.

I continued sorting through the contents, but the rest of it was absolute junk. Boxes and boxes of tat and rubbish which you wouldn't embarrass a charity shop by donating. At the bottom of one box lay a pile of clothes which Maryann obviously hadn't even bothered to wash before she packed them. The filthy minger, there was no excuse for that, she was absolutely disgusting.

I felt sick with rage. The pair of them had brought boxes and boxes of dirty filthy items to my house, which all had to be repacked. I could just imagine the look of distaste on the removal people's faces; they wouldn't know that the items weren't mine. How dare they do this to me?!

Maryann was renting a house round the corner and I had a good mind to go round there and give her a piece of my mind, but I restrained myself. The next time I saw her I would run her down on the street. Of course I'd have to hire a bus to manage it, but I'd deal with the details later.

I eventually composed myself after a stiff gin and a long hot bath. I needed to decontaminate from anything of theirs that I had touched. As I lay in the bath I conceded that there would be gossip all over the office about the bloody boxes. Maryann and Colleen wouldn't miss a chance to badmouth me. I knew that they would try and force the other recruits to take sides, but those who knew me well enough had all said that they thought that Maryann and Colleen had to take some responsibility for what they had done. After all, we were all provided with the same allowance.

I knew that while Maryann would tell everyone that I was holding her things to ransom she wouldn't be broadcasting the fact that she had managed to get new furniture for her house at home and money for a car here. She had saved thousands of dollars while she was sponging off me too. The woman should be a financial consultant. She certainly knew how to beg, borrow or steal to get what she wanted.

Lacey arrived while I had recommenced the unpacking. I was astonished when I opened the door to find her standing there. 'I just thought I'd call on my way home from work and see how you're doing,' she said as she pushed her way into the apartment.

I had been really busy. My suite of furniture had been placed in the living room and I had added the little lamp tables I had bought from a garage sale. I had placed lamps on them and a few little trinkets and I was really pleased with the effect.

Lacey stared at it open mouthed. 'Gee, I never realised you had so much stuff,' she mumbled.

'Well, there's still more furniture downstairs in the garage. I only took up what I could fit in this house.'

Lacey moved into the kitchen area. I had placed my table and chairs there and they looked fabulous. The view of the mountain was spectacular from that position. I had unpacked some of my storage jars which looked brilliant against the white wood of the kitchen cabinets.

Lacey moved around the house and I followed closely behind her. I had taken the single bed from Maryann's room and put it in the smaller bedroom. I had made it up with crisp white cotton sheets and duvet covers and had covered it with a beautiful gingham blanket which I had made. A small white dressing table sat on an angle to the bed with a little stool underneath. I had arranged some perfume bottles and some little painted boxes on it and it looked really pretty.

In the bedroom which Maryann had previously occupied I had placed my king sized bed. I had feared that it might be too large for this room but it fitted it perfectly. My beech bedside tables sat on either side and I had placed red lamps on each one. I had made the bed up here too and had used my Habitat quilt cover which was checked with red, green and yellow squares. The room looked fantastic.

I was exhausted from all the unpacking and I still hadn't even started on the kitchen utensils, crockery or cutlery and my good le Cruset pots and pans which were still downstairs. But I was going to take my time and ensure everything had a place before I brought another box of items upstairs for unpacking. Lacey's face was a picture of misery. Her mouth was pursed into a grimace.

'I didn't know you had so much stuff,' she repeated.

What did she think? That the old sofas and mismatched furniture that had been donated to me was the way I normally lived? I had always been very particular about my home and while I enjoyed buying different things from garage sales and second-hand stores, the majority of the furniture I had bought was expensive. I bought it to last.

'Where did you get the money from to buy all this stuff?' Lacey asked.

'I worked for it,' I answered in surprise. 'You know at home I had a full-time and a part-time job.'

'But I thought...' What did she think? That I extracted money from some guy through subterfuge and deceit? That I didn't pay my own way in the world? That I used my reproductive facilities to trap some man into a relationship? I wasn't like her. I had morals and values and anything I had in this world was earned through honest hard work.

'Has James seen all this stuff?' she asked snippily. She knew rightly she had dragged him away earlier on.

'He was here when the removal men were unloading some of it, but he hasn't seen it all fixed up like this.'

'Has he stayed overnight yet?' she grilled.

'Lacey,' I said in exasperation, 'I told you before I won't talk about anything like that with you.'

'Well, I tell you everything,' she mocked.

'Lacey,' I laughed. 'You tell everybody everything.' She glared at me.

'So you think that you and James might be serious?' she probed. How was I supposed to answer that one? If I said I thought we were becoming serious and he didn't feel like that, then I could end up making a fool out of myself. If I said that it wasn't serious and he wanted it to become serious, it might seem as if I was just stringing him along, just using him for fun. But James was the one who should be asking me these questions, not his bloody ex wife. Surely he hadn't sent her round to try and discover how I felt. Had he? I had never ever been involved in a relationship where the ex-partner was still actively involved in her ex-husband's life. Once again I was out of my depth. It was becoming increasingly difficult to separate my life with either of them. I had decided a long time ago that Lacey was dangerous, that she had the potential to destroy things between James and me. I was going to finally do something about it now.

'Lacey, I don't want to talk about what goes on between James and me and no matter how many times you ask me I still won't. Some things should be private and I'm not going to say anything about James and I don't want you to say anything to him about me.'

'Whadda mean?' she twanged. She had gone behind my back and said all sorts of horrible things about me to James. Did she think I'd never find out? Did she really believe that he would choose her over a relationship with me and that he wouldn't share what she had said? I tried to calm myself. I didn't want to get worked up into a state. I took a deep breath.

'Whadya mean?' she repeated. She looked guilty.

'Lacey,' I exhaled calmly. 'I know you've been talking to James about me. He tells me everything.' Silence. For the first time since I had known her she didn't have a reply.

'Oh, you can't believe him,' she said weakly.

'Lacey, I'm sorry, but I don't think things are going to work out between us,' I said decisively.

'Whadda mean?'

'I mean that I want to be able to trust you but James has repeated things I have said to you. I don't know what's going on with you or why you felt the need to do that. But I think it's getting too complicated with us. I just don't see how our friendship is going to work.'

'Gee, he's just trying to manipulate and control you. You know, he's just so jealous of me. He just said that so you wouldn't like me and you wouldn't hang out with me anymore.'

'I'm sorry, Lacey, but I believe him. You might not know me very well but he does.' She had the grace to look embarrassed. There I said it. I didn't have to have a whole screaming match. I was getting quite good at this assertiveness business.

'Oh, you'll see, just you wait. You'll find out what he's really like. He tried to do the same with all my friends, just 'cos he wanted to keep me all to himself. You'll see, he'll be just the same with you. I know what he's really like and when you find out you'll be sorry you listened to him. Just you wait, you'll be sorry.' She stood up. 'I gotta go now; I gotta go get the boys.' She turned to leave. I walked her to the door. There was no point in saying anything else.

'See ya,' she said brightly and left.

'Yes, I'll see you around, Lacey,' I said as I closed the door quietly behind her. I heaved a sigh of relief as I leaned against the door. That would be the end of that chapter too.

But why had she called round? Because she was curious about what I had? She probably hadn't bargained for the outcome of this little visit when I had taken the opportunity to tell her I didn't want to see her anymore. Now James and I would be able to get on with our lives together.

But what James had said kept ringing through my head. What if she became vindictive? What if she started to cause real problems between us? Well, James and I were strong enough to face whatever she threw at us. Now that I had all my personal stuff I felt stronger and more determined to make a go of my life here. I hoped that with James beside me we would be able to deal with whatever she threw at us.

CHAPTER 30

I went out to the shopping mall to look for bits and pieces for the house. It was really taking shape and I looked forward to coming home at the end of a busy day to my haven. It was a hot day so I bought some gelato and brought it round to James's house. I knew the boys would be there and I really wanted them to like me. It was easy to win with Ashley; all that was required was food. Every time I came over to James's house I brought Ashley some little treat. He had learned to thank me and I praised him for his good manners.

James was delighted to see me. 'I thought the boys could use something cool in this hot weather,' I said.

'Thanks, that's very thoughtful of you.' He smiled. He called the boys into the kitchen. Shirley reluctantly left the computer. James started to share some gelato out for them into bowls. 'I'm not losing out on any computer time.' He looked at his father disdainfully.

While the boys were eating the treat Shirley talked incessantly. 'Shush, Shirley, give other people a chance to speak,' reprimanded James.

'But I like talking all the time,' he said proudly.

'Yes, I can see that, Shirley,' I replied 'but the purpose of a conversation is that you say something and then you have to be quiet so the other person can have a chance to say something too.'

'That's gay,' he retorted in derision. He was just like his bloody mother. He left the table to return to his computer game. The timer on the cooker rang. Ashley moved quickly toward the bedroom. 'Get off now, it's my turn,' he whined.

'Get out, get out,' screamed Shirley at the top of his lungs kicking the door shut in Ashley's face.

'Dad, Dad, Shirley won't give me a turn on the computer; he's had his turn, Dad, Dad,' Ashley whinged, jumping up and down in agitation. James went into the bedroom and took Shirley out by the arm.

'It's Ashley's turn now, you can go on it later,' he said firmly. Shirley stared angrily at me; he pushed open the kitchen door and slammed the screen door as he stomped outside noisily. I was standing at the kitchen window. I looked round; he walked up to the dog and kicked her hard in the belly. The dog yelped in pain, and putting her head down she slunk off to her kennel. Shirley aimed another kick at her but missed; the dog had managed to escape. Little thug. He glowered up at me defiantly. He had no shame or remorse for what he had done. I couldn't get out of the house fast enough. God only knew what the little horror had planned next.

I arrived home and put my parcels on the kitchen table. The phone rang but when I answered it I heard only silence. 'Hello,' I said idiotically to nothingness. This was the second silent call this week. Was someone trying to get through from overseas? The caller display said private caller. They didn't have the 1471 system that we had at home. I put the phone down silently, but it unnerved me. Was it a client? Maybe that new case I was working on? They had threatened me but my phone number was unlisted. Had they managed to trace it? I'd better talk to Tom about it tomorrow when I went back to work.

I arranged to meet up with James the following week. It was frustrating trying to adhere to his custody schedule. He had the children for two days one week and five the next. It was difficult for him to get away from them for even a quick cup of coffee as Shirley was so demanding.

'You know, it's really strange,' said James when we were sitting outside on the porch 'I haven't seen Lacey for weeks but she's started calling round at the house again.'

'She's just fishing for information,' I said casually as I watched people walking their dogs, and bicycling on the mountain behind us.

'She doesn't seem to be willing to let go of you. She comes round only to find out stuff about you.'

'What sort of stuff does she ask?' I asked curiously.

'She always wants to know where we are going and what we are doing. She's always asking questions about you. She seems obsessed with you. I think she wants to be with you,' he said silently.

'Don't James.' I shuddered. I was beginning to think that myself. 'Do you remember the day that she came over and was rambling about going to Ireland? That wasn't about two friends going, that was more of a partnership thing she wanted. I felt so uncomfortable that day. I didn't want to see her after that. I was really surprised when she called round when my stuff arrived.'

'She probably wanted to see if she could get a glimpse into your life there. So now that you won't give her any information she's been forced to ask me.'

'Yes, but you know, James, we both promised each other that we wouldn't let her interfere in our life together and we really need to stick to that.' I didn't want that whole business starting up again. I felt a real sense of relief that I wasn't immersed in all her filth and dirt.

'I think I'll just tell her that there's no point calling round as I'm not prepared to talk to her about anything to do with us.'

'Well, she probably needs to hear it, James, because hints don't work with her. But you know,' I said slowly, 'I just remembered something you told me ages ago about her turning. Do you think that's what is going to happen now? Do you think that she's going to start hating me as much as she …em, loved me, as it were?'

'She swings from one extreme to the other; I've seen her do it with friends in the past. But most of her friends were just burnt out after spending time with her. I'm not surprised you couldn't sustain it either. That's what Lacey does to people. She then goes to the opposite extreme and starts to resent them for not giving her what she wants.'

'Well, she can't do much to us now, can she?' I said confidently, reaching over to kiss him. I didn't realise that those words spoken innocently enough, would come back to haunt me.

James and I had spent a lovely evening together. We had dinner followed by a movie. James stayed at my house that night. I woke up next morning wrapped in his arms. Next morning he gave me a lift to work. He kissed me before I got out of the car.

'I'll see you about five o clock then, sweetheart,' he said smiling. I was determined that no matter how busy it was today, I was going to stick to that time. I needed to balance the two parts of my life. I was not going to let work take over my life completely. I didn't mind putting in some extra hours when James was with the children. I often did some overtime and I had worked the odd weekend shift when the out of hour's service was short-staffed. But time with James was precious to me, and I didn't want work to encroach on that.

Katie arrived as I was getting out of the car. She came over to speak to James and we walked into the office together.

'You know, I was really worried about you for a while there?' she said.

'Why?' I looked at her in surprise.

'When that bloody nutter was ringing you all the time and calling round to your house you looked like you had the worries of the world on your shoulders. But I've noticed since she's left you alone you seem to be much happier.'

'I feel happier now, Katie. That woman wasn't a friend. I can see that now. In a friendship it should be equal, you talk to each other and you share stuff, but you don't just regurgitate all your past and throw it all over them whether they like it or not.'

'Some of that stuff she told you would have made me sick. I would have told her there and then to just fuck off. You gave her too many chances.' I felt ashamed to admit that Katie was right. Now that I've had time away from her I realise just how horrible it all was. But it was like Stockholm syndrome where the captives identified themselves with their captors. It was like a survival instinct.

'And you and James?' she asked quizzically. 'What's happening there?'

'We're good. He's lovely, Katie,' I beamed. 'Honestly he's too good to me. He spoils me rotten. I've never felt so relaxed with someone in my whole life before. There's passion there too, but we hardly ever fight. We are just so compatible. He's just so easy to love.'

'It's a pity you can't say the same about his fucking kids,' Katie said tightly.

'I know. I could do without them. They are so horrible to each other, it's painful to watch and I've never heard children who are so nasty. But at the minute I only see them in short doses and it's enough for me. But you never know, maybe once she realizes that she isn't going to meet the man of her dreams here, she'll take off with them and then it will be just us, left to get on with our lives without any of them. It would be perfect.'

'But what about her studies? She can't leave before that finishes, can she?'

'As far as I can see, she has been at university for the last thirty years and she hasn't a qualification to her name. She just drops out. She'll probably do the same thing here too. Do you know that she blames James for the fact she doesn't have a degree. She says that he didn't encourage her and that if it wasn't for him she would have a degree by now.'

'I can't see how James wouldn't have encouraged her,' Katie protested. 'He thinks education is so important.'

'Yes, that's why I asked him about it. He said that she had started university when he was still a child at school. He was in ankle socks, for God's sake. I keep forgetting there is such a huge age difference there. But he was raging that she said that. He told me that he used to write up her assignments at night when he came home from work, and after he had finished cooking and cleaning.'

'Why, what was she doing?' Katie inquired.

'Lying in her smelly bed as usual.'

'The lazy bitch. She's probably finding it tough to get some man to impregnate her now so she can get child maintenance and alimony.'

'Well, she might not have that many eggs to fertilize now,' I agreed, 'so the gravy train must be racing past the stop.' We sniggered.

'What have you got lined up for today?' Katie asked me. 'I have to go out to see how Nicholas is getting on. Can you still come with me?'

'Only if you do that other one with me afterwards,' I agreed.

We needed to visit Nicholas who was twelve. His mother was an alcoholic who had undertaken a treatment programme when she was pregnant with Nicholas and had successfully recovered. But she had started to relapse now, arguing that she could manage to drink socially without becoming addicted again.

When Katie and I arrived at the house his mother was not there and Nicholas was alone. I contacted her on her mobile phone; she was in one of the local football clubs. She was paralytic. There was no one else to care for Nicholas so Katie and I placed him in foster care. He was nervous at first; but before we left he acknowledged that he was safe, he didn't have to be the adult any more. He could be what he was, a child. Now all that remained to do was to deal with all the necessary paperwork.

CHAPTER 31

Katie and I were still dealing with initial assessments on top of our own caseload. Although we were supposed to forward these cases to another team for longer intervention, we had both been stuck with them.

Katie's case concerned domestic violence and an alcoholic mother. Katie and I had met with the father. We had been cynical from the start, let's face it, we had heard the same story hundreds of times. 'It wasn't my fault, she drove me to it, there's something wrong with her. She provoked me.' The husband ticked all the boxes for a typical case, with one exception. He was the one who had asked for help. He acknowledged that he had anger management issues; he had been struggling to control his temper which erupted whenever he came home and found his wife passed out drunk on the floor, with the children having to fend for themselves. He recounted that he worked long hours to provide for his family and that she was pouring all the profits of the business down her throat. He agreed to move out of the house, and have no contact with his wife until things could be improved for the children. That would reduce the likelihood of further violence erupting. Katie organised regular contact between the children and their father.

The children were provided with individual therapeutic support. The mother was referred to a women's group who provided assertiveness training and emotional support. She also started to attend an addiction specialist. The father attended a programme of work on anger management. Katie and I had visited on a regular basis and we were going out today to review the case.

The mother had stopped drinking. Already she looked better, her eyes were clear and shining and she looked as if she was enjoying life more than on the previous visits. Katie advised the family that she would continue to be involved for another couple of months, but that she was really impressed with their commitment to change. It was one of the few success stories we had experienced together since we commenced work with the Children's Bureau. We returned to the office feeling more positive than we had done in a long time. We would even be able to finish on time today. I was relieved, as James was collecting me.

At five o'clock James was waiting in the foyer of the office when I emerged from the lift. He bent his head to kiss me. He looked genuinely pleased to see me.

Even if I was late getting out, he didn't complain. He really was one in a million. We went to my favourite noodle house and ordered laksa.

'I just want to get this out of the way now, before we can talk about nicer things, like us,' said James holding my hand. 'Lacey phoned today. She's demanding more maintenance for the children.'

'But you already give her half of your salary. What more does she want? Blood?'

'Seems so,' he sighed.

'You know, James, you've been questioning whether any of the children are actually yours. Maybe you should refuse to give her any more money until she proves they are.'

'She wouldn't agree to that. There's only one way round it. There's an Internet site which sends you the kit and you take a swabs from both you and the child. They conduct tests to see if they match. I've been thinking I really need to do one on Shirley. If it is negative it means that I'm not the father and someone else can take responsibility for him. But if that happens then I'll do one on Ashley too. It costs a fortune, and technically it's not legal but if the result is negative, then I can contact the child support agency and send them the findings. I'm under no onus to pay her maintenance for a child that isn't mine. She would have to complete a test and prove he is mine if she wanted me to continue sending her money.'

I considered what he had told me. 'How would you feel if you discovered Shirley wasn't yours?' I asked quietly.

'To be honest,' he admitted, 'I would feel relieved. His behaviour has deteriorated to the point where I don't enjoy his company any more. He reminds me more and more of the way she behaved, and I'm finding it difficult to see beyond that.'

'If you aren't his father, then who is?' I asked appalled.

'I don't honestly know. I know that before he was conceived we weren't having an intimate relationship. We were living in a housing cooperative at the time, and everyone there absolutely hated her. They used to give me these pitying looks. I thought it was just because I was married to her, but I wonder now if they knew that she was having a relationship with one of the neighbours.' He continued, 'From what I remember, Shirley has the exact same colouring and build that he had. And Lacey was always over there at his house. I think we had sex just once in all the time we lived there. So when she announced that she was pregnant I was delighted. But thinking back now, she wanted to leave there immediately. She didn't want to stay. I wonder now if she was afraid that this man might confront me about the situation and possibly tell me the truth.'

'Ashley would be relieved too. He hates Shirley so much, and that way he would be able to step back, if he found out that Shirley was only his half brother.'

'And Shirley?' I looked at James closely. Shirley might be a spoiled brat, but he was only a wee boy. He wouldn't understand what was happening. Would he? It would be hard for him to come to terms with that.

'I don't think it would bother him as long as he got time on the computer and his routine wasn't affected.'

'I feel really sorry for you, James,' I said compassionately. 'It must be awful to begin to realise that you didn't really know the person you were married to. She seems to have lied to you about so much about herself.' He bowed his head. 'I'm not saying she's a tramp, but her idea of safe sex is to lock the car doors. Did you not realise how promiscuous she was when you met her?'

James looked at me carefully. 'Well, it was bad enough having those doubts when we were living in Western Australia. But when we moved to America I got a real eye opener. People used come up to me all the time and say, you know, we can't believe Lacey has met such a nice man; she had an awful lot of boyfriends, you know. But I didn't realise how chequered it was until we went for counselling.'

'Counselling? What brought that on?'

'She wouldn't have sex with me. She had sex only once the year before Shirley was born and she wouldn't do it afterwards at all. She seemed to have major issues there.' He paled as he recalled what life with Lacey had really been like. 'But she used to go to parties all the time and say I'm going to be the party drunk today. Then she'd tell everyone that she was going to fuck my brains out when she went home. But she never did. She used to go to bed immediately and if I tried to initiate anything she would push me away. I was getting tired of it, especially when she told me that she wanted to sleep with other men.'

'Did counselling help?' I asked tentatively. I didn't want to be an information junkie, and pry into the intimate aspects of their life together. I didn't want to be like her.

'She didn't really engage and only went along to complain about me. The therapist told us that sometimes things we do in our past can influence our future. The therapist then asked her how many sexual partners she had had and she said about eighty.'

'Eighty?' Jesus Christ, I wouldn't even know eighty men.

242

James saw the look of disgust on my face. 'I know, even the therapist was horrified. I remember she said to Lacey, you know, Lacey, it's polite to divide by four.'

'But she couldn't possibly have had sex with eighty people, could she?'

'Actually I think it was more than that. Because I asked her again after the session how many men she had been with and she asked if oral sex counted too? I told her it did and she began to name all these men. Once she got to one hundred and twenty I made her stop counting. Though I knew she probably hadn't covered even the half of them.'

'That's so disgusting.' I was scandalized. 'She's like feckin train tracks; she's been laid across the country. But does that not make you feel used?'

'It was really hard when we went out in America because she would point out men all the time and say things like, I sucked him, I fucked him. She even told me that she had anal sex with some blind guy on the beach.'

'Yes she seems to have a bit of a proclivity for that,' I said tightly. James looked surprised. 'I mean that seems to be her favourite pastime.'

'No, it isn't, she never did that with me. I would have been horrified,' James said confidently.

'But, James, she told me she did it with every single man she had ever been with except you.' His face paled. He looked revolted. 'It's true,' I insisted. Sure she even had unprotected anal sex with that bloke, Pete, that Laura and I fixed her up with, on a first date.'

After dinner James left me at home. 'So do you want to stay over?' I asked him.

'I'd love to,' he said.

'Good,' I smiled, 'I bought you a toothbrush yesterday.'

A few days later James and I arranged to meet for a drink. It was Friday afternoon and I hadn't seen him for a couple of days. 'So what's happening with you?' I asked as I hugged him.

'Just the usual stuff. The boys take over my entire life when they come over. It takes them a couple of days to settle down and not be screaming at each other and fighting. They used to be better, but I think their mother is starting to wind them up a bit.' I looked at him curiously. 'Well, it's clear that you don't want anything more to do with her, so she's taking it out on the boys. I think she hopes that if they cause enough trouble between us then you will just give up and leave me, and,' he looked at me carefully, 'go back to being her friend.'

'And is that what you want?' I asked realising just how much I loved this man, and how I couldn't imagine a life without him.

'No, of course it isn't. I've never loved anyone like I love you. I just think that you deserve better. It's bad enough that you have to deal with all my baggage but you have to deal with Lacey as well.'

'I love you, James, you know I think you are worth it, I don't think that things will get better by themselves. We are open to any help being offered out there.'

CHAPTER 32

In work things were no better. I had heard from a lot of people that when Lizzie one of my team mates, first started in the Children's Bureau she was a lovely warm and friendly woman, but now she was a real hard ticket. Maybe working in this place did that to you. For her empathy meant shouting at her clients and bossing them about to within an inch of their lives. The two worst things about her were her faces. She was a cruel and heartless bitch but I had to admit she was damn good at it.

Sally was one of my colleagues and she was one of the few professionals I had met in the organisation. She was always impeccably dressed and she concentrated completely on her work. But Lizzie hated her. Whenever Sally walked past our pod Lizzie always made some derogatory remark. I didn't think that it was warranted, especially since Sally was clearly working while Lizzie spent most of the day creeping about between all the other pods trying to gather information on people, which she would relay immediately to anyone who would listen. She would never tell a lie if the truth would do more damage. I'm not saying she was a gossip but she had a great sense of rumour.

Lizzie was very friendly with Cheryl and Bianca and she too had started to complain about Tom's management style within hours of me starting the job. She had more faces than the town clock. If anyone in our team went on annual leave and a case subsequently blew up, the rest of us pulled together and tried to manage it as best we could. I knew I had managed quite a few of Lizzie's cases in her absence. But when I was on sick leave after the car accident, she complained to everyone within earshot that she had to do so much of my work and that I was obviously incompetent.

She tried hard to be accepted by the operations manager and would sycophantically simper up to her, constantly trying hard to fulfil a role as her snivelling sidekick. It was apparent to me that people seemed to be promoted in this place, not because of their skills or experience, but because of their relationships with their superiors. I refused to play those games. If I didn't get anywhere on my own merits then I didn't want to.

Tom was off work for a couple of weeks on holiday and things were busy. Sally was acting up as manager. She had been pleasant and efficient the first week she had taken over, and I was impressed with her performance. She called me into the office.

'You'd better sit down I've something important to discuss with you,' she said conspiratorially.

'Oh, right,' Jesus, was this about me? Had I done something wrong? My God, was I going to be sacked. 'What is it?' I asked hesitatingly.

'I've been asked to undertake an investigation,' she said proudly.

'Really? On me?' I was incredulous.

'No,' she shook her head. 'It's about Tom.'

'Tom!' Why would anyone be interested in investigating Tom? 'What about him?' I asked shocked. What on earth was going on here?

'Well, I have been asked to collate some information about his management, and whether any staff have any issues.' I looked at her blankly. 'I don't want to influence you, but do you think he has been supportive to you? Do you get regular supervision? Does he give you proper direction in your cases? That type of thing.' She produced a notepad.

'What has brought this on?' I asked carefully.

'Oh, well,' she flicked her hair over her shoulder. 'It's just that some of us have been complaining about him for ages so this seems like a good idea to really find out what is going on. Go ahead,' she smiled, like some empathetic therapist. 'Tell me what you think.' Her pen was poised. She was ready for my dictation.

'I'll tell you what I think,' I said forcefully. 'I think this is a load of bollocks.' Sally looked horrified. 'What the hell is this Bureau up to now.' I asked, 'waiting until the manager goes off on leave and then going on a fishing expedition to get some information to use against him.'

'But this is serious,' interjected Sally, 'really serious. You know,' she whispered conspiratorially, 'after this, Tom may not be coming back here at all.'

'What are you saying? That he's likely to get fired if we come up with a load of grievances against him? As far as I can see the only problem Tom has is that he's stretched too thin. He's under enough pressure trying to manage this team, and then they go and ask him to spend some of that time on another department as well. If there are any problems, it's because management have set him up to fail. And,' I looked at her in disgust, 'I can't believe that you are letting yourself be used in the middle of this, Sally.'

246

'I didn't have a choice, you know,' she said sternly. 'I didn't do this by myself. My manager put me in this position.'

Her manager? Muriel. I might have known it would be her. There was always one more imbecile than you could count on. The baldy bastard Muriel. She had a visit from the fat fairy and used all her wishes. She was so fat she needed one bathroom scale for each foot. When she went to a restaurant, they didn't give her a menu, they give her an estimate. She also had the personality of a snail on Valium and her sole purpose in life was simply to serve as a warning to others. You know, you can always tell the quality of a person by how they treat people they don't need, and her attitude towards her staff was, save time, see it my way.

'Why am I not surprised to hear that? Do you know that she's been saying all sorts of stuff in public about Tom?' Sally had the grace to look embarrassed.

'Don't tell me you don't know what's going on. I took you for better, Sally, you are just being used, and I tell you what I won't take any part of it. Where I come from people are usually advised first that there has been a complaint made against them. You might find that managers all pull ranks and join together, regardless of whether one of them isn't fit to manage himself, but in this place you have been put in that position. Well, you can just tell whoever set this dirty business up that I'm taking no part of it.' Sally blushed. 'Would you not be better off as an acting manager to find out what is actually going on in this team before you start on the manager. Surely this would be a perfect opportunity to address the fact that Lizzie hates you, and that she stops speaking to anyone in the team who talks to you. And what about that other one, Linda, who is always either on sick leave or carer's leave. What's being done about the fact that she hasn't worked a complete week in all the time I've been here and we've been left to pick up her cases. That amount of work isn't reflected in our caseloads. Why don't you address that type of thing, that's more important that this nonsense?' I left her office.

Katie had just come in from a meeting. I was furious. 'Have you got time for a coffee?' I asked. She looked at me, realising that this was important. I was fit to be tied.

'I'll just grab my bag,' she said. We left the office and walked across the road to a coffee shop which the staff didn't use much. We ordered coffee and sat down.

'They are trying to get rid of Tom,' I finally said.

'No,' gasped Katie. 'The bastards. So they wait until he's away and then stick the knife in.' I told Katie all I'd been told by Sally. 'Christ, she's only acting up for a week and already she's power hungry. I don't know what it is about this place, people would step over each other to get promotion, they are always backbiting and trying to undermine each other. There's no team spirit in the place and I'm getting sick of it. Christ, if they've turned on Tom, who's going to be next? You couldn't trust them as far as you could throw them.'

'I know. I'll probably get into trouble for refusing to take part in the investigation, but I don't care. They can send me home if they like, in fact they'd be doing me a favour if they did.'

'Well, I'm with you on this one,' said Katie. I'm not taking him down behind his back. If I've something to say to Tom I'll tell him it myself. Who do you think is behind it all?'

'I think it was Muriel,' I confided.

'The baldy bastard,' said Katie echoing my sentiments exactly. 'Sure Mandy told me that she was out for dinner recently and Baldy was there. During the meal she went on and on about how useless Tom was, and that he shouldn't be allowed to work in the Children's Bureau. I mean, she didn't even know Mandy; she just came out and said all this horrible stuff about him. And do you know who else was there?'

'No? Who?' I asked.

'That chavvy bitch, Bianca. She was apparently hanging on to every word that Baldy was saying. She's so desperate to be promoted, she wouldn't care who she has to sleep with.'

'Yeah, she's Muriel's bitch, innit.' We laughed. 'It's not funny.' I confided, 'She's driving me nuts. I have to sit on the other side of the cubicle from her. Her bloody mobile goes off constantly. She obviously shows the same restraint, discrimination and refinement with her ring tones as she does with her clothes. It's always belting out chavvy house music.'

'Did you see the state of her today?' asked Katie sipping her coffee.

'Yes. I had to turn away so I wouldn't laugh in her face.' Today Bianca's choice of dress was a tight white T-shirt, a pair of knickerbockers, black fish net stockings and stilettos. 'She looks like she should be hanging around a street corner,' said Katie.

'I know, and all that gold jewellery must weigh her down. But you're just jealous because you don't look proper bling.'

We laughed. 'That cheap gold is the only thing that keeps her weighed down, skinny chav slag. I wonder where she put her twelve kids?'

'They are probably in care at home or with all twelve fathers.' We laughed again.

Tom returned to work earlier than expected. I saw Sally and Muriel exchange a look of horror. He wasn't due to return to work for another two days. I met him at the door.

'Hi, boss,' I said greeting him with a hug. 'Welcome back, but I don't think you should be here.'

'I know, I've just realised that. I think I'll just go home.'

'Have you time for a cup of coffee?' I asked.

'Well, if I'm not working I may as well go home.'

'I know, I understand that, but can you spare ten minutes for a cup of coffee? It might be worth your while.'

He looked at me puzzled. 'What's going on, Louise?'

'Not here,' I said shaking my head slowly. 'I'll meet you in the coffee shop in five minutes.'

I grabbed my purse and travelled down in the lift to the coffee shop next door. I ordered a cup of coffee for each of us and sat down. My heart was racing. This was it. I knew that what I was going to do would cause ructions but I had to tell Tom the truth. I had to warn him about what was going on.

Tom joined me. He looked worried. 'I've ordered a coffee already for you. This one is on me.' We waited until Jeffery, the manager, had brought over our coffees. 'Right, Tom.' I took a deep breath. 'I'll just get this out as quickly as possible. The way I see it is that the suits have been ganging up against you. They have been trying to undertake some kind of investigation into you.'

'Me?' Tom asked incredulously.

'Yes, as far as I know there have been some questions which have arisen about your practice. So they waited until you were on annual leave, and Sally was acting up as manager and then they ordered her to talk to the staff and see if we have any concerns about your practice.'

'Christ,' said Tom. He looked as if he had been hit over the head with a hammer. 'You know, I'm sick of this. Why can't they just come to me directly if they are concerned about anything? Why do they have to do this under cloak and dagger.'

'I don't know what's going on, but I can tell you that both Katie and I told them to stick their investigation up their arses. We both said that that isn't the way it's done when social workers are qualified and we wouldn't take any part of it. I know they talked to Janet and she said the same.'

'What about the other team members?' Tom asked.

'That was the funny part,' I replied. 'They didn't ask anybody else. We were all told not to tell the others, but you know how tight Katie and I are and Janet as well. I can trust the both of them. But as for the rest of them, forget it.'

'When were you going to tell me?' he asked cautiously.

'I was going to phone you today. I only found out about the whole thing yesterday. I told them it was a load of bollocks and that I wouldn't be helping to put that baldy bastard further up the ladder.'

'What? Who?' Tom looked confused.

'You know who I mean, Tom. Think about it. Who had the most to gain here? There's a job coming up in management. You are the ideal candidate for it. But there's another team leader who is prepared to get it, even if she does it maliciously.'

Tom gasped. He had begun to realise just what was going on. 'Look, Tom,' I said gently, 'you are my team leader and I have a loyalty to you. But I have to tell you the truth. I had to sleep on this one last night. In the past I was loyal to a team leader who turned out to be a tyrant and a bully. I was reluctant to go down that road again. But fair is fair, and I won't have people treating you that way. You're my team leader, you work bloody hard and if I had any concerns about your practice I'm big enough and ugly enough to tell you myself. And you are big enough to take that. I wouldn't be involved in this underhand sneaky business.'

'Thanks Louise I really appreciate you being so honest,' he confided.

'As long as you don't go and shoot the messenger I'll be all right,' I said jokingly. 'At least you will be prepared for when you return to work. Did you not see the look of shock on Sally and Baldy's faces when they saw you today? They nearly wet themselves.'

'I thought they were surprised because I'd made a mistake and came in before I was due to.'

'No, they were surprised because Sally hasn't had a chance to complete her report because we won't cooperate with her. I'll stand over whatever I've said. You know I've always been honest with you right from the start.'

'I know. I appreciate that. Leave it with me. I'll deal with this. I'll make sure that this ends now.'

'Now just remember you have another two days off on leave. Don't do anything now. Just wait until you come back from work and then deal with it. I won't repeat what I have discussed with you but I'll have to tell Katie and Janet. You could trust those women with your life. They will be on your side in this.'

'OK, thanks, Louise,' he said getting up to leave. 'I'll think about it and I'll see you on Wednesday.' He looked like a little boy who has just had his toys stolen from him. I felt so sorry for him. What a despicable thing for them to do. Did they really think he wouldn't find out? Well, that was beyond my control. I'd done what I thought was right. I'd deal with the consequences.

I didn't have to wait long. I was summoned to the manager's office the next afternoon. 'I just wanted to talk to you about this business with Tom,' said Martin.

'Good,' I replied sweetly 'I was hoping somebody would be giving us some type of explanation soon.'

'Well, I need you to know that there isn't any investigation ongoing, and that a casual remark has been taken out of context,' he said firmly.

'Would you mind explaining that to me in more detail, Martin?'

'Well, Sally is not an experienced manager.' He smiled jovially at me. 'She reported to her manager that she was concerned about Tom's practice, and she was simply told to come back with specific details of what the issues were. Sally took it upon herself to undertake an investigation and things seem to have spiralled out of control since then.'

'So Sally wasn't specifically told to do this?'

'No, of course she wasn't,' he confirmed.

'That's funny because that is the story that she told me. As you say, Sally isn't experienced, so she wouldn't have made that story up on her own. She was told to conduct an investigation, and she told me who ordered her to do it.' I wouldn't accept some company line that he was trying to feed me now. I continued, 'I have to say, Martin, I'm really seriously considering whether I want to stay and work for an organization that is so underhand that it conducts investigations when there hasn't even been a complaint.'

'Well, really, Louise. I wouldn't want you to think badly of this department just because of some mistake which was made by an inexperienced manager.'

'You know, Martin, I hadn't realised until I came over here that I would be working with so many unqualified social workers. But where I come from we have a code of conduct we have to adhere to. I don't want any part of this organization if this is the type of thing that happens.'

'I can assure you that I am completely open and honest in all my interactions. I take pride in that.' He smiled stiffly. 'And I'm telling you that things have spiralled out of control, and I don't appreciate the fact that I had to deal with Tom last night. You know he phoned me and told me what you had told him,' he confided.

'Good. I'm glad he got the chance to speak to you about it.' I simmered back at him. I wasn't going to let him intimidate me.

'Well, you know, Louise, I would have appreciated if it we could have dealt with this matter during business hours when Tom was here.'

'Well, maybe the investigation should have taken place when Tom was here.' I smiled coyly at him. Martin frowned at me. It was clear that I was not going to accept the bullshit that he was trying to feed me.

'Well,' he smiled, a frozen gash on his face 'I just wanted to let you know that if you want to talk to me at anytime about this matter, or if you need someone to mediate between you and Sally then I'll be happy to do that too.' He smirked at me. He looked like the cat who has just swallowed a canary. There was no way I would be talking to him again if I could help it.

'Thanks, Martin, I'll remember that, but I'm a big girl, I can fight my own battles.' I stood up. 'I hope you don't mind but I'm due in court in ten minutes.' I smiled and left the room. Those penis enlargement pills he took must be working. He was a bigger dick now than he was last week.

CHAPTER 33

After court I waited in the office for Katie to return from her meeting with him. I was sitting at the computer as usual, trying to type up my notes when she arrived.

'Did you meet up with Martin?' she whispered as she approached my desk. If Lizzie heard anything about this it would be all over the office in a flash.

'Yes, I'm not long back, why, did you?' I turned round in my chair to look at her.

'Did he give you a bollocking?'

'No, he just gave me some guff about Sally not being experienced and that she hadn't been told to undertake any type of investigation.'

'What did you say to him?' she whispered looking over my shoulder to see Lizzie approaching her desk. I shrugged.

'I told him it was a load of bollocks and that I was questioning whether I wanted to work in an organization which was so underhand and sneaky.'

Katie giggled. 'I said that too. I told him that I was going home soon and that I would have to think about whether I wanted to come back.'

'Jesus, Katie, that's brilliant.' God, she was so clever. I wish I had said that. 'Maybe they'll think a bit more about what they are dealing with now. They'll probably hate us now.'

'Does that matter?' Katie asked. 'I don't want to be promoted in this place. Look what a fortnight's promotion did to Sally and she seemed to be one of the more decent ones here.' We both looked toward the manager's office where Sally was ensconced with Muriel. Katie was right. Sally had changed completely when she had been temporarily promoted. What was it about this place that created monsters out of the nicest people? Sally wasn't speaking to me because she didn't get round to telling me that the investigation was supposed to be confidential and I had told Tom about it as soon as I found out.

'That other baldy bastard, Muriel, gave me the dirtiest look today when she was walking past my desk,' confided Katie.

'I'm not surprised,' I replied. 'It probably scared the shit out of her, knowing that all her scheming had come to nothing.'

As Muriel emerged from Sally's office we both turned round quickly to get on with our work. They didn't need any more excuses to harass us. We had probably provided them with enough ammunition to last them for a lifetime.

It was Monday morning. Again. Weren't Mondays a terrible way to start the week? They were the potholes in the road of life. I had just returned from court and was looking forward to my first cup of coffee of the day.

Before I could even get my jacket off I received a report which needed to be acted on immediately. A mother had contacted the police to report that she had left her two children with their father for the weekend and he was now refusing to return them. The mother eventually disclosed that she shouldn't have left the children there, as her boyfriend was a paedophile who had been convicted for sexually assaulting another child. The police brought the children to the police station. The father was still refusing to let the children be returned to the mother because he alleged she had spent the entire weekend using drugs.

Katie and I travelled to the police station to assess the situation and ascertain if they needed to be placed in foster care. Judging by the information we had received we believed that the children would be at risk of significant harm if they were returned to their mother at this time.

The three-year-old girl sat on the floor with a dummy in her mouth, unmoving. She was clutching a dolly in her arms. The baby smiled happily in the police officer's arms. She was a bonny little thing who smiled placidly at anyone who approached her. We discussed what was going to happen with the police officers and one of them got down on his hunkers to say goodbye to the older girl. She popped her dummy out of her mouth and pointed it at his groin. He looked uncomfortable. The child moved over toward the officer and began to make smacking sounds with her lips. She touched him on the groin and put her hand there to try and fiddle with the zip of his trousers. The police officer was frozen in horror. His face was white. Katie and I had witnessed the whole thing. Jesus, what had the wee mite been subjected to? I lifted the child who reached forward in my arms to try and kiss the police officer on the mouth; she began to move her head from side to side as she tried to kiss him. The officer was clearly shocked.

I pulled the child gently toward me. It was evident that she had been exposed to something untoward and she might require a medical examination. Katie phoned the office to outline our concerns while I held the child in my arms. She tried to kiss me on the mouth, but I managed to divert her with a few toys. Katie returned and informed me that we had been able to get an appointment at the assessment unit. We drove there in silence. The medical examiner listened quietly to our concerns. She started her assessment of the older child, cajoling her to sit still while she measured her and examined her body. The child didn't flinch when the doctor removed her panties. Katie knew from the look I gave her that it was not good news. Katie left the room to phone the office. The police would have to be involved again. The child didn't protest when she was examined as she lay on the examination couch; she was completely unresponsive and compliant. The medical examiner exchanged worrying glances with me. So what the mother had alleged was completely correct, but if she had known that this might happen why had she placed her daughters at risk? The medical examiner began to take photographs while the child lay there, with her legs splayed like some quiescent model in a porn film. The doctor completed her examination quietly.

Meanwhile the baby began to protest. I found a bottle of milk in her changing bag, which was still warm. I began to feed her, and she sucked at the milk greedily. A nurse came in and gave the older child some milk and biscuits. She ate them quickly. She was a small pale little girl; we hadn't even asked her mother when she had been last fed. Though she wouldn't know herself.

The doctor returned. I had just finished winding the baby. She was a very contented little girl. 'I think it might be appropriate to examine the baby, too,' she said calmly. I nodded. I helped to undress her and set her down gently on the examination couch. She continued to smile and gurgle, even when the doctor removed her nappy and discovered that she wasn't unscathed either.

Katie returned to the examining room and started to play with the older child, She lifted a Barbie doll and began to dress her up; the child joined in the game. Katie handed her the doll. 'Now doesn't she look just as pretty as you,' smiled Katie. The child smiled back at her. She selected the Ken doll and began to grind the two dolls' bodies together. Katie and I exchanged a look of horror. Then the child lifted the Ken doll to her face. She laughed and began to lick and suck at the doll's genitals while the doctor looked on unsmiling. This, unfortunately, was part of her daily work too.

After the examinations had been completed we brought the children to foster care. The younger child clung to me initially but she settled into her placement quickly when she was given some toys to play with. The older child gravitated immediately to the foster father. She removed her dummy and tried to reach up to kiss him. He gently pulled her away. We advised the foster carers of what we had suspected and encouraged safe caring practices with the child; she would probably continue to act out in this manner for some time.

As we were leaving I turned around. Both children were smiling and happy, and more importantly safe. The children would be protected now, but we still had to deal with the business of ensuring that a full investigation was completed. It had taken us most of the day to get the examinations done and we needed to liaise with the police when we returned to the office, and start the endless paperwork which was required. But for a while Katie and I sat in the car in silence. We both needed time to consider what had happened, to come to terms with what we had seen. You would have to be inhuman if something like that didn't affect you deeply. I turned and noticed that, like me, Katie was sitting there with the tears quietly streaming down her face.

I met her in the car park next morning. We were leaving immediately to undertake a visit to a nursery school which one of the little boys in her care attended. Katie and I booked out a car and left the office. As we stopped at the traffic lights we saw a hearse up ahead. The family was riding in the car behind, a limousine which contained four men. One of the men smiled and waved at Katie, then he wound down his window. 'Hey, pretty ladies,' he called to Katie and me. 'Do you want to come out for a drink?' Katie gasped. He was on his way to an internment and he was flirting with us? What the hell kind of a country was this.

I snickered. 'It's probably his wife up ahead in the hearse,' I said sarcastically. 'Looks like he's looking for a replacement.' Despite the gesturing and calling of the men, we ignored them, wishing and praying that the lights would change so we could move on.

We arrived at the nursery placement where Tommy attended. He was two years old. He was always grubby and sweaty. It wasn't surprising. On our previous visits we had observed that his house was filthy. The windows had not been opened for years and an accumulation of grime had sealed them further. Bits of broken furniture were scattered over the living room, a mattress lay in the middle of the floor. The kitchen contained drug paraphernalia. There was no evidence of food. Upstairs the child's bedroom contained a cot, which was thick with grunge. There were no blankets. There was one tatty old teddy bear lying on the uncarpeted floor. The spare room could not be accessed due to the accumulation of broken furniture and clothing which threatened to spill out of it when the door was opened. The main bedroom contained a bed base; the mattress from the bed had been removed and brought downstairs to the living room, where the couple slept. The parents had been referred to the office a few months previously, but as far as I could see there hadn't been any improvement since that time.

Katie had organised day care for the child. At least someone would be able to give a daily account of how he presented. She also referred Tommy to the paediatrician. He was underdeveloped in many ways. In the nursery he was violent to the other children. He repeatedly punched them and pulled their hair. He was probably just acting out what he saw at home.

It was nearly impossible to meet with the parents; they were never at home for arranged home visits and would not agree to come to the office. Any time that Katie and I had called out at the house and the parents were there, we always knew they were present before we got out of the car. We could hear them screaming at each other. There was always some dispute going on. The mother would present in tears, and the father was very intimidating to us as well as to the nursery staff. To make matters worse the mother had just disclosed that she was pregnant again.

We arrived at the nursery. Things had deteriorated. The staff told us that Tommy had to be bathed daily when he arrived and they had to wash his clothing and put it back on him before the parents called to collect him. They always came together. That was part of the problem; the father wouldn't let the mother out of his sight. She needed him to get the drugs that were so essential to her daily living. Her drug of choice was ice. His was cocaine. She had all the hallmarks of an ice junkie. Her skin was greasy and lank and she had huge blotches and spots and tears all over her face where she had probably tried to scratch at the imaginary bugs which always surfaced with this particular drug. Users would scratch until their nails bled trying to get the imagined parasite out of their skin.

Today Tommy had purple bruises all over his back; we could see the outline of a fist. We took emergency action. The parents would now have to make changes before he would be allowed home. By the time we placed him in foster care we had lost the best part of the day. Now came the laborious task of recording each and every action we had taken.

CHAPTER 34

James came with me to view houses. I was reluctant to continue to pay the exorbitant rents for a property when it would be cheaper to buy one and now that I had finally sold my house I could afford it. We had looked at one house. It was larger than I wanted but it seemed to be in a good area.

'It's a great house,' agreed James. 'I think you will be really happy here.'

'And you? Do you think you might like to move here someday too?' I asked apprehensively.

'With you? There's nothing I would like better,' he said tenderly.

'Really,' I asked looking at him carefully.

'Look, it might be a bit premature, but I know I want to be with you for the rest of my life, so why don't we start now. Could we not buy this house together?'

'Really? That would be wonderful.' I hugged him tightly.

I missed the time I spent away from him and we were just so compatible in every way. I know that I wanted to be with him for ever and he was right, we should start now. We arranged to return the following week to look at the house again. We wanted Carmella's opinion; she knew a lot about property in the area and would be able to tell us whether she thought it was worth buying.

Carmella and Joseph thought it was in a good location, and it seemed to be without any obvious structural problems. I noticed that I hadn't felt as excited while looking at the property as I had on the first visit. There were some obvious things that needed to be changed. As we were leaving the property Carmella and Joseph stopped to chat with James and me. The next door neighbour appeared. She stood in the driveway of her home and began to rock her pelvis backwards and forwards.

'Show us your balls,' she shouted. That decided it; I didn't want to live next door to some madwoman. I had enough dealing with Lacey. We didn't put an offer on that house. We would just have to keep looking.

I couldn't wait to see Paula. We had worked together in Ireland for a couple of years and had established a great friendship. She was on holiday in Australia with her niece and was staying in the town for a couple of days with her cousin. We arranged to meet up for dinner. I hugged her tightly when I saw her. She was the first person from home I had met since I came here. Seeing her brought back all the feelings I had of being lost, without my people. We went out to dinner with James and had a wonderful time. She updated me on all that was happening at home. Paula told me that as soon as I left Kevin started to pick on Stacey who had only recently joined the team. Stacey had made a complaint against him and he had now been moved to another area where he would have no direct contact with colleagues.

'It's a pity they didn't do that before he ruined my life,' I said bitterly.

'Well, hasn't it worked out well for you now?' asked Carmel. 'You wouldn't have met James otherwise.' She smiled at him. 'And I can see how happy he has made you.' James hugged me; he was so unselfconscious about demonstrating his affection and love for me. I excused myself to go to the bathroom and when I returned Paula and James were engaged in conversation. They became silent when I joined the table. 'I hope you two weren't talking about me,' I said.

'Don't worry, it was all good,' Paula insisted.

Next day James brought me to the Botanical Gardens. We had lunch and a lovely glass of white wine. We played chess and read the Sunday papers. A jazz band began to play and people gathered round with their picnic rugs and listened. It was perfect.

'I love being with you, Louise,' James whispered, 'in fact,' he hesitated, 'I was wondering if we could make it a bit more permanent.' He looked awkward.

'What are you trying to say, James?' I asked him carefully, hardly daring to breathe.

'Well,' he said nervously, 'I wanted to ask you if you would marry me.'

'Are you serious, James?' I was dragging this out of him, but I needed him to say it, I didn't want any ambiguity.

'I've never been more serious about anything in my life,' he said softly.

He looked so nervous; my heart went out to him. He was the most wonderful man I had ever met, and he treated me like a goddess. I had no hesitation at all when I said, 'I think that's a wonderful idea, James, the answer is yes.' He kissed me and held me and I felt safe, warm and protected in his arms. He exhaled loudly.

'Thank God for that,' he said, 'I don't think I could go through another interrogation session.'

'What do you mean?' I asked, confused.

'Paula questioned me last night. She wanted to know what my intentions were towards you. She said that you were a wonderful woman and that you deserved only the best.'

'So you asked me to marry you because Paula bullied you into it?' I laughed.

'No, of course not, I'd been thinking about it for ages, but the time never seemed right before.'

We went for a walk. There were all sorts of strange plants and flowers, which I'd never seen before. There was a recreated rainforest which we walked through hand in hand. We weren't long tearing through it when the sprinklers came on and we got soaked. By the time we had emerged I was like a drowned rat, raindrops dripping off my nose. James laughed. It reminded him of the first time he had met me.

James's family were delighted when we told them our news. They had welcomed me into their home and shown me nothing but love and kindness. I was proud that I would be accepted on a more permanent basis.

James told the children. They were less than pleased. Naturally Ashley ran home to his mother to relay the gossip. She was on the phone in minutes. 'I hear y'all are getting married,' she shrieked. 'Well, you done better not give me any less money.' Thanks for the heartfelt congratulations Lacey, very noble.

James and I went to the posh end of town, where all the beautiful people hung out. We looked around at all the jewellers but only one specialized in Australian diamonds which were mined in the Kimberley Mountains. I picked out the most beautiful ring. It was a trinity ring with a white diamond in the middle and two pink diamonds on either side. It was gorgeous.

I checked the Internet and was looking at the local housing property site when I noticed a gorgeous house. I rang James and asked him to check it on the Internet. He did and he also thought it was beautiful.

'Why don't you ring up and see if you can get an appointment?' he suggested.

I rang the estate agent who informed me that a couple was due to visit the house that evening and we could come along at the same time too. We viewed the house while the other couple was admiring the garden. It was beautiful. It had four bedrooms. The master bedroom was the biggest room I had ever seen. It had floor to ceiling windows which overlooked the back garden and faced directly on to the swimming pool. It had a sitting room, a dining room, a utility room and a family room. It was perfect. I could imagine all my furnishings in this house. It had a lovely homely feeling and didn't need anything changed at all.

We were told that there would be an open day that weekend and we agreed to return with Carmella who would give us her opinion of the property.

Carmella also thought it was wonderful. We put in an offer that afternoon and after a bit of negotiation our offer was accepted. I was delighted. I couldn't wait to move in. We immediately called round to Susan and Henry's house to tell them the good news.

'Why don't you come and see it before we move in,' I suggested. 'Sure the boys have to see it as well.' We arranged a visit with the estate agent.

I drove round to James's house after work where we had arranged to travel to the new house together. Shirley was on the computer as usual, and Ashley was eating in the kitchen, as usual. 'We will need to hurry up, James,' I said, 'otherwise we will be late.' I hated being late. It was the height of bad manners.

James told Shirley to get off the computer and to come and get ready but there was no sign of the child. I was getting impatient. James eventually went into the bedroom and took him off the computer. He had to practically carry him into the living room where Shirley threw himself on the sofa in a huff.

'Put your shoes on, we have to go now,' James said firmly. Shirley ignored this instruction. James repeated it, moving toward him as he did so and picking up the shoes from the floor where they had been lying.

'Put them on now, Shirley, your grandma and grandpa will be waiting.'

'I don't care,' mocked Shirley, clearly meaning everything he said.

'Put your shoes on now,' ordered his father, his intonation rising slightly, as he tried to keep the tension from his voice.

'But I don't have any socks on,' smirked Shirley.

'Yes, you do,' said his father. 'Now don't be difficult, just put your shoes on.'

'But I don't have any socks on,' Shirley repeated as he reached down and pulled the socks from his feet and threw them on the floor. He smirked up at his father defiantly.

'Now you're not going to make us late, get ready immediately.'

'Huh, you're only trying to be a good parent 'cos she's here,' he sneered at me.

Eventually James managed to get him into the car. By this time I was a nervous wreck, the lining of my stomach felt as if it was coming apart. Shirley spent the journey to the house hurling insults at his brother and complaining that everything was shit and crap. Ashley pinched him and tried to kick him and they wrestled with each other in the back of the car.

We eventually arrived at the house where Susan and Henry had been waiting patiently outside along with the estate agent.

'I'm really sorry,' I apologised to everyone. The estate agent looked at the two boys as they spilled out of the car, hitting each other and hurling insults. She clutched her clipboard towards her and sighed.

'Don't worry,' she said. 'I can see you have had your hands full.' She looked towards the house; she was probably trying to figure out what damage they could do to the property before we had even signed the legal papers.

Susan and Henry waited until the boys approached. 'Hello, boys,' said Susan cheerfully. 'How are my lovely grandsons?' They ignored her.

Henry put his hand out towards Shirley. 'Hello, young man,' he said as he waited for Shirley to put his hand out and return the handshake. Shirley stood with his hands wrapped around him staring defiantly at him from under his dirty fringe. I was embarrassed for Susan and Henry. Their own children were impeccably mannered. It must be embarrassing to realise that your grandchildren were so obnoxious and rude.

We moved towards the house and looked around. Susan and Henry seemed very pleased with it, and they commented appropriately on the lovely garden, the light bright rooms and especially the swimming pool which was glistening in the sunshine.

The estate agent talked knowledgeably about the area and how it was close to schools, as the boys continued to make their presence felt by shouting loudly at each other, 'cock sucker, dick head, faggot,' and a great assortment of other insults. I was mortified. The estate agent looked at me and obviously having gone to a really good estate agent school where they teach you courtesy and the value of tact and diplomacy, she asked what age my sons are.

'They're not mine,' I snapped quickly, mortified by the thought that anyone would even believe I was related to them. Susan and Henry hung their heads in shame; they couldn't get out of this one as easily as me.

'Oh, I see, and will they be living, em, here with you?' she asked politely.

'As little as possible unless their behaviour changes,' I stated firmly.

'Quite right too,' repeated Henry and Susan.

I was distraught by the children's appalling behaviour. James and I had already made an offer on the house which had been accepted. There would be financial penalties if we pulled out of the sale. I knew that we would have to pursue it. I hoped and prayed that things would improve when we moved in together. Surely the children would change for the better when they had firm and consistent boundaries.

James contacted Lacey to let her know that he would be moving house but that the current contact arrangements with the children would not be changed. She replied that he hadn't even told her the new address and she accused him of deserting the boys to have a new life with me.

'Don't be ridiculous,' said James. 'I'll still be able to spend as much time with the boys and they will have more room to play here as there's a bigger garden than my last house. And,' he continued, 'they can spend the summer swimming in the pool.'

'You have a pool?' she asked incredulously. 'Well, I won't be setting foot in that house,' she said sulkily.

'I know you won't,' James said calmly, 'we won't be giving you an invitation.'

James and I agreed that I would move in first and that he would move in on the following week when the boys were due to be with him for only two days. This way it would be less unsettling for them.

'There had better be firm rules in our house James,' I insisted. 'I'm not having your boys treating either of us with disrespect. I don't care what they get up to in their mother's house but I won't be running after them here.'

We agreed that when we moved in we would sit down with the children and explain the type of behaviour we expected from them. The rules weren't too punitive either, we just wanted them to tidy their own beds and put their dirty washing in the linen basket. I had standards of hygiene that they might not have been familiar with in their mother's house but they would have to get used to it here. I told James that the children needed to have showers regularly, particularly Shirley, and that he needed to wash his hair on a regular basis. I had never seen it clean.

I felt as if I was drawing up a contract of work with one of my families. I'd never had to apply my social work skills to my home life. It was a very humbling experience. We also agreed that one of the rules would be that they would have to have respect for each other and everyone else in the house. I was determined that they would not carry on in our house the way they did in hers.

I knew we would be facing an uphill battle. Normally children were taught manners when they were little while I would be trying to start to socialize them as adolescents. I was not naive, I knew it would take time for the boys to settle in and feel comfortable, and we were prepared for a few hiccups along the way. But nothing could have prepared us for the onslaught that was to face us when the boys eventually moved in.

CHAPTER 35

It started immediately they came home from school where James had collected them. I had taken the afternoon off work to welcome them, but they ignored me. James showed them their rooms which we had spent a lot of time preparing in readiness for their arrival. We had bought black quilt covers and sheets for them, their favourite colour. I had also made some artwork for them which looked fantastic. Shirley never even noticed his surroundings; he dumped all his things on the floor of his bedroom and went hunting for the computer. It was sitting in the dining room, unplugged. He started banging at the keys.

'This is crap, this thing won't work,' he shouted as he continued to batter at the machine.

James went to him immediately. 'The broadband won't be connected for another couple of weeks so you will just have to find something else to do.' Shirley stared fiercely at him.

'I'm not fucking doing nothing and you can't make me,' he screamed into his father's face.

'Don't you dare speak to me like that young man,' James said firmly. 'I think now might be a good time to talk to you both about what the rules are in this house.'

James called out to Ashley who was lying on his bed staring at the ceiling. He was lost in thought. It was probably unfamiliar territory. He was probably getting used to the fact that a woman actually cleaned her house. James explained to the boys what we had already discussed. 'I know it will be hard for you boys, you have to get used to a new house, and a new suburb, but if we all work together we can make this work.' The boys were silent.

'Now why don't you both go for a swim?' asked James cheerfully. The weather was beautiful outside. Ashley stood at the side of the pool. 'But it's wet,' he whined. He was dumber than a box of hair.

When Fifi saw Shirley come towards her she ran yelping to the safety of her kennel. Shirley smirked. But when he eventually got into the water he seemed to enjoy it.

While James was preparing dinner I asked each of the boys to take the dog for a walk. They refused; they lay there on the sofas, more interested in trading insults with each other. 'Look boys,' I urged, 'Fifi needs exercise every day, it isn't fair on her if she doesn't get a chance to run around.' They shrugged, uncaring. James eventually said he would do it. I thought he was giving in too easily, but this was their first day here and I wanted them to feel as comfortable as possible.

At dinner time James had gone to a considerable effort to make something special. Ashley pushed his way to the table and started to tuck in; there was nothing wrong with his appetite judging by the smacks and slops of him. I could see the food swirl around in his mouth as he didn't close it when he chewed. Shirley started to pick through it. He glowered at his father.

'I want sausages,' he snapped as he squirmed around in his seat. He probably wasn't used to sitting at a table.

'Well, you can't have sausages today,' said James firmly. 'Eat your dinner.'

'I want sausages,' he said, this time louder.

'I told you already you can't have sausages today. Now eat what you have been given.'

Shirley looked daggers at me. I stared back, waiting and watching, wondering what he was going to do next. He didn't pursue it. He sat there ignoring the food in front of him. Eventually he tramped off to his room. James and I cleared up the dinner dishes. I covered Shirley's dinner and put it in the fridge.

'What happens in your house if he doesn't eat his dinner?' I asked.

'Well, he doesn't normally eat with us. He's usually on the computer or he's not hungry. He doesn't eat much. And then if he gets hungry later I just make him something.'

'So he doesn't eat the food you prepare for him, but he expects to be waited on later?' I wasn't going to have some despot in this house; I'd be putting a stop to this behaviour straight away.

'Well, he's just so picky with his food anyway. He won't eat food that touches each other, so that rules out curries and stews and casseroles.'

'Well, he's going to have to learn that in this house we eat dinner in the evening and if you don't eat it you don't get anything.'

'I know, I've tried to do that in my house too, but it's just impossible. He just starts whingeing and whining and he goes on all night until I give in.'

'But you are just as bad as her then,' I said in frustration. 'You know, James, it's a pity the pair of you couldn't act as parents instead of trying to be his friend. It's not fair on Ashley, you know, he doesn't get rewarded for coming to the table. Shirley gets even more attention by being difficult. What does Ashley have to do then?' As far as I could see, he was the only one who was usually ignored because Shirley wouldn't let him get a look in. 'If he refuses to eat it later, then he will have to go to bed without. I'm not trying to be cruel here, James, I'm trying desperately to teach him some manners.' Manners which should have been taught when he was little, by the person who spent most of the time with him, his mother. But she was too busy chatting to guys on the Internet and running around trying to have anal sex to do that.

Shirley came into the kitchen; he went straight to the larder and started to pull out a packet of biscuits. 'Are you hungry?' I asked him.

'I'm starving,' he grunted.

'Good. Well, you go and sit down over there and I'll heat up your dinner.'

'I don't want no dinner,' he protested, 'I want candy. Where do you keep the candy in this house?' He started rummaging around in the cupboards.

'You won't be getting candy in this house, not until you've finished your meal,' I said steadily. 'You can have your dinner, which your dad cooked for you or you can go to bed without anything.' He stared at me. He was clearly trying to size me up. Well, he would soon find that I didn't want to be his friend; I didn't care if he hated me. If I was going to be a stepparent I was going to behave as a good parent should.

'I mean it, Shirley.' I said firmly. 'You can have your dinner or you can have nothing. You decide.'

'I'll have the dinner,' he said quietly.

'Good boy,' I smiled, 'now you go and sit at the table and I'll bring it over to you.' I prepared the food and watched as he ate it, all of it.

'I can't believe it,' said James. 'That's the first time I've ever seen him do what he was told like that.'

'You have to be firm and consistent. You know, if you want your children to respect you it's the only way to do it,' I said smugly. Now that Shirley realised that there would be someone in charge it would be easier for him too.

Next morning James was in the kitchen making coffee. I was rushing around trying to get ready for work. 'Dad, Dad, Dad, Dad,' the call was repeated incessantly by Shirley who was shouting at his father from his bedroom.

'You'd better go and see what's wrong with him,' I said. James went to Shirley's bedroom and returned a moment later. 'Well, what's wrong with his majesty this time?'

'He wanted clean socks. He has a drawer full of them, but I had to get them out for him.'

'You're kidding? I swear to God, James, that child can't do a thing for himself. It's an absolute disgrace. He's nearly thirteen years old and he can't even open a fecking drawer. He's not bloody handicapped.' I looked up. Ashley was loitering in the corner listening intently, spying. He was probably on some reconnaissance mission for his mother.

James brought the children to school. I was relieved. It had been stressful having to deal with their repeated complaints of boredom. Why couldn't they read or do something constructive? I went to tidy up before I left for work myself. Their bedrooms were like tips. They had dumped everything they had taken from their mother's house on the floor. What did the woman hope to achieve by doing everything for them? She had not encouraged them to be independent but had made them completely dependent on her. Was she afraid they would leave her someday? Or was she making sure they never would?

That was it! Lacey had been determined to get pregnant. She treated her children like possessions. But I realised while she had given them girls' names although they were boys, they would grow up to be men. If she couldn't have a man in her life in the way she wanted, she would have the next best thing. I had believed on some unconscious level that these children would grow up and eventually leave home, like everyone else, but it wouldn't happen. It couldn't because of the way she treated them. Lacey must have planned to leave James all along. She knew that eventually she would be alone, but she would have two men who would depend on her forever and never leave her, her sons.

I picked up their clothing from the floor. As it had come from their mother's house I didn't want it here unless it had been boil washed. I didn't want my house to smell of cat's piss like hers. I took everything they had dropped and scrubbed it to within an inch of its life. I went into Shirley's room and pulled back the duvet to see a large dark patch on the bed. He had wet himself. No wonder Lacey's house smelt of piss if this was what she had to contend with every day.

I put the new sheets and duvet cover into the hottest wash on the machine. I put a couple of hot water bottles on the mattress. The bed was brand new. I would have to get a plastic sheet on the way home from work. I couldn't leave the windows open during the day as we might be burgled.

I changed Ashley's sheets and vacuumed both bedrooms thoroughly. I had stocked up on flea repellent; I was taking no chances with anything they had. I knew that if I had to keep up this level of hygiene I would have to get up earlier in the morning, otherwise I would be late for work, but I was determined my house wouldn't start smelling like a client's house, like hers.

I had to scour the toilet and scrub the floor. Those boys couldn't even aim into a hole which was bigger than their heads. Jesus, if men had to clean their own bathrooms, we'd already have disposable toilets.

I returned home from work and turned my key in the lock and opened the front door. I could see the pair of them lying sprawled all over the sofa trying to kick each other. James was in the kitchen preparing dinner. I went over and kissed him and said hello to the children. They ignored me. I was the invisible woman. 'You've timed it well,' James said, 'I'm just about to serve dinner.' My stomach lurched to my feet. I couldn't face another episode like yesterday but I forced myself to sit at the table.

James told the boys that their dinner was ready. The pattern was forming quickly. Ashley pushed and elbowed Shirley out of the way and raced across the room throwing himself into a chair and grabbing the food as it was set on the table. He didn't even wait for utensils. Shirley sat there, squirming in his seat.

'I'm not hungry, Dad, Dad I'm not hungry.'

'Just try some of it,' James tried to persuade him, 'just eat what you can.' Shirley stabbed at the food with a fork, but didn't eat it. 'If you don't eat it now you will be getting it later,' James reminded him. Shirley glared at me; clearly this was all my fault.

We were still sitting at the dinner table; Shirley had finally managed to eat some food and was now playing with his play station. Ashley looked anxious though he had managed to eat my dinner as well as his own.

'Are you all right?' I asked him quietly.

'Mom says she's gonna get a new boyfriend and he's going to beat Dad up,' he said. James and I exchanged a look of dismay. 'Don't you be worrying

269

yourself about that,' I reassured him. 'Sure your daddy can handle anyone, and he has the sense to call the police if anyone touched him.'

'But what if he gets killed?' he pleaded. Ashley had obviously been giving what his mother had told him some thought. I tried to reassure him but he interrupted. 'You don't know what Mom's like when she gets a boyfriend. Wayne hated us you know, he was always screaming at us,' he said defiantly. Lacey had told me that Wayne didn't like kids but I hadn't realised how much he detested the boys. I knew their behaviour was bad, but what woman would continue a relationship with a man who hated her sons so much?

James again reassured Ashley that it wouldn't happen. Sure what man would want her?

I checked that Shirley's mattress was dry and put clean sheets on his bed. I was glad of something to do; I couldn't sit with them anymore. Shirley had provided the entertainment for his dopey brother by passing wind while Ashley reciprocated by picking his nose and eating the snot.

The boys refused to walk the dog again, but at one stage when I went outside, I found Shirley trying to set fire to her hair. I grabbed the matches from him. 'Don't do that again, Shirley,' I ordered, 'you might have hurt her.'

'I don't care,' he smirked lifting his foot and kicking the dog in the back. I pulled Fifi away from him and called for James. Shirley smiled while James started to scold him. He didn't flinch. With the computer not working we were limited in the sanctions we could set up.

'You're going to bed early, young man,' I said sternly.

'Fuck off, cunt,' he sneered. I felt as if I had been slapped.

James grabbed Shirley by the arm and shook him. 'Don't you ever speak to Louise like that again,' he ordered. Shirley shrugged again. James sent him to his room.

'That's it, James.' I insisted. 'That poor dog has to go. It's not safe for her to be here with that monster around.'

'OK, I'll phone Mum, she loves that dog, maybe she might want her.' Susan was delighted to take her; she disclosed that she was afraid of what Shirley would do to her.

We managed to get through the night. Next morning I repeated the same cleaning routine as Shirley had wet the bed again, but I had to hurry as James was giving me a lift to work. I noticed that Shirley had written on the wall behind his bed, 'Louise will die.' Dear God, I was horrified, and I felt frightened. This child was capable of anything. But I couldn't dwell on it now; I'd discuss it with James later.

Shirley was going to the dentist that morning, so we dropped him off at his mother's house. The abandoned shopping trolley and the rubbish which had been lying in the front garden on my first visit months earlier were still there for all the world to see. James drove towards the school.

'So we'll just drop you off here, Ashley,' James said as he pulled up to the side of the kerb. It was eight o'clock in the morning, and the area was full of children on their way to school which was only twenty feet away.

'But you can't,' Ashley replied in panic, his voice rising in anxiety. 'I will be raped.' What? James and I both asked him. 'Mom says that if I ever have to walk anywhere that someone will get me and rape me.' No wonder the child was so nervous about social interaction. On top of everything else she had created an irrational fear of the outside world. James reassured him and I watched him walk off towards the school. His shoulders were hunched in misery and he repeatedly looked furtively over his shoulder.

At least they would be staying with their mother for a while now, so we could get a bit of peace. Later James and I were sitting in the living room having a glass of wine and listening to some music, the telephone rang.

'It's Ashley,' I said as I handed the phone to James. The smile dropped from his face as he left the room with the phone in his hand. There was only one person who had that kind of effect on him – Lacey. What the hell was wrong now? Why couldn't she use the phone herself? It was so juvenile to hide behind the children. James returned to the room and sat down quietly.

'Well,' I asked, anxious to break the silence. 'Was it the good Lacey or the bad one?' I wondered if someone with multiple personalities threatened to kill themselves, was it considered a hostage situation.

'This time it was the good one,' James replied. 'She says she's been reading up on nutrition and has asked us not to give children soda when they are here. She says that it makes their behaviour go off the wall.'

'Oh, so things aren't perfect in her house then?' I said unkindly. 'Well, I agree with her for once. Shirley is addicted to sugar. The other night he wanted me to put eight spoons of sugar in his hot chocolate. I wouldn't, I told him he didn't need it, but he says he always gets that much at his mother's. She wouldn't really give him that much, would she?'

'She probably does. I've seen him come into the house and just eat spoonfuls of sugar out of the packet.'

'Well, maybe we need to think about sweets again, though they don't get many here. Maybe this time she's working with us for what's best for the boys. Hmm,' I replied unconvincingly, 'We'll see.'

CHAPTER 36

The following week the boys arrived spilling into the house, pushing and shoving and calling each other names. James separated them and arranged for Shirley to have a turn on the computer. Thank goodness it was now connected. Ashley could have the chance to do his homework in peace. I had repainted Shirley's room. I told James not to mention it to Shirley. He was probably finding it difficult to come to terms with the fact that there was some kind of order in our house, and he was taking it out on me, the reason for his discontent.

James prepared dinner while I busied myself by cleaning and tidying the house. At dinner time James told the boys to wash their hands. He had poured water for them. 'Where's the soda?' asked Shirley getting up from his chair to go to the fridge.

'There is none,' replied James.

'That's crap,' snapped Shirley. 'I wanna drink of soda. I wanna drink of soda now.'

'Well, your mum has asked us not to give you any,' I explained. 'She says that it affects you both and that she doesn't want you to have any.'

'That's crap,' screeched Shirley.

'I know it might not be what you want, but you can have water or fruit juice if you want.'

'No, that's shit,' reiterated Shirley. 'Mom gives us soda all the time. She gave us some for breakfast today.'

'What?'

'Yeah,' interrupted Ashley, 'she said that it was crap that we wouldn't be having any soda in Dad's house and that we could have it there whenever we wanted.'

Bitch. I looked at James. She was now playing dirty tricks and using the boys to do so. 'I don't know what she hoped to get out of this,' said James later. I didn't either; she was behaving like a child. Was she afraid that the children

273

would like it better at our house? Was she so insecure as a mother that she had to win them over with sweets and lemonade? Let her get on with it. I was staying out of it from now on.

Shirley skulked into the kitchen next morning while I was preparing breakfast. He looked dishevelled. 'Here, let me fix your shirt. It's sticking up at the back.' I moved toward him. Shirley recoiled in horror.

'Get your goddamn hands off me,' he screamed menacingly into my face. He was almost the same size as me and with his level of aggression he could do a lot of damage if he wanted to.

I stepped back. For a moment I felt genuinely frightened. 'Jesus, Shirley, I was only trying to fix your shirt,' I explained.

'I told you, motherfucker, get your fucking hands offa me,' he shrieked.

'Jesus, James, what the hell is wrong with that child?' I asked James who had just entered the kitchen. James looked stunned. He shouted at Shirley and sent him to his bedroom. I could hear him kicking the walls, the sound reverberating through the house.

'You know,' he said, 'I've just remembered that one of Lacey's friends, Jeanette, confronted Lacey once when Shirley was rude to her. She told Lacey that she worked with a lot of kids who had assaulted their parents. She told Lacey that if she didn't do something about it soon, he would end up punching her when he was an adolescent. I think he was about nine years old at the time.'

'And didn't Lacey do anything?'

'No, she put it down to Shirley's blood sugar levels and made excuses that he was tired. So what Jeanette prophesized might just come true? Do you think I should take him to see someone?'

'Yes, I do, it's not normal for a child to behave like he does. He becomes aggressive at the slightest thing, and he has no social skills whatsoever. He doesn't seem to be able to pick up on the social clues that people give him. He's always interrupting or repeating the end of people's sentences. And what's wrong with him that he wouldn't shake his grandfather's hand? That's more than just being rude. You know, I think the danger is that we look at Lacey and think well, he's not as bad as her so he can't be that bad, but we're using the wrong frame of reference. We should be comparing him with another child the same age, not her.'

'You're right. Look, what if I take him to a doctor and see if we can get a referral to a paediatrician and consult with the school as well?'

'I don't think you have any choice. This child is clearly being neglected. He needs help and support to improve his behaviour. And I'll tell you something, James,' I said firmly, 'I'm not going to sit around here waiting to be his punch bag; if you don't do something soon then I'm out of here.'

The only thing Shirley liked apart from the computer was violent films which I refused to buy. He was only twelve and I didn't want to encourage him to be any more aggressive than he was. I felt he had the potential for that already. He would glower at me constantly, and push against me as he brushed past. He gave me the creeps. I knew it must be difficult for him; I was some stranger who had come into his dad's life and tried to change it, when he wanted and needed it to remain just the same.

In the beginning he had tolerated me but when I stopped having contact with his mother, he became openly hostile. He didn't hide the fact that he resented me. The looks he gave me nearly floored me; they were filled with such abhorrence and contempt. Every time he glared at me dread crept along my spine and raised the hairs on the back of my neck. I found myself having to psychically brace myself every time I had to encounter him. I always came away feeling contaminated, sullied, and unnerved. I know you think I was being ridiculous, I thought so myself. How could such a small child generate such terror in a grown adult? I had encountered this level of fear only once in my life, when I had met a convicted paedophile. He displayed the same level of contempt for me that Shirley did, and I knew that like Shirley he didn't care how he was perceived. They shared a physical manifestation of evil.

I was very busy at work during the rest of the time the boys spent with us, so I managed to avoid them in the evenings. I was so tired I went straight to bed as soon as I had remade Shirley's bed. Then it was up early for the washing, which was relentless. The weather was lovely so there was no problem with drying the sheets, but it wouldn't be so easy in the winter. Maybe James should talk to a professional about this too.

Something woke me, a feeling that crept through my consciousness, grabbing my attention. Someone was in the room. I opened one eye slowly and looked into the face of evil. It had a name – Shirley. He was looming over me. I bolted upright quickly, feeling vulnerable and frightened. I clasped the duvet to my chest. He didn't move, he stood there staring, a half smirk playing on his lips. I was petrified.

'Jesus, James, wake up,' I prodded James who was deep in sleep beside me. I never lost contact with Shirley's eyes. He smiled menacingly at me.

'What, what is it?' James sat up, trying to shake the sleep from his body and stared around; the early morning light peeked in between the edges of the window blinds, clearly illuminating Shirley who continued to stand by my side. James jumped out of bed. 'What is it mate?' he asked. 'Are you feeling sick?'

Shirley shrugged his shoulders, never taking his eyes off me. James led him back to his bed. I lay back, quaking, my heart racing. I pulled the blankets over me tightly. How long had he been standing there? He could have done anything; he could literally have murdered me in my bed. What the hell was wrong with that child? His behaviour was getting beyond a joke.

When James returned he shook his head. 'He's not sick,' he said, 'he just couldn't sleep.'

'But he was just staring at me,' I squeaked. 'I've never felt as frightened in all my life. Push that chest of drawers over a bit in front of the door; I don't want him coming in here again.' James started to protest but looking at my pale white frightened face must have convinced him otherwise. 'And first thing tomorrow, James, I'm getting a lock put on that door.'

'It's OK, I'll do it. I'll have a word with him in the morning and see what he has to say. He must have had a nightmare.' Nightmare! He would certainly be causing a few for me. I lay back on the pillows. Was this the first time it had happened? Had he done it before? I lay awake for the rest of the night, too afraid to go to sleep. What was that child going to do next?

I knew it would be difficult to build up a relationship with children with whom I shared no history. I wasn't a complete gombeen. I knew that it would take time for them to get over their fears about losing their father, for us all to adapt as a family. I took things really slowly to begin with. I never rushed them. It wasn't my job to correct their behaviour or to discipline them, I wasn't their parent. Over time I hoped that they would learn to respect me, and to accept that I intended to be with James forever. I read everything I could on step families, trying to assess things from their point of view. I was patient and tolerant, and I tried to inject as much humour into the relationship as I could which seemed to lighten the tension. But every time the boys left and spent any time with their mother we would have to begin all over again on their return. We always seemed to be taking two steps back for every forward movement.

Lacey would interrogate the boys. They were held to account for every minute of the time they spent with us. I think they began to resent it, but instead of reacting against their mother, they took their rage out against me. Ashley began to steal. He was always poking and prodding around in drawers. In the beginning when James and I had moved in together we were very organised.

When bills arrived we put them in the kitchen drawer and they were paid promptly. But some of them went missing; I assumed James had paid them while he assumed the same of me. When we started to receive reminder notices from utility companies we were alarmed. James eventually found some of them crumpled up in Ashley's jeans; they hadn't been washed since he went to his mother's house two weekends before.

We had to squirrel the bills away in my dressing table drawer until Ashley returned to his mother's house. James talked to Ashley at length about respecting people's privacy, but it was futile; he was a nosey little git. We always seemed to be frantically searching for things every time Ashley left. I started to notice that little trinkets were missing, mainly perfume and sentimental items which I treasured. I didn't want to accuse him and have him resent me; there had to be a reason why he needed to hold on to my things. I didn't know if he was bringing them home to his mother, like a trophy, or whether he was saving them for himself.

I bought a small vanity case and locked all my personal things away for safekeeping; I put it in the top of the wardrobe where he couldn't reach. I never left Ashley alone in the house; it just wasn't worth the upset which followed.

As for Shirley, his party trick was to break things and he did it with alarming regularity. I watched him throw himself against the kitchen table where I had placed my Waterford crystal vase which contained roses which James had bought for me. I wasn't quick enough to catch it before it smashed into smithereens on the tiled floor. Shirley grinned, happy with his achievement. I was devastated; I had been attached to it as it had been a present from my sister. He seemed to know instinctively what was precious to me. I wasn't prepared to go through that again so I took all my pictures and mementos and packed them into a box and placed them safely in the garage. The house felt bare, sterile and I hated the fact that my family photographs couldn't be displayed in public, but I knew I would be devastated if he damaged them too.

He then started on the crockery and glassware. I came into the kitchen once to find him bouncing plates off the floor, a sadistic look on his face. I scolded him, but it had no effect. He just shouted at me that he didn't care. I tried not to let him know how upset I was. He had gone through half a dinner set before I could stop him. I noticed that he only broke my things, never his father's. He was clearly angry with me and this was how he displayed that. I packed away the rest of my dinner set and my glasses. But these little things had always given me pleasure and I began to resent the fact that I was being deprived of them.

One day as I brought the washing in, and I went to set it down I saw Shirley standing in the hall poking around in my bag. 'What are you doing with my handbag?' I asked sharply. What on earth was he looking for? Was he looking for my purse?

'I haven't got your handbag,' he protested though his hand was still poised right inside it. I noticed it was one of the few times he had maintained eye contact. I walked over and pulled it away from him.

'Please don't touch anything of mine again,' I said gently.

'But I didn't,' he continued to protest. I walked away and put my bag in the bedroom. I was going to have to put a lock on the outside of the door now too. I might as well be living in prison.

I never saw Shirley with a pen in his hand, but we would find drawings all over the house. They were horrific, huge monsters with blood dripping from their eyes while they devoured their prey, usually characters which resembled his brother or his mother. I was just relieved he hadn't included me in these depictions. The only time he went outdoors was when a cat had been run over just outside the house. He was out there poking it with a big stick and marvelling at all the gore. He protested when James took him indoors.

A couple of weeks later I kissed James as he left to go to the paediatrician's appointment with Shirley.

'So how did it go then?' I asked him when he returned, but I could tell from the resigned look on his face that it hadn't been a positive experience.

'Lacey showed up and she sabotaged the entire thing.' I plonked down heavily on the chair and waited for him to continue. 'The paediatrician kept asking Shirley if he suffered from particular behaviours and he said he did, but she kept interrupting and saying that he didn't do those things in her house.'

'So what was the outcome?'

'The paediatrician said that there were clearly no issues when Shirley was with his mum and that the problems at our house needed to be explored further.'

'Well, that was clever of him. That way he's taken her out of the picture, and she won't have to attend another appointment with you.'

'I suppose so,' he replied resignedly. 'But on the way out of the appointment she came over and started sneering and saying I suppose you're going to take him to another specialist until you get him on drugs. She said that she wouldn't let him start drugs as they might have side effects and that there was nothing wrong with him. It was only you and me that have the problem.'

'But, James, if we have a problem it's because the kids don't know whether they are coming or going. They are stuck in the middle listening to all her

278

madness and by the time they get to us they are ready to explode. Sure you know they come in through the front door fighting and hitting each other, they are just so wound up. You know she can't hold her own water, and she burdens the children with all her problems. She is so incensed with jealousy and bitterness against us that it's spilling over onto the children.'

'I know, it's ironic that she was going to leave the children with me and just go off and now she faults my parenting. At the start when we were first divorced she took the kids with her when she went searching for this guy who she had decided was a potential boyfriend for her.'

My mouth opened in surprise. 'Was that a man called Willie?'

'Yes. Did she tell you about him?' I nodded; I remembered the whole sordid tale. 'Well, she wanted a relationship with this man and when she figured out that he might be staying at a friend's house she used to leave the boys and me without a car and drive about eighty miles away in the hope he might be there. Then one time she took the boys with her too. But it wasn't a proper relationship then, I mean, he wasn't her boyfriend. She wanted him to be, and she hung round the house he used to visit in the hope that he might turn up. She was really obsessed with him; she talked about him constantly and drove there most weekends on the chance that she might see him.'

'What age was she then?' I asked curiously.

'About forty-eight.'

'And Willy?'

'He was only twenty-two. She told me that if they hooked up she was just going to leave the boys with me; she was acting really strangely then, and I think she was really unstable. I didn't know what to do. I just tried to be around for the boys as much as possible so that it wouldn't impact on them as much, but it was hard going as she always pulled them into any arguments we had. She used to ridicule me in front of the kids.'

'What happened when she took up with Wayne then?'

'So you know about him too?' he asked his brow rising in surprise.

'Unfortunately, yes.' I nodded.

'When she took off to Western Australia to be with him she just abandoned the kids and we didn't know when or if she would be back. But then she came back and told me that she wanted the boys and me to move there too, so she could get to see the kids sometime.'

'You're joking? But you had a job here, the kids were at school and you were settled.'

'I know that, but she wasn't thinking about that, she was so desperate to be with Wayne she didn't think about what everyone else needed.'

'So she was going to just move the children away from their friends and their family again, when they had already had to move to another country?' James had said that Lacey was unstable then but did he really think that she was any better now?

James and I were preparing dinner. Shirley was on the computer and Ashley was sitting on the sofa watching television, some makeover programme for women. James looked over at him. 'So Ashley, your mum says that Shirley is really well behaved when he's in her house, so we must be doing something wrong here.'

'That's not true,' Ashley whimpered not moving his head from the television screen or his finger from his nose. Was he digging for gold? 'Sure he threw a huge tantrum in the middle of the video store last week 'cos he couldn't get what he wanted and Mom drove off and left him there.'

'She abandoned him?' asked James in disbelief.

'Well, she drove home and put all the goods away but then she went back for him, I mean, like she didn't leave him there all the time,' he protested. Ashley was afraid he had got his mother into trouble. Even though he got all the blame for everything that happened at her house and was expected to care for his younger brother. He was always telling us that he was so embarrassed by Shirley's behaviour.

'You know, Dad, he said quietly, 'sometimes Mom is really strange. She says weird things.' He shrugged his shoulders.

'What about?' James asked warily.

'I dunno, about people. She's even worse when she invites people for dinner and gets drunk.' James and I exchanged a look; obviously the child also needed to get away from his mad mother.

The following morning James and I drove to the shops to get the morning papers. The children wouldn't be out of bed for ages, but I still felt nervous about leaving them alone. If they killed each other we would be responsible. 'Do you know that Lacey is taking the boys to a counsellor?' James asked. 'Ashley told me last night.'

'So everything isn't perfect in her little world? I'm glad, at least that is a good start, it's just a pity she wasn't honest with the paediatrician. Things might have improved by now.'

I went into the house while James parked the car. I moved towards my bedroom only to find Ashley sitting on the stool in front of my dressing table with the contents of my make-up bag scattered all over the surface. 'Ashley, what are you doing in here?' I asked sharply.

He jumped, clearly surprised that I had come home so early. 'I was just playing,' he said guiltily. He was wearing mascara and eye shadow, his eyes were lined with black liner and he was wearing bright pink lipstick, which had been badly applied. Yuck, that was going straight in the bin with all the rest of the stuff he had handled.

James entered the room behind me; he was visibly shocked to see his son sitting there in full make-up.

'Well, Marilyn Manson wears make up,' shrugged Ashley. 'It's no big deal.'

'I don't think he wears pink lipstick,' cautioned James. 'Go and wash that stuff off your face at once.'

'You just don't understand me,' Ashley complained dramatically as he threw his head back and minced his way out of the room.

'Jesus, James, I know we have to lock the room at night in case Shirley strangles me, but I'll have to lock it during the day otherwise that other one will be trying on my frocks.'

It was strange, though, I thought some of my stuff had been moved around the wardrobe on several occasions. I had taken a dress out of the wardrobe to wear to dinner and the neck of it had been greasy, which was strange as I hadn't even worn it yet. I just assumed that some person had been trying it on in a shop with heavy make-up. I had dry cleaned it and returned it to my wardrobe without comment.

Then there was the fact that I had come home one day and my underwear drawer was disorganized. I had always prided myself on having a neat knicker drawer. I had laughed with James and said that we must have some type of a poltergeist in the house. Now I knew that the poltergeist was James's cross-dressing son. When he went home the next day I'd be locking everything away in a safe place. Wait until Katie heard about this one.

One weekend when Henry was away at a conference, Susan suggested she and James and I go out for dinner together with the boys. I was hesitant. If their table manners were disgusting in their own houses, what would they be like in a public place? I told myself that I was being too critical, they were only children and they might enjoy it. James arranged to collect Susan from her home but we were late arriving for her, as Shirley refused to get into the car. He held on to the door frame of the house and refused to let go. He started screaming that he didn't have to go and his dad couldn't make him. James took no nonsense; he prised his fingers from the door frame and carried him into the car, where he proceeded to vent his rage against his brother. Ashley started to shout loudly and the screaming and wailing continued for the ten minutes it took to get to Susan's house.

I got into the back seat and sat between the boys. I hoped this might calm them down a bit; I didn't want their grandmother to see their deplorable behaviour. It made no difference. They hurled obscenities and insults at each other and tried to kick each other, with me acting like some shield in the middle. Susan started the journey being bright and cheerful but by the time we reached the restaurant she was silent.

When we arrived at the restaurant we all got out of the car, except Shirley who refused to budge; he started to kick at James when he tried to pull him. Eventually after a lot of persuasion, while Susan and I looked on taking note of all the pitying looks displayed by passers-by, he leapt out of the car and ran straight onto the public road. James raced after him, though by this stage I was praying a car would get him first. I hated myself instantly for having that thought. I was supposed to protect children, not wish them harm.

Susan looked at me in horror 'I think the only thing to do is get very drunk,' she sighed. I agreed. As soon as we went into the restaurant she immediately asked for a corkscrew. When the waiter arrived Shirley refused to order food and insisted that he wouldn't be eating. He folded his arms and glowered at his grandmother. She was going to get the brunt of his anger as she had suggested the outing in the first place. He began to complain loudly about the amount of computer time he was losing out on, and threatened that he had better be given the time when we returned to the house, or else. Ashley ordered two starters and two main courses; he argued that he should have Shirley's as his brother had kicked him. He was serious.

Every two minutes Shirley would demand to know if we had finished, even though the food hadn't yet arrived. James eventually gave him money to go to the video shop next door and hire a computer game. Susan and I drank our wine in silence. I couldn't bear to look at James. I was seething with anger and embarrassment and I sensed that Susan felt the same.

When the food arrived Ashley got stuck in, snorting and slurping and burping loudly. I moved the food around on my plate, my appetite lost. Other diners turned to stare, drawn by the loud noises he was making. I was mortified; I hoped people didn't think he was mine. Shirley returned with his computer game and demanded we leave. For once he got his wish. We couldn't get out of the place quickly enough, all except Ashley who burst into tears. Despite the fact he had snorted his way through two starters and two main meals he complained that he hadn't had dessert. We were all beyond listening at this stage.

We returned home in silence. Susan gave me a pitying look when she got out of the car. At least she was going home to peace and quiet but I couldn't escape. When we arrived at home James lectured the boys on their behaviour. He was furious with them. But they both complained that he was a weak and dysfunctional man and that they didn't have to listen to him. I went off to the bedroom; I couldn't bear to spend another minute in their company.

CHAPTER 37

I drove home from work, parked the car in the garage and sat there for ages. I couldn't face the thought of getting out of the car and facing the inevitable battle front. I wasn't trained in warfare. I was exhausted after a busy week. When I finally summoned the energy to walk up the front steps and into the house I took a deep breath. For what I was about to receive.

Ashley was lying on the sofa watching a movie, his hands down the front of his trousers, poking around. I looked around cautiously, trying to locate the monster. He wasn't there; he had gone to the shops with his mother who was buying new clothes for him again. Mall rat, it was the best place for him. I had noticed that Ashley always seemed to wear the same clothing and that his mother never took him shopping for anything new.

During the commercial break Ashley rolled over on to his back, and stared at the ceiling 'I wish I had a boyfriend,' he sighed dreamily, 'Mom says that anal sex is awesome.' So Lacey wasn't completely useless, she could set a bad example. James hadn't heard that remark. But what was the bloody point in complaining, it wouldn't do any good.

The peace was broken by Shirley who stormed into the house slamming the front door behind him in his wake. The atmosphere changed immediately. It was palpable. I sat up straight on the sofa, hugging a cushion tightly. He glared over at Ashley who was sitting on the sofa, quietly.

'What are you looking at, you faggot?' he derided his brother. James got up and tried to settle him down.

'Can I have an ice cream, please?' whined Ashley.

'Of course you can,' I replied and he sashayed to the kitchen to get one. I observed Shirley try to trip him up on his way past. 'I'm taking an ice cream too,' he stated and moved towards the freezer.

'Not without saying please first, young man,' I scolded him. Jesus, if this child hadn't been taught manners by adolescence it was nearly pointless trying, but no matter how much it exhausted me I had to continue. I had standards in this house that I wouldn't compromise on.

'Pleeeeease,' he whined in a sing song voice sneering at me. I let it go. Pick your battles, I composed myself carefully. After a few minutes of Shirley snorting and slopping at the ice cream I could bear no more. I went to bed.

Next morning I was sorting through the dirty laundry when I pulled out a huge pair of tattered lace panties from Ashley's jeans. I almost dropped them in surprise. For a minute I thought that Maryann had come back to haunt me. Where did these come from? Was it a memento from a girlfriend? Surely not. He hadn't shown any signs of being interested in girls, in fact I would have thought by his effeminate behaviour that he was a cousin of Dorothy. I washed the clothes anyway. James carried the basket out to the clothes line for me. He lifted the panties from the basket where he was helping me hang the washing on the clothes line. 'I haven't seen you in these before,' he said as he held them up.

'They aren't mine,' I spluttered, my mouth full of clothes pegs. 'I found them in Ashley's jeans; it might be a good time to be talking to him about manly stuff.'

'I'll talk to him when he gets up,' said James, 'but I never thought he was at that stage yet. If either of them was going to be engaging in sex I would have thought it would have been Shirley.'

We were having a cup of coffee on the patio when Ashley finally emerged from his bed. 'I'll just go and tidy up,' I said winking at James as I slid past him.

James joined me in the bedroom a few minutes later. I looked up as I fluffed the pillows on the bed. 'That must have been the quickest talk on contraception ever,' I said.

'There was no need to have that talk with him.' James threw himself on the bed that I had just made.

'Why?' I joined him.

'The panties weren't his girlfriend's, he doesn't have one. They are his mum's.' What? He was wearing woman's knickers? 'He says that they are more comfortable than boxers.'

'Jesus, James, I don't want anything of hers in this house. God knows where they've been. If he wants to wear his mummy's knickers he can wear them in her house, but don't you think there is something a bit sick about that?'

'I don't even want to think of that. The more time I spend with them the weirder I think they are.'

Later James left Ashley at a school friend's house where he was going to stay the night. It was probably some type of make up party, though I was pleased that he had eventually made a friend. It wasn't normal for young people his age to hang around the house all day. Lacey had insisted that Shirley had to stay in her house as she was having friends round. James reluctantly agreed to collect him in the morning.

The telephone rang at 12am as we were preparing for bed. James answered it; I heard a male voice ask if he knew where his son, Ashley, was tonight. 'Who is this?'

'It's the police.'

'He's not here tonight; he's staying at his friend, Brad's house. I left him there earlier tonight,' James explained.

'Your son is in the police station. He was picked up with his friends tonight when they were found drinking alcohol, breaking bottles and lighting fireworks on the grounds of the local primary school. Can you come and collect him?'

'I'm sorry,' stumbled James, 'I've had a couple of glasses of wine and I don't think I should drive.' The police officer agreed that he would return Ashley home as soon as he could. We waited for over an hour before he arrived. Wasn't it strange that we lived in a society where pizza gets to your house before the police? The police car eventually entered the drive and stopped. Ashley got out of the car as James walked to the veranda to greet the police officers.

'Hey, Dad,' he said cheerily as he wiggled up the steps to the veranda with the police officers following closely behind. The officers started to recount the events of the night and what had happened. Ashley kept interrupting them.

'I wasn't lighting fireworks,' he moaned. The police officer glared at him.

'Go to your room, Ashley,' I ordered. Clearly someone had to be the parent around here. He swaggered off dramatically.

The police officer stated that he was prepared not to press charges on this occasion, but that if any further instances of antisocial behaviour occurred he would have no option but to prosecute.

'Don't worry, I'll make sure he's grounded for a very long time,' said James.

'Yes, he'll never be allowed out again if I have anything to do with it, but he's not my child, you know,' I insisted. I was vehemently opposed to having the police officers think that this type of behaviour was acceptable from any child of mine. The police officers left and I went to the bedroom while James agreed to talk to Ashley.

'He's only had one bottle of beer,' he explained later, 'and he's really embarrassed about what he's done.'

'But what happened?'

'I left him at Brad's house and they were having a party when Brad's father showed up and threw them all out. So they all went to the local primary school. Brad's father didn't know that this had been arranged. But I blame myself,' he protested, 'I should have checked that Brad's dad was there and not left Ashley there unless he was.'

'But what did they think they were going to do? Did they think that they would sleep out there all night? They would all have died from hypothermia; it's the middle of winter.'

'I don't think they knew what to do. Ashley has said he knows he should have phoned me, and he's really sorry he didn't but the other boys had about eight bottles of beer and he only had one.'

'Pull the other one, James, don't be so naive, he has had more than one beer. Do you think he would let them think he was a big Ginny? That child couldn't hit sand if he fell off a camel. He wouldn't have been able to come up with any reason not to. He might have fooled you but he didn't fool me.'

Next morning I woke early. James was in the living room. He had collected Shirley, who was still cross that he wasn't going to get a chance to play on the computer. James had drawn up a list of rules which he was going to go through with the boys. I didn't want Shirley to be blamed for something he didn't do, but his behaviour recently had deteriorated further. He needed to be reminded of what we would expect from him.

I tidied our bedroom while I heard James talking to the boys about acceptable behaviour and the consequences if they misbehaved. I could hear raised voices and Shirley screaming at the top of his lungs.

'You can't make me. I don't have to follow no fucking rules. I don't want to live here. I want to live with my mum all the time; she lets me do what I want.'

'Well, you can't do what you want here,' I heard James protest. 'You will follow the rules and every time you do something unacceptable you will lose more computer time.'

'Stuff your computer time and stuff you, butt nugget,' he screamed as he kicked Ashley before storming off to his bedroom and slamming the door behind him.

I emerged into the living room where James and Ashley were both sitting on the sofa. I half expected Ashley to at least attempt to say sorry to me for the previous night's events, but to no avail. Clearly manners weren't compulsory in this family. Well, at least his mother should be proud now she had a delinquent son and another one on the way, according to her predictions.

Shirley returned, storming into the room. 'I wanna go home now,' he screamed. 'Mom said I can go home whenever I want I don't have to stay here if I don't wanna.'

'Actually I think that would be the best thing,' said James. He stood up and walked towards the telephone. He phoned Lacey who complained that she had made plans to go out later. 'Well, then you shouldn't have told him that he could come over whenever he wanted. You are really not helping things you know.'

Lacey started to protest but James cut her short. 'I'll have him over with you in ten minutes. Right,' he said as he put the phone down and turned to the boys. 'Get your shoes on, you're going home.'

I was secretly relieved. At least we wouldn't have to deal with another explosion of temper when he was asked to visit his grandparents. And he had sabotaged Lacey's night out. That would bloody teach her.

'Is Lacey still bringing the boys to counselling?' I asked James when he returned. 'Because I haven't seen any improvement in their behaviour at all. In fact if anything it's deteriorating.'

'No, she told me she can't make them go.'

'Let me get this right. So the boys have no behaviour problems in her house, and they are so helpful and do everything she asks them to do, but she can't make them go to see a counsellor? Is there not something a bit hypocritical about that?'

'I know, but don't you remember that time when her car was being repaired and I agreed to give her a lift. When I got there she started complaining that she couldn't get the children to do anything, and that she wanted them to go swimming but they wouldn't get ready.'

'So she wanted you to act like some sort of referee?'

'The boys were really horrible to her; I just walked out and waited in the car. I didn't sign up for that; I had only agreed to give her a lift, not sort out world war three.'

The following weekend James had planned to take the boys to Sydney for the weekend. 'It will be good for them to spend some time with you.' I said.

'Yes, and it will be good for you to get a bit of peace and quiet too.' We laughed.

'So what will you do?' he asked as he stroked my hair.

'I'll ring Katie and see if she wants to come over for a drink.' I looked up and moved toward the hall quickly. Ashley was standing outside the door in his stocking soles, all the better to creep up on people and hear gossip. 'Heard enough?' I demanded as I pulled the door open quickly. He nearly fell at my feet.

He shuffled back to his bedroom. He was just as nosey as his mother. I had caught him numerous times rummaging around in drawers and cupboards in the house.

On Friday we said goodbye and James left with the boys. I exhaled loudly. I was going to enjoy a bit of peace and quiet. It was a bit strange being without James that night. It was the first time we had been separated since we had started to live together. He phoned me from Sydney to check I was all right, and I could hear the kids in the background fighting and calling each other names. Nothing new there then.

I woke up next morning. The phone had rung twice in the middle of the night, but when I answered it there was no reply. Just breathing. I had eventually pulled the line out. It was hard enough trying to get to sleep worrying about work and the demands it brought, without worrying about some creep who must be getting off at the sound of the anxiety in my voice. It was unnerving; the machine that linked me with home was now seen as something sinister. I had experienced silent calls when I was living in the house, but they had stopped when I moved into the house with James. Had my stalker resumed their activities?

When they returned on Sunday afternoon James told me that they had had a good time though Shirley complained the entire time about the amount of computer time he was losing out on. James left the boys at their mother's house and we spend some quality time together. We were interrupted by the telephone.

'I'd better get that,' said James. He returned later his face pulled into a frown.

'What's the matter? Has something happened to your parents?'

'No, it was Lacey.' I sighed. 'She was screaming at me like some harridan, and saying that I had taken the kids to Sydney because you had planned to have people over and you were ashamed of them. She said you didn't want them to be there.'

'Well, she's right about one thing. I am ashamed of their behaviour but you weren't sent off to Sydney just so that I could invite people over. If that was the case I'd just invite people whenever the boys aren't here. But if she thinks I'm ashamed of them would any other mother not be asking themselves why?' Would any reasonable parent not be telling their children to be on their best behaviour in case it reflected on them? What kind of parent encouraged them to behave as badly as they possibly could?

'She must have grilled the kids when they went back to her house. She's always questioning them about you,' admitted James.

I knew that already. There wasn't a lot happening in her own life, so she had to look outside for a bit of excitement. She came to this place hoping to live some sex in the city existence and she had been constantly disappointed since. She wasn't going to compete with any of the professional woman here. She looked like a bloody transvestite for a start, and she had all the social skills and grace of the typical red-necked hillbilly. And she couldn't be happy with those children; they were horrible to her and to each other. God knows what was going to happen to them but I didn't think it would be good.

Hell hath no fury like a scorned woman, and in her case despite the fact that she ended the relationship with James this was how Lacey reacted. She started to tell the children that their father had left the marriage and that she desperately wanted them all to live together but he wouldn't listen. Ashley was too thick to remember that only four years ago she had dragged them away at the weekend in her chase for boyfriends.

Even though there was an agreement about contact arrangements Lacey changed it. She now only permitted the children to come every other weekend. Even then she tried to make it as difficult as possible. She would contact James and offer the children up for contact, like parcels, when she knew that he was working. Then she would accuse him of being an uncaring father when he couldn't see them at short notice. Lacey gave no priority to James's time with the children and she would often organise an activity which clashed with contact arrangements without discussing it with him. We didn't know if we were coming or going, but James was still determined to spend as much time with them as he could.

CHAPTER 38

James drove to Lacey's house to collect the boys to take them to the movies. When he returned I was still working on a report for work. 'Did you have a nice time with the boys?' I asked.

'Shirley refused to go; he won't leave the house at all now except to go to school. I think he's getting worse. He's practically agoraphobic.'

'Well, everything he needs is in that house, so why should he leave? Would you leave when you had your mother running around meeting your every need?'

'I worry about those boys,' confided James. 'They used to be able to play together and now they just hate each other so much. Ashley told me that Shirley punched him last night when their mother was out. He has a cut and a bruise on his eye.'

'I take it that he didn't get grounded?' James shook his head.

'She never tries to punish Shirley; it's just too difficult for her.'

'She's not brave enough to be a parent; she probably blamed Ashley for walking into Shirley's fist.' I wasn't surprised that Ashley hated his brother. Shirley got away with blue murder in her house. She always accused Ashley of name calling when we both knew that every single time in this house it was Shirley who had done it. Now he had started punching him, what was going to be next?

'I think maybe Ashley might behave that way in her house because he's trying to fight for a bit of justice,' James reasoned, 'but he doesn't need to do it here, because we protect him from Shirley.'

'Well, somebody has to be an adult and stand up to Shirley to try and curb his tyrannical behaviour. She can't. She lets Shirley verbally abuse her and she does nothing about it. She turns a blind eye when he does the same to his brother. She's going to regret that some day when he starts punching her.'

'I thought he was going to do it to me a while ago. I have never felt afraid of a child before in my whole life, but he was so angry, he could hardly contain himself. His fists were clenched and he looked as if he really wanted to do it. I don't do anything to annoy him, I usually stay out of his way, but can you just imagine what he could do if he lost it completely?'

'But maybe she will be forced to get some help for him then.'

'Right, James, and maybe it will be too late and something terrible will have happened. He seems to be having more and more problems controlling himself. I wouldn't be surprised at anything that child would do. She told me that her own mother turned a blind eye when her brothers battered her. She even said that one of her brothers beat her so badly that she was knocked unconscious.'

'Yes, that's true; it happened a few times,' said James. 'She said she woke up once and her brother was lying beside her on the ground, crying and praying that she would get up. He thought he had killed her.' But if her mother didn't protect her, wouldn't you think that she would be trying twice as hard to make sure than nothing like that happens with her own children?'

'Part of that might be because Ashley hasn't suffered the extent of abuse she has suffered so she thinks it isn't too bad. If he hasn't been knocked unconscious then it doesn't really count. But I don't know what more has to happen before she intervenes?' What would it take for Lacey to realise her son was a sociopath? What more would happen before she accepted that he needed help?

It was 11pm and I was half asleep on the sofa watching some old movie while James had given up and gone to bed. The phone rang. It was Shirley. 'I wanna talk to my dad,' he demanded.

'Sorry, you can't, Shirley.' I explained. 'He's in his bed where you should be at this time as it's a school night, and I've told you before you don't get anything in this house unless you say please.' I could hear his mother in the background; there was the sound of splashing water. Surely she couldn't be washing dishes, not at her house?

'Just go and tell him I wanna talk to him now,' he commanded.

'No, Shirley, I won't. If you want something you will just have to learn to ask properly for it.' I put the phone down. The phone rang again immediately and I unplugged it. The cheeky little brat, I'd teach that child to have a bit of respect for me if it was the last thing I did. But I knew that any action I took would be futile. I had no authority as a stepmother; I couldn't correct the children's appalling behaviour without being harangued later by their mother. I don't even think the children intentionally sought to disrespect me; they were just behaving in our house the way they did in theirs.

They would barge into rooms without knocking. When I was in the bath Shirley banged at the door and demanded to be let in. I knew his mother still allowed him to bathe with her. Maybe it was the only way she could get him to go near soap and water, but there was no way he was doing the same with me. I tried as much as possible to give them their own space; I knew it must be so hard on them having to share their father with me.

I knew I had to consider my own self preservation so I began to create some physical and psychological boundaries for myself. Our bedroom was out of bounds to them. It was a sacred place, which James and I shared, and I didn't want that sullied. Sometimes I would go there when I needed to get away from the screaming and the shouting. It became my refuge, my sanctuary. I took the television out of the sitting room and put it there. At least I might have a chance to watch something I liked in peace. I realised I was creating an invisible boundary with the boys, but I forced myself to believe that James needed to spend time alone with them.

I was continually exhausted; despite everything Shirley had done I continued to make an effort. He was only a child and I knew that most of his behaviours were usual in his mother's house. It must have been so confusing coming from one house where there were no rules to another where there was. No matter what I did for him, nothing worked. I bought him the comic books he liked and I had even bought him some of those horrible blood and guts T-shirts he liked, but he never wore them. I had spent the past months trying to get close to him, but he pushed me away every time. He wouldn't talk to me. The only attention he seemed to like was the negative attention he got when he misbehaved. His eyes would shine in glee and he looked as if he had won a prize. He thrived on conflict; he was his mother's son.

James made a pot of coffee and brought it outside. This was our Saturday morning ritual and I loved it. James had risen early and gone to the shop to buy the weekend papers. We settled down to read them.

'You know, I keep thinking of what it was like before Lacey became pregnant with Shirley,' said James. 'At the time we never had sex; she spent most of the time on the Internet while I looked after Ashley and went out to work. She always said she was emailing her family and friends back in America but I checked one day to see what sites she had been on and she was using some Internet dating site. She had been on it all day; I had just come home from work and collected Ashley from day care. The house wasn't clean, the dinner wasn't ready, though she always left most of the cooking and cleaning to me.'

'Yes, she probably hasn't lived in a clean house since you left. Honest, you should see that state of that pigsty she's in now. And it's not the house itself, it was probably clean before she got it. Does she not have an annual inspection like most people who live in rented accommodation here?'

'No, she has this landlord who lives up north. She just pays the rent and he leaves her alone. She doesn't even contact him when something needs fixed, she usually calls me instead.'

'So you are supposed to maintain her house, like some type of husband? Well, I'm telling you now, James, I know she's allegedly the mother of your children but you have no responsibility for her. I'm not putting up with that, it's a load of total bollocks. If she wanted you to be a caretaker, she shouldn't have left you, should she? Why can't she get one of her Internet contacts to come fix things?'

'I don't intend to set foot in that place again. But I was trying to say that I think she might have been meeting people on that site.'

'Let me get this right,' I questioned. 'She left her child in day care all day when she was at home doing nothing but surfing the net?'

'She used to go for drives; I never knew where she went. Whenever I went to use the car the petrol tank was always empty. I was constantly filling it up. I knew then she wasn't sitting in the house all day. So you think she might have been meeting men on sites. She did say that she wanted to have sex with other men,' he pondered.

'Well, that's nice of her to ask her husband's permission first. Then what happened?' I sat down; this whole saga was getting worse. I felt like I was embroiled in the most sordid soap opera ever written, and the sad truth was that it was all real.

'Then one day when I came home she looked really kind of flushed and we had sex that night, and a short while later she told me she was pregnant again.'

'And you never doubted anything?' He couldn't really be so naive, could he?

'I was just so happy about her having another child. I loved caring for Ashley, and I thought it would be even better to have another child. I know we have been talking about getting a DNA test on Shirley, I think I need to get one now. I've been looking it up on the Internet. There's a site in Canada that send you a kit, you send it back to them with a sample of your saliva and the child's and they send you the results.'

'Is it legal?' I asked carefully.

294

'Well, it says on the site that if the result is negative you can apply to the family courts and say that you aren't prepared to pay any more child maintenance so the onus is on the mother to prove that the child is yours, but the test is 99.9% accurate.'

'So are you going to do that?'

Yes, I've already sent away for the kit. I have to know the truth, there's too much at stake here. I'm just so frightened that she has known about this all the time and that she intended telling me the truth when he was eighteen and couldn't do anything about it. It's just the type of low life thing she would do.'

'Maybe you should be worried. It sounds like this pregnancy was completely different; I don't see any photos of her cavorting around the place naked.'

'No,' he agreed, 'she was very subdued with this pregnancy and she was smoking dope all the time. The house was reeking with the smell of it. I had to open the windows and let Ashley play outside before I would let him in. I told her she would have to stop, that it wasn't doing her or the baby any good, but you know what she's like, you couldn't reason with her. And then later when Shirley was born he was so ill we thought we were going to lose him.'

'Did anyone ever consider that he might have been suffering withdrawal from drugs?'

'I don't know what questions they asked her, but I don't think she told them that she was smoking dope all the time.'

And he never spoke up either? Once again, he had let one of his children down. I thought I knew this man, I thought I loved him, but the more I learned about her the more I became concerned about his part in the whole dirty business. Somewhere between each of them the truth of their marriage lay but who could I believe?

CHAPTER 39

I was taking a bubble bath, my daily retreat from life. Stuff their water restrictions, a good book and a bottle of bath foam worked wonders. James came in with a glass of white wine and passed it to me. He sat down on the floor. He seemed very subdued. I waited. I knew if he had something to say he would say it.

'I've never considered it before,' he began, 'but do you think the way that Lacey was abused as a child has affected her now?'

'Well,' I said, 'she has a history of physical and emotional abuse and she was also sexually abused when she was only twelve and her mother didn't believe her. She called her a whore and a slut. Can you imagine what that would do to a young girl growing up? Knowing that you were being blamed and the perpetrator was not.'

'Her mother, Sharon, seemed to really hate her,' agreed James. 'When we lived in America, Sharon always told me that I was too good for Lacey. She was the one who paid for us to return to Australia, but she wanted me to take the boys and leave her behind. She was trying to get Lacey committed to an institution.'

'You know, it's a real tragic story when you hear it, but her family really put the D in dysfunction,' I said caustically.

'Hmm, you're right, you know, she used to say that every night when the family sat down at the dinner table, her father used to come in and start beating up her brother. Every single day. As far back as she can remember, until the dad died when she was fourteen. Nobody said anything about it. They just sat there in silence and waited for it to end so they could start dinner.'

I couldn't begin to imagine what the abuse from that family had done to her. There was also the history of mental health problems in her family. Madness didn't so much run in that family as gallop. Her sister was now on husband number five and each one of her husbands seemed to be worse than the one before. Her latest husband sounded like a real case. He had eighteen children to loads of different women and he didn't have contact with any of them. He didn't even know their names.

Lacey's grandmother appeared to be quite wealthy. But between her sister and her older brothers they managed to drink or inject whatever money she had given them. Or they spent most of it on expensive dogs. Her older brother now lived in a car somewhere. He didn't work, and didn't need to because his mother financially supported him.

I was sure Susan and Henry were really impressed when they met Lacey. They must have thought James had really lost the run of himself taking up with a woman like that. And it wasn't as if she was some teenager who didn't know any better. She was in her late thirties when he was only twenty. Christ, it was only a good pair of shoes away from child abduction.

Then when we move on to their marriage, what was next in the Lacey tale? It sounded like the worst case study from a child protection client file. First there was the determination to get pregnant, even though she didn't have a job, or anything to offer a child. She was just looking around for some man to donate his sperm. And James couldn't flatter himself and say that she was picky. There seemed to be several in the running before one of them hit the jackpot.

So she pranced around the country naked when she was pregnant, not worrying about who might find that type of thing a bit distressing. She didn't tell the medical professionals that she had herpes because she wanted to try natural childbirth. That was the part that made me so angry; she put that baby at risk of blindness just because she was so bloody selfish.

But James was an adult then too; he had some responsibility for this child too. In some way he colluded with her. He didn't speak up. He just allowed it to happen.

When she got pregnant with Shirley, James thought it was a bit strange as they had only had sex once in months. At the time he didn't start to count up the fact that she was disappearing all the time and telling him she wanted to have sex with other blokes. Even though she spent her entire pregnancy stoned on marijuana, ignoring the small matter of the child she already had.

Whoever had dealt with that birth should be prosecuted for not checking that she had given birth naturally before. That should have been followed up. Then when she got Shirley home she lay in her bed all day, ignoring the child. And when James came home from work, and Ashley came home from day care, she took to her bed again and had nothing more to do with either of them.

Had either of them any idea what psychological problems that would cause an infant. He was fed and changed, but infants have died because they weren't given any physical affection. They need it nearly as much as food at that age. I wouldn't be surprised if Shirley had some kind of attachment disorder. And the prognosis for that wasn't particularly positive.

What would happen when it got to the stage when nobody wanted to be around him? Ashley had already said that he couldn't wait to leave home. But that wasn't just because he had to deal with all Shirley's explosive rages and violence without his mother protecting him from that. He had said he was so ashamed of the way she behaved, especially when she drank. But while Ashley might have an escape route I doubted if Shirley would ever be able to leave home. I could just picture Shirley sitting there as an adult in his underpants, scratching himself and playing computer games all hours of the day and night. And his mother would love it; she would have someone to care for. She wouldn't see the fact that she had denied him the opportunity to be with family and friends; she wouldn't see the fact that she had created dependency and robbed him of the chance to live a fulfilling life. She wouldn't care that he would never have significant relationships, the chance to fall in love with someone and have children. She would only see that he stayed with her because he loved her. When the sad truth was that the child didn't seem able to love anyone.

At some level it must be a bit scary for a child knowing that if he flew into a rage people would bend over to do his bidding. This level of power might be a bit scary for a wee boy. What would it be like in her house if the decisions about computer time, what he watched on DVD or television, all those things were taken care of by people who cared about him? Who only wanted the best for him? By adults who were strong enough to take his rage and still be firm and loving? That's what that wee boy was crying out for. But she was just so caught up in indulging him and treating him like a baby. She couldn't see that every time she gave in it was making it more and more difficult for him.

I wondered if Lacey might be afraid that I would do a better job than she had. Was that why she had created this whole wicked stepmother role for me? But I wasn't buying into that. I was not being forced to take that role, just to appease her fears about her own inadequacies. James was right, it was funny that Lacey had no problem at all about James's parenting of the boys when she divorced him, or when she abandoned the boys, and she had only started to raise questions now that he was with me.

For someone who had instigated a divorce Lacey seemed to have a lot of unresolved issues. I knew from personal experience that divorce was a painful, emotional process. It took time for both separated people to recover and get on with their new lives. But some people never did. Even though she instigated it, I think Lacey expected that James would always be there for her in the background. Her plan was to meet all these sexy men and be wined and dined but it hadn't happened. She was reduced to the dregs, trying to have relationships with clients. And to make matters worse, James met someone. He wasn't supposed to, it wasn't in her script. He was supposed to be the one she dumped the kids with when she took up with yet another low life. He was always supposed to be there to see how much she was enjoying her life. But when we met and fell in love she tried to undermine what we had so we had been forced to exclude her. But it didn't have to be that way. She could have been part of our lives on some level and we could have at least had a friendly arrangement which would have been much better for the children.

To make matters worse we had bought this house, which was a long way from the tip she lived in. She still wanted James to be living like some sad old bastard, sitting around waiting for her to drop by for a cup of coffee, or being so grateful for a small kind word from her when he went to collect the children. I knew how bloody self-centred Lacey was. She probably thought we had done all this personally, just to annoy her. And to make matters even worse for her, we had decided we were going to get married, and in Ireland. The place, where in one of her delusions, she was going to build some type of peace community. In some way we were living out her dream, well, only the saner parts of it.

In Lacey's life, all her relationships had been intense and unstable, swinging wildly from love to hate and back again. This time I was the one who had been struck by the hate pendulum. But Lacey viewed herself as a victim of circumstance; she wouldn't accept any responsibility for her behaviour or the reasons our friendship ended. She had never accepted responsibility for any of her problems; she had always blamed other people for all her relationships. I didn't think she could. Every single time the boys went home and said anything positive either about James or me, the jealousy ignited all over again.

'She's more to be pitied than anything else,' I said sadly. 'But it would take the combined efforts of a psychiatrist and a psychoanalyst to sort it all out now.'

'I know, I used to really worry about her,' said James. 'She used to eat and eat and would be sick several times a day. Sometimes she would get up in the middle of the night and make a whole batch of chocolate brownies and eat them all herself. She also used to make this paste stuff from cocoa powder, butter and sugar and she would sit in the kitchen and eat it directly out of the saucepan. I used to find her there all the time. Then I used to hear her in the bathroom afterwards throwing up.'

'She had bulimia?' But she was the size of a detached house. Did she forget to be sick?

'Well, she denied it, she kept saying she wasn't being sick, but it was a small apartment, the walls were thin, and the smell of sick lingered for ages afterwards.'

'You know,' James confided, 'her friend, Jeanie, told me that she thought Lacey was looking down the barrel of being an old woman, living on her own.'

'It's true. It's bloody difficult enough to find someone half attractive when all your bits and pieces are in the right places but when you are fifty? Would you even be bothered?'

He laughed. 'You do make me laugh, even in the middle of all this mess,' he said.

'Yes, well, you know me, James, I always use humour as a defence mechanism, and it stops me from putting my head in the oven and pulling the switch.'

'You don't really think you would ever do that, do you?' he asked horrified.

'No, I bloody wouldn't, she's not worth it. But I do feel embarrassed for you sometimes. When I think of your family and how lovely they are, it must have been horrendous for them when you brought her home.'

'It was,' he agreed. 'The first time we went to my parents' house my mum opened the door and Lacey said, right, show me the photograph of the girl who took his virginity.'

'What a shocking thing to say. I'm sure your mother must have been mortified.'

'She was,' he admitted. 'Mum and Dad paid for us all to come down for Christmas once with the kids. Lacey drank too much champagne and spent the entire night throwing up loudly in the bathroom. The next day when we were just about to sit down to Christmas dinner she said that she wanted to go for a walk and left the house.'

'She claimed afterwards that she got lost, but my dad had to go out looking for her. When he eventually dragged her back she sat at the table and refused to eat. We were sitting there with Joseph and his wife and son, my parents, Carmella's parents and some other guests who had come over especially for dinner. I thought my parents were going to have a fit.'

'Were you not so ashamed of her, James?' I asked sympathetically.

'Yes, of course I was, but for the sake of the boys, I thought it was best for us to be together as a family. I didn't want my children to be part of a broken home.'

'But seriously, James, I think at some level she must regret what she has thrown away. She must have realised that when she first moved here and all these blokes weren't queuing up to date her. She must at some level have wondered if she had done the right thing.'

'I'm not sure if she even knew what she was doing then,' he said sagely. 'Her mother was really worried about her and she had consulted with the psychiatric unit. She was trying to have Lacey committed to an institution because she was behaving so insanely. Sharon told me that Lacey behaved this way when she was younger as well, but that Lacey had run away before she could get her committed and she hadn't returned home for years.'

'Maybe she might have got the help she needed then. I can see some of the signs of severe mental health problems with her now. It's just a pity that it isn't just her that it affects; it affects those boys, you and, unfortunately, me too. God knows how this will all end up, but there will be tears before bedtime.'

'What will happen to her do you think?' he asked sorrowfully.

'I don't honestly know. Maybe she looked a bit better when she was younger, but you have to admit it, she's not the bonniest. She dresses like a transvestite, actually. That's very insulting to guys who cross dress, sorry there, fellas. Even transvestites wear heels, not men's clumpy shoes. She has a poodle perm and a filthy mouth. She has no boundaries. She's into sodomy. Christ, give her a couple more years and she will be wearing nappies with the damage that all that has done to her body, if she doesn't die of AIDS first. She has two children who are horrible to her and each other. She has herpes. When you add it all up, she hasn't got a lot going for her, has she?'

'No she hasn't,' he agreed.

'Is it any wonder she bakes batches of buns in the middle of the night and eats them; it must be the only comfort the poor woman gets in her life. But honestly, James, I can't believe when she realised that all her fantasies weren't going to come true that she never tried to reconcile with you.'

'She did,' he said boldly.

'What?'

'Yes, but after all she'd put me through I didn't want anything to do with her, at all.'

I hoped not.

CHAPTER 40

Katie and I were catching up with a rare cup of coffee. I was updating her on Lacey's latest antics. 'She takes me to the fair, Katie. She's actively encouraging the boys to behave as badly as they can when they are with us. I even caught that wee brat Shirley writing on the walls in the hall that Ashley takes it up the butt. And that other gobshite has been sent to search the place for incriminating information. I took a letter that my father wrote to me out of his hands the other day. I even caught him one day trying to hack into my email account so he could read my emails.'

'You know what her problem is, don't you?' asked Katie.

'You mean apart from the personality disorder, the slovenliness, the irrational behaviour and the harassment?'

'She's so jealous because James took you away from her. How do you save Lacey from drowning?' Katie asked.

'I don't know, you'd better tell me.'

'Take your foot off her head,' laughed Katie and I joined in.

'How do you get Lacey in your bed?' I asked.

'I don't know.'

'Grease her hips so she'll fit through the door and throw a Mars bar on the bed.'

'What do the Bermuda Triangle and Lacey have in common?' asked Katie.

'I give up.'

'They've both swallowed a lot of semen.'

'Right, what about this one? Why is Lacey like a door knob? Because everybody gets a turn.'

We convulsed into giggles. Joking like this with Katie was the only thing that kept me sane. As we were leaving the office Katie asked, 'What's the difference between Lacey and a bowling ball?'

'I don't know, what?'

'There is no difference. They're both round and have three holes to poke.'

'How do you prevent Lacey from having sex?'

'I don't know, Louise, tell me?'

'Marry her.' We snorted with laughter. We were on our way out to visit Jenna, a young mother I was working with. We had visited yesterday but she wasn't home though we had met her Uncle Charlie at the front door. He had been out of it, high as a kite on drugs. If he was living with Jenna it meant that things had deteriorated. I had advised Charlie that I would be back today to see her. I had been trying for a few days now to contact Jenna; if she was ignoring my calls it meant only one thing – she had reconciled with her husband John who had a history of violence.

He had been convicted of attempted murder, and in the short time that I had known him he had knocked his wife from one end of the town to another. I had seen Jenna with black eyes, broken limbs and cut lips. After every reconciliation there was inevitably another pregnancy to contend with. Jenna had three children, Karin was five and lived with her grandmother, Bobby was four and Jason was two. When John left her, as he inevitably did, he took all her electrical appliances with him. Or he would return when she wasn't there and steal everything in sight.

Katie and I arrived at the house. Jenna opened the door. She was dishevelled and looked exhausted. There were huge black rings under her eyes. She tried to block my entrance to the house, but she knew me well enough by now. I wouldn't leave without seeing the children. I asked Jenna if I could come in. She hesitated and then opened the door reluctantly. Jenna's Uncle Charlie was sprawled over the sofa; his girlfriend was on top of him. Jenna turned round. 'Hold on a minute,' she said, and closed the door in my face.

Katie looked at me. 'It doesn't look good, does it?' she asked.

'No, not at the minute,' I replied. We waited. I looked around the garden. The skip which I had ordered for Jenna was sitting in the front driveway; it was only half full of rubbish and junk. Jenna had agreed to clear the house of all the rubbish and broken furniture as it was a health hazard. The skip was due to be collected in another couple of days but there was still a huge pile of rubbish in the back garden. Old kitchen appliances were lying on their side beside mattresses and a broken set of bunk beds.

Jenna let us in to the house. Uncle Charlie and his girlfriend looked distinctly uncomfortable. I had already talked to Jenna about them. They moved around between family members who were expected to feed them. Jenna could just about afford to keep herself and the children; she didn't have the money for another couple of dependants. But she insisted that family was family. She didn't have the heart to send them away.

I noticed immediately that there was considerable damage to the house. Jenna admitted that John had struck again. There were holes in the walls of the front hall and he had kicked holes in the bottom of the doors. The curtains had been ripped off their tracks and he had smashed the air conditioning unit which she had in the living room. She would need this in the hot summer ahead. I also knew that Jenna was due to have a housing inspection. If she didn't pass this she could be evicted. He had stolen her microwave television set and video player, which meant Jason wouldn't get to see his videos again.

The boys appeared, running towards me to give me a hug. They were beautiful children. They were affectionate and loving. I always liked to keep a close eye on them. I asked Jenna why Bobby wasn't at nursery school. 'I don't have money to buy his lunch,' she admitted. That usually meant that John had taken the contents of her purse with him.

'Have you anything in the house for the children's breakfast?' I asked her. She shook her head silently. I had suspected this. I knew it was hard for Jenna to have to admit that she was stuck financially. I had brought out a food voucher for her. I agreed to take her to the shops immediately so she could buy some food for the children. The children came too, all three of them. Karin should have been at school too.

Karin and the boys waited in the car with Katie while I accompanied Jenna to the shops. When we returned she had bought essentials which would keep her going until she was due to get another Centrelink payment. She struggled with the shopping bags and I assisted her, but not before noticing that she had gained considerable weight since I had last seen her. She looked pregnant. I didn't want to confront her with my suspicions, not when the children were there; the priority was to get them home and fed.

We brought the family back to their home and I reminded Jenna that the skip would be collected in two days' time. I encouraged her Uncle Charlie to put all the rubbish in it. He might as well do something to earn his keep. She would need another voucher to purchase items to repair the home. I would have to go back to the office to plead her case. I arranged to call out next day to ascertain how things were. Bobby and Karin would be at school then and I would have the chance to talk to Jenna properly.

'Did you know that Jenna is pregnant?' asked Katie as we drove off to the office.

'I thought so, but how did you know?'

'Karin told me. She said her mummy told her that if it was a baby girl it would live with her grandma and her, but if it was a baby boy it would stay with the boys.' Leave it to Katie; she could get blood out of a stone. I was glad I had arranged to go back. That meant that she had been with John again even though he wasn't allowed to come near her house. This was going to be yet another worry for me on top of everything else.

Next morning I had just parked the car and was walking towards the office when Katie met me. 'You look fed up. What's wrong, is that bitch still causing problems for you and James?'

'Can't you guess? You know we are going to have to tell the children to stop talking about what goes on in that house.'

'Why?'

'Well, Ashley just told me that Lacey destroyed all the family photos in front of him and Shirley. She even destroyed that DVD I bought James which he lent to Ashley. She must have done it with a six inch nail, the groove is so deep. That was no accident. You know she never questioned James's ability to be a good father and to care for the children by himself when they were divorced or when she abandoned them to go off and commit sodomy. But since he met me he has suddenly became totally unreliable and can't be trusted with the children unless she gives him a complete list of do's and don'ts.'

'She's nuts,' said Katie, 'what do you expect?'

'I know that. You know every time I hear something more that she's done to those children it wounds me more and more. I think I'm going to have to make a report about her. I'll probably lose my job if I don't talk to someone about it. I'm not being vindictive or using my position here, but I really think she's abusing those kids.'

'I've been thinking about that too. I think you are right,' replied Katie seriously. 'Look, why don't you talk to Tom about it. That way if he thinks there's enough to report he will tell you to do that, or if he thinks you should wait a while and see what else happens at least you've checked it out with someone in authority.'

Katie was right. I decided to talk to Tom later that week when I had supervision with him. That was if I was lucky enough to get it.

'Tell me this?' asked Katie later as we were going out on another visit. 'If you saw Lacey drowning in a swimming pool, would you go to lunch or the movies?' I laughed.

'Hmm, that's a difficult one. I think I'd go to the movies first; you could get snacks and have the best of both worlds.'

'Good answer, comrade,' she smiled. I knew I was going to miss her desperately when she left at the end of the week for a few weeks' holiday at home.

CHAPTER 41

The report came in late afternoon. It needed to be acted on immediately. An eight year old girl had disclosed that her mother had hit her with a belt. The principal of the school had revealed that there were visible marks on her arms. There were no other available staff; Katie was on holiday and my team mate Larry wouldn't go out on the visit as it was 4.15pm. He finished every day at 4.51pm, public servant hours, and always had a lunch between 12 o'clock and 1.00 o'clock. It was well for him. I was lucky if I had eaten breakfast by the end of the day. I wouldn't have minded that level of choice in my own working life. It wasn't good practice, but I decided to conduct the visit alone.

The house was well-furnished and tastefully decorated. A huge television took up an entire wall of the front living room where Tanya's mother invited me in to. She was angry. She started immediately when I sat down. 'That wee bitch is only trying to get me into trouble, I'm sick, I have enough to do without you people coming out here.'

I tried to calm her down. I needed to know what had happened before she had beaten her daughter. She complained about the fact that she had no social life. She complained that Tanya's father provided no support to her. She was forced to go out to work but the stress of doing everything had made her ill. She had constant migraines which were so bad she couldn't even get out of the bed.

She said that that morning Tanya had insisted on being driven to school but she couldn't get out of bed to do it. She claimed that she had only smacked her with the first thing that had come to hand. She had been exhausted, her boyfriend had left her; it was all Tanya's fault.

She resumed her litany about her daughter. Tanya was nothing but an inconvenience, and she was nothing but trouble. She wished she had never given birth to her. She wanted her taken away. She wanted to relinquish her responsibilities as a mother. She signed the forms for voluntary admission to foster care, and moved quickly around the house to pack a case full of clothing. She didn't want to come with me to place the child or meet the carers. 'Just take the wee bitch away,' she ordered.

I telephoned the office when I returned to the car. I needed to find a placement. Telling an eight-year-old that her mother no longer wanted her was not going to be as easy.

I collected Tanya from school. She was nervous; her hair toggle was hanging onto the ends of an untidy ponytail. 'You look like you are falling apart,' I said gently. 'Do you want me to fix that for you?'

She looked up at me. 'If you like,' she shrugged.

I smoothed her hair into a ponytail. 'Would you like it in a nice plait?' She nodded. I plaited her hair and held it together with the hair accessory. 'Green, that's my favourite colour,' I said approvingly. Tanya moved over in the front seat of the car; she had started to relax.

I knew it would take a while for the office to secure a placement so there was no point in taking her there and making her wait. 'Would you like to go to McDonald's for a milkshake and we can have a little talk?'

Tanya agreed, 'But only if I can have strawberry.'

'We'll just have to drive around and find one that serves it,' I reassured her. We arrived at a local McDonald's, they are always easy to find. I ordered strawberry milkshake and a cup of coffee for myself. When we sat down I started to talk to Tanya about visiting her mother. 'She seems very tired,' I said. 'It must be hard for you. Do you have to be quiet in the house when your mummy is sick?'

'Yes, she always shouts at me if I make a noise, so I have to watch my cartoons with the sound off. I can see the pictures but I don't know the funny things that get said.'

Tanya told me what had happened that morning; her mother's version was much the same up until the part where she had beaten her. 'She told me to bring me over her jeans and I thought she was going to get dressed and take me to school. But she only took the belt out of them and started to hit me with it.' Tanya put her head down and played with the straw of her drink. 'Do you want to see it?' she asked quietly.' I nodded. She looked around her to see if anyone else was watching before she pulled up the sleeve of her sweatshirt. The welts stood out red raw against her pale white skin. 'I have them on my bum too, but I didn't tell Mrs Simpson, because that's rude.' She blushed.

'Did anything else happen before you got to school, pet?' Tanya put her head down. 'Mummy pulled my hair really hard, but it's all my fault. I couldn't put the hair toggle in by myself.'

'Has it happened before?'

Tanya nodded. 'She usually just hits me with her hand or the hairbrush; she never beat me with a belt before,' she said adamantly.

'What about your daddy?' I asked carefully. 'Do you ever see him?'

Tanya's eyes lit up. 'He took me on holiday last summer to his house. I had a great time. I have a new mummy there who's really nice and a new little sister and she's really funny. One day she put her mummy's shoes down the toilet.' Tanya laughed mischievously. 'Can I go and live with him, please?' she wheedled.

'When was the last time you saw him?'

'On my last school holidays, but he phones me all the time but mummy won't let me talk to him.' She shrugged her shoulders. 'Mummy says I have to live with her so that daddy has to give her money but she says I can't see him any more because she's going to get me a new daddy, but I don't want one, I hate them.'

'Who Tanya?'

'Her boyfriends that always come to our house. She writes to people on the Internet. Some of them talk funny, like they are all sleepy.' Hmm, probably drugs or alcohol. 'And then one day Brian got in my bed and my mummy was really cross with me. She said that I had told him to.'

Christ, there was more happening here than I had thought. 'Did he hurt you, Tanya?' She put her head down again. 'He touched my pee pee,' she whispered quietly. On top of everything else the child would need to be interviewed by the police for suspected sexual abuse as well as physical abuse.

'Do you know what I think would be best?' I asked Tanya. She looked up at me quizzically. 'I think that you both could do with a wee holiday away from each other.'

'You mean to another house?'

'Yes.' I nodded. 'I think it might be good for both of you to have a few days away.'

'Who is going to make my mummy her tea in the morning?' Tanya looked worried.

'Don't you worry about that. I'm sure your mummy can get it herself.' Tanya didn't look convinced.

'Maybe she might even miss me a bit then,' said Tanya solemnly.

I talked to Tanya about foster care. I told her that I didn't know where she would be living yet, but she would go to the same school, and she could see her mummy when she wanted to, but that I wanted to make sure she was safe.

'Will they beat me too?' she asked, her eyes wide. 'No, pet,' I reassured her, 'they won't, they'll take good care of you and make your breakfast in the morning, and they'll make dinner for you.'

'Will I have to clean their house too? I can hoover up,' she said proudly.

'No, pet, you might have to keep your own room tidy, but that's all you will have to do. The rest of the time you can play.'

'And can I watch cartoons?'

'Yes, I'm sure you can.'

'Can I have the sound turned up?' she asked in surprise.

'Of course you can darling,' I said. 'We'll make sure of that.'

The office phoned and gave me details of the placement. I could fill out the rest of the details when we got there. 'I've already got some of your clothes and one of your teddies, so do you want to go there and see what it's like?' She put her hand out, reached for mine and held it tightly.

I brought her to her foster placement and introduced her to the foster carer, Emily. I had used Emily before on an emergency basis and I couldn't praise her highly enough. Tanya never left my side. She sat beside me, looking hesitatingly around the room while I completed the required paperwork.

'Maybe you'd like to see your room now?' Emily suggested. Tanya moved slowly towards her.

'I'll just go out and bring in your things,' I said. She hesitated. 'I'll be back in a wee minute, pet,' I reassured her.

I returned with her clothing and heard squeals of laughter coming from the bedroom. Emily indicated that I should come and look. Tanya was tickling Emily's little daughter who was only five. The pair were giggling away.

I set the clothes down and returned to the living room with Emily. I explained that I didn't know how long the placement would last but that I would organize transport to school and would contact her the next day. We chatted for a few minutes and Tanya returned to the living room. She was red-faced and breathless.

'Can I really stay here?' she asked me.

'Of course you can.'

I gave Emily the mother's phone number. 'Now if you want to phone your mummy later on, Emily can dial the number for you.' Tanya nodded. 'Now darling, I have to go back to the office, but Emily will look after you, and I've talked to Emily about putting the cartoons on for a little while after you've done your homework.'

'Can I really?' Tanya's eyes were wide as saucers. 'With the sound up?' Emily nodded.

As I was leaving Tanya ran out of the house towards me, and gave me a big hug. 'Thank you so much for finding me a new family,' she smiled into my arms. I nodded. Unfortunately this would only be a temporary placement. I would have to contact her dad and see if he was in a position to take her on a full time basis.

Tanya was one of the lucky ones. Over the next few weeks I established contact with her father who was anxious to secure custody of her. He told me that he lived in another state and Tanya's mother had repeatedly made it difficult for him to visit her, or have the child stay with him. We arranged for him to come down and meet with me to discuss some of Tanya's recent experiences. He gave his assurances that he would provide a high standard of care to his little girl.

Tanya was delighted when I told her that that she was going to live with her father. 'For ever and ever?' she asked eagerly as she hugged me.

'Yes, Tanya, forever and ever,' I replied as I placed a kiss on her head.

Tanya's mother had made no contact with her daughter since she was placed in foster care, and she hadn't returned any of my calls either. It was clear she had washed her hands completely of her daughter's care.

But that night I was exhausted. I just wanted to get home. I was looking after most of Katie's cases while she was on holiday, as well as two cases from another team member who was on sick leave on top of my own caseload. There just weren't enough hours in the day to do everything that needed to be done. I had accumulated ninety-four hours of overtime, but I wasn't able to use it as we were so short-staffed.

I kissed James when I returned home but I was too exhausted for dinner. I had a bath and he came in to talk to me for a little while, and then went to bed early; I could hardly keep my eyes open.

'You need to look after yourself,' he said worriedly, 'you are doing too much at work.' I knew that, but there was no one else to share the work out with. I fell asleep as soon as my head hit the pillow.

There was a knock at the door, though the sirens that preceded it had already woken me up. James raced to answer the door. It was the fire brigade. Again. This was the second time in as many weeks that they had been called out to our house for a fire which didn't exist. This had to stop. James apologized again, but the fire officers said they would have to trace the calls. They would soon find they didn't come from here. But where?

CHAPTER 42

After three long weeks Katie returned. I hugged her. 'I'm so glad to see you again,' I said. 'Why don't we get coffee now and catch up. We probably won't have time to do it later on.'

'Good idea,' she said and we grabbed our bags and went down to the coffee shop. We ordered coffee and looked around for a table.

'You'd better sit down,' said Katie. Before I could ask her why she blurted out, 'I'm going home.'

'What?'

'Yes, Geoff and I have talked about it, and after all that business with Tom I keep thinking that any of us could be next. We didn't realise until we got here just how incompetent they are. They promote people who don't deserve it, just because they crawl up their arses. They don't offer any support. We are expected to work nearly twice as many hours as they originally indicated, and then they just get rid of people without any explanation. All they tell us is that someone has been sent to Special Projects. But Baldy has said that's a euphemism for being sacked. The work is shite; we farm it out to agencies and have no control over what they do. We don't get to do proper assessments like we would at home. And to top it all they won't even let us use our proper titles in case it hurts somebody's feelings because they aren't properly qualified. When the truth is they aren't bloody properly qualified. I just can't stand it anymore. We're going.'

Katie was right. Most of them haven't a clue, but when all else failed, they would just lower the standards. 'I will be really sorry to lose you; you're the only good thing that has come out of this fucking place. When are you leaving?

'Well, when we were home a few weeks ago we had a look at houses and we've put an offer on one. We're going at the end of the month. I had booked some time off then anyway as Geoff and I were going to go to Perth, but stuff Perth, this place has put me off looking at anywhere else. I just want to go home.'

'When are you going to hand your notice in?'

'When I get to the airport.'

'You're kidding.' I beamed.

'They don't deserve any better than that the way we've been treated. I have no loyalty to them at all. If once, just once, they had met up with us and asked us how it was going, how we were settling in, if we were having any problems, then it might have been different. But they give all their attention to the people who yap the most, and ignore the ones who are struggling quietly in the background.

'You mean like that bitch, Maryann.'

'Yes, she got money for a car, but I was refused. I didn't ask them for money to buy new sofas for my house that I was renting out. I sold up and moved out here believing all that they told me at the interview and it was all a crock of shit. I found that out straight away. They thought that they had us tied here for eighteen months because of some relocation allowance they gave us, but I didn't sign anything. Did you?'

'No, I didn't actually.'

'Well, fuck them then. They can just sing for it,' Katie said sharply.

'You should really be charging them for all the money you will have to spend to get your stuff sent back home again.'

'That's true,' said Katie. 'If they had provided the level of support they had told us they would then I wouldn't be having to pay to have our furniture and all our stuff sent back. Even supervision would be nice. That pisses me off the most. We have to get our supervision notes on the computer, so it looks as if we have had supervision, but there's no bloody tick button to ask if it has actually happened.'

'I usually only get half of it, so I get to talk about some cases, and I'm supposed to talk about the rest in the other half but it never materialises.'

'I take it you haven't talked to Tom about your concerns about those children yet.'

'I wish. He didn't turn up for the supervision session that was been booked and he's cancelled the three previous sessions. I'll be lucky to get supervision this side of Christmas.'

'The same as me. We have huge risks that we are carrying alone. You can guarantee that the minute something goes wrong, it will be our asses on the line, not our bloody managers.' I looked at Katie. I could see she meant it.

'But I'm going to miss you,' I said slowly as I felt a single tear drip down my cheek.

'Oh, don't be bloody daft, we'll keep in touch. We're like people who have survived some siege. We'll be thrown together forever like a survivors' group. We will always be in touch with each other. I just wish that you were coming too.'

'To tell the truth, Katie,' I said reluctantly, 'with all the shit that has happened in this place, and all the crap I have to go through with those ill-reared savages and their whore bag of a mother, I might join you sometime soon.'

'Really?' Katie was really surprised.

'Yes, I just think that all my experience has been useless. I can't cope with those children; I'm a total failure as a stepmother. I have some cheek on me going into peoples' houses and telling them how they should bring up their children when every single thing I have tried with those boys has failed. I am useless. For the first time in my life. I now know why people beat their children. Most of the time I feel like doing it with those two, and I know it isn't their fault they are only children. I just think that woman will always be there causing mischief forever.'

'What about James?'

'I don't know if we will survive here with her and her devil's spawn. Maybe I could deal with it a bit better if work wasn't so stressful.'

'We could all do with therapy,' Katie acknowledged.

'Therapy is expensive. Popping bubble wrap is cheap. You choose, but you are right. You know, I have reached the same level of stress in eight months here that I only reached after eight years of child protection work at home.'

'Well, maybe you had support there.'

'Actually I had less,' I argued. 'My manager there was a bully who was completely incompetent. I didn't get supervision once for six months, and he kept on piling cases on me. When I eventually had supervision he stopped halfway through and said, so let's set a date for your next supervision and I had to tell him he hadn't even covered half the cases.'

'But at least most of the staff there were professionally qualified. They had some kind of clue as to what they should be doing. They don't here.'

'Did I tell you that Lizzie asked me to go out as a secondary person one day to interview a child who had alleged that her father sexually abused her? I was up to my eyes but I agreed anyway. When we got to the door she said, you'd better do it, I've never interviewed a child before.'

'You're fucking kidding?'

'I'm not and we'd already rung the doorbell. I didn't want to be seen arguing with her on the doorstep so I had to do it, while she took notes.'

'That's bloody typical of the people here,' Katie said in disgust. 'I heard that baldy fucker Muriel told people that she wasn't going to have social workers tell her what to do.'

'The only thing she would be told to do was eat all the pies.' We laughed. 'So it sounds as if you have planned your escape?' I said sadly.

'Yes, we're getting people in next week to give us a quote for the removal of the furniture. I'll send my notice from the airport in Sydney when I'm about to board the plane. But as for the relocation, honestly when I think of what I have lost out monetarily then they should be paying me.'

'Do you need me to do anything, Katie? It will break my heart knowing that you are going, but I'll be glad to do what I can.'

'Well, I have to leave the property on the Saturday and the plane doesn't leave for England until Monday afternoon. If we could stay with you on Saturday night that would be a big help if it wouldn't put you out.'

'Put me out? I insist on it. It's the least I can do for you. Look, why don't we get a few people round that you like from here that you trust. It would be nice to have some type of farewell, and acknowledge all you have done since you have been here.'

'You don't have to do that, Louise,' she protested.

'I know, but I want to. I'm only thinking about myself though and how hard it's going to be coming in here and knowing that you aren't here. I have to think about what it's going to be like for you. You have a chance to go back and have a life, and I'm sure your family will be delighted to know that you are coming back home. I think mine would be the same.'

'This place is too far away. It's not like Europe where you could just jump on a plane and travel there cheaply; most people would have to take out a second mortgage to afford the flight here.'

'I know and do you not think they knew it too? They have us trapped.'

We planned Katie's escape and I must admit that I secretly enjoyed it. I admired her for doing what she was doing, having the guts to just take off. I wished I was able to do the same. But what would happen with James? And then there was the house. We were committed to living in it for a year.

If I had to pay back the relocation money, I would have to pay the full amount plus the money that I had to spend on the bitches' stuff. I had lost out financially since I moved to this place. They didn't tell us that tax was higher here and every consultation with a doctor cost a fortune before you even got a prescription. The utilities were more expensive than they were at home and the food was more expensive too. The only thing that was cheap was alcohol. No wonder they had so many social problems with alcohol abuse.

Katie and Geoff were in their own house, packing up their last bits and pieces which would be going on the return journey overseas. Katie was annoyed as Bobs would have to stay in cat foster home for two months before he could return to the UK. 'I like cats, too. Let's exchange recipes,' I said to Katie but while Geoff sniggered she didn't think it was funny.

Bobs was the most well-travelled and expensive cat I'd ever known. She was in quarantine for ages when she came to Australia and she took against Katie after that. She would look at her huffily and sidle up to Geoff and rub herself against his legs. Geoff used to ask her if she wanted to play in the traffic but he knew that if anything happened to her Katie would be devastated. When they decided to go home they knew that Bobs would have to go back into foster care, but at least when they were home in England they would be able to see her on the video camera which the cat carers had set up. The fees were on a sliding scale. If you paid more your cat got to watch TV and have its own seat to curl up on. Katie had chosen these cat carers as she would be able to monitor Bobs through the Internet camera which the cat people had set up.

James and I borrowed Joseph's van and brought them and Bobs to our house. Bobs looked disdainfully round the house. She must have known she was going to move somewhere else again.

We had a farewell party for them. James's mother and father came as did Joseph and Carmella and a couple of people from work that Katie trusted not to reveal her secret. We toasted her and Geoff and wished them all the best, but I knew that while I was smiling and joking, my heart was breaking at the thought that I wouldn't see her again. Unlike Maryann and Colleen, she really had become like family.

James and I brought them to the cat foster carers where Katie was distressed at having to part with Bobs. We then brought them to the bus station from where they would travel to Sydney and stay overnight before they boarded the plane for their long journey home. I hugged Katie tightly, not wanting to let her go. 'You know Katie, someday we'll look back on this, laugh nervously and plough into a parked car.' I hugged her again, but in the end I had to just walk away. I could hardly see a hand in front of me because of my tears.

Katie had been my sounding board for all the turmoil that happened in work and with Lacey and her children. She had kept me sane, she had provided humour, support and understanding and I missed that more than anything. We emailed daily and phoned each other but it wasn't the same as spending time with her here.

Lacey had found out, through the boys probably, her usual source of information, that Katie had gone. She knew that I had spent a lot of time with her when the boys were in our house, and now that she had gone I would be forced to spend more time in the house when they were there. She never missed an opportunity for vengeance.

CHAPTER 43

James and I were alone. The boys had gone home the night before. We usually spent the first couple of days trying to recover from the trauma which they inflicted on us, albeit their behaviour was being dictated by their mother. She treated them like puppets. We had just finished dinner and were sitting at the table chatting. I could see that James was a bit nervous.

'Look, you'd better get it over with. I can see you are anxious about something. Spit it out, I'm a big girl, I can take it.'

'Oh,' said James hesitatingly 'you can read me like a book. Look, I was really reluctant to bring this up with you, in fact, it's taken me a couple of days but Lacey has told me to tell you to wear more appropriate clothing.'

'What?'

'Yes, it seems Shirley gets upset when he sees other women's breasts.'

'And you took this nonsense from that woman? You allowed her to dictate to me?' This from a woman who thought it was all right to prance around butt naked! How bloody dare she? I never ever wore anything inappropriate, and I was very careful when the boys were around. If I thought for one minute that they were even looking at my breasts I'd break both their legs. I didn't want pervy teenagers staring at me. In fact I was so modest when they were around I practically wore a burqa. How dare she dictate to James? She was the one who took her clothes off for money. That's practically prostitution. Does she walk around nude in her own house?' I asked James.

He nodded, 'And she doesn't care what her nudity would do to them?' Christ, had the woman no cop on at all? She really was so self-centred; all she thought of was herself and she had the cheek to complain about the way I dressed. At least I wore fecking clothes. 'What did you say to her?'

'I told her that I wasn't even going to tell you.'

'So why did you. Don't you see, James, you are still allowing her to dictate to you, and she's trying to control me through you. I'm sick to death of it. I don't ever want you to discuss me with her again, do you understand me?'

319

'Yes, I know, she's very wrong,' he conceded.

'Yes, but obviously not so wrong that you would terminate the conversation immediately. Why didn't you just tell her to take a flying fuck? It seems she must have got you thinking, then. I'm telling you now, James, she's not using you to get at me. If she has something to say I'll make sure she says it to my face.'

We spent the rest of the night in total silence. Well, that was, he tried to speak, but I was too angry. I realized the difficulties I was having with his children were causing problems between us, but his ex-wife, while she was a loose cannon, hadn't directly made any remarks about me before. I was damned sure she wasn't going to start now. I simmered furiously. Someday I would write a book about all the experiences I had had since I came to Australia. I didn't think anyone would ever believe half of what I had written. Yes, that's an idea. Everyone's truth exposed for the whole world to see. Imagine the book launch. Big knickers and big dinners would be dying to get a read at it; they wouldn't think I'd ever tell the truth about them. Hmm, what about a title? I know, "Bitches Boxes and Bastards". That would be perfect. I could get most of the page numbers done by the weekend so all I'd have to do would be to just fill in the rest.

The only trouble was that I wouldn't want the whole world to know that I had made such foolish choices with people since I came here. I'd sound like a right eegit. And if I complained about the children everyone would say, sure it's your own fault; you knew he had kids before you started a relationship with him. They would be right, too. But in some ways wasn't it a bit like starting a new job? If your boss turned out to be the biggest power hungry bully in the world, people wouldn't say, well, you should have known. You had an interview before you took the job, didn't you? If your colleagues turned out to be gossips or people who manipulated others to get promoted, people wouldn't say, well, you should have known what you were getting yourself into when you accepted that position.

It was like somebody complaining about how badly their husband treated them. We would show sympathy. We wouldn't say to them, well, you knew what he was like when you married him? It wasn't an arranged marriage, was it? It was a bit like saying to a woman who had been a victim of date rape; well you knew he had a penis when you went out with him.

James and I went to the National Museum of Australia. There was an exhibition of paintings on show called Exiles and Emigrants. Susan and Henry had recommended it. The paintings began showing scenes of the famine in Ireland and then they moved through the process of moving to a new country, the long journey by sea and finally a new life for the emigrants. It was a wonderful exhibition, but I had never felt so homesick in all my life. The paintings of

Ireland showed what a beautiful green and lush country it is in comparison to the dry red heat of Australia.

As we emerged from the exhibition a woman approached me with a clipboard and asked me what I thought of the exhibition. I burst into tears in the poor woman's face and muttered something about homesickness. I was so embarrassed she didn't know what to do. James looked on awkwardly before finally leading me away. 'Great, I bet I won't be allowed in next time,' I said.

'It's really getting to you now, isn't it?'

I nodded. 'I never realised it would be so hard. I feel like I have settled into work really well, and I'm good at what I do there, but my real life is still over there.'

James hugged me. 'Sorry,' I mumbled. 'I'm only feeling sorry for myself because I have nobody to play with.'

It was true. Since Katie left there was no one I could connect with. Work was just, well, work. There wasn't anyone who lightened it. I had gone out a couple of times for a drink after work with some people from the other team, but during the week when things were busy or difficult or if I was worried about something I just had to keep it to myself.

At work it was like the Titanic where the band was still playing while people leapt overboard. I was getting tired of going to afternoon tea, to celebrate the fact that yet another member of staff was leaving. Since Katie had left, another two members of staff had left the team and we were struggling to manage the workload. Even Tom had to carry a caseload as well as try to manage his team. Eventually staff started to protest, and to demand that things should be changed and that management should be concentrating on retaining the staff they had, instead of seeking to recruit new ones. The latest story doing the rounds was that the Children's Bureau was going to Canada to seek to recruit new staff.

Laura informed me that the union had acted on people's dissatisfaction and were seeking information about any issues which people had with working in the Children's Bureau.

'What exactly are you looking for?' I asked her.

'You know a lot of people are complaining to the managers that they are worried that they will be left short-staffed when the overseas recruits all finish their contracts. I think most people feel that the overseas people will just move on and that they will be left carrying heavier caseloads than they are currently doing.'

'Well, I think it's a distinct possibility. I haven't talked to all of them, but I know that most of them are very unhappy with the volume of work they have,' I agreed.

People say that hard work never killed anybody, but did you ever know anybody who rested to death?

'Well,' asked Laura, 'do you think caseloads are too high? Do you think you are getting enough support? Is there anything that you can think of that you are not happy with the organization? We're not nitpicking, we only want genuine concerns.'

'You mean, like the culture of bullying that is promoted here? I could give you reams about that.' I could include the fact I no longer needed to punish, deceive, or compromise myself, unless I wanted to stay employed. 'Leave it with me Laura,' I said. 'I'll work on it at home as I don't have time now, but I'll give you something in writing tomorrow.'

'Oh, you don't have to sign it,' reassured Laura. 'It will all be added to other peoples' issues to see if there is some kind of theme.'

'No, I'd prefer to stand over anything I've written. That way management will know that it's serious. I wouldn't submit something anonymously. That's too sneaky and underhand for me. And you know how I feel about sneaky and underhand people in this place.' We both looked towards Maryann who was waddling down past our desks.

Laura laughed. She had extricated herself from a recent conversation with Maryann who had tried to cry on her shoulder, saying that I had stolen her personal effects.

'What did you say to her?' I asked, amused.

'I just said, well, if you only had two boxes you should just ask Louise to give you your two boxes back. She was stumped.'

'So she didn't happen to tell you that she was afraid that the other nine might contain stuff she needed too?'

'No, she didn't. But she's always hanging out with that Martina now. I wouldn't trust her. She's a gossip; you can guarantee that she'll know the whole saga.'

'You mean, Maryann's version as opposed to the truth? What do you expect from a pig but a grunt?' I didn't trust Martina. She looked like a transvestite with a badly shaved moustache. She was always simpering up to Maryann. God love her if she was reduced to having Maryann for a friend. I knew that on one

322

occasion Martina was at home with Maryann when Janet, my colleague, had called round with her daughter, Chloe. I had already met Chloe, she was a gorgeous child and we had loads of fun together. Chloe had asked Martina why I wasn't there. She had then looked up at Maryann and smirked, 'I don't like you. I just love Louise. She's my friend.'

I laughed out loud when Janet relayed that story to me. Out of the mouths of babes. Good girl, she deserved the latest Barbie for that comment. But have you ever wondered, if Barbie was so popular, why do you have to buy her friends?

I provided two A4 sheets for Laura outlining what I thought were the major issues in the organization. 'That's brilliant, Louise; I didn't think you would be able to list so many. Do you mind if I give this to the union representative and we can incorporate that with some of the issues that other people have raised?'

'Of course you can, Laura, work away with it.'

'You know, I've been thinking we are having that union meeting today and we are going to ask for a meeting with management to discuss some of the issues. I think it would be a good idea to have one of the overseas people there. And I know you've given me more information for this meeting than anyone else so I thought I would see if you could join. That's if you are interested in doing it, of course.'

'I'd be delighted to. I think you are right, the committee needs to be balanced and maybe it might help some of the people here see some of the difficulties we have had since we came here, too.'

'Well, there's a meeting this afternoon so I'll let you know tomorrow what happens.'

'Thanks, Laura,' I said.

She approached me the next morning. 'Hi, Laura, how did your meeting go?' I asked.

'Well, we realised that a lot of people were saying the same things so we're going to categorize them and then meet with management to see what they say.'

'That's brilliant, I'm glad that someone is finally doing something.'

'I asked about you joining the group,' said Laura slowly, 'but I'm afraid that there was an objection.'

'To me? Because I'm from overseas, you mean?' Maybe Colleen was right, maybe the Australian staff were discriminatory toward the overseas recruits.

'Oh no, they all thought that was a good idea. It's just that Martina said we shouldn't pick you because you wouldn't be fair.'

Fair what the hell was she talking about? If life was fair, Elvis would be alive and all the impersonators would be dead. Well, Martina clearly had her own agenda, and she had obviously been listening to that fat bastard complaining all the time about her fecking boxes.

'I don't know what her problem is,' I said to Laura, 'but I'll bet it's hard to pronounce. But don't you worry about it. I don't want to be in any club that she's a member of.'

'I am really sorry, Louise,' Laura apologised. 'I think you would have been brilliant in that group. We really need someone who isn't afraid to challenge the system.'

'No, it would have been too awkward. I'll deal with Martina in my own time. I'm not offended by what she said. I'm just glad that she's stringing words into sentences now.'

I turned away to continue my work. Bloody Martina, bloody moustachioed transvestite. She looked as if her parents were siblings. Long runs the fox, my friend, Leanne, always used to say and it was true. I would get her in the long grass.

Were all the other staff in the Children's Bureau thinking the same thing? Maryann in particular would tell anyone within earshot what had happened to her boxes. She couldn't hold her own water. But when did I get a chance to tell the truth? The real truth, which was that those two bitches had lied through their teeth and used me. They had cost me thousands of dollars and they weren't prepared to put their hands in their own pockets when it came to getting their own stuff back.

I was sure they weren't telling people that part of the story. Was there no end to this bloody saga? I wished for the millionth time that I had never met either of them, and that if I had told them where to put their bloody boxes.

CHAPTER 44

There were other changes afoot in the office. The powers that be had decided that the four teams should be divided into five. Tom had agreed to move his team round the corner. At this point there was only Larry and I left, and we would fit into a stationery cupboard.

I had lost a box of files in the relocation and I really need them to compile a court report. I eventually received an email saying that someone had found it. I walked over to their workstation and saw the box sitting on the desk. I lifted it and carried it about twenty feet to my own desk. As I was placing it on the floor I felt a searing pain in my back. I dropped the box. I felt some pain, but as I needed to get the report finished for court I continued working away. I didn't have time to be sick.

The next day I felt sore and nauseous, but I trundled on. I didn't have time for infirmity; I was busier than Michael Jackson in a day care centre. I lasted until lunch time when Tom came back from a meeting. 'I think I'll have to go home boss,' I sighed painfully. 'My back is killing me.'

I had to phone James at work and ask him to collect me. I hadn't brought my own car and I really didn't feel well enough to get the peasant wagon, the bus. James came and collected me and brought me home. I must have been really sick as I couldn't even sleep and you know how precious an afternoon nap is, especially when you should still be at your work.

That night I tried to sleep but the pain kept me awake. I got up. There was no point lying there tossing and turning. As I stumbled about I discovered that shins were designed for finding furniture in the dark.

The next day I felt no better and my back began to really play up. I couldn't go to work. I phoned and left a message asking them to contact me if they needed me but I was going nowhere. I could hardly manage to drag myself out of bed.

Next day was Saturday and James brought me to the chemist as I wanted to get painkillers. I had just emerged from the car when my back went into some type of seizure. Thank God I was holding on to James at the time otherwise I would have fallen down in the street.

I eventually agreed to go to the doctor at the local medical practice. Isn't it a bit unnerving that doctors call what they do medical practice? The doctor made an appointment for me to come back the next day to have x-rays. The next day??? This was virtually unheard of within the National Health Service. At home what usually happened was that by the time you got your appointment for the tests you needed you had made a complete recovery and had survived several other health scares in the interim. Even if you were admitted to hospital there were no beds so you lay on a trolley somewhere between the canteen and the morgue in your pelt, for all the world to see. But the Australian health service was second to none. I was offered an appointment, not just hanging around the x-ray agency for several days pouring over the out-of-date tatty magazines and watching the radiologists trying their best to ignore you. This was a proper appointment all of my very own.

I hobbled in for the x-ray next morning. Have you noticed that the colder the x-ray table the more of your body is required on it? I was mortified when I couldn't even turn over on my side to allow the radiologist to take some more photographs of my spine.

When we were finished he asked me if I wanted to see the doctor straight away but the shock nearly put me over the edge. I mumbled that I'd already agreed to see the doctor next morning anyway. What a great country, they really take care of their sick. I could imagine all sorts of fun times ahead with the number of infections and injuries I would most likely encounter.

I was very unlucky there. When I was working in Ireland one day I fractured my wrist when I went to visit a client. I tripped over her doorstep and landed like a heap on the step. She opened her door to find me lying there with my skirt over my head, sobbing like a child. Up until then I had been experiencing major problems trying to engage with her but from that moment on she was a changed woman. She even called the office to see how I was doing when I was off on sick leave.

She was a lot more caring than that bloody boss, Kevin. When I returned from the home visit to the office with my left arm hanging there like some kind of withered limb he barked at me for being late. He ranted and raved for ages before I managed to interrupt him and tell him that I needed to go to the hospital. He complained that he couldn't release any staff to come with me. I was devastated as I could hardly change the gears on the car when I had driven back earlier and had completed the entire journey in second gear. When I eventually arrived at casualty I waited for about five hours even though there was no one else there but some yappy schoolboy and his over-indulgent mother. I was off work for ages as the thing wouldn't mend the way it was supposed to.

But this was a new country and a new health system to try, I told myself, as I went to the doctor's next morning, hoping against hope that he wouldn't think I was some type of a malingerer who only wanted time off to lie around in my bed and watch Dr Phil. Isn't it funny the way you always feel better after watching that programme? It isn't just because the man dispenses words of wisdom, but when you saw the state of some of the participants and all their dysfunctional problems you felt immediately smug and superior about your own crappy life.

The doctor looked at the report which had been sent with the x-rays and said I had two ruptured discs in my spine. Wow, a real illness and not some mysterious gynaecological disorder excuse that women use to scare male bosses.

He gave me industrial strength painkillers and arranged for a CT scan the next day. He was lovely and told me to rest and take it easy and gave me the print-out of the report from his computer. What dedication, what caring. I was so impressed.

He asked if I had any further questions. I told him in all seriousness that I would pay him if he told me that the pain would go away eventually and that I wouldn't have to live with this for the rest of my life. He laughed and said I didn't have to blackmail him, but in his experience it took as long as six months before a full recovery could be made. Six months? I couldn't live with this pain for another six months. He reassured me that it would all get better in time.

When I emerged James was waiting. 'Well, where to now?' he asked.

'I need to go to a chemist to get these painkillers. But the doctor wouldn't give me a prescription for arsenic.'

'Arsenic?' he asked cautiously.

'Yes, I was thinking I could slip some to Lacey, but I'm sure a photograph of her is enough for the pharmacist to give me bucket loads of the stuff. I'm only joking,' I said when I saw the look of terror on his face.

I returned for the CT scan next day saying hello to the reception staff as we were all on first name terms by now. They greeted me like an old friend when I came back the following day when the diagnosis was confirmed. I was given a medical certificate for two weeks and instructed not to lift anything and just to rest.

After two weeks things hadn't improved much and to be honest this wasn't just wallowing around in misery. At times the pain was so bad I lay in bed at night sobbing like a small child who wanted her mammy. I went back to the nice sympathetic doctor and got another two weeks' sick leave. But I was conscious that I was letting my team down, all one of him, and I was determined to go back to work as soon as I possibly could.

I was beginning to panic as I had used up all my sick days and I didn't want to call in dead. But Carmella, James's sister-in-law, talked to me about something called workers' compensation.

'But I don't want to sue anyone,' I stated, 'I'm not from America.'

Carmella explained that if the accident happened at work, you applied for workers' compensation. If it was approved they would be able to pay my salary and my medical bills until I had recovered. I contacted the Children's Bureau and spoke to a lovely woman, who talked me through the process and said I would be allocated my own case worker who phoned me only a short time later.

She came out to the house with all the forms I needed to fill in and arranged to collect them the following week. She said that she would refer me to a rehabilitation manager who would be able to accompany me to a doctor and work with all the services to ensure I had proper physiotherapy and could make a full recovery.

After this time I went back to the doctor's where I saw some doctor who could barely speak English. He told me that I could start work the next day, with limited duties. I was not allowed to drive, sit at a desk for periods of time, use the computer or lift any files, or children. So what part of my job did that leave then?

Barbara, the rehabilitation manager, called to my home later that day and she could see by the state of me that I was not putting it on. I showed her the medical certificate from the doctor I had seen that morning. She told me that I shouldn't be accepting the word of some no name doctor and that she would make me an appointment to see a specialist. A proper one. Within minutes she was on the phone organizing an appointment with the sports doctor who worked with all the famous, well, all right then, famous Australian sports stars. She even accompanied me to see him a few days later.

I was a bit worried about having a consultation with him; after all, he was used to working with fit sporty types of people. What was he going to think about me? What if the man had never been exposed to cellulite before? But I needn't have worried, he was lovely. He made me change into a pair of shorts and left the room. I'd never understood that part, sure weren't they going to be examining you anyway? When he returned he asked me to walk across the room then informed me that my left calf was definitely thinner than the right one. He even measured it.

'Yes, I thought so,' he said. 'It's one centimetre smaller.' My God, the man would be brilliant working for an insurance company. He could tell you what weight you were before you could even begin to try to lie on your application form. He started tapping away at my legs with a small hammer type thing and then told me that I had no reflexes in my left ankle which made me feel even more special.

'Of course you can't do your job in that condition,' he stated clearly and authoritatively and I was so impressed. He even reassured me that my pain would diminish over time and that I was not to worry that I would have this injury for the rest of my life. He referred me to hydrotherapy sessions, but in the meantime all I could do was rest.

I went home determined to follow his directions to the letter. Surely on some subliminal level he really meant that I was to be treated to chocolate and glossy magazines. I was going to make the most of this.

I attended hydrotherapy sessions. That was a laugh and a half, trying to splash around in the water like some beached whale. My fellow patients included two women in their sixties and two men with hip injuries. Caroline, the physiotherapist, was lovely. Not just helpful and kind but gorgeous as well. I tried to hide my cellulite as best I could in the water, but no one even noticed. They were all experiencing some degree of pain themselves. Caroline gave me a series of exercises to do and I performed them diligently. The water was lovely and warm and the people were friendly. It was a bit like sharing a hospital ward. Within minutes they had discovered what was wrong with me and they all told me that my ruptured discs were much more serious than their sprained ankles. The only one who could compete with me was a guy called Terry who also had ruptured discs in his spine.

After a couple of weeks I didn't feel any better. In fact I felt worse. I was completing my exercises in the water but I had to stop. I told Caroline that the exercises were really hurting. She tried to tell me that a little bit of pain was a good thing. When I finally emerged from the pool I took a whole succession of spasms in my back and landed on my knees on the side of the pool. I had to wait until the pain subsided, worrying that they might send for the fire brigade. Can you imagine how mortifying that would be and me without any nail polish on my toes?

I finally managed to crawl up the side of the pool into the changing room. I was in agony. Whoever was sticking pins in that voodoo doll can stop now, I prayed, as I tried to change out of my swimming costume.

I went to the doctor's the next day where he had the results of the MRI. He held my hand, which I didn't think was a good sign, and then he told me that he hadn't realised that I had been in as much pain until he had seen the scan.

'What, the fact that you touched me and I cried didn't give you a bit of a clue?' I asked.

He referred me to a neurosurgeon. James came with me and before we had our bums on the seat he got down to business 'We have some good news and some bad news,' he informed me seriously. The good news was he was going to buy that new BMW, and the bad news was I was going to pay for it.

'The bad news is you might need surgery and the good news is that we can try a course of injections into your joints first to see if they are effective as there are side effects with surgery.'

'Such as?' I asked nonchalantly.

'Well, incontinence, infection which could lead to meningitis and of course paralysis.' Paralysis? What the hell would I do with my shoes?

'I'll take the injections.' I informed him.

I thought that it would be a bit like pethidine or morphine, you know, something blurry to get rid of the pain quickly. I hadn't realised that they injected you through an x-ray machine, so there would be less chance of paralysis. The doctor told me it might smart a little. He didn't tell me that the week before two patients had bitten through their tongues. They injected right into the joints of my spine. I lay there in agony thinking, please God, that's enough, just take me away now, please. But he must have been busy. Afterwards I hobbled out of the building.

I had previously arranged to have a hairdresser's appointment. My roots hadn't been touched since the day of my injury eight weeks before and the top of my head looked like a landing strip. James dropped me off. I managed quite well in the hairdresser's until it was time to leave when I discovered that my legs wouldn't work. I couldn't stand up. No matter how much I wriggled and squirmed, nothing happened; I was stuck to my chair like superglue.

I could see the hairdresser look at his watch. It was nearly five o'clock and he obviously wanted to get home for his dinner. They didn't have time to cater for people who were temporarily disabled. What would they do with me? I had already phoned James who came to the rescue as usual. The staff were so grateful to him for rescuing me I don't think they charged me for half of the treatments I had. At least my hair looked good. These things are important no matter how sick you are.

330

James drove me home and when we had pulled into the driveway I discovered that once again my back had seized up and I couldn't get out of the car. I had to sit there in the driveway of my house like I didn't have a place to go. I had bought an old doll's pram a few months earlier in a recycling shop, which I intended to renovate. I considered using it, but unfortunately I was heavier than Tiny Tears and I would probably have buckled it. There weren't even any empty shopping trolleys sitting outside the bus stop in our street where they normally lived. Eventually the pain subsided and I managed, with James's help, to struggle up the steps to the house.

'I don't know how you can put up with this,' I said. 'Any other man would have run for the hills.'

'Well, any other woman would have left me because of the children, never mind their crazy mother. I don't care what happens to you, if you end up in a wheelchair, if you get meningitis, whatever. I love you and I don't want to be without you.'

The next morning I was still in really bad pain. What was the point in putting myself through that? It hadn't made a blind bit of difference. But by the evening I noticed I had more mobility than I had had for ages. I felt practically normal. Great, it worked; I didn't have to go through surgery. Next morning I got up feeling pain free for the first time in months. Great, now I could lead a relatively normal life again.

But by lunch time I was on my hands and knees crawling on the floor as I couldn't stand up. The pain was excruciating, like being jabbed with an electric prod. The injections hadn't worked at all. What had the doctor lined up for plan B?

CHAPTER 45

James was painting the garden room. I was lying on the sofa. I had been awake all night as the pain in my back was unbearable. But I supposed after a certain age, if you didn't wake up aching in every joint, you were probably dead.

There was a knock at the door. I tried to rise in an effort to answer it but the pain in my back was excruciating.

'Don't you move,' scolded James gently, 'I'll see who it is.'

'It's probably Brian,' I said. 'He told me he'd be out some time today.' Brian was a police officer who had assisted me with one of the cases I had in court. He phoned last week to tell me that he was preparing a report for the Court and needed my statement. When I told him that I couldn't drive or travel into the police station to complete it, he had arranged to come out to the house.

James opened the door and I heard a male voice ask if I was at home. 'Yes, of course, she's in here,' said James stepping back to let two police officers into the house. I didn't recognise either of them, but I assumed that Brian had sent them to get my statement signed. They approached me and asked me to confirm my name. I did so. I was puzzled, what was going on?

'Is this to do with the statement?' I asked warily.

'What statement?' one of the officers asked.

'I've been putting together a statement for the Court.' I explained.

'We don't know anything about that,' he said looking at his colleague. 'We've come to talk to you about a report we have received.'

A report about me? I was incredulous. What was this about? 'Please,' I said remembering my manners, 'please sit down.'

'Do you want your partner to be here?' the officer asked turning around to see that James had resumed his painting.

'No, it's OK, go ahead.' The police officer referred to his notebook.

'We have received some information to suggest that you tried to run another motorist off the road.' What? I was incredulous. There must be some mistake.

'When was this supposed to have happened?'

'Well, it is alleged that the incident happened yesterday afternoon.'

'Oh, what time?' I asked casually.

'The victim has said that the incident occurred when she was coming home from work which was approximately at four o'clock. Can you tell me where you were at that time?'

'Yes, I can actually and I can tell you who was with me. Maybe you should ring one of your officers, Brian Chaney, and ask him what he was doing at the same time.'

'Why? What do you mean?' He looked at his colleague guardedly.

'I was here yesterday afternoon at that time with one of your officers because he was taking a statement from me for a case we have been working on.' The officer looked sceptical. 'Please, go on, ring him. I'll get you his mobile number.'

I reached across to the coffee table and passed the officer Brian's business card. The officer rang Brian and asked him where he was yesterday afternoon at four o'clock. 'Right, I see,' he said. Then he began to explain to Brian the nature of the complaint he had received against me.

'Um,' he said. 'No worries. I'll tell her.' The officer turned off his mobile phone.

'You are right,' he accepted. 'Brian said that he was here with Officer Riggings between 3.45pm and 4.30pm and that they were taking a statement from you. He also said that your partner, James, was here as well.' I nodded. 'He also said that he has never taken a statement from anyone in their own home before as people come into the station. He said that because you couldn't drive he came out here to you. Is that right?' he asked.

'Yes,' I confirmed. 'Can you tell me who made this allegation?' I asked judiciously.

'The alleged victim is a woman by the name of Lacey Bones.' Lacey. The bloody malignant bitch. I would kill her with my bare hands, just as soon as I was able to stand up unaided. But there were very few personal problems that couldn't be solved through a suitable application of high explosives. I wondered just how much I could get away with and still go to heaven.

'Hold on a minute, will you, please,' I interrupted. 'James,' I called, 'you'd better come in here. Can you repeat what you just told me?' I asked the officer when James came into the room.

He looked at his jotter and read. 'We received some information from a Miss Lacey Bones who has stated that Louise tried to run her off the road yesterday at approximately four o'clock in the afternoon.'

'You must be joking,' stated James. 'You can't seriously believe this, can you? That's the most ridiculous thing I have ever heard.' The paint dripped from the brush he was holding in his hand. 'You do know she is my ex-wife?'

The officer looked uncomfortable. 'Well, sir, we have to investigate all reports which are given to us.'

'Did she say anything else?' I asked.

'Ms Bones has alleged that you have been stalking her.'

'Stalking how?'

'Ms Bones has alleged that you have been driving your car in her neighbourhood and outside the vicinity of her workplace. She has also alleged that you have been slowing the car down when you have been driving past her house and that you have been following her to work.'

'When is this supposed to have happened?'

'Well,' he said referring to his notes. 'Ms Bones says it has been occurring on a regular basis for the past two weeks.'

I smiled calmly even though I was shaking inside. 'I'll tell you where I have been for the last two weeks, and the two weeks before that if you want to know about it. I've been here, in this house and I'm not allowed to drive.'

'What exactly do you mean?'

'If James's sons had been allowed to visit, Lacey would know I hurt myself at work and I have two prolapsed discs in my back. The only time I have left the house is to go to the doctor's or to go for a CT scan or an MRI. Oh, and there was that time I had injections into the joints of my back. But apart from that I have been housebound. I don't know if you noticed, but I can hardly walk from one end of the house to the other, never mind get into a car and drive.' The officer looked mortified.

'I can give you medical certificates; I have copies of them here.' I reached for the papers on the coffee table and handed them to the officer who looked at them closely. 'These will show the only times I have been able to leave the house,

334

and to tell the truth it nearly killed me to get down the steps from the front door. I don't know if you know anything about spinal injuries, but sitting in a car is the most painful thing I can do. My back keeps going into muscle spasms and my doctor told me the first day he diagnosed me that I wasn't allowed to drive.'

'So you haven't been driving at all?' He scribbled in his notebook.

In fact if James isn't able to drive me I have a rehabilitation officer. Here's her card.' I handed it to him. 'She will confirm that she has to collect me to take me to the doctor's. In fact I think she will tell you that I am the only person she brings to the doctor. Her other clients have to make their own way there.'

'I see,' the officer said as he continued to take notes.

'In fact, if you want to know the truth,' I continued 'Ms Bones is the one who has driven past our house over and over again to try to spy on us. James's car was badly damaged one night when someone threw a brick through the back window. He reported it to the police immediately and James didn't tell the children that it had happened, yet when they came here a few days later they knew all about it because their mother had told them all about it.'

'Do you wish to make a complaint against her, sir?' he asked turning to James.

'No,' said James firmly, 'to tell you the truth we have enough problems with that woman without making it worse.'

'So what happens now?' I asked.

'Well, clearly we will have to talk to Ms Bones,' he said commandingly. 'It's a very serious matter, wasting police time, you know.'

'So it should be,' I agreed.

'I'm really sorry to have disturbed you,' he said apologetically. 'We'll be on our way now.'

'So is that the end of it?'

'We might need to take a statement. Would you be prepared to do that?'

'Yes, of course I will as long as you know you will have to come out here to get it.'

'That's fine,' he agreed.

'Actually you could get Brian to take it; he's due to come out here later on anyway. He could have saved you the trip.'

335

'Yes, well, obviously we didn't know that at the time,' he conceded. He looked embarrassed as he left the house.

'Is that the start of it or the end of it now?' I asked James.

'Well, they obviously won't be doing anything with that information; you have more alibis than anyone.'

'No, I don't mean with the police,' I insisted, 'I mean with Lacey?'

'I was just wondering that myself.'

'God knows what her next trick will be. She is turning into a vindictive malicious bitch,' I said bitterly. 'How dare she do this to me, making up false allegations like that?'

'Don't worry, baby, things will get better,' James said putting his arms around me. 'There is a light at the end of the tunnel.'

'Yes,' I sighed, 'but it's probably just the headlights of an oncoming train.'

A few days later I was in the bath when there was a knock at the door. Bugger. I stepped out of the bath and draped a towel round myself and stumbled up the hall to answer it. 'Oh it's you again,' I said in disappointment.

'Pizza delivery,' said the man casually, proffering a box of pizzas.

'But I didn't order it.' He looked frustrated.

'Look, doll, it was ordered for this address, just pay for it.'

'But I didn't order a pizza.'

'Well, someone else here did then, just give us the money, doll,' he said shuffling his feet as he forced the pizza box closer to me.

'You'll have to take it back,' I said firmly. 'I didn't order it.'

'Don't ya want it then, darlin'?'

'No thanks. I don't know who phoned in an order but it wasn't me. You don't have the phone number for the delivery, do you?' I asked.

'Yeah, it's here on the order form.'

'Can I have it? I'll try and find out who's doing this.' He exhaled loudly, gave me a copy of the order and walked away in annoyance.

I looked at the number in my hand. I didn't recognise it. It was a mobile number so it could have been anyone. I dialled the number, my fingers tensing with every digit. The phone went straight to answer service and I listened carefully to the message. That explained it. I didn't hesitate. I phoned the police. I explained about the fire brigade, the pizza deliveries, the ambulance and police who had all been called out to the house within the past weeks. I gave them the number I had obtained tonight. Let them deal with her now, she was becoming a bloody nuisance. Yes, Lacey.

I was determined to build on the friendships I had made since Katie had left. I had invited Janet and Chloe round for the afternoon. I had bought Chloe a new Barbie doll, and she was delighted. We played with the doll for a while and because it was such a hot day, we splashed round in the pool; Chloe was really excited at being in the water.

Then James arrived with Shirley. I froze. What was he doing here? It wasn't our turn to have him. Why shouldn't someone else be punished for a change? James explained that he had called round to the boy's house to deliver some school books and Shirley had asked if he could come over to cool down in the pool. James believed that he was finally making some progress with him and he had readily agreed, but I didn't feel comfortable having Chloe and Janet here. I could see Janet move protectively towards her daughter the minute she saw him. I wasn't surprised. Anyone I worked with refused to come to the house when the boys were here. Their mother's tales had already scared them off.

Shirley went into the water while I prepared coffee for Janet and some snacks for Chloe. Chloe ran outside and got into the water and we kept an eye on her from the living room which looked directly on to it.

I was just asking Janet a question when she bolted out of the room. I turned round. Shirley was trying to push Chloe under the water. Janet jumped right into the pool and pulled her daughter to safety.

'Don't you ever touch my daughter again,' she screamed at him as she dragged Chloe to the edge of the pool. Chloe was spluttering and crying. She looked at Shirley in abject terror.

'Just get him out of here,' I shouted at James who dragged him out of the water and drove him straight home. No matter how much I apologised I could see that Janet had been terrified by Shirley's behaviour.

'You know that kid is going to kill someone if something isn't done about it soon,' Janet protested as she took Chloe home. After Shirley's behaviour there would be no way she would be coming back to this house again.

When James returned I was still livid. 'When are you going to realise that there is something very wrong with that child?' I demanded. 'I'm sick of it, James. Things are spiralling out of control. He could have drowned that wee girl.

I don't want to be part of this anymore. If there isn't an improvement soon then I'm out of here.'

James was devastated but I could see that no matter what he did Lacey was the one who had the final say. She was the only one who had the chance to change Shirley's behaviour and she clearly wasn't interested in doing that.

'For a start if they come this weekend, I don't want that computer on. After the way he has behaved he doesn't deserve it. You have little enough time with him as it is. It seems pointless when he comes here and all he wants to do is play computer games.' James agreed. He released that he was losing control and if there were no changes he was in danger of losing absolutely everything, including me.

CHAPTER 46

I was trying to talk to Katie on the telephone but the noise in the living room was escalating and I couldn't hear myself speak. I opened the living room door to request that the boys keep the noise down. They were both lying on the sofas, like a pair of mismatched bookends, shouting at their father.

'It's all your fault,' spat Shirley, 'you left Mom to be with Louise. If it wasn't for her we would all be living together.'

Ashley joined in, 'Yeah,' he groaned as he sprawled on the sofa, 'she controls you, Dad, and you've really changed since you met her.'

'That's because I'm happy now, boys, James explained. 'Don't you see that? Don't you remember how sad I was before I met Louise? I was miserable all the time.'

'No, you weren't,' retorted the children in unison.

'Yes, I was, boys, and you are just going to have to accept that Louise and I are getting married. We love each other, and I did not leave your mother to be with Louise. We divorced four years ago.'

'Yeah, but you must have been writing to her on the Internet,' barked Shirley animatedly.

'Look, boys, you are being ridiculous,' explained James. 'I only met Louise when your mother brought her to the house. You were there, Ashley. He looked at his son. 'You remember, Ashley? It was the first time I had ever met her.'

'Well, if it wasn't for her, we would all be together as a family, and Mom would be happy', Shirley moaned.

'Yeah,' said Ashley, 'and she's not our mother.' The child was so slow; he had to speed up to stop.

'Look, boys,' James said in total exasperation. 'I don't know what your mother has told you about our divorce but I didn't leave your mother. She left me so she could go and have sex with other men.' The boys' mouths opened in surprise. They were stunned into silence. 'And you must remember what it was

339

like each weekend after we divorced, when your mother drove for miles so she could meet up with one of her boyfriends.' Ashley sat back on the sofa looking conspicuously awkward.

Shirley spent the rest of the morning skulking about and scowling at anyone who even glanced at him. Later on, Susan and Henry arrived to take me out to lunch. They were clearly concerned that I wouldn't be able to get out much because of my injury.

'Come and say hello to your grandparents,' I said to Shirley who was sitting on the sofa, arms folded and in a black humour. He looked like that character out of the Snoopy cartoon that was surrounded with a halo of dust. He muttered something under his breath.

'Go on,' I urged and opened the back door so he could go outside. He skulked outdoors and plonked himself down on one of the chairs at the picnic table. His grandparents greeted him warmly but he ignored them completely. He stared through them as if they didn't exist.

'I hear you are going to start learning the drums soon,' said Susan smiling at the boy. 'Shut up,' he shouted, 'you don't know nuthin' about me.' Susan flinched.

Henry reached him before James did. 'Don't you ever speak to your grandmother like that, young man,' he said firmly. Shirley shrugged. James ordered him to apologise to his grandmother.

'I don't care,' he simpered as James forcefully dragged him to his bedroom.

Susan and Henry brought me to lunch. They chatted away but I could see that Shirley's outburst had upset both of them. After a while they relaxed and we had a wonderful time.

They returned me to the house, but understandably they didn't come in. I couldn't blame them. I took a deep breath and opened the front door to be met with an avalanche of noise from Shirley. Please God, no. There would never be enough alcohol at lunch to get anyone through this.

'Dad, Dad,' he was screaming opening his mouth so wide I could see his fillings. 'Phone Mom, phone Mom.' Christ, it was ET. I moved out of the room as swiftly as I could. I had learned very quickly to leave the scene of the crime as quickly as possible once he started on one of his temper tantrums. I shuffled outside, wishing not for the first time since I had met that child that I hadn't stopped smoking.

He was used to getting his own way in everything he did. He would throw himself to the floor and thrash his arms and legs about screaming at the top of his lungs until his request had been met. My plans for consistent boundaries had fallen by the wayside. I just couldn't deal with the level of aggression I had to face every single time he was here. I felt like I had been pushed into the role of super nanny, and I was beginning to resent it. It was bad enough dealing with children with behavioural problems on their own, but their mother was the one who was promoting antisocial behaviour and undermining everything James and I had tried to set up.

'But you've already called your mother, she's not home,' James asserted to him; I could still hear the commotion in the room behind me.

'Phone Mom, phone Mom,' he repeated becoming more and more uptight, hopping from one foot to another in an agitated manner. He would probably wet himself next. He had done that a couple of times when he was on the computer. Even though he knew that he had to go to the toilet, he would rather piss his pants than lose out on one minute of his precious computer time.

'What's the matter?' I asked James as he came outside to join me. 'Is he unwell?'

'No, he's fine; he says his mother told him that if he didn't want to stay here he didn't have to. He's phoned her but she's not home.'

'But it's your time with the boys,' I said in dismay.

'I know, she's not helping anyone with that attitude.'

'I'm sure she needs some time alone too. After all he's so demanding. Are you sure she even said this?'

'I'll have to talk to her, try to reason with her again, but you know it's all pointless.'

I knew full well how pointless it was trying to negotiate with Lacey. Once she made her mind up about something she went ahead, regardless of the consequences. I must admit Lacey brought religion into my life. I never believed in hell until I met her.

James continued to phone Lacey's house. I could see that Shirley was becoming increasingly agitated. He could hardly contain himself; he was hopping from foot to foot, screaming at James to keep trying. I went to get a drink of water to swallow a handful of aspirin; he had given me a headache.

'What are you looking at, motherfucker?' He looked menacingly at me.

'Don't you speak to me like that, young man,' I said sharply. He wasn't going to treat me the way he did his mother.

'Why, what you gonna do about it, fuckbag?' he derided.

I flinched and tried to take a step back, but he was too fast. He moved quickly towards me and punched me hard on the stomach. I stumbled against the fridge and slid to the floor. He came towards me and started flailing his fists at my arms and shoulders while I tried to defend myself.

James came tearing into the kitchen. He wrenched Shirley away from me by the arm and shouted at him to get to his room. 'Baby, are you all right?' he asked, fear written all over his face. He helped me to my feet. My back had gone into spasm again. I must have hurt it when I fell against the fridge. I felt sick to my stomach and was shaking like a leaf.

'Just get him out of here, now,' I cried. James went into the bedroom and grabbed Shirley and he frogmarched him out of the house, holding onto his arm. The child's feet didn't even hit the floor. James shoved him into the car, and drove him round to his mother's house.

When he returned his face was grim. 'I'm so sorry that happened, baby.' He wrapped his arms round me as I sat on the bed. I was still weeping, a soggy tissue clutched between my fingers. 'He won't hurt you again, but you should ring the police, you should report him. He has assaulted you and he's old enough to take responsibility for that.'

'No, James, just leave it,' I implored. I couldn't face the thought of going to court and seeing him or his maniacal mother there.

'I told Lacey what had happened and that I was going to encourage you to make a complaint to the police but she still managed to turn this around and blame you.'

My stomach started to do belly flips. 'What do you mean, she blamed me?' I asked incredulously.

'She wanted to know what you had done to her son, and screamed that she was going to ring family services and tell them you hit her child.' Bitch. I hoped she would. Maybe they would do something about it, and hopefully it would backfire on her in the long run.

I took a long hot bath. I locked the door. Ashley was still in the house and even though he hadn't done anything, I didn't want to see him for the rest of the night. James fussed about, trying to meet my every need, but I just wanted to be by myself. I explained to him that I needed time alone and went off to bed, leaving him and Ashley in the sitting room.

I had recovered; I'd been assaulted by bigger and better than that wee bastard. The last time was just before I lifted the boxes in work. A client had slammed me up against the wall. I had reported it to Tom, but he didn't even give me an incident form to complete. It showed the level of compassion that the Children's Bureau had for its staff.

As I lay there I remembered that time Shirley had been standing over me in bed. I started to quiver in fear again. He was like some wild animal; you couldn't predict when he was going to pounce next. Should I just leave and go home now? I started to cry again. I knew that I wasn't able to even climb the steps of an aircraft. I was stuck here, trapped until my back recovered, or I killed myself, whichever came first.

I lay there with the quilt in my mouth, trying to control the sobs which wrenched through my body. I wanted my mother and my family now, more than I had ever done before. But I couldn't even be honest with them. I knew when I spoke to them I had to sound upbeat. I couldn't have them worrying needlessly. Why did I ever come to this bloody country in the first place? Why hadn't I just stayed at home? James. That was the answer. I loved him, but I knew that time was running out for us. I was not prepared to deal with much more of the baggage, which should have stayed in the past.

I knew that the children had been encouraged to be disobedient; they wanted things to go back to what they were like before, with James running after both them and her. I didn't want them to win; I knew that Lacey would be delighted if I ran out on James. It would reinforce all her arguments that he was impossible to live with.

Now that I knew that Shirley wouldn't be coming back to the house I felt an enormous sense of relief. I hadn't realised just how tense I was around him until James finally brought him home that day. Whether it was on the phone or in person, he frightened me; I always knew he had the potential for violence. Thank God, I wouldn't have to deal with that again. As for that other one, Ashley was just a whingey effeminate little boy; as long as I kept him out of my knicker drawer and away from my personal stuff, I would be able to manage him. I took a painkiller and a sleeping tablet; I could sleep knowing that Shirley wouldn't sneak into the room in the darkness.

When Ashley began to come alone we thought he would thrive with the individual attention he got. Shirley had always hogged the limelight, leaving Ashley floundering on the sidelines. But instead of becoming more secure around his father, Ashley became really clinging and wouldn't let James out of his sight.

Ashley had come into the kitchen once and wrapped his arms round James waist and slid his hands down below the waistband of his trousers. James was horrified. But he was very sensitive in his handling of the situation. He didn't want Ashley to feel rejected, but he talked to him about acceptable ways of affection.

Ashley would loll on the sofa and try and put his head on James's lap if he sat beside him to watch television. James squirmed; he didn't know how to react. He patted Ashley's hair stiffly then told him to get up and sit up properly. I noticed after this that James always sat beside me.

'Ashley is probably just jealous,' I reassured James. 'Just try and spend more time with him alone, he seems to really need that.' James agreed. He arranged to take Ashley to the coast for a few days. It was the summer holidays and Ashley was going to be with us for a week anyway.

I was glad of the peace and quiet, and was relieved that I wouldn't have to spend that amount of time with Ashley. When we were alone he talked away to me maturely, but as soon as James entered the room, Ashley transformed, his behaviour regressed and he acted like a small child.

James returned from the coast with Ashley. He talked animatedly about his trip and then went off to contact his cyber friends. He still hadn't any real ones. James and I were reading. Ashley came into the room and walked towards him. 'Dada,' he simpered as he slid his hands round James's waist. James squirmed with embarrassment. I could feel it across the room. The blush rose from under his shirt and spread up to his cheeks.

'You haven't called me that since you were two,' James said pointedly.

'But you're my dada, aren't you, dada?' He began to tickle James. That wasn't going to endear him to anyone; James hated being tickled more than anyone I knew.

'Stop that please, Ashley,' he said gently trying to pull his body out of reach but Ashley held on like a limpet. I lowered my book. There was something very disturbing about the whole scene. I'd never seen a sixteen-year-old boy act like that. He was an imbecile.

Then Ashley uttered the immortal words, 'I'm feeling kinda peckish.' This translated roughly as, bring me a field of potatoes and a cow.

'Help yourself to a snack,' James stated.

'But I want my dada to do it,' he whimpered.

'Ashley, you're old enough to get yourself something,' said James firmly. 'I'll make your dinner later.' Ashley reluctantly unwrapped himself from James's arms.

While before at dinner time he just shovelled the food into his mouth and never took his eyes off his plate, now he started to interact a bit more. But this was usually communicated through belching, interrupting or speaking with his mouth full. He started to act more and more like Shirley. James became exasperated trying to teach him appropriate social skills and manners. It was a hard slog.

CHAPTER 47

The phone rang; it was Jack, one of the managers from work. 'Hello, Jack,' I said, feeling pleased that he had phoned me. I assumed that he wanted to enquire after my health as I was still on sick leave. I still hadn't received a card or a phone call from any of the staff since I had been injured at work, and I was feeling a bit miffed about it.

'What a lovely thought,' I started to say but I was silenced when he told me the real reason for his call.

'We have received a report about you from Lacey Bones. She has alleged that you have abused her children.' Although it wasn't entirely unexpected, it still came as a surprise. I was horrified. I was a child protection officer, this was absolutely ludicrous and I would never do anything that would jeopardize my job. How could anyone ever begin to believe that I could harm a child when I had spent most of my adult life trying hard to protect them?

Jack told me that he couldn't give out any details of the allegations over the phone. He said that he would be calling at Lacey's home first to clarify some of the issues with her and would visit me afterwards.

James tried to reassure me. 'You know you have nothing to worry about,' he said gently. 'You have always been patient with the boys, and she's just being vindictive. Don't let it upset you.'

He tried to cajole me but I couldn't get the worry out of my head. What if I lost my job? What if they believed her? What if she encouraged the children to tell lies about me? I knew how much the children hated me.

I spent the entire weekend in tears, wondering what she had told the boys to say. I was racked with nerves by the time Jack came out to the house. He was accompanied by another team manager, Nadia. James invited them into the house and they sat down in the living room.

Jack said that he wanted to talk to me alone before speaking to James so James went into the sitting room. I was even more nervous as James wasn't there by my side. I felt like Daniel in the den of the lions. Jack began by saying that only Nadia and he and their immediate line manager knew about the report, and that it was confidential and not shared out among the teams.

I was angry as Jack started to list the allegations which Lacey had made against me. 'Miss Bones has claimed that you are a heavy drug user and that you often smoke marijuana in front of the children.'

I laughed out loud, partly in surprise and partly in relief. 'Actually,' I said, 'if Lacey had any knowledge of me at all she would know that I am vehemently opposed to illicit drugs and I have never used them in my life. Well, that isn't strictly true,' I said cautiously. 'I had one puff of a joint once, about ten years ago, and I promptly vomited all over my shoes. You can check it out with the children or with James, but no one smokes anything in this house.'

Nadia began to scribble furiously in her jotter. 'Right, well,' Jack continued, 'Miss Jones has alleged that you forced the children to go to Sydney with their father for the weekend because you had arranged to have friends over for dinner and you were too ashamed of the boys to have them meet them.'

'That's not true either,' I said. 'James took the boys to Sydney for a weekend but he went to get some new clothes for them as they wouldn't wear anything in the shops here. James even managed to get Ashley's hair cut when they were there. As far as I know, the children enjoyed the break, and I didn't go so that they could spend some quality time together. And I didn't have any friends over then,' I clarified. 'I usually only invite friends when the boys aren't here so their routine isn't disrupted.'

The next allegation was even more comical. By this time I had started to relax a bit, knowing that Lacey was scraping the bottom of a barrel if she had to make up all these lies about me. 'Miss Bones has alleged that her marriage broke up because you had embarked on an affair with her husband. She said that the children had become aware of this but that you had forced them to keep it a secret.'

I burst out laughing. 'That's the most ludicrous thing I have ever heard. They were living in America before they got divorced so it might have been a bit hard to have a relationship with James, given that I lived in Ireland up until last year. I only met Lacey through work last year here and then I met James shortly after that.'

Jack loosened his tie; he was beginning to look distinctly uncomfortable. 'Well, the next allegation we have is that you walk around the house naked in front of the children.'

I was beginning to enjoy myself, especially with this allegation. Had she never heard of projection? 'Whenever the boys are here, or even when they aren't, I usually wear tracksuit pants and a T-shirt round the house. I have never walked around my house naked and never will. In fact, Jack,' I said slowly, 'I have a very prominent birthmark on my body and I'm very conscious of it. So if the boys can tell me where it is then maybe you can take this allegation seriously.'

'I see,' said Jack. He looked over at Nadia who was taking copious notes.

'In fact', I continued, 'the boys have told me that they feel uncomfortable when their mother walks around the house in the nude.' I saw Jack give Nadia a strange look. 'You do know that she works as a nude model?' I asked.

'No. I wasn't aware of that,' Jack said carefully.

'In fact,' I said, 'James has photos over there in the family album of her prancing around naked when she was pregnant. Maybe you'd like to take a look at them.'

'No, no, I don't think so,' Jack said quickly squirming uncomfortably in his seat.

'I don't blame you,' I agreed. 'They aren't a pretty sight.'

Jack cleared his throat. 'Miss Bones has also reported to us that James has changed since he met you, and that you control him.'

'You can't be serious, Jack,' I laughed. 'There's no doubt James has changed since I met him, but that's because he's happy now. As for controlling him, he's an adult and makes his own decisions. I don't control anyone.'

I could see that Jack looked confused. 'Is that it?' I asked.

'No, em, the final allegation which Miss Bones has made is that you force the children to stay up late on school nights and that as a result they aren't able to concentrate in school the next day.'

I shook my head in despair. This was a complete reversal of the truth. 'We have clear bedtimes in this house,' I said slowly, 'especially when the children have to go to school next day. If anything they should be complaining that I send them to bed too early.'

I was enraged. I had hardly slept all weekend worrying what she might have said, worrying that I might lose my job, and she had come up with the most ridiculous allegations I had ever heard. Meanwhile every allegation she had made against me could all be directed to her. I had suspected that Lacey was mentally unwell, but I hadn't realised she was just so unbalanced. She had projected all her failings onto me.

'If you must know,' I continued, 'Shirley phoned here last week at eleven o'clock at night to tell his father to collect him the next morning for school. James was in bed and I refused to wake him, but he couldn't do it anyway as he was training next day. I know that when Shirley has to get the bus he has to leave his home at 7.00am to be on time for school, which probably means he went to school exhausted from his mother's house, not from here. In fact,' I confided, 'the children have told us that they just go to bed when they are tired and that they stay up as late as they want to in her house.'

Jack put down his notes. 'Perhaps you should tell me yourself if you think there are any difficulties in your relationship with Miss Bones. Maybe then we can begin to make sense of why the report was made.'

'I'd be glad to,' I smiled. 'In the beginning the boys were accepting of the relationship between James and me. In fact Lacey was the one who promoted it. She then tried to sabotage it when she realised we were getting on with our lives without her. But, Jack, child protection reports shouldn't be about couples in some type of conflict. They should be made when there are concerns about children. Now that you are here maybe you should be exploring our concerns about the children while they are in their mother's care.'

'What do you mean?' asked Jack cautiously.

'Well, for a start, Shirley has presented with behavioural difficulties from the first day I met him. I have seen him with each of his parents and I have major concerns about how she manages him.'

'What type of behaviour are you talking about?' Jack questioned.

'They are really strange behaviours. He won't eat food that touches each other on the plate and he has this strange aversion to shoes and socks. He explodes with rage whenever he doesn't get his own way. He won't go outside, and we have to force him to go to the movies. We can't take him to a restaurant as he won't eat anything at all. He's always interrupting people and he talks incessantly. He's physically and verbally abusive. He spits and punches when he has to leave the house to visit his grandmother. He's also addicted to the computer. Everything he does is measured out in how much computer time he can get. I heard him get up in the night once and I went to see if he needed anything and he was sitting at the computer. It was two o'clock in the morning and I sent him back to bed.'

'How do you manage all this?' he asked in disbelief.

349

'When we moved in here he seemed to respond really well to tight boundaries. We made him go to bed at the same time each night. And if he misbehaved then he lost out on computer time. He started to read comics and he was a lot more pleasant. But then he started to tell us that he didn't have to stay here, that he could go to his mother's house any time he liked. Then he said he didn't have to do what we said, that his mother had told him that the rules in our house were crap.'

'Have you thought about professional help?' asked Jack gently.

'Yes, of course we have,' I insisted. 'James brought Shirley to the paediatrician's for an assessment but Lacey sabotaged that.' Jack look confused. 'When the paediatrician asked if Shirley did particular things both James and he agreed that he did,' I explained, 'but Lacey said that he didn't. You know, Jack,' I continued, 'I've seen Shirley in his mother's house and he's a million times worse there than he is here. Sure she used to tell everyone in work about how dysfunctional her children were. She was always saying that they hated each other. Why don't you check it out with anyone who was working there before me? If that wasn't bad enough, both boys have said that when they go home after the weekend their mother asks them all sorts of questions about me. Then every Monday evening, without fail one of the children will phone, and if I answer they ask to speak to their father, but it's always Lacey waiting in the wings ready to give out to James about something or other that allegedly happened when the boys were here.'

'So when did your friendship with Lacey start to go sour?' Jack asked leaning towards me in his seat.

'Friendship? It wasn't friendship,' I protested. 'I was an audience. The other staff at work told me that she was mad and warned me to stay away from her. But I believe in giving people a chance. But when she told me that she wanted to have a sexual relationship with a client and bring him home I lost it with her.'

'What do you mean?' Jack exchanged a look of horror with Nadia.

'I mean this wasn't just any old client, but a man with a history of violence and severe mental health problems. I told her that the children needed to be protected, but she was only interested in the cuteness of this man's butt.' Nadia was scribbling away furiously. 'I'm sure you know that there were concerns about her behaviour when she was on placement.'

'What do you mean?' asked Jack guardedly. He was becoming increasingly uncomfortable with every piece of information I provided him.

'Lacey was obsessed with talking about sex,' I explained. 'She received complaints when she was on her placement about this behaviour. Why don't you speak to her practice teacher about that? You could also speak to the secretarial staff; she tortured them by asking if they knew of any single men she could date. Just ask any of the team members who were in the team before I started. They will all confirm that she presented with boundary issues.'

I could see by Jack's face that Lacey hadn't shared any of this with him either. I was beginning to enjoy this. 'Then there was the time that she called at my house in a delusional state and she was rambling on about moving to Ireland and building a peace community. She took it badly when I refused to become involved.'

'So what do you think the main problem here is?' Jack asked shaking his head.

'I think that Lacey seems to be having difficulty coming to terms with the fact that James and I are happy together, and I believe she's using the children as pawns. She denigrates their father continuously so the children will lose respect for him and become alienated from them.'

'What would you like to happen?' Jack asked.

'The main problem is Shirley. He obviously needs help from a qualified professional and the least that should happen is that he attends a paediatrician for a proper assessment. This is starting to affect his self-esteem. He has said that he doesn't want to have children when he grows up because they might turn out like him. Can you imagine how bad things are when a wee boy says something like that? It might be useful to talk to his teacher. The poor woman has had major problems with his behaviour, so it's not just happening here.'

Jack then asked to speak to James. James reiterated exactly what I had said.

'So, James, what do you think is the main problem here?' asked Jack.

'I think that Lacey is toxic. She burdens the children with her problems and actively encourages deterioration in their behaviour when they are here. I think she hopes that Louise will eventually give up and just leave. She doesn't seem to be putting the children's interests first.'

'What do you mean?' Jack asked warily.

'Well, Lacey specifically asked us not to give the boys lemonade as it really changed their behaviour and affected them negatively. We both thought it was a good idea. But both boys have said that she told them it sucked that they didn't get lemonade in our house and she bought it for them there.'

'I see,' said Jack slowly.

'You know, when the boys come here they are completely wound up. They both gang up and accuse me of all sorts of things.'

'What sort of accusations do they make?'

'They say that Louise controls me, that I left their mother to be with Louise. That if it wasn't for Louise we would all be a family. But I didn't get involved with Louise when I was with her. I wouldn't do that. She was the one who left me so she could pursue sexual relationships with other men. Nadia squirmed uncomfortably in her seat.

It was clear that Jack and Nadia had no further questions. 'We'll just go back to the office but we might need to meet up with you again to clarify some of the issues,' Jack explained.

'No worries,' said James, 'call out anytime you like.'

When they left I turned to James. 'This would be really funny if it weren't happening to us. Is there going to be no end to this? If it's not the police it's family services. She's determined to try to split us up.'

'I know. I would understand if you just left now, Louise. I don't know of any other woman who would wait around for the next instalment from her.'

I had questioned this myself but every time I thought of life without James I became overcome with such sadness. The thought of losing him left me feeling so bereft I knew I would never recover. I loved him more than I had ever loved any man, and I wasn't prepared to let her take this away from me. 'I won't let her beat me, James, I won't let her do this. She would be delighted if you went back to the way it was before, but would either of us be happy?'

'I don't think so,' said James. 'But I can't believe that she actually told lies about you using drugs when she was the one who had the problem. I can't believe she could get so low.'

'I know I tried sniffing Coke once, but the ice cubes got stuck in my nose. It's true,' I laughed. 'I don't do drugs because I find I get the same effect just by standing up really fast.' We both laughed but it was brought on by hysteria. I hoped that this would backfire on her, and that now someone else would have a chance to see what was really going on for those children. Although they had been horrible to me, I knew that most of it was because they are only following her orders. Shirley enjoyed conflict just as much as his mother, he thrived on it, while Ashley was so stupid he couldn't see he was being used. The child was so thick, he could carry on conversations with bushes.

CHAPTER 48

We hadn't heard back from the Children's Bureau, but about a week later we were preparing dinner when Lacey phoned, using one of the boys as cover as usual.

'You thought you were getting me into trouble by talking to the Children's Bureau about me,' she shrieked. 'Well, they've proved that I haven't abused my kids. You are going to pay for this big time. I'll make you so sorry you and your girlfriend did this to me. I'm going to the papers; I'm going to phone her work every week. I'm going to make sure that that bitch loses her job!'

I heard every word. James sat down beside me. 'You don't think that's the end of it do you?' he asked sceptically.

'It can't be,' I replied confidently. 'If they spoke to the paediatrician or the school they will have realised that we aren't overreacting that we have some serious concerns. That can't be the end of the investigation.'

'But they can't just drop it now without doing anything or telling us, can they?' asked James with a worried expression on his face.

'They have to tell you what the outcome is. But Jack has been trained in the UK. He's used to undertaking thorough assessments. Part of any assessment is to try and get information which might throw a bit of light on the situation, and they will have realised how bad the problem is the minute they phoned the school. Sure the last time you spoke to Shirley's teacher the poor woman was tearing her hair out and was on the verge of a nervous breakdown because of his terrible behaviour in class. That will have to be considered.'

James still looked worried. 'Look,' I tried to reassure him. 'They know what they are doing. I wouldn't be working for them if they weren't fit to undertake a basic assessment. She's only saying that to wind you up. It doesn't mean anything.'

The following week we were just sitting down to dinner when Jack phoned. He told James that they weren't going to be doing any further work with the family and he suggested family mediation.

'But this isn't about a custody battle,' said James slowly. 'This is about a child who is being neglected and harmed by her refusal to acknowledge any problems.'

'Well, we've decided we won't be investigating the matter further,' said Jack nervously and he terminated the conversation.

Jesus Christ. We both sat there too stunned to move. 'I can't believe it. Did they speak to the school?' I asked James.

'No,' he replied despondently.

'Did they talk to the paediatrician?'

'No.' He shook his head.

'Well, what kind of a half arsed assessment is that? I wouldn't accept it from a student. Jesus Christ James, if that's the way they conduct their business I don't want to have anything more to do with them. I feel so ashamed that they can leave things like that without even coming back to clarify issues, or checking out some facts with professionals involved in the case. As soon as I'm well enough to return to work I'll just resign. They can stick their job up their arse.'

'I don't know what to say,' said James. 'I thought this would be the best thing for Shirley. I thought he would get the chance to be properly assessed and given whatever support he needs. This will only make things worse. You can bet that she will use this against both of us and we will never hear the end of it.'

James was right. Shirley refused to come back to the house. When James went to collect the boys Lacey stood between Shirley and his father and insisted that he didn't have to go if he didn't want to.

'You know you won't get any computer time there, because they are always grounding you, poor child,' she cajoled. That did it. Shirley turned and stormed back into the house.

'I've lost my son,' James sighed as he returned to the house with Ashley, who came skipping up the steps to the house, his overnight bag strung over his shoulder like some big handbag.

'Don't worry,' I insisted confidently. 'She will get what she deserves. There is going to come a day when the children will tell her that she has poisoned them against their father. They will resent her for the rest of her life because she's been instrumental in taking you away from them.'

'Do you think so?' James asked disbelievingly.

'I believe so. She's going to regret that she has forced the children to choose sides.' I believed what I had said but I was torn apart for James. Why couldn't she just accept that the children had a right to have a happy relationship with their father? She was doing what she could to make life a misery, and because he would always be concerned about the children's wellbeing, she would always have the chance to hurt him.

The following weekend, Shirley phoned. 'Mom said I had to phone you, and that you have to take me out somewhere now,' he demanded of his father.

'Sorry, Shirley,' said James. 'I've made other plans, but when you come to my house next week we can do something together.'

Shirley hesitated. 'I'm not going back to your house again,' he spat furiously.

'Why not?' James asked questioningly. Silence.

'Well…em…because she manipulates you. That's why!' The child was clearly only repeating what he had been told to say, even if he didn't even have the intelligence to realise what it meant.

James came home from work. I was still on sick leave and longing for news of the outside world. The human race was faced with a cruel choice: work or daytime television, but after three months I realised that Australian television didn't count; it was terrible. I had cabin fever. While the sun was brilliant you couldn't leave a door open in case the cockroaches flew in. Dirty filthy things, they were huge, you had to batter the bastards to death. And the ants, trails of them marching right into the house, into your cupboards, everywhere, crawling over you as you sat on the sofa. I had more time to think, now that I was at home alone, and every day I used it to berate myself for coming over here in the first place. I looked forward to James returning from work.

'Well did you have a nice day,' I asked him as I kissed him.

'It was a strange day,' he replied. 'I received an email from my friend, Sam, who is working in Sri Lanka, trying to rebuild houses and help the people who have been so badly affected by the tsunami.'

'That is nice of him. How is he doing?' I smiled.

'He's well but he forwarded an email he had received from Lacey. She complained to him that we were trying to wreck her life and her family.'

'What?' Was there no end to the mischief this woman would engage in?

'She told Sam that every time poor Shirley came to our house he was grounded.'

355

'He's never been grounded in this house.' I laughed. 'Sure you couldn't get him to leave the house. The only sanction he gets is loss of computer time, but why would Sam be interested in that?'

'Well, he isn't. He told me that he hadn't had any contact with her for years and he couldn't understand why she was writing to him out of the blue to complain about some domestic issues.'

'I'm sure the man has more important things to be thinking about,' I said positively.

'Sam said that he knows there are two sides to every story. He said he remembered when Lacey first moved back to Australia she lived in his house with his mates. He said that she told so many lies and made so many allegations about me that they wanted to beat me up.'

'I remember you telling me that story,' I agreed. Lacey had alleged that James had raped her throughout her entire marriage to him.

'He said that there wasn't any truth to it then and he couldn't believe that there was any truth to it now and that he could only assume that the same thing was happening again.'

'So if she's been writing to Sam out of the blue, then she's probably written to everybody you know, including all the people in Arkansas,' I said guardedly. 'But surely they will realise there are two sides to every story too?'

'I hope so,' said James, 'but the way she distorts the story and goes on and on relentlessly about things, they will probably be forced to believe it.'

'You don't want to get into some email war by trying to put your side across. Anyone who knows you knows what a decent man you are and that you wouldn't try to ruin anyone's life. I think you should just leave it.' I shrugged. It was easy for me to say. This was his reputation, and these were his friends.

James sat down beside me and took my hand. 'I've been thinking, if I had been a bit more honest about her behaviour and brought it to the attention of the judges when we divorced, the outcome might have been completely different.'

'It's true, I'm sure they wouldn't be too pleased about having some whore bag of a woman in the role of mother.'

'I've regretted that ever since,' he said sadly, 'but at the time she had the upper hand. She kept saying she would return to Australia, but then next minute she would say she wasn't going to go. I wasn't completely sure until we got on that plane that she would actually go. In fact on the day that we were leaving we arrived at the airport and she said, no, I've changed my mind, I'm staying here. I had the agreement from the judge which said that the boys would be returning to Australia with me, so I just left her there and took them on the plane. It wasn't until the plane took off that I realised she had actually boarded.'

'Those children's lives would have been so much different without her, you know, James; at least they wouldn't have to listen to all this poison now.'

'I know,' he acknowledged. 'But it will be different when she meets someone. She will suddenly realise that the boys are in the way and she will demand that I start spending more time with them. Even though Shirley has been saying he doesn't want to come, he will suddenly be told he has to. She abandoned the children when she met Wayne. She just got up and left, not caring what was going to happen to them. She only came back because he dumped her. All she was interested in was bloody anal sex,' he said bitterly. As soon as she finds someone she'll be off again.'

'It's going to be harder now for her though,' I contended. 'If any poor man who hasn't had a full frontal lobotomy does become interested in her, and isn't put off by her madness, then he will have to face Shirley. That child would turn you off living.'

'I know, there are no rewards with him now. The more I spend time with him the more I realise that he's not my son. He's hers.'

'Well, hers and possibly someone else's,' I said sarcastically.

'Don't remind me. I have to live with that every day of my life too. But the child needs a father, or a father figure, wouldn't it be worse if I wasn't around? If there was only her?' I had to agree.

CHAPTER 49

James came into the kitchen; I was having a cup of coffee and reading the newspaper. He was carrying a letter in his hand. He looked completely deflated, like a balloon with all the air out of it. 'What is it, James?' I asked struggling to get into an upright position.

'It's the DNA test, it's come back.' He was fuming. He threw it on the table and stormed out of the room. What had happened? It wasn't like him to be bad tempered. He had the sweetest nature of anyone I had ever known. I lifted the white page toward me and tried to decipher the rows of columns and numbers which were swimming before my eyes.

There was no match in any of the eight levels which had been tested. This meant that James was not Shirley's father. Oh God, what now? Had he not suffered enough from this woman? Would she go on deliberately causing him pain for the rest of his life? I walked into the bedroom. James lay on his back staring at the ceiling. I moved toward him and reached out my arms to embrace him. He accepted the embrace; he turned in my arms and sobbed.

'She lied, she cheated, but I'm the one, who has lost out,' he exploded. 'I will never have any say in his life any more. After all the time I spent with him, it was all for nothing.'

'Shush, James, don't say that,' I implored. 'He still needs a father and you are the only one he has known. That must give you some rights.'

'I'll see what bloody rights I have.' He rose from the bed his face etched in stone.

'Where are you going?' I asked stupidly, knowing what the answer would be.

'I'm going to see what she has to say about this. I'm going to sort this out once and for all.'

He was out of the room and into the car before I could move. I ran out towards the front porch but his car was already tearing out of the driveway. To be honest I'm not sure I would have stopped him anyway. This was one battle he had to fight on his own. There was nothing to do now but wait.

By the time James returned I was frantic with worry. Anything could have happened to him. He finally came into the kitchen and opened the fridge. He poured himself some gin and added some tonic. 'Do you want one?' he asked calmly.

'No thanks,' I replied, my heart racing. 'What on earth has happened?' He came towards me and sat down stiffly beside me.

'I'm sorry if I scared you,' he said slowly and reached out and held my hand.

'Don't worry,' I assured him wrapping my arms round him. 'I was just worried about you. Do you want to talk about it?' He heaved a sigh which came from the depths of his soul.

'She knew,' he confessed. 'She knew the whole time. She said she was going to tell me when he was eighteen.'

'No?' I gasped. There must be some mistake, surely this couldn't be right? It was all my fault, if I hadn't come along there would never have been any questions about his parentage. If Lacey hadn't confided so much in me at the beginning there might not have been any doubts raised in James's mind. I was the one who was instrumental in him losing his son. James hung his head in despair.

'She wasn't even embarrassed about it. She said that she didn't want me to have anything more to do with him, and that she was going to the courts to get her own test done to prove I wasn't the father.'

'Christ, James. I'm so sorry. I know things have been really difficult with Shirley lately, but you don't deserve this.'

'I can't get over how callous she has been about the whole thing. I was just a meal ticket for her. When I think of all I put up with when I was with her, just to ensure that the boys were all right, I could cry.' He was devastated. He had aged since he had read that paper earlier on that morning.

'So what are you going to do now?' I asked carefully.

'I'm going to contact the child support agency tomorrow for a start. She can pay me back all the money she owes me,' he said firmly.

'What about Shirley? Do you think she will really go to court, or will you get to see him?' I struggled to come to terms with what had happened.

'She told him right in front of me,' he exclaimed.

'Oh God, James, no.' My heart was breaking for him, the pain was written all over his face. Surely even Lacey would have prepared the child for this bombshell?

'She called him out to the door when I was there and she told him that I wasn't his father,' he declared. 'She said that meant he didn't have to come to my house anymore. She told him that legally I couldn't have any say in his life.'

'What did the child do?' I asked in disbelief.

'He didn't do anything, he just said that he was missing out on his computer time and turned and went back in doors.' Was this a normal reaction? Maybe the child already suspected something was wrong. Had she already told him? Did he know about this before James did?

'You might need to get some legal advice yourself,' I insisted. 'You've been a father to him all this time.' Surely all those years couldn't be thrown aside like a pair of old shoes.

'What's the point? You know, in some way I was relieved. I have been concerned more and more about his behaviour because it's as strange as hers used to be. Now I know that he's nothing to do with me, that some other man is responsible, it kind of lets me off the hook,' he sighed.

I could see that James was trying his best to put a brave face on things, but it was clear that he was struggling. His entire life had been turned upside down. In the space of the year I had known him, he had learned that his ex-wife had engaged in sodomy with masses of men; she had tried to get pregnant so she wouldn't have to go out to work and, more importantly, the child he had claimed as a son had never been his. The woman was toxic.

'It gets worse,' he said slowly. How could anything be worse than losing a son? Dear God, no, not...

'Ashley's not mine either, apparently,' he said calmly. 'She said that she was going to tell me when I'd stopped paying child maintenance for him in another two years.'

'But you haven't done a DNA test on him,' I asserted. 'She might be lying. You know how vindictive she is.' He looked at me carefully.

'I know it, I've always known it. Do you think either of them even looks like me?'

'Well, no, I don't.' I replied slowly, 'but that doesn't necessarily mean anything. And even if it does, Ashley needs to make his own mind up about whether he keeps in contact with you.'

'I think while Shirley didn't react to the knowledge that I'm not his father, Ashley might be more affected, but she's probably told him by now. She won't wait to stick in the knife, no matter who gets hurt. I'm sorry,' James said wearily, 'I just want to go to bed. I'm really tired.' He kissed me briefly and went to the bedroom. He looked crushed. So this was it? On a personal level it would be like a dream come true, not to have contact with her or them again. But I knew I was being selfish. I would have coped with anything they threw at me, just to have things back to when James believed that he was their father. Why did the outcome have to be so tragic for him? He had lost everything he had been committed to for the last sixteen years. It had all been torn away from him.

Did he regret submitting that DNA test? If he hadn't done that he would have had Ashley for another couple of years, before she told him the truth. I know he would probably have demanded a test for Shirley, but he might have been able to cope with it better then. Or would he? Knowing that he had invested his life and soul into those boys made it even harder for him to come to terms with this news. Lacey had proved, yet again, that she was a hard mercenary bitch. I hoped she died screaming, she deserved it.

I knew that James hadn't slept properly; he tossed and turned all night. Eventually he got up in the early hours of the morning. I joined him in the kitchen wrapping my dressing gown around me as I tried to stifle a yawn.

'Do you want coffee?' he asked.

'I would love some; it might wake me up a bit.' I looked at him carefully, trying to assess just how damaged he was by the blow he had received the previous night. 'Aren't you tired today, darling?'

'Sorry, did I keep you awake?' he asked as he poured coffee into a cup and handed it to me. As usual in the middle of a crisis James always thought of other people.

'No,' I protested. 'I'm just worried about you. You never slept a wink.'

'I just keep thinking about everything that has happened and I'm trying to make some decisions about what I want to do now,' he said steadily as he sat down at the kitchen table.

'What do you mean?' I asked stirring the coffee slowly.

'I mean that so far Lacey has sent out the police and the Children's Bureau to this house, and after everything we have gone through with Shirley we discover that he isn't mine. I don't need to do a DNA on Ashley; she's already told me he isn't mine either. My entire life to date has been a complete lie. But now that I've lost them I still believe that she won't ever let up. She may not be able to do it through the boys, but she will continue to cause problems for us while we are here. I think the only thing to do is to move away, but I don't know how you might feel about that.' He looked at me warily.

'Are you joking, James?' I protested, 'I'd leave in the morning if I could. After that botched assessment that the Children's Bureau did I don't want anything more to do with them. I don't want to be working for them if another child dies, in case people associate me with them. But what about your family?'

'I will have to tell them that they don't have grandsons. I think they are going to be relieved about Shirley, but they will be devastated that they are losing Ashley as well. The only good thing is that I won't have to have anything more to do with Lacey. I'm going to pack the kids' clothing and take it round to her house with their bicycles today. I don't want anything of theirs here any more, it's unbearable.'

'And then what, James?' I asked apprehensively. 'What do we do next?'

'I've already been on the Internet. There's an employment agency that is coming over to Australia to interview people for posts in the UK and Ireland. I think I might apply. Maybe I'll be able to get a job in Ireland.'

'Really, you mean you'd go home with me?' I grinned. I couldn't imagine anything more wonderful. I'd be able to put this horrible experience behind me and even better we would never be annoyed by Lacey again. But wait a minute, hadn't I said the same thing months ago when I was trying to get away from Kevin? I hadn't realised at the time that I would be jumping from the frying pan into the fire. Please God, let this be the right decision for us both I prayed.

James submitted his resume immediately. He received an email inviting him to attend for an interview in Sydney the following Sunday. We travelled to Sydney together and stayed with friends of James, Sophie and Dario. I had met them before; they had come round to our house for dinner and we had a great time. They were lovely people who were clearly very fond of James. I was glad of the opportunity to see James with his friends. They were intelligent caring people. Sophie confided that none of their circle of friends had ever liked Lacey and they were all so relieved when she and James had split up. They were shocked when James told him about Lacey's recent exploits. Dario wisely said, 'Once a nutter always a nutter.' Dario and Sophie had their own problems. Dario was Greek. He had moved to Australia when he was only seventeen. He and Sophie had been a couple now for about ten years and they were committed to each other but they were both totally opposed to a having baby. Because he was an only child Dario's parents had put enormous pressure on him to have a child. Sophie told us that when she last went to stay with Dario's mother she constantly urged them to go into the bedroom and make babies. She had purchased a house full of baby toys and clothing for the grandchild she hoped to have. When she realised that her dearest wish was not to be realised she had been inconsolable. She had returned to Greece for a holiday last year where she had announced to her family that Sophie and Dario had finally had a baby, a son. Dario's relatives all phoned him to congratulate him. Poor Dario was shocked, but he had gone along with it, not wanting his mother to lose face. The imaginary baby was now two years old. We all looked at each other. This was surely a desperate act but what did the grandmother do for photographs of the child? Did she take random pictures of babies and send them overseas?

Next morning we left early. James looked so smart in his suit and tie. We went to the opera house and had a cup of coffee. We watched the ferries travel across to Manly. James had already taken me there.

He went off to the interview while I went for a coffee. I was afraid of moving too far away from the hotel in case my back packed up again. James was taking ages. I walked back to the hotel and sat in the lobby. I read every Sunday paper in the place and was halfway through a magazine when James eventually appeared. He looked pleased with himself. He kissed me and we walked out of the hotel together. I was dying to ask him all about it.

'Just wait until we sit down, I think you might need to. I've loads of things to tell you,' he teased. We walked towards a Japanese restaurant and sat down. We ordered lunch and a glass of wine.

'Right,' I said impatiently. 'I can't wait any longer. What did they say?'

'They have loads of posts all over, but one of the interviewers is a manager and he offered me a job in a leadership post developing overseas marketing on the spot.'

'You're kidding. Already? Christ, where is it?'

'Belfast!' he smiled. Home! This was too good to be true. I might be able to recapture some of the life I had before this whole saga started. 'Oh, James,' I hugged him, 'I think it would be fantastic. It would be new start for us. What do you think?'

'I think it would be amazing,' he agreed. He seemed really excited. This would be a new opportunity for him, and more importantly we would be able to leave everything to do with Lacey behind. 'They want me to start right away,' he said animatedly, 'but I told them we couldn't sell the house until March so I probably wouldn't be able to start until April. I think they were so pleased with my experience that they will be prepared to wait.'

'But that's even better; my contract with the Children's Bureau ends in March too, so I would be able to go with a clean slate. I wouldn't have to send them a letter of resignation from the airport like Katie did.'

We spent the rest of the day discussing what we thought it would be like, planning and scheming.

'We can't tell anyone until it's all finalised, James.' I said firmly. 'I don't want Lacey to get wind of it; God knows what she would be likely to do to sabotage it.'

'You're right, and I think it will be hard enough telling my parents, though I think they will be more annoyed about you leaving than me. They have been really taken with you. Dad goes on at me all the time about how wonderful you are and Mum thinks you are the best thing that has ever happened to me. She keeps saying it's a great pity that I hadn't met you before that horrible woman; she doesn't even call Lacey by her name now.'

'Well, I can think of a few names I'd like to call her too,' I agreed. I hoped this would be the last conversation we would have about her. She had assumed far too much power in this relationship; I wasn't going to allow her to do it now. I breathed a sigh of relief. I felt like a burden had been lifted from my shoulders. We were going to get rid of her, the Children's Bureau and the bitches. We would have the chance to have a new life together. A new life which didn't include any of them.

CHAPTER 50

I was sitting at home reading a book, but I couldn't concentrate. I was thinking of everything that had happened since I came to Australia. I had read somewhere that you were supposed to meet people for a reason. Usually it is when you are ready to learn some life lesson or when you require particular support or help with something. My life lesson must have been my realisation of what I had left behind. But what a painful way to learn this truth. The reason for everything was clear – James. If the bitches hadn't been so horrible to me I wouldn't have agreed to go to Lacey's house for dinner. If I hadn't gone for dinner I wouldn't have met James. So the early stuff led me to him. But what about the rest? If everything I had to go through led me to James, then why did all the other horrendous stuff have to happen as well? Why had I been investigated by both the police and the Children's Bureau? What did I need to learn from that, other than I didn't want to work for any organization that couldn't be relied on to complete a decent assessment? Why had I been exposed to such hostility from James's children? The main problem had been and always would be Lacey. If I was being truthful I would have to admit that despite everything she had done, my relationship with James was probably stronger than it might have been, because we had to fight every step of the way to be together.

I wondered how Lacey was managing now. At least when the children came here, she was able to get a bit of peace. She wouldn't have that reprieve now. And financially she must be suffering as well as she was no longer able to extract child maintenance and alimony. James hadn't pursued the money which she owed him; he felt it would be unfair to the children. We hadn't seen the children for weeks, but I still couldn't believe that it was all over, that everything we had been through had finally come to an end.

There was a knock at the door. It was the postman who was a regular visitor. My sister's children had sent me little gifts and other family and friends had also been sending me books and presents to wish me a speedy recovery. It was probably something from home. I took the fat package, noting from the logo that it was from the Children's Bureau. Good, they had finally remembered about me. The application for workers' compensation had been submitted months ago, but it hadn't been approved yet, and I hadn't been paid for months. We were really struggling financially. Maybe this was the good news I had been waiting for.

So far I had been disgusted by the Children's Bureau response when I had finally asked them for some support. I had been redirected to several people, but no one was able to help. Kylie's role as relocation manager had ended, and it looked like we were just supposed to get on with things ourselves. It was a long way from the support which they promised would be available when I had my interview.

As Tom had moved to another department, and the rest of the team had all left no one had even sent a get well soon card. I was disgusted, especially since my injury had been sustained at work. Was this the way they treated people who had been hurt while working for them? I wasn't impressed. But maybe I had misjudged them; maybe this parcel was just that. I opened the envelope carefully. It contained two letters from the Director, Seamus. He had written that he had received a complaint from Lacey Bones. Jesus! Would that woman never leave us alone? Seamus wrote that he believed that I had made a false report against her. He stated that if I was found guilty, my employment might be terminated and I would be deported.

On top of all of that he had written that he believed that I had a medical condition which I hadn't disclosed on my health assessment form when I had applied for the job. What medical condition? There was nothing wrong with me until I came to this bloody place. Jesus, if I needed any more evidence that I had made the biggest mistake of my life, here it was in front of me now. Seamus claimed that I had been fraudulent and that I had sought to benefit financially from the situation because I had a medical condition and I knew that it would deteriorate. Benefit? He must be bloody joking. I was in debt to the tune of thousands of dollars now with all the medical appointments I had to attend, and all the tests I had had to undertake. If I'd wanted to benefit I would have made a claim following the car accident. I hadn't received any salary for three months and was living on the scrapings of tin. It's not hard to meet expenses, you know. They're everywhere.

I had met Seamus when he travelled to Belfast to interview applicants for the posts. He looked like a leprechaun with his wee short legs and his beard. He had been more interested in meeting his mates for a drink than about asking questions in my interview. Seamus was the one who hadn't been honest about working conditions. He hadn't told us that the tax was significantly higher than at home, he didn't tell us that utility bills would be higher than anywhere else, he didn't tell us that property prices were the third most expensive in Australia. All the things he had promised at that interview had not materialized. There was no regular supervision, or support. Sure no one even cared when I had been assaulted, or when I had been injured. If I hadn't been so conscientious I wouldn't have moved that box which contained files I needed to write up a report for the Children's Bureau. So Seamus actually believed that I came to this godforsaken country to make money out of some health situation. That carried the same kind of logic as saying to someone who was diagnosed with cancer, well you should have known that you might get it. I wished the buck stopped here. I could certainly use a few.

I sat down on the sofa clutching the letters to my chest. Thanks God, I was becoming increasingly worried that there wasn't enough anxiety in my life. It was happening all over again. I was being harassed and bullied by yet another male manager. Was there no end to this? Was I going to have to live out the rest of my life fleeing from country to country to avoid bullies?

I was devastated by the tone of the letter. It was really hostile. There didn't appear to have been any consideration of the facts. I had always believed that people were supposed to be innocent until proved guilty. Hadn't they realised the trouble that Lacey had already caused when she accused me of all sorts of horrific things? Despite the fact that the Children's Bureau had never formally apologized to me, or admitted that she had been vindictive I knew I had been exonerated. But here they were again. Lacey must have realised that she couldn't accuse me of abusing her children now, so she was submitting a complaint instead. Was this not further evidence of her instability?

Seamus had written that he had organized a meeting with himself and Martin, another manager at the office, when I would be given the opportunity to respond to all the allegations. I was incensed. I had left my own country because of a thug in a suit and I wasn't going to do the same again. But I was determined that I wasn't going to give up without a fight. I was going to be prepared. I took half a Valium before I got there, my nerves were in tatters. I didn't want to show them any weakness. I knew I was fighting for my right to stay in Australia, for my professional reputation and my credibility. They must have thought I was going to just lie there and let them walk all over me. They probably thought I was some wee gombeen just off the boat but I'd learned a lot in the year I had been here about treachery and deceit. I was ready for them.

James and I finally met with Martin and Seamus and I lambasted the lot of them. I argued that they had given a platform to a woman with serious mental health problems instead of a professional who had made sacrifices to work for their Bureau. I protested that I was the one who had been a victim of fraud. I had been lied to about caseloads, about hours and conditions of work. I pointed out that I had reached the same level of stress after eight months of work here as I had after eight years of work at home. I affirmed that I rarely received supervision, and that I hadn't attended any training due to the pressures of work. I cited the number of hours I worked each week as opposed to what my contract had set out. I talked about the fact that I was expected to compromise my professional opinions. I argued that I had been forced to close cases when my assessment had been that children were still at risk.

I declared that I was being harassed and intimidated. Their behaviour was not only grossly offensive and humiliating; it constituted direct discrimination. I maintained that their threats to have my employment terminated or to have me deported had done nothing but exacerbate my level of pain and had only increased my level of stress significantly. I threw in my trump card. Was it any wonder they had had so many child deaths that year when their standards were so low? To err might be human, but to rub it in was divine. James provided the counter-attack, the fact that he had written to all the ministers, both state and federal. That he had contacted the media who were eagerly awaiting the outcome of this meeting today. He also argued that they had made things worse by telling Lacey I was going to be sacked before we had even had a meeting. She had already told James. Martin and the other manager looked guilty.

Seamus told me that it would take some time to compile a report and he reiterated that they would be in touch with me as soon as possible. We rose to leave 'Sure I can always ask Lacey about the outcome,' I smirked, 'she seems to know more about my life than me.' Seamus looked horrified. James tried to stifle a smile.

We waited patiently for the outcome which was delayed as the tape recorder they had used had not taped correctly and the answers to the questions they had asked me had 'gone missing'. Finally, after two anxious weeks, they sent me a letter. They had found me guilty of misconduct and my employment had been terminated. I was sacked! Although I was shocked, in some perverted sense of reasoning I was relieved as I realised that I wouldn't have to have anything more to do with the Children's Bureau again. But after everything I had been through I wasn't prepared to let them try to ruin my life like that. I had lost too much in coming here; I wasn't going to let them get away with that.

James's friend recommended a lawyer and we arranged to meet with him. Thankfully Donald had had experience of dealing with this Children's Bureau in the past and he was wise to every move they made. Apparently they were notorious for bullying staff and getting rid of anyone who voiced a complaint. I was determined that I would be professional and just lay the facts out for Donald to explore, but retelling all that had happened, the injustices and the betrayal, brought it all home to me just how awful everything had been to date. I burst into tears and Donald listened sympathetically as I described my experiences in between sobs. There was something so comforting in the fact that he was appalled by the way an Australian employer had treated me. This was confirmation that not all employers were the same.

Donald prepared a wonderful response to all the allegations that the Children's Bureau had made. He appealed the decision and submitted a claim for unfair dismissal. As Lacey had made a formal complaint against me, she would be their star witness. I was looking forward to her taking the stand; she wouldn't be able to contain herself and would be an embarrassment both to herself and them. They must have realised that too. After four long agonizing weeks the Children's Bureau decided to settle out of court. I wished we had gone to see Donald in the beginning instead of assuming naively that justice would prevail. But at last I was free to leave. But before we got out of the country there was more to come.

James and I had begun to clear out the garage and pack our belongings. It is amazing the junk you collect in a short period of time, but most of the stuff belonged to Maryann and Colleen. I had ignored it when we first moved into the house but it sat there. Every day I went into the garage it seemed to taunt me. Maryann had sent me an email telling me that she was preparing papers and that she intended going to the small claims court to get her goods returned to her. But that had been months earlier. I decided to use that weekend to pack everything up and dump it; I would be too embarrassed to send it to a charity shop as it was full of rubbish.

The postman arrived. At this point I was dreading his every visit. Surely there couldn't be more bad news, could there? I accepted the letter from him. It was from the small claims court. Maryann was suing me for $10,000. Maryann had claimed that I had agreed to transport all her goods to Australia for free and that I had illegally held her goods and wouldn't return them to her. I couldn't believe it. It was utterly illogical and unreasonable for anyone to believe that I would agree to carry such a large volume of goods halfway across the world on behalf of someone else, knowing that they had been provided with monies for this specific purpose.

As if that wasn't bad enough, Maryann had provided a huge list of items for court which she claimed were in my possession. It bore no resemblance to the items she had sent to Australia. Apparently she had expensive perfumes, clothing, shoes and CDs which amounted to the value of $10,000. She had to be bloody joking. There wasn't anything in there worth more than twenty pence. Maryann alleged that she had to purchase these items in order to replace the items which I withheld from her, but the receipt clearly showed that she had bought these items when she had just arrived in Australia, months before the shipment arrived. I

369

examined it closely; she had submitted the receipt for the curling tongs and CD player for which she had already been reimbursed by the Children's Bureau. Jesus, the cheek of her, she was trying to get money again for goods she had already been paid for. I was the one who should be suing her. Her Coca Cola had destroyed my good computer and the engineer later said that it was beyond repair. I had to destroy loads of my clothes due to cross contamination by her soiled clothing.

The timing of her legal proceedings was particularly interesting. Maryann was aware that she had to remain with the Children's Bureau for eighteen months otherwise she would have to repay a proportion of her relocation fees. As her eighteen months was almost up it seemed that she was seeking money in order to return to Ireland. I wasn't going to let her get away with this either. I knew I couldn't take much more.

With the last reserve of energy I could muster I completed the response form. I included a statement from my sister saying that Maryann had confirmed that she had agreed to pay for the goods when they arrived in Australia. I provided the quote from the shipping company and the report from the computer engineer and I counter-sued for $10,000. I stated that I was disgusted that Maryann was using the Australian Court as a facility for engaging in fraudulent behaviour. I also stated that I had written a letter of complaint to the Children's Bureau about this matter. Let her sweat and have a few sleepless nights. She deserved it after all she had put me through. I didn't want to think of myself as a victim. I wanted to put it all behind me, but everything was pulling me back, not letting me go. Was Australia determined to pull me down completely? Surely there was some justice in this country.

As it turned out there was. The court agreed that Maryann had reneged on a verbal agreement with me and she was instructed to pay me $10,000. She didn't have a choice about repaying this. I didn't ask but she must have used some of the money she got from her claim for bullying. I returned her goods to her. I was happy to do so. I didn't want to look at them ever again.

Donald insisted on the Children's Bureau conducting an investigation based on the complaint I made against her. As it turned out, I had been right; the Children's Bureau had already reimbursed her for the goods on the invoice which she had submitted to the courts. They contacted her former employer and discovered that she had been off on sick leave for over a year, and that she had not disclosed this in her medical assessment form. Her employment was terminated and the Children's Bureau took legal action to secure the relocation monies they had provided to her in the first place.

While money wasn't everything I felt that I had been vindicated. I had learned that if you had money in this country you could make it, but after five and a half months without any income and the solicitor's bills I had accrued, there was nothing left. We put the house up for sale, but due to the huge amount of stamp duty and the fact that the property market hadn't increased significantly there would be no equity.

I had always prided myself that that was one thing in my life I had done well – renovating houses for profit. Now with solicitors and estate agents' fees, and having to pay to relocate my stuff back to Ireland I wouldn't even break even. But this experience had taught me that living the dream wasn't everything. I knew that many people aspired to have the huge house with the swimming pool and endless sunshine, but the reality was completely different. No matter where you lived, happiness came from within.

I knew that if James and I were going to survive we would have to get away from this place. We deserved a chance. If we stayed we would only be destroyed by all the negative memories and associations. James had lost so much too. His children didn't want to maintain any further contact with him. He was bitterly disappointed, but there was nothing he could do about it. While Lacey might have won the battle, she had lost the war. Things must have been difficult for her, having to deal with the children without a break and without James's financial commitment.

James had met Shirley one day in the mall where he was buying lunch at McDonald's. Shirley seemed uncomfortable and was eager to get away. Maybe he was embarrassed because he knew he should have been at school. James was aware that the children hadn't been attending regularly but James said it had been difficult to see Shirley as he was filthy. His hair was unwashed and his clothes were smelly and soiled.

We repainted the children's rooms and changed the furniture around. It was too difficult for James to walk past them every day without thinking of what might have been. Whether it was psychological or not, once we had no further contact from Lacey, my back began to improve. I was delighted when the neurosurgeon reported that I wouldn't require surgery. At least that was one piece of good news.

We listed the house for auction and prepared it for sale. It was going to be sad leaving the house behind, but after everything that had happened I think we were both keen for a new start. James and I made plans to travel to Ireland. At least I wasn't worried about meeting Colleen there as she had moved to London. Apparently her mother insisted that she would be more likely to meet some man there who might marry her, with all the immigrants there wanting citizenship in the UK. Maryann wouldn't be allowed to leave Australia until she had repaid all the monies she owed them but as she was unable to work as her working visa had been cancelled she had been forced to sell her house in order to recoup the money she needed to repay.

It had been a long hot summer, due to the drought; we were down to stage four of water restrictions. Even the kangaroos had come closer to the suburbs in a bid to get fresh water and eat the grass from the lawns, as their usual habitat was dry and barren. Gardens died in the heat, cars went unwashed and baths were not permitted. People were being fined huge sums of money for lighting fires as any spark could make the place go up like a tinderbox. There had been a huge bush fire a few years ago which went out of control and hundreds of houses were destroyed and lives were lost. The emergency state services were determined to be a bit more vigilant this time. James had cleared dead leaves from the gutters and drains. We had both prepared an emergency pack to take with us if we needed to leave the house in a hurry.

After a long tiring day, we went to bed exhausted. Packing was a tiring business. Wasn't moving supposed to be one of the stressful things in life, up there with divorce and bereavement?

The telephone woke us. James reached across and answered it. The next moment he jumped out of bed and began to rush around the bedroom grabbing clothes and dressing quickly.

'What's wrong, James, what's happened?' I sat up and squinted at him my eyes adjusting to the bedside light.

'That was Dad. There was a fire at Lacey's house; the children have been taken to hospital. I'm going to go and make sure the boys are all right.' I knew that even if the boys didn't want him, he needed to make sure they were safe.

He was away for ages, and he hadn't taken his mobile so I had no way of contacting him. When he eventually returned he walked into the house slowly.

'Are you all right?' I asked him, getting up and wrapping my dressing gown around me tightly. 'What about the boys, are they all right?'

'They were both taken to hospital with smoke inhalation and Ashley has burns to his body,' James exhaled noisily.

'But what happened, James?' I asked cautiously. I was afraid of the answer he might provide. James turned towards me with tears glistening in his eyes.

'The police officer thinks that Shirley did it. He poured lighter fluid over Ashley when he was in bed and then set him on fire.' Shirley had set his brother on fire? Jesus Christ, this was the most horrific thing I had ever heard. James swallowed a sob and continued. 'The police said that the house was littered with rubbish so the fire spread quickly. They were lucky a neighbour phoned the fire brigade. They are still there battling the blaze; they're trying to prevent the fire from spreading to the other houses. The house backs on to the bush so they have to be really careful, everything is so dry now.'

There was something missing here, what was it? 'But Lacey?' I finally stumbled over the name. 'Where was she when it happened?' Had she left them alone again?

James shook his head in despair. 'She's with her boyfriend Seamus.'

'Not Seamus from the Children's Bureau,' I questioned. James nodded. So that explained a lot. 'Apparently the police have been trying to find her all night.'

When Lacey finally returned home she was advised by the police to contact the hospital where her children had been for hours. Before she had sight of her children she was interviewed by the Children's Bureau. They had to conduct another investigation, as the children had been left alone all night.

Lacey was eventually prosecuted and convicted of neglect. She was unable to continue her social work course. When Ashley was discharged from hospital he was placed in care. Lacey's prediction for Shirley had finally come true as he was convicted and sent to the kiddie jail. He would not be discharged without a full psychiatric assessment.

After everything that happened James and I needed to get away from everything we knew in Australia. There were too many memories which would only poison us if we remained. Susan and Henry were devastated when we told them we were moving to Ireland but they understood why we had to leave. They supported us in our decision.

It was strange returning to my homeland after everything that had happened. I was worried that people would think I had failed, that I couldn't hack it in another country. But I knew I wouldn't settle anywhere else. I just wanted to be back, among friends, among people I could trust. They were all there to celebrate with us when James and I were married. Despite all that has happened, all the obstacles we have had to overcome, James and I have still retained that degree of passion which we both felt at the beginning. It might not have been the most mature solution to a problem, and I'm not sure I would recommend it again, but in the end running away from Kevin completely transformed my life.